CW01216759

Praise for *Scraps of Grace*

An inspiring spiritual journey driven by relatable characters facing real-life struggles. *Scraps of Grace* captures a turbulent moment in time while exploring timeless questions of faith.

- Chuck Snearly, author of *The Guardian of Detritus* and *Far Out Man*

Jon Harmon creates a young, single-father character hoisted by his own petard, explores how conviction can enable us to navigate escalating life issues, and sets it all against the sports-mad world of recent yesteryear Detroit. Fascinating and recommended.

- Tom Morrisey, bestselling novelist and author of *The Art of the Tale*

In a time when pro-life values are often overlooked in mainstream entertainment, *Scraps of Grace* emerges as a poignant tribute to the complexity of life. What a beautiful story, so artfully written. We follow the main character's spiritual journey as his path converges with others to reveal the strength that comes from embracing his deep but nearly forgotten convictions.

- Amy Drake, Director - Patient Client Service, Waterleaf Women's Center, Aurora, IL

The author leads us masterfully on a true-to-life journey of ordinary people experiencing the challenges of everyday life. Hidden within is the important reminder that God is present through life's struggles; that His grace is being poured into us, especially through those around us, and often by people from whom we may least expect it. *Scrapes of Grace* beautifully reminds us of what we already know in our hearts—we are made for communion with one another; we are a Eucharistic people.

- Deacon Matthew Napoli, Diocese of Joliet, IL

A heart-warming, relatable story of an 'average joe' trying to recover from the storms of life. Through unlikely friendships, love, faith and grace, Tyler shows us what it's like to walk through Romans 5:3-4 (NCB), where: "… suffering develops perseverance, and perseverance produces character, and character produces hope." This is a story to inspire those who are afraid to get out of the rocky boat of life, to step out onto the water with faith in Jesus.

- Gregory McDonald, Founder, Men As Christ

Tackling some weighty issues, *Scraps of Grace* benefits from a fluid prose style punctuated with moments of clarity and beauty. Tyler's car-obsessed brain deploys some arresting (and laugh-out-loud funny) descriptive language, as when a Chevy Caprice Classic is painted as "an ugly whale abortion of a car." … But the key is a fine ear for rhythm and the sonic qualities of words, elevating even straightforward thoughts like, "Her green eyes glow intensely now. It's not just the light; there's a confidence behind them he's never seen in her." The novel is worth reading for these nuggets of particularly excellent prose. For readers who enjoy a conventional narrative done very well, *Scraps of Grace* more than delivers.

Verdict: A detailed period piece set in a crucial moment in modern American history, Jon F. Harmon's *Scraps of Grace* compassionately and movingly portrays an average American man struggling with the failures of contemporary models of masculinity. (4.3 stars out of 5)

- Indie Reader

SCRAPS of GRACE

A NOVEL

JON F. HARMON

To Mary, the love of my life,
who has taught me to trust always
in the goodness of the Lord,
even when there's no break in the clouds

Copyright © 2024 by Jon F. Harmon

All rights reserved.

This book or any portion of it may not be reproduced or used in any manner without the written permission of the author, except in brief quotations as Fair Use.

The opening chapter in an earlier form was published in 1992 in the inaugural issue of [SIC], the literary journal of University of Detroit-Mercy, as "Channel Surfer."

Fair Use: Contemporaneous newspaper and magazine articles, music lyrics, billboard copy and other copyrighted material has been referenced, sampled and/or briefly quoted in this work as Fair Use as defined by Section 107 of the U.S. Copyright Act.

Most of the places referenced, news articles quoted, and world events described as historical or contemporary to the story have been accurately represented. However, the work's characters and their actions are fictional; any resemblance to actual living persons is coincidental and unintentional. The opinions of the book's narrator and characters do not necessarily reflect the views of the author or publisher.

Hardcover ISBN: 9798822964082
Paperback ISBN: 9798822964099
eBook ISBN: 9798822964105

PALMETTO
PUBLISHING
Charleston, SC
www.PalmettoPublishing.com

SCRAPS of GRACE
A NOVEL

I. CHANNEL SURFER	1
II. IN THE WHITE ROOM	89
III. KODACHROME	213
IV. MOONSHOT	419
EPILOGUE	479

All science, even the divine science, is a sublime detective story.
Only it is not set to detect why a man is dead,
but the darker secret of why he is alive.

G. K. CHESTERTON

I. CHANNEL SURFER

August 1990

The pity he imagines in her downcast eyes as she waits to be paid irritates him. Tyler fights the urge to explain to the babysitter that his wife's death hasn't crippled him, that he is still whole. Really.

His right hand tries to free his wallet from the tight grip of a rear jeans pocket.

"When'd Robbie go down for you?"

"Like around eight-thirty. About when he usually does."

"Did he eat okay?"

"Uh-huh. Some hamburger meat with ketchup. Lotsa ketchup. And a whole thing of applesauce."

"What'd he have to drink?" Tyler asks, running out of questions, but still struggling with his wallet.

"Some milk at supper. And a box of juice right before he fell asleep."

The babysitter looks down at the living room carpet throughout this exchange. Her loose jeans and oversized sweatshirt, sleeves rolled up to her elbows, cannot conceal her lean athletic tautness. She seems somehow taller than the last time she babysat for him, just last week. She has become his regular sitter, promoted from the once-a-month-or-so status she held when Tyler's wife, Christie, made the arrangements. Her fingers fidget, pulling at a dangling earring. She works the gum in her mouth.

Since she got her license a few months ago, he doesn't have to drive her home and he's lost track of the things they used to talk about. Tyler can only vaguely remember conversational dead ends during awkward five-minute drives to the neighboring subdivision where the girl lives with her parents. And a younger brother, maybe. Plodding through a dense fog, Tyler was just going through the motions, especially those first two months. After Christie left him.

"You gonna play basketball this year at school?" he asks, recalling some distant connection.

She looks up, green eyes opening noticeably wider, and she smiles slightly, perhaps pleased he remembers. "Yeah, I got a pretty good chance to make the team. Varsity," she adds with emphasis. "Three of the girls that started last year graduated, you know, so maybe I'll even start."

Tyler opens his wallet. Several bills, but they're all singles. Not enough. He roots through his gym bag for his checkbook, blocking for now the babysitter's path to the half-open door. Behind him crickets sing from his thick, dewy lawn and from the lawns of each of his neighbors.

"You got much of an outside shot, Nicki?"

He likes the tomboyish sound of the babysitter's name, cute for a teenage girl. She'll outgrow it soon enough. At college in a few years, pledging some sorority, her name will fill out to keep pace with her maturing bust and hips, Nicolette. Still, Tyler seldom calls her anything, except when phoning her house to ask for her to sit. When there's no one else around, you don't use names. And she doesn't seem to know what to call him—he's too young to be Mr. Manion, but Tyler doesn't fit right, either.

"That's funny you ask. Last year, I hardly shot. I played a lot—on the sophomore team—because I hustled. Coach liked that, you know, but I didn't start." She speaks in short, rapid bursts. "But I've been practicing, working on my shot all summer. And I'm getting pretty good. For real. I'm gonna be ready this fall."

He seems to have discovered an untapped nerve, this basketball tack. The little jockette even demonstrates the shooting motion her father has taught her—right hand cocked, palm up, slightly above her right ear, while the soft curve of her left hand steadies the left side of the imaginary ball. Her knees bend and straighten as she rises up on the toes of her little white Converse sneakers. Then her right arm releases and she flicks her wrist in a smooth, practiced motion. Tyler can almost see the ball come off her hand with familiar masculine backspin. *Swish*.

"We should play a little HORSE sometime," he offers. "I used to have a sweet jumper myself." At a stocky six-foot-two, Tyler is five or six inches taller than the girl, heavier, and much stronger, certainly. But none of that matters in the shooting game HORSE.

"Yeah, that'd be fun. Next time, you know, before you go out. Tomorrow. I'm not kidding. I can hit from the top of the key. Most girls can't even reach."

Tyler has never seen her this enthused; her unblemished brown face beaming. He thinks about turning on the light over the garage and asking her to play a quick game in his driveway before she goes, but doesn't press it. He writes out a check for twelve dollars—three bucks an hour for three-and-a-half hours rounded to four.

The babysitter looks down at her tennis shoes and mumbles an embarrassed "thank you"; the spell already broken. Then she walks through his door and down his front walkway into the night, rolling her narrow hips just a bit. She opens the driver's door of the white Mustang at the end of his short driveway. It looks too new to be her car, but perhaps it is. Tossing back the wild tangles of her shoulder-length hair with well-practiced nonchalance, she slides into the car and shuts the door. The Mustang shudders. Then its headlights explode the darkness like twin supernovas, so that he has to look away. He turns back in time to watch the car's red taillights disappear around the corner.

Tyler leans against the wrought iron railing on his porch, sucking in cool air, his eyes still readjusting to the night. A gibbous moon glows warmly just above the trees in the eastern sky, bloated and pale, like a pregnant woman's belly, obscuring the stars around it with its brightness. Will we ever return to our nearest neighbor in the heavens? More than twenty years since man first stepped on the moon and it's still the signature human achievement of the century. *If we can put a man on the moon, why can't we...* remains our standard expression of impatience with everything else in life.

Chalky white moths beat their wings against Tyler's porch light, leaving dusty stains. Across the street, the blue haze of a television glows through sheer living room drapes. A bug zapper next door with its purple glow makes a chaotic *zing-zing-zzzinckk-zing* as it electrocutes a steady stream of gnats, mosquitoes and an occasional larger insect. Evening dew glistens on his freshly cut lawn. He breathes through his nose to smell the sweet wet grass. Somehow through it all this summer he's found time to water and fertilize, cut and edge, and he's been rewarded with thick, even grass—just like every other yard in the subdivision. He's proud to not be an embarrassment. He even planted a few flowers in front of the house, not as many as she used to put out, but respectable. Already feeling like a former self, this Tyler who lived here and took for granted that his Christie would be together with him a lifetime and more.

Yes, the yard is looking good, he thinks as he stretches his arms back and up until his fingertips graze the porch's uneven ceiling. Except for that tree. A crippled oak mars his front yard. About this time a year ago lightning amputated the upper half of the tree. Now only two stumpy branches remain, one on either side. Like a telephone pole, only shorter. A few leaves grow on tender green shoots off each branch, but you could call the tree dead and be more right than wrong. Tyler again reminds himself to cut it down like he had promised Christie, before the neighbors get on his case.

"Come inside now, Ty. It's getting late, love." Her voice from somewhere behind or beyond him, full of warmth, even when she's letting him know she's feeling more urgency than he does without her. Gently shaking him from his mind's hiding spot. He peers through the windowpane into his living room, hoping to catch a glimpse of her.

Tyler frowns. She remains in his head, of course, but it's no good. Out here on this porch that used to be theirs together, he feels Christie's absence, the loss of the arc they had together, streaming along like a Saturn V rocket oblivious to the danger and disappointment all about them. It hurts to think of her, so he doesn't allow his mind to linger there, escaping quickly to an easier place. Still there inside him, but he can forget her for a while if he tries.

* * *

Inside, Robbie sleeps. Tyler reaches into the crib, pulling his son's chubby hand from his mouth. He wipes away a thin strand of spittle that extends from tiny lips to a crooked wet thumb. Robbie's white cheeks and neck, soft as warm pudding against Tyler's open palm, take on a slightly jaundiced hue in the yellow glow of the cartoon bird nightlight, Woodstock from the Peanuts series. A pastel green blanket tucked over the child's shoulders continues far beyond thick, clumsy feet. A cloth mobile, more pastels, slowly rotates above his head: Bert, Ernie, Big Bird and Cookie Monster dancing on invisible strings, hanging from the battery-power carousel.

This little one, at peace for now in his crib, carries an immeasurable weight as Christie's sole legacy and the only lasting evidence of the brief, blessed union of two love-drenched twenty-somethings. It will become his mission, Tyler vows again to himself in the dark silence, to be Robbie's bodyguard and coach, his guardian angel, mentor and wingman. *No matter what.* So that they both will make Christie proud. He owes her that, he knows.

Tyler hops in the shower and washes away the sweat and dust of another softball game. Three or four routine balls hit his way in right-centerfield. He replays each catch in his mind. Four of them, now he remembers. He scoots gracefully under one after another, watching in his mind's eye as if from a network camera high above the pitcher's mound. Four easy plays, though one had ended disastrously. He gets a good jump on the pop-fly, slows for a moment, then accelerates to catch the ball on a dead run, his momentum carrying him toward the infield as he pulls the ball out of his glove, cocks his arm, daring the runner on second to tag. The runner does tag up, starting toward third with a little jump, then launching into long, fitful strides. Tyler's right arm unsprings, firing the ball, angrily. He has the runner by a mile. Except his throw keeps carrying, well over the head of the third baseman, into the old rusty bleachers where a couple of mothers shield infant children with their own flabby bodies.

He towels off and reaches down into the top drawer of the vanity for a Q-tip, turns the cotton swab in the canal of his right ear, withdraws it and examines the frayed cotton end. A disappointing white, not even a trace of waxy yellowness. Then he inserts the opposite end of the Q-tip into his other ear. Again, nothing. Tyler secretly loves the sensation of the cotton twirling inside his ears. Tickling. He goes through several dozen swabs each month, though the enormous blue box holds so many it lasts half a year.

In cotton pajama bottoms, Tyler walks across the kitchen linoleum and opens the refrigerator. He reaches for a beer, then reconsiders. He drank enough with his teammates after the game, and he has to get up in the morning to go to work one last time. So, he pours himself some grape Kool-Aid, finishing off the pitcher, and carries the plastic cup into the living room. Sinking into his recliner, he flicks the remote control, checking ESPN for a late ball game, but finds only soccer. If soccer really is the most popular spectator sport in the world, hundreds of millions of people's lives must be far duller than his own, he thinks. He taps the remote, cycling through the channels looking for something interesting. *Channel surfing*. Of the forty-two channels, eleven or twelve feature nothing but motionless text. He never stays on any of them long enough to read the text, so he can't really be sure, but it seems they never change, the same blue background and dreary letters. Who do they think watches this?

Three or four televangelistic channels are sprinkled throughout the forty-two, each with a 900-number prayer line at the bottom of the screen. On one channel, two massive bodybuilders perform impressive feats of strength in the name of the Lord. One steroid-abusing but otherwise clean-cut young man kneels on a stage in front of what appears to be an altar, struggling against heavy black chains. He grunts and sweats trying to break free while his partner stands behind him, pulling on the chains to prove they're real. Tyler keeps watching, dazed. The one who's standing prays over his hulking friend and invites him to give the chains one more try. *Presto!* The iron chains tear apart, and the two sweaty hulks jump up and down triumphantly, praising God for their muscular magic trick. Tyler can be saved too, the talkative one tells him, if he commits his soul this minute to the Lord. Right now, he says; it has to be right now.

He presses the clicker and lands for a moment on a commercial, a pitch from Toyota that snidely bites at Tyler, laid off from his human resources job at a General Motors manufacturing plant. Tomorrow is his last day. *I love what you do for me, Toyota*. On another channel, a nun wearing a brown and white habit prays the rosary. Her face is replaced by painted images of suffering saints hanging on the screen, a low-tech slide show, her voice-over droning on. Taking him back to his Catholic grade school days in Akron, and the no-nonsense teaching style practiced by the nuns at St. Michael the Archangel. Faith wasn't something to embrace individually so much as a set of rules everybody had to follow. Then it was off to public high school. Sometime during his senior year, Tyler stopped going to church on Sundays with his mother because, he told her, he wasn't getting anything out of it. Like a summer rerun of a show that wasn't too interesting in the first place. Tyler's mother hadn't tried to argue with him; it would have seemed futile to her. Tyler's father, who had never been much of a churchgoer, had by this time disappeared from their lives, and Tyler's sister, Celia, was away at college. Later, off himself to the Ohio State University, he began occasionally attending mass again, at the campus Newman Center, still not getting much from it, but secretly afraid of missing out on something important. Even now, Tyler won't let go of his Catholic beliefs. Like an apprehended suspect who gets a static-filled line on the one call he's allowed, it is his only connection to God and he's not going to be the one who hangs up.

He surfs through the rest of the channels, but doesn't find anything remotely entertaining. He can't get into the late-night fare: professional wrestling; prerecorded and mostly lip-synced music videos; black-and-white reruns of shows baby boomers ten years older than he grew up with—*Donna Reed, My Three Sons, Mister Ed*. Tyler turns off the television, checks the front door's deadbolt and walks slowly to the half-bath off his bedroom. He pulls the contact lenses off his dry, red eyes and pops them into their little boiler bed, brushes his teeth, then takes one more good leak to get him through the night. He slides under a thin cotton sheet on his queen-sized bed, head buzzing slightly, still swimming in the beer. Sweet currents of color roll behind his closed eyelids, his arms and legs and chest pleasantly warm beneath the single sheet. Slowly sinking. Into the softness of the pillow.

It takes effort to lift himself out of the near sleep to silently recite a prayer. Though he feels a little guilty talking to God after he has been drinking, he feels guiltier when he doesn't pray before sleep. He opens his eyes to the room's darkness to clear his mind, then reshuts them, tightly, focusing on stain-glassed thoughts. *Our Father, who art in heaven…*

As he thinks the words, his mind wanders; he can't stop it. He watches himself circle under a high pop fly. Higher and higher it climbs, then begins to drop where he stands waiting, glove raised. The ball settles into his mitt and he throws it home, perfectly, just in time to nab the sliding runner…. He shakes free of the little dream and fashions an appropriate mental picture: a bearded God the Father in a long, brown robe, sitting sternly on a heavy wooden chair. This image quickly fades to a picture of his front door. Did he lock the deadbolt? *Yes.* Then he sees Nicki, the babysitter, admiring the bookshelves he's making for Robbie downstairs. In his workshop in the basement. Her thin, brown fingers with closely trimmed unpainted nails trace the grain in the wood. Once he's sanded it just a little smoother, he tells her, he'll dust the wood and stain it a nice light oak. Then a matte varnish to give it a soft, glowing… *deliver us from evil. Amen.*

As he finishes this prayer that he has silently spoken thousands of times before, that he can recite flawlessly even when he's nine-tenths asleep, Tyler realizes he has once again failed to stay focused for the forty-five seconds he gives his maker each day. Nothing against God, it's just the way his brain works. He opens his eyes to the darkness and clears his mind blank. Clamping eyes shut, he begins again. *Our Father, who art in heav*

Body and mind slide down into the warm whirlpool of sleep; Tyler rests in peace.

2

Christie swims in the ocean shallows while Tyler kneels on wet Florida sand building a castle, or rather a sort of mushroom-shaped mound with a moat circling it. He works water into the sand to give it the consistency of mortar and compresses the brownish mixture between his two large hands. Warm saltwater runs up the beach between pulsing waves, through unseen openings in Tyler's bathing suit, and laps away, leaving behind sand and finely ground seashells.

A teenage couple walks up the beach, holding hands, then stop to watch Tyler shape the sand mound. The boy turns to his girlfriend, covering his mouth with his free hand, then bursts out laughing and runs tugging the girl behind him.

The salty wind and the sun have dried the skin on his face so that it feels pleasantly tight. He looks out across the ocean's blue-green waters through six-dollar sunglasses, purchased at the 7-Eleven. You can spend a lot more on fancy shades, but why? You just lose them anyway. Beyond the breaking waves, there's water as far as you can see. You'd swim for thousands of miles on wind-whipped waves and jellyfish before finally hitting land again. Portugal. Or Africa maybe.

Christie floats on her back near a sand bar, kicking up spray that refracts the late afternoon sunlight into a hazy rainbow. Then she stands and walks toward him through the shallows, droplets of water shimmering on her legs, beading like raindrops on the hood of a newly waxed Corvette. Her milky white one-piece suit makes her look darker, more exotic, than he remembers her. *She has come back.* Tyler opens his mouth to ask her where she's been, to tell her he's taking good care of Robbie and that the boy's talking now, the words coming so fast, a few more each day it seems. To tell her she looks more beautiful than ever, her wet reddish hair glowing in the setting sunlight. But his parched mouth cannot form the words. His nearly silent rasping wheeze is drowned out by seagulls *crying, crying*.... He looks again at her, to soak in her image, to study her one last time before she disappears again, but she's already gone.

Crying, Robbie's crying.

The digital clock radio on the bedstand says 2:44. There's no second hand to stare at, nor digital record of the seconds that still tick away like the evenly spaced orange barrels along a highway construction zone that he's always wanting to side-swipe as he drives by, like a hockey hip check, but is afraid to because the one he'd hit wouldn't be hollow plastic at all but solid concrete. Tyler forces his numb body out of bed, urinates in the small bathroom off his bedroom and staggers into Robbie's room. Sesame Street characters spin and wobble in a crazy orbit over the bawling toddler, his arms flailing, his shrill cry piercing Tyler's foggy consciousness. Father lifts son over the wooden bars of the crib and immediately the child is still, deadweight against his shoulder and neck, transformed in an instant from outrage to contentment. With his free hand, Tyler steadies the mobile. He had raised it high above the crib when Robbie learned to stand. Now the boy must be able to reach it again. He holds Cookie Monster for a moment, noticing the irregular stitching around its fat blue body. Christie had made the mobile from a kit she bought at the craft store when she was pregnant, not a very good job, really. The fronts and backs come together too sharply; there should be more stuffing inside to make a more rounded side. She was a little careless like that, more important for her to finish the job and move on to the next one than to do it really well. Tyler is a frustrated perfectionist and a bit of a neat freak, qualities lost on Christie.

His eyes grow moist. A solitary droplet runs down his left cheek, curving its way to his upper lip. Then another follows the same salty path. The boy needs his mother, Tyler sees with gloomy, middle-of-the-night clarity. How could he think he might somehow conjure up life's answers without her? He doesn't even know the questions. Stumbling through it alone. It had been all new to her, too, of course, but she had the natural instincts and intuition to get it mostly right as a mother and still have enough left inside her to guide him to become a seemingly capable parenting partner, just beginning to trust his own nascent fathering instincts. Without her, what chance does he have? To protect his son from every freakish danger lurking unseen is challenging enough. He knows he must do so much more than that during these crucial early months and years when the boy's malleable brain is forming. Don't they say, the experts, the psychologists who write the parenting books he has just begun to crack open but can't quite get into, that now is the critical time when the tracks are laid down, connecting all his tiny neurons, determining if he will grow up to be the mentally stable man he should become or instead one who will never quite adjust to the ups and downs of adult life, the fleeting moments of happiness along with the crushing responsibilities and inevitable heartache and loss? Destined to failure, loneliness and neurosis, even if he doesn't become a psycho killer shooting a semi-automatic rifle from a clock tower, like in that movie *Parenthood* that he and Christie had seen last fall when Robbie was not yet one, his life a barely begun book of possibilities. They had laughed at that exaggerated scene, Steve Martin in his daydreamed future being shot at by his grown-up son, Christie squeezing his arm in the theater with unspoken reassurance: *Don't worry; we'll get it right, the two of us together.*

He lays Robbie on his back on the tiny white mattress atop the changing table, and the boy begins to cry again, but with less force and venom. "Easy, now. Gotta check your diaper," he mumbles. "After I give you something to drink, you're gonna pee up a storm. So, we got to start you off dry again." Tyler undoes little white adhesive strips and removes the heavy, yellowed diaper. "Good thing we got rid of that one. Now, you gonna give me trouble about going back to bed?"

Robbie has no answer, but Tyler can see in his son's now wide-open eyes that he's not thinking sleep. "Not getting up twice in one night. Sorry, one time's my limit, kid."

Robbie had been sleeping through the night, but lately he wakes up screaming just before three, like clockwork. Maybe he's teething again; maybe he's testing his father's love. Or regressing. Tyler remembers now the pediatrician a few months ago telling him not to worry if his son *regresses* over the coming weeks and months. It would be normal, she had said, if the boy's development took a step backward as he dealt in his own way with the loss of his mother. Too young to understand, of course; he just feels her absence, missing his Mommy. Tyler can only do so much to fill the void. He won't let on, but he misses her, too, of course. Terribly so. Supposed well-wishers just don't know what to say to him, and what does come out of their mouths can be so wrong it's painful, their words an ice pick to his ears. It was easy enough for them at the funeral. *Our condolences, Tyler.... We're so sorry.* Like the bland sympathy cards that filled his mailbox—Christie had so many friends; the letters came from everywhere—these canned expressions of consolation required no originality or effort.

But then the awkwardness set in. A few days later in the supermarket with Robbie along in the cart, little dangling legs kicking away obliviously, a woman he barely knew from church had actually said: "But you must believe it's for the best. She's in heaven away from all the pain and troubles in life."

For the best! Does Robbie think it's for the best? The one who brought him into this world surely did not ask to be taken away so soon. When in a weak moment he allows his mind to wander back to the time and place she was ripped away from Robbie and him, to chew on the sheer arbitrariness of it all, he finds himself running down despairing, bitter roads that he refuses to travel. So, he won't think of her at all, for now.

This latest loss—of his rightful position at General Motors—eats away further at the core of who he is. Or at least who he is in the eyes of others, his professional identity. *So, what do you do? Where do you work?* Just small-talk icebreakers but so jarring when you don't have a ready answer. He will not let it sap his confidence, this second wound. No one wants to hire a loser from the ranks of the unemployed. He cannot allow himself to worry that it is his career that might be regressing.

He steps with his left foot on the little accelerator pedal that opens the lid on the plastic wastebasket and flips the wet disposable diaper with an end-over-end spin. *Two points*. Sure, these plastic diapers won't ever break down in the overcrowded landfills, not for ten thousand years anyway. He really should switch to washable cloth diapers, but he figures he handles enough crap as it is.

Will Robbie's mind as it matures have the same flighty tendencies as Tyler's? Perhaps the medical authorities will put an attention deficit disorder label on the boy someday; it seems all the rage these days. Tyler himself was never diagnosed with ADD. Back then, kids were just kids. He zips up Robbie's one-piece pajamas over the bulk of the puffy new diaper and carries the boy into the kitchen, heats up six ounces of two percent milk in the microwave, thirty-two seconds, not too hot, screws on the top of the bottle, and settles into his recliner just in time to catch the *Headline News* sports segment, the usual highlights for baseball season: home runs, strikeouts and sliding runners beating catchers' tags at home plate.

"Milk, milk," Robbie insists.

Tyler hands him the bottle without testing its temperature. Darryl Strawberry rips a low pitch into the upper decks. Tom Browning strikes out an unlucky Cub, Mark Grace, who lunges for a nasty slider that will keep breaking away from his bat every half hour, striking him out again and again to help entertain insomniacs across the country. No highlights for the Tigers; must not have played last night.

"I got to cut you off these baby bottles," Tyler says. "You're too old."

As if to confirm this, Robbie clamps down on the rubber nipple with his tiny white teeth as he pushes the bottle away. The nipple stretches, then snaps out of his mouth. Milk dribbles out the corners of Robbie's giggling mouth.

"Hey, cut that out," Tyler scolds. "You're gonna tear off a little piece of that rubber thing and swallow it. Then you'll be sorry. What am I supposed to do if you get something like that caught in your windpipe, huh?"

The kid's twenty-two months old now, nearly two. Is that too old for a bottle? But how else can he get Robbie back to sleep? This warm milk-in-a-bottle routine always does the trick, knocks him out for the rest of the night.

CNN's sports update is over. Time for the "The Hollywood Minute" with Sandy Kenyon—the film and TV star gossip that to Tyler isn't just dull, it's irritating. But he makes no effort to zap the channel. Some new controversy about that all-time over-exposed bore, Madonna. These one-name celebrities, like Cher and Sting and Bono, all seem to have egos as big as Elvis, and the ignorant public just laps it up. Madonna, so cold and calculatingly deliberate, undoubtedly having some brains behind that pouting face, has made a video too explicit for MTV's standards, "Justify My Love." Feigning outrage, she cries censorship. So, she sells the video direct to the public, cutting out the middleman. The media must know they're getting suckered, but they play along anyway, covering the controversy, hoping to ride Madonna's gravy train, pick up some Nielsen points.

After a series of inane commercials, a bright-eyed *Headline News* anchorwoman resets the lead story at the top of the hour: New evidence of Congressional payoffs in the savings-and-loan scandal. The "Keating Five" exposed now as corrupt "public servants" who looked the other way while crooks mismanaged some bank—Silverado Savings and Loan—and took it on a government-insured, multi-billion-dollar dive. *Silverado, like Eldorado*. A Cadillac with quality problems. Tyler looks at the still-frame pictures, mugshots really, of the five men, including Michigan Senator Don Riegle, who Tyler voted for two years ago. Like some shady law firm, the Five: Riegle, Glenn, McCain, Cranston & DeConcini. It's too early in the morning for outrage, and when they're talking about billions it seems remote and untouchable, like Carl Sagan's stars, but his stomach feels unsettled just the same. He burps, but doesn't feel relieved. Instead, he's left with a sour aftertaste in his mouth. As he flicks off the TV with his remote, he reminds himself to chew a couple of Tums before going back to bed. If he's got any left.

Robbie's eyes are tightly closed, his breathing rhythmic. Tyler carries him into the boy's bedroom and lays him in the crib. Then he slips under the blankets in his own bed and tries to welcome *death's sweet sister*, sleep. But at three a.m., the problems in his life seem impossibly immense. He doesn't want to think about Christie, nor his lost job. He closes his eyes to an image of a baseball player, himself, born again with an untouchably wicked fastball. Blessed with a cannon for a right arm, he can throw a baseball harder than anyone else in the big leagues, one hundred and five miles an hour. A scout from the Tigers points a jugs gun while Tyler throws to a trembling catcher. The scout's impressed, of course, and signs him to a semi-lucrative one-year contract. Here he is now walking in from the bullpen, the eighth inning of a tight game against the Yankees.... It's a well-worn fantasy Tyler uses whenever he hopes to escape from disturbing thoughts that might keep him awake. The cozy familiarity of his 105-mph fastball striking hot, hard leather behind the plate while an array of opposing hitters swing blindly, too late, lulls Tyler through familiar gates of sleep.

3

Tyler brushes away most of the crumbs that have collected in Robbie's car seat, slides his silent son into the protective plastic bucket, and lowers the seat's clunky armrest piece that keeps the kid in place. *Click.*

"Want my … tur-tull," Robbie says, fumbling with the last word.

Tyler retrieves the hard plastic Ninja Turtle figurine with a red bandanna—Raphael—and hands it to his son. Then Tyler walks around the car and hops into the driver's bucket seat. He still has to wiggle his butt, arch his back and roll his shoulders back and forth each morning before he feels comfortable in this car, Christie's little Sunbird. He kept the Sunbird, a woman's car, because it was newer, in better shape and more practical than his red two-seater Fiero, which was kind of a woman's car, too, actually. He'd bought the under-powered Fiero when it was just a year old from Celia who had suddenly decided to join some kind of missionary group in the Philippines, or Singapore, Tyler can't remember, hasn't heard from her in ages. He bought the car off her as a favor and because his old '76 Camaro with a screaming V-8, definitely a guy's car, was thoroughly beat. *Pontiac Fiero.* It was supposed to be a hot car, a flaming hot car. The name wasn't supposed to make you think of fire in the sense of an engine fire, but that's what the car had become known for. They stopped making the dogs after only four model years, a ruined car line even though GM had fixed the problem after the first two model years, adding an extra quart capacity to the ridiculously small three-quart oil pan—undersized on the original because it was the easiest way to accommodate the car's radical flying wedge design. *Form over function.* His sister's was built in the spring of '85, one of the last ones made with the too-small oil pan. He sold the Fiero five months ago, a couple of weeks after Christie died, to a girl from Ann Arbor, a U-M student, who paid him three or four hundred more than the car was worth. Tyler had shined it up nice, made it look sexy sitting in his driveway, a car she couldn't resist, bright red like her fingernails.

    He backs the car out of the garage and taps the button on the remote clipped to his visor. The garage door lowers slowly. "Bye, bye," Robbie whispers as they back out of the driveway. Tyler glances in his rearview mirror and catches a glimpse of Robbie's little hand waving to the empty house.

    Curtains are drawn in each neighbor's front windows and nobody's out for a walk to wave to him this morning, his last as an employee of the largest corporation in the world. Neighbors staying to themselves these days, avoiding the one who has lost his wife and must be spoken to gently. Or perhaps tense as they talk to each other about what has them most worried, the neighborhood going to hell now that these Arab families, at least a dozen of them, have moved lately into nearby subdivisions; they used to stay down in East Dearborn with its mosques and *shish kafta.* Lebanese mostly, it seems. They move, quietly at first, into what had been stalwart "all-American" neighborhoods. The extended family, multiple generations with cousins and in-laws, overflowing one house and then moving into another nearby. And then, the seal broken, another family moves in, and another. They don't keep up their lawns very well, Tyler has heard people at his workplace say. Almost immediately you can see a difference, the grass scrabbly along their driveways and sidewalks where they should be edging and using weed killer; they must not have lawns in the desert countries they come from. Word goes around that the neighborhood is going Arab and some of the white homeowners panic, like skinny gray worms in the pouring rain that wriggle free of their flooded underground tunnels in a desperate attempt at escape, ending up on sidewalks where they're mercilessly squished by children stomping like giants in cheerfully colored plastic boots: yellow and blue and pink. Where can they go, these homeowners with their fleeting prosperity and quaint ideas of patriotic, homogeneous seclusion, but farther out from frightful Detroit to leafy Bloomfield Hills or Troy, maybe, Orchard Lake or Northville, with inflated home prices and property taxes, signing on to crushing mortgages and killer commutes until they succumb like worms without refuge in the rain. No sanctuary after all.

With his right index finger, Tyler punches the buttons on the radio each time a commercial comes on, jumping from music to talk to music, but then landing only on commercials. The stations often play their ads at the same time as each other, a conspiracy to thwart the jumpy listener. Then at the top of the hour, seven o'clock, the news. Never very interesting, yet seemingly important and real, so he lingers there. Something about the Middle East, but the traffic ahead jams up, his lane stops moving, and then he can't remember what he just heard. It's always coming at you, all this information, layered on top of what it takes just to live in the world these days. No wonder he misses so much.

The ladies at the daycare center are extra patient with Tyler. Dads at daycare are a rarity still, even after two-and-a-half decades of women's lib. They're treated like children, the dads here, patronized by the staff, who can't quite forgive them for not being women, not being moms. And Tyler is given special attention. They know Robbie has no behind-the-scenes mom, packing an extra set of clothes and boots and gloves in the winter, like the other kids whose dads drop them off in the morning and return in the evening to bring them home so their working wives can take over again.

Tyler writes on a sheet of a spiral notebook, "Robbie Manion, 7:10," and initials it, "TGM." He holds his boy's hand, and they walk together to Robbie's room, the Penguin Room. Seven or eight boys and girls his age already are playing with yellow Tonka trucks and red and blue Duplo blocks or climbing on a tiny plastic gym set that sits on a padded mat. Lots of bright primary colors. A little Asian boy—he looks Japanese but maybe Korean—reaches on his tippy toes for a familiar tall yellow bird sitting on the desk of one of the "teachers." He pulls at it but misjudges its weight.

Big Bird falls to the floor with a crash, exploding into little pieces and a cloud of dust. Not the stuffed animal the kid thought he was reaching for, but a ceramic bank, heavy and fragile, even without any coins. A tall, skinny woman in her thirties, brown hair pulled back in a bun, hurries over with a broom and dustpan and a mild reproach for the boy who just stands there stunned, his hands still high over his head. Three other children who had been playing near the desk, startled by the crash, flee to bury their heads into the wide embrace of a portly teacher who comforts them against the soft mass of her body in a generous, grandmotherly hug.

"How's my big boy doin'?" asks another lady, mid-forties with glasses and a little too much makeup, her red cheeks glowing in a pasty texture.

"Fine. Good. If only I could get him to sleep through the night again." They fight it like death, the little ones, when their indulgent parents desire nothing so much for themselves as the soft caressing release of sleep and their fondest hope in those early hours after midnight is to put the crying child down without a fight. We pretend to forget this infantile lesson when we grow up, the forbidding darkness that sleep and death have in common. But it's

21

embedded in our very language as when we speak of a rabid dog that has to be *put to sleep*.

"Oh, that's normal," she reassures him. "All kids go through stages where something or other wakes them up. Don't worry. He'll grow out of it."

"Yeah, I'm sure he will."

The woman looks at Tyler through round wire glasses. "Robert is just so advanced for his age. It's incredible. He's the best talker in this room, definitely. In fact, he already speaks better than most of the kids in the Giraffe Room," she says, lowering her voice, speaking confidentially. "I think he's gifted."

Tyler smiles. In Livonia, like Farmington and Farmington Hills and the other comfortable suburbs here in southeastern Michigan, every parent whose child isn't a complete lummox thinks their kid is *gifted*. Still, Tyler can't help but be pleased when others notice how quick Robbie is.

"Thanks. Yeah, he's something all right. Hey, Robbie. C'mon over here and give me a hug goodbye."

Robbie already has wandered off to play with his classmates, but he turns and dutifully walks back to where Tyler bends down, crouching on one knee to return to his son's world. The same size now. For a moment, they're one body, arms clinging to each other's sides and back, eyes shut. No one else there. Tyler feels an urge to whisper into the little warm ear that is touching his nose. *Dreams sometimes break*, he might whisper. Like a clay bird they get broken and can't be fixed because the pieces won't fit anymore. The warning goes unspoken; there's no room for it in their silent embrace.

Tyler cannot stay. He stands up, six feet tall and more, a grownup, waving to his son. But the boy already has slipped away into the excitement. He doesn't notice his father leave.

4

Tyler parks the Sunbird in one of the employee lots behind the General Motors Garden City Stamping Plant. Whoever named this wasteland *Garden City* had an ironic sense of humor, like those responsible for nick-naming New Jersey the *Garden State*. It's nothing but a shabby, industrial parcel of land between Detroit and the livable suburbs to the west. "Morning," he mumbles to the pale, middle-aged receptionist at the secondary lobby off the plant's rear entrance.

"Good morning, Tyler," she returns cheerfully, still operating in yesterday's reality when she was expected to be pleasant to him.

He walks down the hall to the staff offices. *Industrial Relations*, an old, faded sign declares, what Human Resources used to be called at General Motors, or rather, the part of HR dealing with hourly workers. Tyler's name plate already has been removed from the cubicle wall. He sets down the empty cardboard box he's brought from home to clean out his desk, to retrieve the few personal belongings he's kept at work these four years. Although he technically is being laid off, with the unofficial expectation that he will be called back when the "economic downturn" ends, Tyler knows he's unlikely to ever get his job back. He is low man on the totem pole of seniority, the only criterion that matters. He hopes that long before GM gets around to calling him back, he will have found a better place to work, at a company where Human Resources means something closer to the profession he aspired to in his college days.

There is a note lying face up on the seat of Tyler's well-worn swivel chair. A "buck slip" emblazoned with *A. M. Schulous* at the top left in blue printer's ink, the GM logo on the right. "Tyler: See me."—it reads in typed letters, undoubtedly dictated to his secretary. Those three short words too much to be hand-written; a hurried "S" scribbled below. What's that bastard Schulous want now? Tyler crumples the note and flicks the tiny wad into his gray steel wastebasket. He takes a handful of pens and pencils from his desk drawer, binds them with a red rubber band, and sets the bundle into his box. A framed photograph—Robbie when he turned one—is next. Then some books and notepads. He reaches to the bulletin board behind his desk and unpins some more photos, him and Christie on vacation, at a wedding, in a sports bar yucking it up after one of his softball games. And two faded Calvin and Hobbes cartoons. They don't strike him as funny anymore, so he crumples the comics together in a tight ball to be tossed in the basket. That reminds him of the note from Schulous. Might as well see what he wants.

Tyler walks through the quiet cubicles in the staff area, the silence broken only by the pecking of keyboards on either side of him. He walks down Executive Row. Schulous's secretary is not at her desk. A small, printed sign standing on her desk facing any visitor who would approach indicates that she and her boss can be found today in the other row of executive offices at the front of the plant. When Tyler reaches the doorway to the plant floor, he plugs his ears with yellow rubber inserts. Then he puts on a set of safety goggles—thick, black Buddy Holly glasses with protective side pieces of clear acrylic.

He opens a heavy steel door encased in a giant rubber gasket and is greeted by the familiar blast of hot noise. He grabs a bike off a rack and pedals slowly into the bowels of the stamping plant. Workers in soiled green jumpsuit coveralls pay him no heed as he pedals past. Sweat dampens his white shirt and his eyes begin to sting from the foul factory air; the safety glasses don't stop the smog from quickly coating his eyes. But it is the noise he feels. It never lets up. Noise from everywhere all at once. The ear plugs don't stop the noise. They just spread it out, so that every square inch of his skin all over his body feels the ugly, incessant vibrations. After four years of countless trips on the plant floor, traveling by bicycle because the distance would take you forever if you walked, several hundred yards from end to end and a thousand yards deep, he has never gotten used to the noise inside the stamping plant. A steadily erratic bass beat of metal thumping, pounding and grinding. On and on.

Tyler rides the blue single-speed bike over the factory floor, past one giant press, and another, then another. Pale green under thick layers of dust and grime from forty-five or so years of stamping steel, the presses work hard and steady, just as they did when they were new, bright symbols of American industrial dominance. Must have been something to see in those first years, stamping steel for post-war Chevrolets. Tyler knows the stories from the glory days of this plant, twenty years before he was born, when Detroit was all muscle, full of energy and promise. If you wanted a car during the war, you bought used; the auto plants were busy building tanks, jeeps and airplanes. After the war if you wanted a car, you probably had to wait for it, whether you wanted a Chevy, Olds, Buick, Packard, Desoto, Chrysler or Ford. Plenty of choices, all American. With the rest of the world's industry obliterated by the war, American factories were humming three eight-hour shifts a day to fill the void. Industrial dominance fit America like a handsome leather glove, and Detroit was its index finger, waggling at the world: Number One, baby!

Tyler pedals past shiny coils of corrugated steel, four feet in diameter, unrolling as they feed into the presses. A massive hammer, the size of a baby grand piano, rises out of the top of each machine, twenty-five feet above the plant floor, and comes crashing down onto a die resting just above a length of sheet steel pulled taut and ready for the punishing blow. A precise, three-dimensional cookie cutter, pounding and cutting the flat steel, giving it shape and purpose. Fenders for Chevies, Pontiacs and Oldsmobiles are spit out the other end of each machine. Fenders for Buicks and Cadillacs come out of another line.

Two men in grease-stained green coveralls stack the newly formed fenders on a wooden pallet, putting a cardboard spacer between each one. A bright orange plastic spacer marks each dozen; twelve not ten in unspoken defiance of the metric system favored in Europe and Asia. The men fill the crate until another worker comes by on a hi-lo. The tractor's steel tongs spear the pallet under the crate and lift it six feet above the floor. The hi-lo backs up and lurches around a corner, out of sight. The men begin to fill another crate. How do they stand the noise?

In the Seventies, the American companies grew complacent and careless. Pintos exploding, Corvairs unsafe at any speed, Ralph Nader showing up the Big Three in court and in the market of public opinion. The Japanese are the quality leaders now and somehow their boring designs underscore a basic competence. *They belong*. Next it will be the Koreans. Like an endless series of waves spreading from a powerful earthquake on the other side of the ocean, they're coming. And not just into the U.S. They're crafty, these relentless Asians, already moving into developing markets where they undersell the American companies, which don't even notice they're there. Like a giraffe content to eat the remaining leaves on the highest branches of the only tree in its zoo pen, GM cannot see the competition moving underneath it, forever taking away opportunities in these new automotive markets: Eastern Europe starting to break free from decades of Soviet stagnation, the East Asian Five Tigers with their insane appetite for economic growth, and the Latin America nations with so much potential if they could just keep a government in place for more than a year or two.

Tyler pedals the bike, counting the presses he passes. Thirty-four, thirty-five, thirty-six. Fenders, hoods, trunk lids, body panels and roofs to supply GM assembly plants all over the U.S. and Canada. Finally, he reaches the front of the building—a thousand yards from the back entrance. Outside, where it's sunny and the air is fresh and mostly clean, seems like a hundred miles away.

He turns right and pedals past another dozen presses before coming to the executive offices off the plant's main lobby. As he closes the heavy steel door behind him, Tyler pulls out his ear plugs.

"Is Art Schulous in?" he asks the secretary, a short, bloated woman he doesn't recognize. Must be a temp. The secretary slowly turns in her swivel chair away from a video terminal, revealing the secret of her heaviness—she's pregnant, probably in her seventh or eighth month. Now she looks vaguely familiar. Tyler has never been good at remembering faces.

"You're Tyler Manion?" she asks, smiling cautiously. He nods. "He's in, but he's talking to somebody. On the phone. Please have a seat. He'll be right with you."

Tyler settles into an orange chair. Back issues of the company's employee newsletter lie on the coffee table in front of him, but he's not interested. Just as well; the dim light in this outer office would make it difficult to read. Two of the fluorescent tubes above have burnt out. The secretary peers into a bright word processor screen that lights the pale profile of her face with a sickly greenish-white glow. Something about her is familiar. She glances over at him, feeling his stare. He looks past her, at a calendar from a Dearborn florist. Pink and white flowers, carnations maybe, brighten the upper half of the calendar. Below, numbers arranged in seven columns represent the month of July. A month behind.

He looks at the secretary's face again. Then he remembers. She was here that first day he came to Schulous's office eighteen or nineteen months ago when he was told about his new assignment within the department, his last assignment as it turned out. She was pregnant then, too. Must be some kind of baby machine.

Something on the secretary's desk buzzes. She lifts a phone from the cradle within a multi-buttoned plastic unit, and whispers into it. Then she turns to Tyler, giving him a disapproving frown, still holding the phone to her ear. "Mr. Schulous will see you now," she says flatly.

Tyler opens the door to Schulous office. A large oil painting in a heavy, dark walnut frame hangs on the wall behind his desk.

"How are you, Tyler?" Schulous asks pleasantly, as if nothing's changed between them. He shakes Tyler's hand. They both sit down. A frail and balding man of about fifty-five with a bushy gray mustache and dots of stubble all over his cheeks, chin and neck, Schulous slouches to one side as he sits. A half-burnt cigarette smolders from a crowded ashtray.

"Fine," Tyler lies, looking at the eagle in the painting behind Schulous. The one thing he has respected about his boss, this finely detailed, seemingly original oil painting. Unusual for someone below a vice president to have a real painting in his office. More likely a nondescript poster print in a metal-and-glass frame. But now it's not what he expects to see. Not the painting of a majestic eagle soaring over amber waves of grain that he remembers hanging here. An eagle yes, but a vicious, hungry eagle bearing its talons, swooping down onto an open meadow of high grasses where unseen rabbits and field mice undoubtedly run for cover.

"I've got some paperwork for you to sign," Schulous says. As if on cue, the pregnant secretary appears with a manila folder which she hands to Tyler.

Three thick, multi-colored forms await his signature. He scans the legalese formalizing the layoff. Schulous explains that if he will give up any expectation of being called back, Tyler will receive a severance payment equal to twelve weeks of his salary—not bad, Schulous says, considering that Tyler has worked for General Motors for only four years. *Might as well*, he thinks, already having resigned himself to the idea that he is never coming back to GM. Just like that, the layoff becomes a *separation*.

"Press hard with your pen, it has to go through all those carbons," the secretary advises solemnly. She tears off the bottom copy of each form. The faint sloppy curves of his signed name look timid on the thin pink sheets, his copies.

"Let me know if there's anything I can do to help you," Schulous says, leaning over the desk, his face close enough that Tyler can smell his stale smoker's breath. "Just say the word."

"Okay," Tyler mumbles.

"I always liked you," Schulous is saying. "You just got caught in a bad time. I'm sure you'll find a better position somewhere else."

He pauses. Silence fouls the air between them. Time all but stops; the awkwardness lingers. Tyler tries to conjure thoughts of the dominating pitcher standing on the mound, staring at his catcher, waiting for the sign, a single index finger calling for the heat, but the confining immediacy of the old manager's lair won't permit it. The eagle stares down on him, as he tries to hide in the weeds. Why can't this be like *Good Morning America*? Where even the most heart-wrenching stories don't last more than three minutes. *Thank you for joining us, Art Schulous. I'm sorry, that's all the time we have. When we come back from the station break, we'll hear from Joan Lunden in Hawaii.* Short and sweet and we're outta here.

Into the clouds of silence, Schulous bleats: "Any leads yet?"

Tyler tugs at his tie. "No. I've been talking to those two head-hunters you told me about. Plus another one, out of Atlanta. Nothing yet," he says. Truth is, professional recruiters don't bother with lower-level jobs for relative newbies like Tyler. Then he fills the silence with the expected explanation: "The economy," he says.

"You're smart not to limit yourself to Michigan," Schulous says, stroking the coarse, gray hairs of his mustache. "You're better off outside the auto industry. Unless you're thinking of hooking up with one of the transplants."

Tyler knows what Schulous thinks of anyone who'd even consider working for one of the invading Japanese *transplant* auto assembly plants springing up throughout the non-union rural Midwest and South, welcomed with massive tax abatements by governors happy to bring in some jobs to replace those lost with each closing textile mill, tool and die shop, or cluster of abandoned family farms.

"I don't think so," is all Tyler says, breathing in hot, dry air through his mouth. He looks past Schulous at the hungry eagle in the painting. Yellow eyes focusing on a helpless mouse running crazed through an open field just beyond the border of the painting, the crops already harvested, an occasional clump of weeds the only cover. *Each and every one of us is prey to somebody flying higher*, he imagines Schulous saying.

"Well, don't hesitate to use me as a reference," Schulous is actually saying, as he rises to his feet. It's over. Tyler shakes the older man's bony hand and turns away, making for the door. "Hey, good luck, Tyler. It was a pleasure."

Tyler turns and offers Schulous a small smile as a peace offering. *Don't burn any bridges.*

"Thank you, sir. I learned a lot from you." He looks into Schulous's sad eyes and adds bravely: "I'm not worried about finding a new job."

The secretary's fingers are a pink blur across her keyboard. She doesn't look up from her work as Tyler passes through the outer office. He finds his plugs and returns them to his ears just before he opens the heavy door.

5

Robbie doesn't act surprised to see his father picking him up so early. When you're his age, you're flexible. He says goodbye to his daycare friends and walks with his father to their car, his hand wrapped around Tyler's index finger. They drive up Telegraph Road, not the usual way home. Robbie spots the Golden Arches long before Tyler signals the turn.

"Happy Meal," the boy announces.

Tyler has finished his Big Mac and fries before Robbie has made much of a dent in his food. Mostly he's played with the plastic toy that came with his meal and sucked ketchup off a French fry, dipping the same fry over and over into a little red puddle his father had made on the paper place mat.

Tyler grabs a *Free Press* lying abandoned on a bright blue plastic bench in a neighboring booth, the main headline on page one in bigger type than normal, crying out to be noticed:

INVASION JOLTS WORLD ECONOMY
Double-Dip Recession Feared in the U.S.; Oil Price Already Spurting

The story is date-lined Washington. The White House has denounced the "naked aggression" of Iraq in its invasion of tiny Kuwait, frozen U.S. assets of the Iraqi government, banned most imports from Iraq, and called for an international isolation of the Mideast oil power. Kuwait begs for U.S. military intervention. A little map shows where these countries are. Over by Iran, wouldn't you know. Tyler scans down the page to a related story with the local angle:

SOME IRAQI-AMERICANS CHEER INVASION
Many Iraqi Chaldeans in Michigan feel part of a historic victory. "It's great," says Willam Saleh at a Middle Eastern market in Southfield, buying flat bread. "If you go back in history, it's ours."

The article notes that the Detroit area has one of the largest Iraqi populations in the United States, estimated at 75,000. Virtually all are Chaldeans, a Christian sect in the predominantly Muslim nation. A photo shows a smiling Saleh, raising a fist, Chaldean bakery in the background, just like the story mentioned.

Tyler skims the news stories for the same reason he still goes to church; he's afraid of missing out on something important. The news around the world must matter, must somehow pertain to him, he feels, or else it wouldn't be there, right? But now he looks for something different, not-so-hard news. Page three has something about golf:

PANEL TELLS NOMINEES TO QUIT BIASED CLUBS BY '91

The controversy over exclusive clubs that discriminate against women and minorities surfaced in the Senate, the story says, as the Judiciary Committee warned potential candidates for federal judgeships or senior Justice Department posts, against joining them. Ever since that redneck down at Shoal Creek said something about not having black members, a couple weeks or so ago, and the PGA threatened to hold the Masters somewhere else,

Tyler is thinking, everybody's outraged about all-white country clubs. As if it had been a big secret that they excluded blacks. He, on the other hand, is no bigot, having played golf with a black guy at least a couple of times just this summer. Ed, from the softball team. A tall, athletic dude with a long, fluid swing of his wood driver. Persimmons. You don't see that much anymore in this age of metal woods. Club head raised up and then back down in a big, smooth arc, colliding with the ball on the tee with a crack like a dry branch snapping. Then the perfect follow-through, hands and wrists coming up across his chest and over his left shoulder, only then looking up to catch the disappearing ball still climbing against the deep blue sky, such discipline. The rest of us so often lift our heads too early. Tyler does it once or twice a round, it seems, topping the ball, sending a screaming grounder that gets caught up in the tall grass and hardly goes anywhere. But not Ed, keeping his head down in studied obedience to some long-ago lesson, not falling prey to the tempestuous desire to sneak a peek, to lose focus. Why do most of us find it so hard to concentrate for the few seconds within a single golf swing? The only thing that matters at that moment, and yet we can't hold our focus there where it needs to be. The mind wanders where it wants to go, has a mind of its own.

Tyler pushes the paper aside and coaxes Robbie into eating most of his food. He dabs the red ketchup stains on either side of the boy's mouth with a paper napkin. What chance in life's merciless rat race does this little one have without a mother's soothing embrace and gentle doting? A mother to encourage his better angels to the forefront of an emerging personality, his first real self, so he will be secure enough in his home and in her love that he can venture out to make friends with children from other homes, to discover new worlds with cheerful curiosity, without cowering in fear of the unknown. Then a father can do the work of building and shaping the character of this future citizen, so that, if all goes well, he will mature into an adult self that is principled, disciplined and dependable, becoming a worthy husband and father of his own someday. But character is built upon a foundation of nurturing that comes naturally from a mother. How can Tyler be both father and mother to this little one when he still has so much to learn just being a dad?

They return to the car. Robbie's eyes look heavy and Tyler thinks about taking him home for his nap, but instead makes a quick run for the library. He hasn't spent much time with his son lately, and he'll be going out again tonight. Now's his opportunity to cram in some quick quality time.

The kid is loud and bratty in the library, over-tired. He pulls a half-dozen books off a shelf and starts crying when they fall to the floor. "*Shhh*. You have to be *quiet* in here," Tyler whispers loudly.

"Wwwwan dab bbb," Robbie stammers between tears. "Want da bbbear one."

"Which bear book, Robbie?" Tyler pleads. Each of the books on the floor, it seems, has something to do with bears. They must be in the bear section. "This one?"

"No!" the boy yells. He gulps his breath in quick, emphatic teary staggers, the quiet before the storm. Tyler points at several books but can't find the one his son wants. Then the boy's floodgates burst open. His bawling shatters the library's musty silence. Tyler scoops up his son with his right arm, grabs three books with his left hand and carries boy and books to the checkout desk. A librarian with closely cropped white hair frowns as she runs the books and Tyler's library card under an optical scanner. It's all computers now, everywhere you go. She rubs her nose absent-mindedly while she stares into the large cube of a monitor taking up nearly half her desk. A few keystrokes complete the transaction.

Then she looks up at Robbie, hesitating before she returns Tyler's library card. "In the future," she says dryly, still looking at Robbie, "please try to do better in keeping your child quiet."

Tyler holds his tongue, and they leave peacefully, Robbie catching his breath. Soon after they reach the car and Robbie is strapped into his car seat, he falls asleep. Tyler carries him into the house and lays him down in his crib, untying the white laces on the boy's Reeboks and covering him with a cotton crib sheet. Robbie doesn't fight it.

Tyler changes into a pair of blue jeans and an old red, white and blue Detroit Pistons tee shirt and goes downstairs to his basement workshop. Smiles as he walks past a half-finished set of bookshelves. A present he's making for Robbie's second birthday in two months. Plenty of time left. Tyler's already bought some of the picture books he'll wrap up for Robbie to add to the gift. He stops to examine the piece of pine impaled on the lathe. It will be one of the struts for a little rocking chair he's making for Robbie—another present, perhaps to be saved for Christmas. He can't work on it now; the lathe makes too much noise. He reaches instead into the top drawer of an old, press-wood dresser he had once used in the bedroom of his first apartment while still a college student, now exiled to the basement and filled with tools and work supplies rather than clothes and linen, for a sheet of sandpaper to put the finishing touches on the soft curves of the pine boards that will be the chair's seat and back.

Time slips away as he strokes the wood, pausing periodically to blow dust from his work. He wanted to stain the wood today and let it dry overnight, but already he hears Robbie stirring. He returns the sheet of sandpaper, hardly used, to the top drawer of the cheap, old dresser. Then he sweeps up the little pile of sawdust.

6

Tyler and Robbie are waiting on the front porch steps when the babysitter arrives. She parks the Mustang on the street and walks up the driveway, wearing lime green sweatpants and a white short-sleeved shirt. Robbie in a blue-and-red Pistons outfit runs down the walk toward her.

"Hi, Nicki!" he shouts.

"Hey, squirt. Think I can beat your dad in a game of basketball?"

Robbie stops to consider this. "No… think so," he says finally.

Tyler smiles; he was hoping she would remember their basketball date. "Hey, your dad hasn't shot a basketball in months," he says to Robbie. "And this girl claims she's hot stuff."

The babysitter blushes and does not reply.

"I'll get the ball," Tyler says, ducking into the garage. He finds the orange Wilson NBA in a sturdy cardboard box that contains an assortment of sports equipment—a football and tee, a pump, a tennis racket, half a dozen softballs and a couple of old bats. He bounces the ball to her, an easy pass. She snatches it out of the air and jumps, pumping and releasing in the same motion she showed him last night, this time aiming at the goal attached to Tyler's garage. The ball swishes through the nylon net.

"Not bad. Bet you can't get that lucky again," Tyler teases her. He gives her another bounce pass. She grabs the ball, dribbles to her right a few steps, then kisses the ball softly off the white plastic backboard through the iron rim.

"Hey, nice shot, Nicki," Tyler says.

The ball bounces back to the girl. "Let's see what you got," she says, flicking him a waist-high pass that smacks against the palms of his hands. Tyler dribbles out a few feet past the faded white stripe that marks the foul line on his asphalt driveway. He rocks up on his toes and sends the ball on a graceful arc. The aim is true, but there's too much on it. The ball strikes the crotch of the rim and rockets over the girl's head, bouncing on the lawn over where Robbie sits watching.

"Brick!" the girl taunts.

Tyler retrieves the ball, dribbles in a little closer, and launches another shot. It skitters around the rim, but drops through. "Okay, I'm warmed up," he says. "Take a shot."

The game is no contest. Tyler is down H-O-R to nothing before he makes a shot. The girl doesn't miss. And, as she lets him know, the basketball they're using is a bit bigger than the girls' ball she's used to shooting. Finally, he makes a little double-pump layup she can't quite duplicate.

"At least you didn't get shut out," she says.

He dribbles the ball out to the far corner of his driveway, beyond NBA three-point range, rises up and shoots the ball on a high curving trail that ends with the ball cleanly piercing the circular plane of air in the middle of the rim and whipping through the net. *Swish.*

"Hey!" she exclaims.

"Move in a few steps," he offers. But the girl stubbornly walks out to the corner, turns and eyes the distant goal. She throws her shot like a baseball. It looks to be on the right line, but falls short.

Just as Tyler thinks he can feel it, like the old days after school at the Armory in Akron, he grows cold again. His shot from along the right baseline, his feet planted on the grass beside his driveway, has too much on it and doesn't even hit the rim. A moment later, he picks up another letter, missing an easy shot from the foul line. Then the girl walks out well beyond the foul stripe, to about the top of the key like she bragged about last night. She holds the big boys' ball above her head, her eyes wide open, unblinking, focusing on the target. Behind her, the sinking sun burns red and orange highlights through the thick tangles of her hair. Silhouetted in this dim light, her small, soft lips are brown. She rises up on the balls of her sneakers' soles and sinks the shot, all net, as advertised.

Tyler misses for the final letter. "Hey, good game, Nicki," he says, walking over to where she stands, beaming. "You've really got some range to your shot. You been working out or something?" His hand rests on her upper arm. "Let me see you make a muscle."

The girl blushes, hesitates, then flexes her right arm, drawing her hand into a tight little fist. Tyler squeezes the hard lump of her tensed bicep.

"Hey, not bad," he says. Then she opens her fist, and the strong boyish muscle relaxes into feminine flesh still covered by his fingers. Soft, warm and a little sweaty.

"Oh, I don't know," she says. "I don't always shoot like that. Sometimes it just feels right."

Tyler's hand falls from her arm. "Well, you were making them just now."

"I'll tell you what it really is," she says, as if about to confide some dark secret. Her green eyes glow intensely now. It's not just the light; there's a confidence behind them he's never seen in her. Not the cocky false bravado she had earlier, but a quiet surety of a knowledge in something beyond the here and now.

"What?" he asks.

"What do you aim at when you shoot?" she asks him back.

"At the goal, the basket. The big hole up there inside the rim."

"Yeah, that's what I used to do. But I'm shooting way better this summer because I don't just throw it toward the goal. I focus on the back of the rim. On a little piece of the inside of the back part of the rim, actually. On the opposite side of whichever way I'm coming in at it. I give it a nice high arc and good follow-through. But the real secret is zeroing in on a spot at the back of the rim. Like aiming at a bullseye."

"Let me try it," he says. His shooting used to be automatic, the strongest part of his so-so game in high school. He never really had to aim. The rainbow path of his shot found the bottom of the net more often than not. His Dad had worked with him on it, and he had practiced, sure, practiced a lot. But his shooting was *natural*, something he was born with. Now he squints at the back of the iron ring, but his shot from just beyond the foul line is too flat. It strikes the back of the rim hard and ricochets right back to him.

"It takes some practice. Let me show you. Of course, you're looking under the front of the rim to see the back part of the rim, especially from my height. But you ignore that. You don't even see the front. Because when the ball is on a nice rainbow, it just…" No need for her to finish the sentence; her graceful shot is perfect. *Swish.*

"Your coach teach you that?"

"Nah. It just came to me one day when I was shooting by myself. I needed to focus my aim. It makes all the difference for me."

Robbie has moved over to join them. "Nicki beat?" he asks.

Tyler laughs. "She sure did. I guess it's my turn to practice. Crap, I couldn't hit anything."

He changes into a collared golf shirt while the babysitter fixes Robbie's dinner. "You be good for Nicki," Tyler tells his son as he scoots out the door.

***

Aaron Foster and Webb Rucker have already drunk half a pitcher by the time Tyler finds their table at the Turnstile. Foster is an

MBA from GM's Controller's Office, a fast-tracking bean counter on special assignment at the Garden City Plant. He's twenty-six and single, same as Tyler. Rucker is five years older, divorced, a computer operator in Inventory Control, in the part of the plant where Tyler worked until a year and a half ago.

"So, this is my farewell party, huh? Two guys," Tyler says, not really complaining.

"Told you not to expect many," Foster says. "Tried talking you up, but you know how people are." Foster often drops the first syllable or two leading off a string of words; it somehow gets lopped off before he gets going. *Neticut* is his nickname at the plant—a chopped form of Connecticut, where Foster is from. Tyler and the others don't know anyone else from the little New England state, so they're unsure if it's just Foster or if everyone from Connecticut speaks in the same, clipped style. Foster doesn't mind the nickname. He views his peculiar speech pattern as the hallmark of genius. His mouth simply cannot keep up with the quickness of his brain.

"You mean they don't want to be associated with someone who's been axed," Tyler says.

"Remember you as the guy holding the ax in the first place," Neticut reminds him.

"And that your ax beheaded a few of their own dear departed," Rucker adds stiffly, trying too hard to be witty.

Tyler feels like a luckless wrestler caught in a tag-team mugging. "Well, aren't you two just terrific pick-me-ups. Hey, pour me a beer and change the subject."

Rucker takes it upon himself to comply with both requests. "How's your little kid doing?" he asks as he fills Tyler's glass with foaming Budweiser. With a sudden jerk he stops pouring, but the head keeps rising. Its overflow makes a white puddle on the brown vinyl tabletop.

"That's enough, Rucker!" Tyler scolds. "You did go to college, right?" He leans over and sips a little from the glass without moving it. "Robbie's doing great. It's really something to follow him around and just watch him. He gets all enthusiastic about stuff that's nothing special to us. Like the moon, changing shapes from night to night. Or blades of grass bending to his touch."

"It's all new to him, right?" Rucker adds, trying to make amends.

"Now that he's starting to talk, it's like I've got this window into his thoughts. Turns out he understands a lot. He just couldn't put it into words back to me. Kind of like the first thought in a Neticut sentence."

Foster doesn't seem to hear this. A red-haired girl, no way she's twenty-one, walks toward them. With each step she takes, the rounded fullness of her chest bounces and settles. She moves past their table. A short, brown skirt barely covers the smooth curve of her bottom. She tugs at it with her right hand as she walks. Back to the pool tables in the rear of the bar she goes, throwing her arms around a bearded guy in a checked corduroy shirt and ripped jeans.

The three pairs of eyes at Tyler's table each return to the glasses of beer in front of them. "Got any leads on jobs, Tyler?" Rucker asks.

"I've talked to a few headhunters. I'm not worried. Companies are always going to need HR people."

"Isn't a good time," Neticut says gloomily. "Economy's looking worse every day. Talking about oil prices going up again, account of this Kuwait thing."

"Well, I've got three months' severance pay to blow before I get too nervous." Tyler isn't so much an optimist as a procrastinator. No use worrying before you have to.

A waitress in black pants and a black-and-gray striped top—the Turnstile uniform—appears with another pitcher, her top blouse button unfastened. Rucker slides her a ten-dollar bill and admires the view as she stoops over the table to make change. Tyler silently snickers. Like most of his male friends, he notices the women all around him, everywhere he goes. The background colors that decorate his life's television set, women with their bright smiles, their curves, their hip-rolling walks you notice from behind. Even the fat ones and plain ones, the awkward, self-conscious ones with bad hair and glasses, filling up the screen of Tyler's mind in ways that men simply do not; he hardly sees them, like washed-out photographs in an otherwise brightly colorful magazine. Women are more interesting because they are *so unlike us*, he thinks.

Someone turns the sound system up a little louder. Friday night, moving into *prime time*. The low-lifes who frequent the Turnstile all week now out-numbered by cleaner, flashier yuppies.

"Schulous called me into his office today," Tyler announces loud enough to be heard. "Couldn't just let me go in peace."

Rucker leans in toward the center of the table. "What'd he have to say?"

"That I could use him for a reference and to just ask him if there was anything he could do for me."

"I hope you told Schulous to kiss your butt. Then you could tell him that you always knew he was just an ass wipe, right?" Rucker says brashly. It's easy to come up with something memorable when you're telling somebody else what they should have said, after the fact. Webb Rucker isn't so bold when it's him on the spot. Deflects questions with questions. High strung and nervous, like a little toad that's so frightened when you pick it up from its hiding place in the grass it pees on your hand, even if you're just trying to save it from the lawn mower.

"Not exactly. It wasn't like I gave him a hug goodbye, but I guess I didn't see any use in pissing him off, either." Keeping things cordial didn't necessarily mean he was ready to forgive and forget. What was that JFK quote? *Forgive your enemies, but never forget their names.*

"He sends you packing, and you're worried about *his* feelings," Rucker says. Then lowering his voice, he adds: "Hey, looking sweet." Behind wireframe glasses, his dark eyes roll tellingly to the right.

A tall blonde wearing form-fitting slacks leans over the bar nearby, her back to their table. Standing on impossibly high heels, she sips a mixed drink and listens to a large, black-haired woman in a purplish dress. A silk scarf pinned over one of the big woman's shoulders looks like a blue and green flag that got stuck to her chest as she pushed through the clearance racks at K-mart. *Blue Light Special,* coming through. The two women move closer together. The fat woman from K-mart intrudes into Tyler's line of sight no matter how tightly he tries to crop his focus.

"Before you got here," Rucker says to Tyler, "Neticut was telling me that evolution is the mother of life."

"Guess you got an early start on the beer," Tyler replies.

"Natural selection is the guiding hand of the universe," Foster says. "Evolution leaves God with nothing to do. Absurd to believe in a pointless god."

"And what do you say to all that?" Tyler asks Rucker, not really wanting to get pulled into this.

"It's science, so you can't argue with it, I guess. I mean, what do you think?"

Tyler shakes his head. Rucker has no convictions.

"I was hoping you could tell me why I should disagree with Neticut," Rucker adds. "You being a church-goer and all."

This last comment is accurate, most Sundays anyway. But how does Rucker know that? It's not something Tyler wears on his sleeves; you get grief from the likes of these two who see church as quaint and old-fashioned at best, more likely ridiculous or even vaguely threatening, an impediment to progress. Faith's *melancholy long, withdrawing roar* from our so-called advanced society. Why would rational people still interrupt their weekends to attend a ritual reenactment with boring music when there is so much living to do?

"Don't even start with that bit about a tornado in a junkyard or a bunch of watch parts shook up in a drawer," Foster says loudly to Tyler, before he even has a chance to say anything. "Tired arguments make evolution seen impossible, since even billions of random acts won't put together a complex organism, or a 747 or a watch." He catches his breath and adds: "Absolute beauty of evolution is that it isn't random at all, but a deliberate march forward by millions of instances of natural selection."

Tyler sighs. He has no bone to pick with evolution, Charles Darwin, the proof of fossils, the rise and fall of the dinosaurs. None of it contradicts, in Tyler's mind, the notion of a Creator, hiding behind the curtains. Otherwise, where did it all begin? That's the question science can't get past. All matter got together and collapsed on itself, leading to the Big Bang and the expanding universe. Okay. But *where did all that matter come from?* And even if you somehow look past that, *what about the beginning of life itself?*

"So, evolution brought some fish out of the lakes and eventually there were salamanders. An amazing thing, no doubt. But how did life begin in the first place? You can have all the swamp water you want and a trillion years of lightning strikes and whatever. You're still left with a lifeless swamp."

"Going to be able to create living creatures someday in a lab and prove that life did, in fact, emerge and evolve," Neticut says firmly, quite sure of himself. His faith in science is self-evident. Every day, somewhere in the world, scientists discover new insights into the physical world, unlock new truths. What can religious zealots do to compare with that? Nothing. They just quote from the Bible, crusty old sentiments written by primitives two thousand years ago or more. They could have at least added some modern new chapters to the Bible, as human knowledge expanded exponentially, an unstoppable march of progress to today's computers and television and the Space Shuttle. People today are nothing like their superstitious ancestors two thousand years ago, Neticut must be thinking. How could the Bible never need updating?

"Nah, I don't think so. Life isn't just another form of rock or mineral. Nobody's going to mix some chemicals together, swish it around and create life," Tyler says, growing tired of this conversation. "I don't see it happening."

"Already talking about making life in the lab, cloning," Foster counters. "Done it with simple organisms already and they'll soon clone a mammal. Maybe they'll make a new kind of animal."

"It still starts with something that's living. It isn't pulling life out of swampy soup."

Tyler would like to poke a final hole in Neticut's arrogant science. The unstoppable expansion of all that we know means that whatever we understand now, or at any time before or in the future, is necessarily incomplete. There is always more to know. The ever-expanding finite will never catch the infinite. But Tyler's heart isn't in it. He has no intention of getting all churchy on them. He refills his glass and looks out across the bar away from his two friends. That ends it. In the haze and the noise of the bar, with the welcome distraction of under-dressed women coming and going, the unfinished debate is quickly forgotten.

Rucker leaves the table to use the bathroom. Tyler and Neticut rehash last night's softball game, a safer topic. Aaron Foster is perhaps the best player on the team. A shortstop who covers half the infield, and a consistent hitter with surprising power.

"You hit a couple of rockets. They won't cheat in close on you again," Tyler tells him. "But I can't believe you booted that grounder." He can't resist bringing up Foster's error. The guy's such a jock you've got to put him in his place when you get a chance.

"Don't know what I was thinking," Neticut admits. "But nothing compared to your throw on that tag up. Know how close you came to nailing that lady in the stands? Lucky you didn't orphan some kid." Instead of leaving it at that, he adds a little taunt, unthinkingly: "Gonna try to kill some other kid's mother next week?" This remark hits way too close to home.

Tyler glares at him, teeth clenching, nostrils flared. It's been just under six months since Christie's sudden death. Silence, like the stale smoke from an untended cigarette, grows awkward until Foster chirps: "Hey, I didn't mean anything. I'm sorry."

"What do you mean? Forget it," Tyler replies irritably. "Don't think I'm so freakin' sensitive. My wife's dead. I miss her. I miss her a whole hell of a lot. But I can deal with it. What am I supposed to do? Dress in black and have everybody walk on pins and needles around me, afraid to say anything?"

The waitress appears again, asking if they need another pitcher. "Give us five minutes," Tyler says, raising his glass to his lips. Rucker returns from the can. He takes off his glasses and wipes them with a paper napkin the waitress left.

"You dating anybody yet?" he asks Tyler. Neticut tries to make eye contact with Rucker to signal that he may be steering the conversation into dangerous waters.

But Tyler answers the question matter-of-factly. "Not yet. Tomorrow, actually is my first date since Christie died. Her name's Candice."

"That's great," Rucker says enthusiastically. "Where'd you meet her?"

"We got introduced by a mutual friend," Tyler lies. In fact, he's meeting a blind date. He placed an ad in the *Detroit News* "Companion Column" ten days ago. He heard from four women. They sent their letters to a post office box at the newspaper, without knowing his identity. The letters are forwarded to Tyler in batches. That means he can pick who he wants to call and, well, piss on the rest.

He had second-guessed himself as soon as he wrote the copy for his ad and mailed his check to the *News*; he should have asked for a photo. Didn't want to seem superficial. But you can tell so much from a picture. Harder from just a letter. Once you get a girl on the phone and tell her your name, you're pretty much committed to meeting her, he thinks. This one, Candice, a nurse from

Lincoln Park, seems to be the best bet. Her letter makes her sound like a cross between Florence Nightingale and a young Sally Field. She gives no physical description other than her age, twenty-eight. But her handwriting was the neatest of the four, its curvy letters somehow sexy and inviting. Two of the others hinted at weight problems. The fourth letter had a couple of spelling errors. Maybe that fourth one's a fox; he'll never know. When all you have to go on is a letter, literacy counts.

He talked to this Candice on the phone for about ten minutes, and she seemed okay. Relaxed, confident, funny. Kidded him good-naturedly about her Buick Skylark, how it had given her nothing but trouble since she bought it. This in reference to his ad, where he'd written that he worked in a salaried position for GM, not mentioning that his days there were rapidly coming to an end. He didn't get into his joblessness on the phone, either. Why screw up a first impression?

"What's she look like?" Rucker asks.

"Brown hair, average height, okay-looking," Tyler guesses. "Kind of cute," he adds, like a car salesman describing next year's model before he's seen it. He has been trying not to think about her too much, not really sure he's ready to be dating again, not looking to get stuck somewhere he's not prepared to be, the give-and-take sparring of two people getting to know each other, the physical awkwardness of it all. Sex he's ready for; it's all the pretext that scares him.

"Where you taking her?" Foster wants to know.

"To the Attic Theater downtown to see something called *Nomadic Gestures*," Tyler says. The truth again. "I checked the paper for something to do before I called her. Hope it's a comedy." Tickets are reasonable at the Attic, a small repertory theater in Detroit, unlike the Fox or the Masonic Temple, where he'd really have had to shell out. That would have been way overboard for a first, blind date.

Tyler looks to change the subject. You talk too much, you get caught in your lies. He turns away to look at the grainy image on the big-screen projection TV where cute, little Chrissie Hynde sings while she chokes the neck of her electric guitar. She's from the same part of Ohio as Tyler, but she's older by twelve years or so. A Pretenders video from around 1982. She must have been thirty or thirty-one, but they made her look younger.

"You remember this song?" Tyler asks the others. He used to like the Pretenders. You never hear them anymore.

Neither Neticut nor Rucker responds.

"'Back on the Chain Gang,'" Tyler says, answering himself, just before Chrissie gets to the title lyric. "It reminds me of college. We played this song to death my sophomore year. We thought we had it rough, going to class, taking tests. Nobody told us that the chain gang is the working world."

The other two don't seem interested in Tyler's Ohio State days and has-been bands. They drink their beers and look around the bar. Getting crowded. Smokey and loud.

Rucker raises his voice to ask Tyler: "Why'd you take the assignment with Schulous in the first place?"

"He didn't exactly ask me," Tyler answers, thinking back to that day in Schulous's office a year and a half ago. The pregnant secretary and the benign eagle painting. "He told me he wanted me to help with a special assignment. And that he'd move me into Labor Relations within two years. It was a promotion. You'd have done it."

Rucker doesn't challenge this. "What did he say you'd be doing?"

"He wanted me to develop a system to identify poor performers and guys whose jobs weren't necessary anymore." Tyler can almost remember Schulous exact words. "He wanted it *air-tight*. It had to be *objective* and *statistically valid*. He said the computer would take the heat for headcount reductions that were needed to save the plant."

"Could have turned him down," Neticut says. Easy for him to say, Tyler thinks. With his MBA from Wharton, Foster won't have to endure any unpleasant assignments. Finance Staff takes care of its own. Foster's success is assured, as long as he toes the corporate line.

"How'd he get away with having you do something for Garden City that was different from the rest of GM?" Rucker asks, setting his glass down on the table loudly, misjudging just a bit the distance to the tabletop.

Monolithic GM is built on procedures, rigidly duplicated throughout the company. Nowhere is this more true than in Human Resources. A huge manual of two volumes, each over eight hundred pages, last updated in the late Seventies, gathers dust in every HR manager's bookcase. Now a team of scriveners somewhere in the New Center of Detroit, home of GM's headquarters and associated bureaucracies, has the task of keying in the text of both volumes into a computerized manual that will still have to be printed and bound because so few HR managers use personal computers, just now being purchased for some non-clericals. Computers and word processors carry the stigma of being a tool of the lowest and most female class of white-collar worker, the secretary. The scriveners, most of them women, dutifully copy the text, fingers flying over keyboards while their minds are on anything other than the ponderous, monotonous words, thickly detailing the prescriptive policies that aim to ensure the company's people management is conducted in a predictable, uniform manner, just as a McDonald's hamburger patty is fried exactly the same length of time whether in Dallas or Denver, never different, no questioning, never bending the rules, never veering from the prescribed path. A few in the HR committee assigned to reprint the policy manual wanted to take the opportunity to completely rewrite the rules, and in fact, a subcommittee has been appointed to study what changes should be made, but they will be minor and subject to long debate. In the end, the "new" policy manual will not be much different from the old manual. GM has no appetite for unsettling change. HR exists to protect the corporate status quo from disruption, mediocrity knowing nothing higher than itself, preserving the steady and predictable systems and processes that have served the company well for decades, solid and unyielding.

"Schulous had approval to run a pilot project at Garden City that could've been rolled out company wide. He said I could live out every hard-working employee's dream by helping get rid of the slouches that weren't pulling their weight."

The other GM plants and offices were cutting their salaried staff by seniority; last hired, first fired. Seniority was the job-preservation principle prescribed somewhere in the policy manual supposedly because it was predictable and fair, the just reward for dutiful service to the company. In reality, it was a concession to cowardice. Like many programs for salaried employees, it mirrored what was in place for hourly workers as dictated by the powerful union, the United Auto Workers. The company was so worried that its salaried employees might someday unionize that it preemptively granted them the same raises, benefits and holiday schedule that the union had won for the hourly people. Likewise, for the layoff policy. In lean times, the company would shed its youngest, most energetic salaried employees, who were typically earning a good deal less than their more senior counterparts. Instead, Schulous wanted to get rid of the entrenched old-timers, many of whom, he said, hadn't done an honest day's work in years. Deadwood, he had called them. "Tyler, you and me are going to clean out the damn *deadwood* around here."

Of course, none of the cuts Schulous envisioned would affect the hourly workers who greatly outnumbered the salaried employees at the plant; they were staunchly protected by the UAW. The worst salaried employees couldn't compete as true deadwood with the worst hourly workers, who would routinely miss work or come in drunk or too hungover to care. The union made sure you didn't touch their brother workers. Everybody knew that working on the floor of a stamping plant was a frightening kind of hell, and most of the guys did their jobs well enough, so Schulous let the union protect the truants and the drunks, looking the other way so he wouldn't have a strike that'd be a bear to explain to the vice president who always seemed to have his ass in a sling. Anyway, there was plenty to be gained by cleaning out the salaried slackers. This pilot program was Schulous's last chance to get promoted to a soft headquarters job he could retire from, and he needed Tyler to get it done.

Tyler swallows another couple gulps of beer.

"There was nothing to do but act excited by the challenge of something new."

"Sucked up to him," Neticut says, never one to beat around the bush.

"You could say that, I guess. It didn't really matter what I thought. He just wanted the process set up before word got out what we were up to."

Tyler tries to imitate Schulous raspy old smoker's voice: "'I know this isn't an assignment you'd choose on your own, Manion. But you'll help us out and it will be good experience for you.' What was I going to say?"

Neither of them answers. They know what happened. Tyler developed a system, a complex matrix measuring several aspects of performance and utility. It was all very clinical. Schulous made sure there was one column of input for intangible performance, allowing him to protect his favored few who might otherwise be on the bubble. But the computer made the final calculations. Those who performed the most essential tasks best were rewarded by being allowed to keep their jobs. Forty-two others were handed their walking papers. Once the head count goal had been reached, Tyler's computer turned on him, identifying Tyler's work as expendable. Schulous had stood by the computer. "I can't make an exception for you, Manion, or else we'd be sued by every geezer we dumped over the last eighteen months. Age discrimination suits could be the undoing of the pilot."

Neticut excuses himself from the table to go hit on the blonde they'd noticed earlier.

Rucker starts off on a new subject. "I read a story in the *USA Today* about a guy who walked into a Las Vegas casino with a suitcase filled with a million dollars in cash and gold coins, Krugerrands. He bet the whole wad on one roll of the dice. And he lost. They found his body the next day in the bathtub of his hotel room. He'd slit his wrists with a three-inch pocket knife. Can you imagine putting that much money on one roll of the dice?"

"People do it all the time," Tyler says, looking down at his beer. "Maybe not one roll, but over a lifetime. And not just guys like Pete Rose, either. Think of all the poor saps at the plant who buy bunches of Lotto tickets every week. If they'd ever add up all the dough they've blown over their whole lives, they'd slit their wrists, too." That comes out harsher than he intends. Maybe he should keep his mouth shut.

The waitress with the top button undone appears, setting two shot glasses on their table. "What's this?" Rucker asks her loudly.

"Courtesy of your friend at that table there," she says, pointing to where Aaron Foster sits with the blonde and the dumpy woman from K-mart. Rucker swallows his drink in a quick rush and sets the empty shot glass on the waitress' tray before she can leave. So, she waits for Tyler to drink his. The whiskey leaps down his throat. He inhales between pursed lips and his chest fills with a hot glow. Rucker orders another pitcher.

"I wonder if Neticut wants us to join them at that table?" he asks.

"God, I hope not," Tyler answers. "The fat one's nobody's prize. Besides, the numbers are wrong. That's our excuse."

Rucker nods, looking relieved at Tyler's response.

They finish the pitcher. The bar has become too loud. Tyler doesn't feel like striking up a shouted conversation with some new woman, and he's growing tired of Rucker, too. "Want to leave?" he asks. Rucker nods. They head toward the front door looking for Foster, but don't see him. The blonde and the dumpy woman seem to be missing, too.

Outside, it's quiet. Tyler draws in a deep breath, the first smoke-free air he has breathed in three hours. A few stars above shine through the murky, humid August air. Rucker's new Chevy Caprice Classic, an ugly whale abortion of a car, not the kind of inspired design GM needs to pull itself out of the recessionary funk, is parked near the side door where they came out. They pause behind its elongated rear end. Tyler hunts for Neticut's candy-apple red Corvette, its vanity license plate brashly asking the ultimate come-on question: WET YET. The car's not there.

"I'm going to take Robbie swimming tomorrow, want to come with us?" he asks.

"Where're you going?" Rucker wants to know. He can't give an answer without asking another question.

"I thought we'd try Metro Beach," Tyler says, referring to a huge city park on Lake St. Clair, to the north of Detroit. And more than 30 miles east of the western suburbs where they live.

"Oh, that's a forty-five-minute drive, at least," Rucker complains. "And always so many blacks there."

"So what? It's something different. I haven't been there in a couple of years."

"What time you leaving?" Rucker asks.

"Probably right after a late breakfast so Robbie can get his nap in on the drive there. You coming?" Tyler asks again as he pulls out his car keys.

"Give me a call in the morning, not too early. I'll let you know," Rucker says, not one for spontaneous decisions.

***

Tyler drives the Sunbird cautiously, watching his rearview mirror for police cruisers. He stays in the far-right lane of the boulevard, creeping along, not wanting to make a mistake. After a few miles he begins to relax and picks up his speed a little. He pops a cassette tape into the player. Then an on-coming car flashes its headlights and Tyler realizes he's been driving with his own headlights off. He reaches for the little knob and slows down again.

As he pulls into his driveway, he cuts the corner a little too sharply and catches the curb with his back right tire. The sudden jolt throws his body against his now-taut shoulder belt. He brings the car to a complete stop. Breathes in deeply. Then he reaches up to the visor and clicks the opener. The garage door rises, slowly. He creeps the car in, being careful to miss his son's plastic Big Wheel trike. Why is it always in the way? Robbie doesn't even ride it; he still can't figure out the pedals.

Nicki is in the family room watching MTV. A bony white guy with long, thin hair and tattoos all over his chest plays heavy metal guitar in front of a fake audience. A nice-looking braless blonde groupie jumps up in the front row. The camera hangs on her body for a teasing second or two before returning to the thin-haired lead singer.

"How'd he do?" Tyler asks the babysitter.

"Oh, he was fine. I read him a bunch of stories, you know? He went to sleep around nine-thirty." She lifts her windbreaker off the couch and pulls it over her arms and shoulders. Then she reaches her arms in back of her neck, and with the in-turned thumbs of both hands lifts her long, kinky hair from underneath the jacket. She clicks the jacket's zipper together, but doesn't zip it up.

"I guess he's entitled to a late night once in a while," Tyler says. Feeling guilty about the lack of time he's spent with Robbie lately, he adds: "I'm taking him to the beach tomorrow."

"I bet he likes the water," Nicki says, edging toward the front of the room, the exit. Then stopping when Tyler makes no move.

"Oh, yeah. He's a regular water rat. He likes to sit on the edge of the shore and let the little waves wash over his legs. I've got to take him to the ocean someday so he can see some real waves."

"In November, they're already got it all planned, my family's going to Padre Island. In Texas." Her green eyes watch him carefully.

"That sounds like fun," Tyler says. The heavy metal video ends and a fat black man with ridiculously thick gold chains begins an irritating rap. "Do you want anything to drink? I'm going to have a glass of Kool-Aid."

She follows him into the kitchen. "No, thanks. I just had a can of pop. You don't mind, right?"

"You can help yourself to anything I've got, you know that. Except my beer," he adds, smiling at her. "I don't want to get in trouble with your parents."

She doesn't know if he's kidding. "Oh, I don't like beer."

"You've tried it then?" he asks.

"Oh, you know, at parties I've been to, yeah. Somebody usually sneaks in some beer."

He'd like to ask her what other forbidden things she's tried. *Switch the subject*, he tells himself.

"How long you gonna be down at Padre Island?" Tyler asks, reaching for the refrigerator door handle. But it's closer than it looked. His open hand bangs against it clumsily.

"A whole week," Nicki answers. "It'll probably be boring, actually. With my parents and little brother." She pockets the roll of small bills Tyler hands her without counting it.

"Maybe you'll meet a boy there, and you won't want to come back." Like an episode on *The Wonder Years*.

"Yeah, right. With my mom and dad around? No way."

Tyler sips his Kool-Aid from a blue plastic Detroit Tigers cup. After all the beer, the cherry drink is refreshing at first but then too sweet. He can almost feel it staining his teeth.

"But I love the ocean," she adds. "I don't mind just sitting in the sun and reading a good book, you know?"

"What're you reading now?" he asks. *Sexy Jackie Collins trash? Or a who-dunnit mystery?*

She looks at him then, past the glassy red eyes to the back part of the inside of his head, seemingly, and perhaps sees something worth saving.

"Right now, I'm just finishing a book from my summer reading list from school, *The Hiding Place*. This Christian girl and her family live in Holland. Back in World War II. They're protecting some Jewish people. From the Germans." She speaks in rapid clips again, enthused. "They have to become sneaky, this girl and her family. Lying, cheating, stealing, like that. You ever read it?"

"Nope," he says. "When I was your age, we had to read stuff like *Catcher in the Rye* and *Lord of the Flies*."

"Oh, we read both of those in eighth grade," she says dismissively. "They were okay, I guess. Stories about boys trying to grow up and all. But sometimes these books that you always hear are classics, *The Old Man and the Sea* and all that, the ones that you just have to read because they're so important, turn out to be kinda, I don't know, overrated."

She backs up against the kitchen counter and hops up on it, using her arms to help lift her. Must feel like talking. Sitting there, she's just about his height.

7

The ten-speed bike's pedals offer little resistance against Tyler's pumping legs. There's no challenge in these streets. Like the rest of southeast Michigan, Livonia is flat and featureless. The tallest hill within thirty miles is a made-over landfill, rehabilitated with a couple of ski lifts. *Mt. Trashmore*, they call it.

Livonia is a collection of middle-class subdivisions, a bedroom community of mostly semi-prosperous, mostly white people who work somewhere else. In the factories and office towers in Detroit or in the older suburbs. Or in the fashionable new suburbs where the high-tech jobs are. Livonia has plenty of 7-Elevens, gas stations and video rental stores. But no industry. Livonia has no downtown. No history. And no hills.

Robbie is Tyler's silent payload. Riding in the little white plastic child's seat above the ten-speed's rear wheel, he wears a white styrofoam safety helmet. Tyler wears a helmet, too—hard black plastic. You can't expect the boy to wear his if you don't wear yours. Robbie adds just enough weight to make the bike ride seem like real exercise.

They don't see many cars about. Good time for biking—seven-thirty on a Saturday morning. If your son won't let you sleep in, might as well get out in the fresh air. The summer slips away whether we're outside or not. Tyler pedals up one street and then another, rows of brick ranches in one subdivision. Then smaller wood bungalows, ranches again, bigger and more expensive on this street, smaller but still kept up nicely on the next. Then a sub with rows of two-story colonials each with a two-car, attached garage. Each neighborhood taking comfort in its uniformity. Nobody rocks the boat.

Tyler looks over his shoulder at Robbie to make sure he hasn't fallen asleep. The boy's brown eyes watch the passing houses, hunting for something interesting. Tyler first took his son for a bike ride last July, just a few months after Robbie learned to sit up, a soft foam insert providing just the right amount of stuffing to hold his little body in place. The motion of the ride quickly put the little boy to sleep. The baby seat's safety harness had kept his body in place, but Tyler didn't like the way his tiny head was hanging, forward and to one side, unsupported in his sleep, the weight of head and helmet tugging on his little neck. Tyler didn't take Robbie out on the bike again for almost a year. Now the boy is much bigger and doesn't need the cushion insert. But Tyler still doesn't like the idea of him sleeping back there. Straining backward, Tyler feels his balance slipping away. He snaps his head around and instinctively shifts his weight just enough to right the bike's wobble. Then another near disaster: he veers abruptly to miss a deep pothole. What does his son think of this wild ride?

They pull into their driveway twenty minutes later, Tyler just beginning to sweat. He unbuckles their helmets and unsnaps his son's harness, setting him back down on solid earth. The boy is unusually quiet, standing there looking down at his little stubby sneakers. Toddlers often get quiet, Tyler knows, when their diapers need changing. "Is your diaper wet?" he asks his son.

"Okay," Robbie says, his way of answering yes.

"Well then, we'll get you changed. Then let's get some breakfast. I don't know about you, but I'm hungry."

Robbie fusses with his Cheerios, so Tyler gives him a Pop-tart and lets him sit in the recliner watching cartoons. Care Bears and Gummi Bears have displaced Bugs Bunny and Road Runner. They've got all the product endorsements, like Michael Jordan, so they call the shots.

Tyler hunches over the kitchen table, reading his morning *Free Press*. More about those crazy Arab countries, Iraq and Kuwait.

U.S. ANGER RISES AT IRAQ, GAS PUMP

World oil prices have surged because of the invasion, and retail gas prices in Michigan have already jumped even though it will be weeks before that pricier oil reaches the United States, the paper says. Legislators are investigating the apparent price-gouging. What a surprise, Tyler thinks, the oil companies giving us the shaft. Tyler scans the other news on the front page.

BUSH CONSIDERS ALL OPTIONS
AS IRAQI TROOPS NEAR SAUDI BORDER

What's the president going to do about it, Tyler wonders. Nuke 'em? The paper says Iraq already has 100,000 soldiers in Kuwait. Baghdad Radio is said to be reporting that Iraq plans to withdraw its troops from Kuwait, beginning next Sunday. "Well, let's see them haul out right now," President Bush says in the story.

Tyler pictures Dana Carvey looking presidential and staring down at another *Saturday Night Live* actor playing a plump Saddam Hussein. *Let's see you do that withdrawal thing.* They're already working on the skit, for sure.

NATION'S JOBLESS RATE AT 2-YEAR HIGH

An alarming number of Americans lost their jobs in July – 200,000 – as the national unemployment rate jumped to 5.5

percent, the highest level in two years, according to the Labor Department. In Michigan, the jobless rate hit 7.4 percent…

Tyler finds little satisfaction knowing he's been joined by 199,999 others.

BOTH GERMANYS URGE EARLY ELECTIONS

Leaders of both East Germany and West Germany are pushing for joint elections nearly two months earlier than planned, and the two countries have agreed to make Berlin their united capital. Amazing how such bitter adversaries are coming together so quickly now that they have embraced the plan for a single Germany, not even arguing about who first had the idea.

Tyler pushes the front pages away and hunts for the sports section, E.

BOSOX BATTER TIGERS, 14-5

No point in reading about that mess; Tyler caught the wrap-up on TV last night after Nicki left. Wasn't pretty. He glances at the standings. Detroit's seven and a half games behind Boston, fourth place in a weak division. Since the Tigers' magical 1984 season—the incredible 35-5 start, Jack Morris' clutch pitching all year, Gibby's dramatic homers—they've dropped back to mediocrity. That dominant '84 wire-to-wire run seemed to bring together city and suburbs—*Bless you boys!* was a local television station's unapologetically cheesy slogan—but then the World Series clincher set off a crazy reverie of drunken bedlam that ended badly: a downtown riot, stores looted, and that police car, upside down and burning behind the deranged presence of an obese fan named Bubba in a photo featured in newspapers and magazines across the world. Even in its moment of supreme glory, Detroit managed to cover itself in ugliness.

Tyler clears the few dishes they've dirtied—Robbie's little plastic cereal bowl, Tyler's considerably bigger ceramic bowl, a coffee mug, a spoon and a little breakfast plate where Tyler set his Pop-tart between bites. The plate's clean except for a couple of crumbs which he brushes away. He returns the plate to the cupboard and puts the other pieces in the dishwasher. Still only half-full. He'll run it tonight.

Tyler leaves Robbie watching cartoons while he takes his shower. No need to shave until later, closer to his date. After he towels off, he twists a Q-tip inside his right ear, flips it around as he passes it to his left hand, and cleans out imagined wax from his other ear. The blue box lying there, split open like a wounded animal in his vanity's top drawer, with these cautionary words: *Do not insert into ear canal*. The Q-tip company's lawyers made the company put the warning on the box, no doubt, after paying a huge settlement to some cluck who poked a hole through his eardrum. Words the company hopes go unheeded. If people didn't use the swabs to clean out their ears, why would anybody buy them?

He pulls on a pair of blue jean cut-offs and the Pistons tee shirt. Then he goes downstairs to his workshop for some tools. He's finally going to fix the outlet in Robbie's bedroom that's never worked since Christie and Tyler moved here three years ago. Their first house—three bedrooms and one and a half baths. It seemed so big then, after the apartment. When Robbie came, and then all his toys, it no longer felt so spacious. Now with Christie gone, it should seem big again, but it doesn't really. You get used to the space you're in, like tropical fish raised in an aquarium growing only as big as the space allows; ones in a crowded tank stay smaller than ones that can swim freely. Yet, there's an undeniable emptiness in the many reminders that she's not there anymore.

Insulated screwdriver, pliers, snippers, electrical tape, flashlight. And a new outlet. That should be all he needs. No need to solder; he's never been very good at the tricky art of joining wires together with molten lead. The lead balls up without sticking to the wires if you don't heat it all to just the right temperature. Twisting the wires together and wrapping them with electrical tape is just as good for a connection that will never be stressed inside the wall. Pretty simple job; should have done it long ago. The only trick will be to turn off the right breaker. The circuit box in a dark corner of the basement isn't marked clearly. The previous owner was no handyman and Tyler hasn't gotten around yet to marking the breaker switches himself. He could turn off the whole set just to be safe, but then he'd have to reset digital clocks all over the house.

The doorbell rings; he can hear it even from the basement. Tyler sets down his tools and climbs the stairs. As he crosses the living room to his front door, he can see through a crack in the curtain it's a neighbor lady. A black-haired woman in her mid-thirties or so, who's married to a much older man, Johnston, who must be pushing sixty. Tyler opens the door. "Well, hello," he says, trying to be friendly.

"Hello, Tyler." She surprises him with his first name. He can't remember hers; maybe he's never known it. "We've been meaning to bring something over to you ever since we heard the sad news…" Her voice trails off as she hands him some kind of browned meringue thing in a round glass dish. *Who's the we?* he wonders. She's the only one at his door.

"Well, thanks," Tyler says, still holding the screen door open. "You want to come in for a minute?"

She steps through his door. Thin pink stripes on her black spandex running suit bend with her body's curves, not bad for a woman married to such a geezer. Tyler often has seen her and the old man walking briskly, aerobically, up and down the neighborhood sidewalks. Tyler waves and they nod back cheerfully without breaking stride. Subdivision harmony nurtures in such feigned familiarity.

"Would you like some coffee?" he asks her.

"Sure, that would be nice." She follows him across the toy-strewn living room into Tyler's kitchen. He fills two mugs with water and puts them in the microwave. On high for a full five minutes. Water takes longer to heat up because the microwaves can't seem to find it. They bounce around inside the oven, mostly warming nothing.

"Instant okay?" he thinks to ask, a little bit after-the-fact.

"That'd be fine," she says, squinting just a bit, a tell, maybe, when she's lying. "How's your little boy doing?"

"Super. Robbie's really a great kid. He's in the family room now watching cartoons."

The scent of expensive-smelling perfume reaches Tyler's nose. Pleasant, at first, but then too strong. He leads the woman to the room off the kitchen. The overstuffed recliner has nearly swallowed the boy, only the profile of Robbie's face, one arm and his two bare feet are visible. He stares reverently into the TV.

"Hi, Robbie," she calls to the boy. "Whatcha watching?"

Robbie turns his head slowly and looks for a moment, saying nothing. No recognition in his glassy eyes. He turns back to the familiar figures of the Gummi Bears, up to their little necks in trouble with a fat, green troll.

"Do you have kids, Mrs. Johnston?" Tyler asks, looking for safe common ground.

"Nora. Please. I'm not that much older than you. No. Unfortunately, Stan and I haven't been blessed with children." She fidgets a bit with one of her shoulder straps and switches the subject. "Did you get down to the fireworks in the city for the Fourth?"

Before he can answer, *No*, she goes on herself: "I was disappointed, frankly. I thought they were extremely mediocre. And the crowds were just awful. There was a stabbing even, did you hear on the news after? We didn't see it, but I can believe it. We hardly ever go into Detroit anymore. I don't know what we were thinking."

Tyler can't help frowning at *extremely mediocre*. Christie would have cringed at the nonsensical expression. But he says nothing.

Nora lifts both her elbows up as she draws her fingers with their pink nails through thick black hair. Her brown eyes catch

Tyler noticing as the elastic material in her running suit tenses across the expanse of her breasts; like a trampoline it propels a little jade pendant dangling there on a thin, gold chain upward for a moment before it settles back below her neckline. She reaches down to a kidney-shaped pink pouch strapped to her waist and tugs at the zipper. Her fingers dip inside the pouch and reappear with a black cigarette case. They snap the case open and withdraw a single brown "woman's" cigarette—long and slender and sad.

"You don't mind, do you?" Nora Johnston asks, digging in her pouch for her lighter.

"Actually, I do," Tyler says, jerking his head toward the living room. "You know, the kid."

"Oh, yes, I'm sorry," she says, just as she finds the lighter. Her fingers hurriedly place the cigarette back in the case and zip up the pouch. She exhales loudly.

The microwave beeps. Tyler dumps a plastic tablespoon of instant coffee grains into the hot water in each mug. She takes hers black; he spoons sugar and non-dairy creamer powder into his.

"It's just amazing how you can live right next door to someone for several years and never really get to know them," Nora says. *Is she irritated?* Tyler wonders, that he didn't know she is childless? Maybe she's going to have some kind of nicotine fit.

"Yeah, well. I guess we're all so busy." It doesn't sound like much of an excuse.

"But I'm going to make a point of getting to know you better, Tyler," she promises, as they sit down at the kitchen table. "I think you must be a very interesting person." He doesn't know how to respond to this. She sips her coffee without lifting her eyes off him. He breathes lightly through his mouth; her perfume is too strong when she's sitting this close. Nora's smoking must have choked off her sense of smell. "It's got to have been hard on you since your wife died," she continues, bent on taking their conversation on a new journey. Into deeper, more personal and intimate waters that really aren't any of her damn business. Everyone in the neighborhood must know about Christie's death, though he's told none of them.

"Yeah, it's an adjustment," he says. Then silence. She waits for him to elaborate. He doesn't.

"Stan and I could watch your little boy when you need a night out," she says finally. Tyler's glad to hear her mention the husband's name again. It makes him feel less like a conspirator.

"That's thoughtful. Thanks. Maybe I'll take you up on that someday. I've got a babysitter, though."

"Oh, of course you must. Who is it?" she asks.

"Nicki Saliba," Tyler says. Seeing no recognition on Nora Johnston's face, he adds: "She goes to Divine Mercy High."

"Suh-lee-bah," Nora repeats slowly. "Is she an Arab?"

"I don't think so. Maybe her father is. I'm not sure."

"She must drive that little white sporty car," Nora says knowingly. What else has she observed of his life from her window across the street?

"Yeah, that's right."

Nora finishes her coffee before Tyler's has cooled enough for him to drink it. "Well, I really don't want to intrude on your weekend," she says.

Tyler seizes this opportunity to get rid of her, getting up and stepping toward the living room, the front door. "Thanks for stopping over. And thanks for the pie. I'll return the dish when we've finished it."

"There's no hurry. I'm sure I'll be seeing you," she says, waving to him neighborly as she scoots out his door into the already hot, muggy air.

Tyler returns to his project. He finds the right circuit breaker, replaces the outlet, and turns the power back on. It works. Simple enough. He'd like to get another job done. Not enough time to cut down that ugly tree in the front yard; he'll get to that tomorrow. Instead, he finds some wallpaper cement in one of the drawers of his workbench and re-adheres some peeling corners in the kitchen. A Wedgwood blue floral print. Christie picked it out, of course. He's got flowers on the walls in just about every room of the house. Not exactly a bachelor pad.

At ten-thirty, he calls Webb Rucker. "It's beautiful out. Supposed to reach eighty-seven. So, you coming, or what?"

Rucker asks him back: "What time you leaving?"

"How about half an hour? Eat something quick, then we'll go. It's a little early for Robbie's nap, but I have to get back. I've got that date."

"Oh, yeah. Your date with Candy the nurse."

"Candice. So, you coming?"

"You driving?" Rucker wants to know.

* * *

Tyler picks Webb up in the Sunbird. They get on the eastbound Fisher freeway and Robbie falls asleep. Mission accomplished.

"Haven't you got anything in here besides Springsteen?" Rucker complains, hunting through the top layer of Tyler's shoe box of cassettes. He selects an old Police album with a funny name, Zenyatta Mondatta, and pops it into the player. Tyler rarely listens to this tape anymore. He soured on Sting when he made that record with Dire Straits a few years back, "Money for Nothing." Howling like a dog and cry-babying something about wanting his MTV. The cassette player comes to life with a simple repetitious beat as one of the songs that became a hit single, "De Do Do Do, De Da Da Da," begins to play.

"Classic rock," Tyler says with exaggerated disdain. "More like baby talk. They don't write 'em like that anymore."

Webb snorts, his way of laughing. "At least you can hear the words. With Springsteen, I don't know what he's saying. Just grunts with that New Jersey accent."

"You can hear the words if you listen," Tyler argues. "Hey, how do you think Aaron made out last night?"

"Same thing I was wondering. So, I called him before you came by."

"What did he say? How did he get rid of the fat one?"

"He couldn't say much," Rucker explains. "The blonde was still over, in the bathroom, so he couldn't give me any details."

The Sunbird follows the freeway into the west side of Detroit. Other than the deepening trash along the roadside, and the occasional abandoned building visible from the freeway, you're insulated from the city's decay and you could easily miss it. To see the vacant lots overgrown with weeds, the burnt-out houses and the junked cars, you have to get off one of these exits. Decay. It's there, but you don't have to see it if you're just passing through.

"Squankkkk." Rucker blows his nose into a yellow Kleenex he's pulled from a little pocket in his bathing suit. Then, with an unused corner of the tissue, he wipes his glasses. "What do you think of all this about East and West Germany coming together?" he asks. "You been following it?"

"It's hard to miss," Tyler replies. "Seems like everybody and his brother has shown up at the Berlin Wall. What do they call that place they all go to? Sounds like from Vietnam?"

"Check-point Charlie," Rucker answers.

"Yeah, that's it. Chisel a chunk out of the wall there and you make it on the TV news back home. It's kind of getting old, if you ask me."

"But it's amazing, really," Webb says. It's his job to stay enthused about this subject since he brought it up. "That wall's been there for thirty years and it comes down in a matter of weeks. The whole Eastern Bloc is going down. Communism is dead. It doesn't work."

"It does seem pretty historic," Tyler admits. "The wall coming down and all."

"Darn right. Your kid will read about this in history class. He'll remember 1990 as the year the world moved closer to lasting peace. We've been living with this atomic cloud hanging over our heads for way too long. Do you know what they used to call a backyard fallout shelter back in the Fifties and Sixties? *The family room of tomorrow.* That's no way to live."

Tyler watches the highway signs, keeping track of his progress, though his exit isn't for another twelve or fifteen miles.

"How long before those Communist countries start asking us for money?" Rucker continues. "Their state-run factories just can't compete in a free market. We ought to insist on some military cutbacks, concessions, if we help Eastern Europe rebuild. Don't you think we ought to rub it in, just a little?"

Tyler doesn't answer this. He can't get worked up over this Commie talk. It seems so overblown, and his own sense of politics doesn't run very deep. Voted for Bush and for Reagan before that, but who did they run against? Mondale and Dukakis. Mister Excitement I and II. Tyler would have voted for Reagan the first time, but he was too young, having just turned seventeen the month before the election. Still, he never did buy into all that *Evil Empire* stuff. As long as they stay over on their side of the world and have plenty of their own troubles to keep them occupied, why should we mess with them? But something is unsettling about all this change in the air. Walls are crumbling all around him. Remote people with their gut-wrenching problems don't feel quite so distant anymore. His world is getting uncomfortably crowded, like the mall right before Christmas.

The tape ends. Half a minute later, something inside the player clicks and the Police start up again. The other side of the tape. Auto reverse; flawless Japanese technology.

"And you have to wonder if we're creating a monster in a united Germany." Rucker says, still trying to milk this German reunification thing. "Don't you think we ought to do something before they get visions of empires all over again? And death camps?"

"I don't think we need to do anything," Tyler says, intent on passing a red VW Jetta. "Just let them be."

"But what about the Jews? Wonder what a guy like Aaron thinks when he sees Germany getting big and strong all over again? Pretty scary."

"Ask Neticut, not me. Are you sure he's even Jewish? And why does it matter anyway if the Germans get back on their feet? If you think there's something in their German blood that makes them power-hungry killers then maybe you're a racist yourself," Tyler says. "Odds are the next Hitler won't be a German. Maybe he'll be a Frenchman or an American, even. A Jew. Or an Arab. Maybe even a woman."

"The Germans now are saying 1945 was their Zero Hour," Rucker says. "The beginning of a real change for them becoming a good nation, a force for good in the world. We probably should take them on their word, give them a chance at least."

"Now you're arguing both ways, aren't you?"

"Yeah, why not?" Rucker asks back.

Near the end of the first song on this side of the tape, "Don't Stand So Close to Me," Sting shows off, letting us know how well read he is, reaching for the rhyme, "*He starts to shake and cough. Just like the old man in that book by Nabokov.*"

"He's trying too hard to make up for the nonsense in the last song," Tyler complains. He passes another slow-moving car, thinking back to last night. Nicki the babysitter had surprised him when she hopped up on the kitchen counter, and then put him on the spot.

"How much did you drink tonight?" she'd asked him point blank, not like her.

"Quite a bit, actually. More than I'd intended."

"Maybe you shouldn't drive like that," she said quietly.

She was right, of course. He had told himself that it was only a few miles, that he would drive carefully, and keep an eye out for cops. But he had no business getting behind the wheel when he was pretty well hammered. "You're totally right," he had told the girl.

And just like that, she slid off his counter and disappeared into the night.

Tyler steps harder on the gas pedal and gets ready to pass a green Skylark, looks to be an '86 or '87 model, an early version of the current generation, decorated with a single black-and-white bumper sticker with the letters MIA*POW above the shape of a man's closely cropped head, bent over; an image of a guard tower ominously in the background. *More than fifteen years since the end of the Vietnam War; are some of our soldiers really still there?* But the faceless silhouette doesn't remind Tyler of anyone. Guys like him have never had to fear being drafted into combat. The question recedes from his consciousness as quickly as the Skylark fades from his read-view mirror.

He comes up on a Ford Taurus, plodding along in the far right lane, with a *Choose Life* sticker on its rear bumper, complete with a simple drawing of a little fetus baby curled up inside a red circle.

Tyler glances down at the little digital clock in the center of the Sunbird's dashboard. They're going to have to keep their time at the beach to a couple of hours or so. He had told Nicki to come over at seven to watch Robbie while he goes out on his date. Three nights in a row she'll have been over. He's ruining the girl's social life.

Tyler speeds up a bit. Then he reaches over to press a button on the cassette deck, ejecting the Police tape, abruptly cutting Sting off. He grabs one of the older Springsteen cassettes from the box on Rucker's lap, and pops it in. The Boss's distinct voice growls mid-verse:

"*…a notion deep inside*
That it ain't no sin to be glad you're alive"

"Hear that? You can understand him just fine," Tyler insists.

"Yeah," Rucker concedes. "But who wants to listen to what these rock stars have to say, anyway? Who says they've got any better idea than the rest of us about what's important and how to think about it?"

"Maybe not how to think about anything. If they get you to think at all, maybe that's the point. Maybe that's all there is."

A car that's been just ahead of them in the center lane these last few minutes, a blue Toyota Corolla, one of the newer ones with the slightly rounded corners but still a crappy subcompact with a sewing machine for an engine smoothly humming yet so underpowered, until now keeping a good pace of sixty-five or so, has come upon a slower-moving truck. *You see these Japanese cars a lot these days, even around Detroit,* Tyler thinks to himself. *How does anyone who lives in Michigan have the nerve to drive an import?* Even if they don't work for one of the American auto companies or their suppliers or dealers, somebody in their family does surely, and their neighborhood restaurants and dry cleaners and liquor stores all depend on auto people for customers. The Corolla begins to slow, dutifully staying in the center lane. Tailgating the truck now, maintaining the bigger vehicle's same slow-speed pace. *Bet it's a woman driver*, he says to himself, *afraid to make her move*. He flips on his left-turn blinker, switches lanes smoothly and comes up alongside the Corolla.

He's wrong. Not a woman, but a white-haired old man, gripping the steering wheel for dear life, eyes pasted straight ahead. As Tyler passes the truck, he keeps checking his rear-view mirror. The old duffer still makes no move to get around the dawdling truck and now other cars have moved into the left-hand lane to get around the Corolla. Some people just allow themselves to get stuck in a rut, making no effort to steer themselves around it. They don't see a big loafing truck until they're close behind it and then they feel trapped by the impatient drivers rushing past. Same way some people can't see change coming when it should be clear as day. Others side-step smoothly. Tyler's one of those people, he thinks, the side-steppers. The way he embraced cassettes when they first came out, a number of years ago. Anyone paying attention should have seen that the cassette tape was going to win out as a technology over scratchy, poppy vinyl because you could put whatever music you wanted on them, recording off the radio or from albums borrowed from a friend. Still, there were plenty of people who continued to buy record albums, clinging to their vinyl, resisting the changing tide like a sightless starfish clinging to the drying leg of a vast wooden pier, stubbornly expecting the briny water to still be there but it's not anymore. Tyler could see that cassettes had another advantage over record albums or even clever but bulky 8-track tapes, recognizing early on that smaller was becoming a virtue in this new world. And now compact discs coming on strong and making the cassette tape itself already look like a tired old technology.

The march of progress continues inevitably and unyielding. Yet you can miss the signposts along the way. They aren't always recognizable until they appear in your rearview mirror like the big, block letters helpfully printed backwards on the windshield of an emergency medical van coming up behind you and gaining fast, so that the letters make sense in your mirror: AMBULANCE. Like VHS over Betamax; you couldn't know which technology was going to win until it played out. *You have to be nimble, have some agility.* And that's where Tyler has the leg up on his slow-moving colleagues in the human resources world. As stewards of the status quo, bureaucratic enforcers of corporate steadiness and predictability, HR people are entrenched in the way things are, blind to the ways things are going to be. Tyler is *agile*. His short attention span is his secret weapon. When he grows bored with something, it's a leading-edge signal to change, to swerve to the left and hit the gas. The world is changing. He can see it clear as the bug splat on his windshield—more global and more fluid, faster-paced. And unlike the tide that the stubborn starfish can wait out, eventually returning to the level where it was stranded, this world is not going back to the old way. The Information Age is replacing the Age of Manufacturing. They've been saying it for a while, but now it's really coming; ideas and creativity will be more important than bigness. Even still, it will come as a surprise to those who can't see ahead very far. Or don't want to. For decades, General Motors has been the biggest company in the world, more employees, more factories, and an entrenched HR staff set up to manage all that bigness without any surprises. The elephant on the playing field seems unstoppable, but now the little guys are running circles around it and what can it do? The high tide is not returning. Getting laid off was annoying to be sure, but it's going to lead to new opportunity, Tyler feels, where his agility will be an asset, where he can be an agent of change without having to swim against the corporate riptide. In this last decade of the Twentieth Century, change is in the air. Opportunities will abound, he can see, for the agile-minded.

Tyler comes up on a slow-moving semi-trailer truck and puts on his blinkers to pass on the left even though a lane is wide open to the right of the truck. Not supposed to pass on the right. *Sherwin-Williams Paint*, it says on the truck's side. That explains the strange picture he'd seen on the back of the truck: an enormous globe representing the world and a giant bucket labeled SWP somehow hovering above the world, inverted and dumping immense amounts of thick red paint over an entire hemisphere, *Cover the Earth*. Some of the paint spilling off the globe and continuing in a red tidal wave past Antarctica and into outer space below the Earth, as if there was still a *down* beyond the Earth and its gravity to make it keep falling that way. *They'll have to change that slogan now that we're all getting environmentally responsible,* he thinks. That massive spill of red muck, somehow done on purpose to fulfill the mysterious and sinister command, *Cover the Earth*. How does that make anyone want to buy their paint?

The east side's billboards, cigarettes and booze, booze and cigarettes, tell you this isn't the place for car trouble. The neighborhoods are tougher here. In Detroit's west side neighborhoods, people won't bother you, even if you're white, if you don't bother them. But the blacks living on the east side, Tyler thinks, have a chip on their shoulder. It says, *Don't mess*. Maybe it's because they live so close to the Grosse Pointe money, they feel their noses rubbed in it, like Rucker said we should do to the East Germans. Even from the freeway, just passing by, Tyler can sense the resentment. It hangs in the air like the thick, foul smoke from a smoldering tire in a garbage dump. Resentment encouraged by old, hateful Coleman Young, mayor of Detroit since the mid-Seventies, re-elected time after time by blacks who applaud his profane moxie, standing up to perceived white oppression and stoking an increasingly heated divide between city and suburbs. The Young years have been devastating to the city as white flight and corporate evacuation destroyed the tax base, accelerating a downward cycle of worsening schools, chronic unemployment, emboldened gangs and an epidemic of drugs and violence.

The freeway is not the only way to Metro Beach. They could take Jefferson Avenue along the Detroit River, the scenic route. If you follow Jefferson past the UAW headquarters and the old Chrysler plant, you pass through neighborhoods that look like Beirut on the evening news. Bombed-out, burned-down, broken houses that once were homes. Dirt and shattered glass. Then just as the Detroit River on the right turns into Lake St. Clair, Jefferson Avenue becomes Lake Shore Drive, and Beirut turns into Grosse Pointe Park. Huge old oak trees line the boulevard on both sides. No dirt on the street here, no broken glass. The homes are large, then immense, set back behind manicured green lawns. Grosse Pointe Park becomes Grosse Pointe, then Grosse Pointe Farms, Grosse Pointe Woods and Grosse Pointe Shore, distinctions for the social register, lost on Tyler. These people, too, have a chip on their shoulder. It says, *Don't trespass.* You pass the Detroit Yacht Club, then St. Clair Shores, before finally reaching Metro Beach. A huge, thoroughly public park, an oasis from all the exclusiveness.

Tyler would prefer to take Jefferson/Lake Shore Drive, to gawk at the mansions: Which one is Diana Ross's mother's house? Which is Edsel Ford's? But he stays on the freeway to save time.

He exits St. Clair Shores/Metro Beach, drives along the tree-lined road to the park, pays the rangerette in the guard shack three bucks and parks the Sunbird what seems like a quarter mile from the beach.

"Wake up, Robbie. We're here."

It's no use. Tyler puts his limp son over one of his shoulders and grabs the gym bag with his free hand. Webb lifts a Playmate cooler out of the trunk and follows a few steps behind. Three seagulls fly overhead. Just to Tyler's right, a Nissan Sentra takes a direct hit of white bird droppings on its polished blue hood. "You see that?" Tyler asks.

Rucker nods. "Beautiful, wasn't it?"

The black pavement feels hot to Tyler's feet, right through the rubber soles of his sneakers. Robbie begins to weigh on his shoulder and back. They reach the end of the parking lot, finally, and Tyler sets the boy down on the sidewalk, shaded by a large maple tree. Robbie looks up with groggy eyes. "Aaaaaayyy," he begins to whine, a reflex action to the unexpected awakening, but his heart isn't in it.

"Drink," he says to his father.

"I'm thirsty, too, Robbie," Webb says. "Don't worry. Inside this old cooler is lots of good stuff to drink."

"Juice," Robbie guesses.

"Yeah, I think we even have juice," Webb says.

Robbie stoops down to poke at a shiny piece of broken glass.

"No, Robbie, leave that alone," his father scolds, throwing the chunk of glass toward a trash basket; missing. "C'mon. Let's keep going."

They walk over the grassy park onto the beach. It's like a big party; everyone's smiling. Exposed flesh—from the darkest black to pale, freckled white, and every tan and brown in between. They find a patch of unoccupied sand big enough for three beach blankets, and stake their claim.

"A woman's legs are a beautiful thing, a wonder of creation," Rucker says looking up the beach twenty yards or so at a particularly tall young woman in a yellow one-piece, with shapely, brown legs. Walking slowly up the beach with a bit of a smug smile, towering above the beach blanket citizens all around her. She gazes through designer sunglasses, out at the glistening water's rolling waves and distant silent sailboats.

"They can be, at times," Tyler says with less enthusiasm, looking out in the opposite direction where two chunky teenage white girls make their way toward them, plodding through the deep sand. Rap music from jam boxes overwhelms an occasional pop song.

Then he feels it coming on, the panic, like an edgy agitation in his spine. Not that he's afraid of anyone or anything here at the beach. Fearful instead of an enveloping despair he tries so hard to avoid. Everything at once, crowding him in, taking away his oxygen, or his sense of self. That all the loss has left him lost. Without the bearings that rooted and shaped his life, defining him as husband and corporate employee, what hope has he of finding his way? With invisible effort, Tyler sits himself down on a beach towel between his son and Rucker, waiting for the feeling to pass.

Robbie pushes a yellow plastic shovel into the soft sand. "You still thirsty, Robbie?" Tyler asks his boy, the lone remaining signpost he has, marking him a father at least.

"Okay, Daddy," the boy answers cheerfully without looking up from the sand slipping out of the shovel's mouth. Tyler finds a purple juice box in the cooler, disconnects the little straw glued to the box with a single dot of adhesive goop, and frees the straw from its clear plastic shroud.

As Robbie drinks the juice with one, long continuous draw on the straw, Tyler finds a large, pink bottle of sunscreen, SPF 50, claiming to be water repellant and made especially for kids. He squirts a gob half the size of a golf ball into his right palm and begins to rub it all over Robbie's back and neck, then his little chest and all over and around both his arms. Another smaller gob to cover his legs and feet. Sand quickly finds its way onto the white goo covering much of Robbie's skin, but he doesn't make a peep of protest. He says nothing even as Tyler takes the box and straw away long enough to smear sunscreen on the boy's face, not quite as heavy here, being careful not to get any in his eyes or mouth. The boy's father then coats the top of his little head, smearing it through thin brown hairs. The sunlight can get through, and the top of the head is the worst because it's perpendicular to the sun rays beating straight down, or at least tied for worst with the top of one's shoulders. Tyler slips a little blue sun hat on the boy's head, drawing the elastic band underneath his chin. Robbie paws at it with a white-coated, sandy hand but doesn't take it off.

Tyler wears a navy blue baseball cap with an old-English script capital "D," signifying the Detroit Tigers, and inexpensive, wire-framed sunglasses that color his world green—he could have bought ones with yellow lenses but why would he want everything to look sickly yellow? Rucker wears a red cap with the Chevrolet logo, similarly cheap sunglasses and a white Oldsmobile tee shirt. Tyler puts a thin coat of the toddler's sunscreen on his own shoulders and then dabs some on both his ears. As one of the songs in the chaotic concert of competing jam boxes comes to an end, Tyler can distinctly hear the cheerful American Top 40 jingle and then the voice of the radio show's announcer, Shadoe Stevens, who's not nearly as memorable as Casey Kasum was when Tyler was a teen and tuned in weekly. *With this week's Number 27 hit, here's Aerosmith with "Janie's Got a Gun."*

Rucker gulps his beer, from a can hiding inside a Koozie Sleeve. Tyler slurps his ice-cold Mountain Dew, also within an insulated Koozie, even though there's no need to hide the pop can from the park rangers.

"Aren't you gonna help me drink these beers?" Rucker wants to know.

"Nah, I got to drive us home before too long," Tyler responds matter-of-factly.

Robbie studies an ant, then another and another, racing crazily in zigs and zags over the waves of sand. Tyler and Rucker scope the beach for attractive female bodies, but don't see any worth noting, the long-legged, yellow one-piece girl long gone. What becomes of the countless people who pass through our lives in an instant, never to be encountered again? Fading so quickly, into *bolivion,* as Mike Tyson has said. Nothing outstanding here at all. In a sea of flesh, a desert of unsexiness. Thousands of people at the beach today, at least half of them women. Have to be some real babes here somewhere, you'd think.

8

Showered, shaved and wearing a buttoned-down striped shirt and khaki slacks, Tyler parks the Sunbird in a lot across the street from the Attic Theater. Little purple banners with fancy script type hang from street poles calling this area of the city, *The Theater District*. An exaggeration. The truly impressive Fisher and tiny Attic are the only theaters in the "district." The Fox is several blocks away in one direction; the recently restored Masonic Temple at least as far in another direction.

Tyler's supposed to meet this Candice by the popcorn vendor in the Attic's lobby. His idea. He was here once, years ago with Christie, and seems to remember they sold popcorn in the lobby. She'll be wearing a turquoise dress, Candice had said.

He sees the snag in the plan as soon as he gets to the front entrance; you need to show your ticket to enter the lobby where the popcorn must be. But he's got both tickets. He decides to hang around outside, by the ticket window. A mixed collection of theater patrons pass by: a stylish, gray-haired couple, the woman wearing a long green dress and pearls, the man a navy blue suit, conservative red tie, probably an executive for one of the auto companies; a thirtyish black couple, much more casual but stylish, she in a pale green pant suit, he in a summer sweater and stone-washed jeans; another older, white couple. Everyone in pairs. Across the street, a construction worker with an orange vest and a yellow hard hat sits on the curb, smoking a cigarette, collecting overtime. Behind him, some street punks loiter. Strangers they all are, brushing up against Tyler—or at least invading his peripheral vision—at some arbitrary intersection of their lives, whom he'll never see again, never know their names. The disagreeable family he avoids in the mall; the fat woman with a cold in the next seat on the plane for three hours he doesn't talk to, pretending to read; the homeless guy on the corner he hurries past. Drab, forgettable sections of the scenery of his life and memories, like the commercials he fast-forwards when watching something he has taped on his VCR.

He sees her then, crossing the street, and nearly turns to escape before she sees him. *Too late.* She hurries right toward him, somehow picking him out from his description: six-foot-two with shortish, straight brown hair, one hundred ninety-five pounds, he said, although he's really more like two-ten. Wearing a yellow shirt with thin, blue stripes, just like he promised. She must be honing in on his clothes. She's wearing the turquoise dress all right, but it's what's inside the dress that makes him want to run. She's big. Not fat, exactly, just big. She must be five-foot-eleven and, well, beefy. Her dress's shoulder pads don't help either; she looks like she might crush him if she gets angry. Why didn't he ask for more physical description on the phone? He told her what he looked like, fair's fair. He could have got sick or had a funeral come up.

She thrusts a meaty hand at him. "Tyler, I presume?" she says in the voice that sounded cute and sexy on the phone. He shakes her hand like a man's.

"Candice," he says, not asking, knowing his fate is sealed, for this one night anyway. Then he adds, explaining, "I waited out here because you need your ticket to get in."

"No problem. It was easy to spot you. Everybody else is with somebody." Then she laughs, more of a bray, really, like a donkey, all teeth. It's new; she didn't laugh like that on the phone. Again, he fights the urge to run away. He hands their tickets to the man at the door and then they're inside, buying popcorn and Cokes, finding their seats. She shovels the buttery popcorn into her mouth, two and three at a time.

"Did you have any problem finding this place?" he asks her, determined to be friendly. Once the play starts, he won't have to worry about trying to keep up conversation. After it's over, he'll walk her to her car as quickly as he can, then bolt.

"No, it was simple. And I didn't have any trouble today with my fine General Motors car," she says, smiling. "I really do like my car, I was just kidding you on the phone."

This GM banter could grow old fast. "Great. So, how you been? How's your job at the hospital?" He can't remember which hospital, he knew a minute ago. *Doesn't matter; this will get her talking.*

"Ok, I'm doing good. I've been looking forward to meeting you. It's all I've been thinking about. I told my girlfriends at St. John's…" *That's it—St. John's Hospital, east side suburbs somewhere.* "…they all think I'm crazy. Meeting a stranger. In the city, at night no less. It sounds so dangerous to them. But I figure, you seemed pretty normal on the phone, and we're meeting at a public place, people all around. They worry about rape," she adds this last bit in a hushed whisper, close to his ear. Furthest thing from his mind, raping her. He wishes she would give him more room. The seats are small and tight.

"Well, I guess you can never be too careful," Tyler says, wondering where to go with this. "But I'm not really a violent person."

"What kind of person are you, *Tyler?*" She says his name with a little too much emphasis; it's not comfortable to her yet. And what's this question about, really?

"Oh, I don't know," he says. "I like sports. I told you about the softball team I play on. I do okay, but I'm no great athlete or anything."

"But what kind of *person* are you?" she presses, digging. What does she want from him anyway?

He pauses, pretending to be in deep thought. "I'm a good person, I guess. A good father…" he adds, remembering just after he says this that he hasn't told her yet about Robbie, or about Christie. He was going to wait on all that. How long until the play starts?

"You have a child?" she says, pulling her head back. Giving him space at last.

"Yeah, a boy. Twenty-two months old. I'm a single father. I didn't get a chance to tell you on the phone. My wife died about eight months ago," he says, stretching the truth a bit. Six months doesn't seem that long ago if he's saying it out loud. "I'm just starting to go out again."

"I had no idea," she says. Peach-colored makeup around her eyes stretches back in true surprise. "I'm so sorry. This must be very hard for you." She leans closer and puts a thick arm on his back, just below the neck. He tenses and she must feel him tense. She pulls her arm back to her seat.

A woman in a red dress that doesn't quite extend to her knees steps down the aisle, looking at the numbers on the end seats. Matching red pumps, with a bit of a heel and a thin strap around the ankle. Sheer white pantyhose on her sleek legs, not exactly slender, there's a little more curve to them than that. Nice rear end, Tyler notices as she descends the steps of the aisle past him. She turns around then, having gone too far apparently, and walks back up toward Tyler and his big date. She's wearing a round hat the same dark shade of red as her dress and shoes, with a wide brim that dips down in the front and a white ribbon. He can make out a striking face in the shadows under the hat: sharply defined cheekbones around tiny red lips, white cheeks and neck framed by shoulder-length, auburn hair. Not much makeup. Young twenties, Tyler guesses. She glances up and sees his eyes on her while his date continues to talk, oblivious. The girl in the red hat smiles, just a bit, then looks down and finds her seat—in the next row directly in front of Candice. She seems, for the moment at least, to be alone. Tyler's date pauses, waiting for an answer, something about his wife.

"Christina. She was great. We were happy together. Had a good marriage. No problems." *Are these the right answers?*

"What did she look like?"

"She had wavy, reddish hair. Short, about five-four. Kind of petite." Describing Christie's figure to this large woman seems rude or unfair, but she asked. Christie was undeniably a fox, even when she was pregnant with Robbie and afterward. Her figure came right back. You could fit one and half Christies inside this one Candice, easy.

"What was Christina like? I hope you don't mind me asking so many questions, but I think it's important that I learn a bit about someone who must have meant so much to you. Still does, I'm sure." *Why is it important?* How does he let this Candice know that after tonight, that's it, she won't be hearing from him again? Tyler looks down at the top of the round red hat with the white ribbon in the seat in front of his date, wishing he could jump ahead one row to the empty seat beside her. So far, no one has joined her. Every so often she turns her head to the side enough that he can see a soft white cheek.

"She was smart. Really well-read. She was an English major at Ohio State. That's where we met. She was quiet, you know, kind of shy."

Candice starts to ask him something else, but then, mercifully, the lights come down. A spotlight shines on a far corner of the stage where a bearded man dressed as a cowboy begins to speak to the crowd, as if to his wife. Or maybe his horse. You can't be sure at first.

Then another man comes out. Another cowboy. Two arrows stick out of his back. But he's not dying; he seems unaware that anything's amiss. It's a comedy. Tyler sinks back in his chair, relieved. The cowboys are brothers, Oklahoma homesteaders. The bearded one tries to convince his younger brother to move their families back east, to New York City, where it's safe. The brother insists they have nothing to fear in Oklahoma. "Nothing to fear?" the bearded one roars, losing his patience.

The younger one throws up his fists, as if to ward off an attack from his brother. "True nobility is exempt from fear," he says, switching to an exaggerated British accent, must be quoting somebody. "More can I bear than you dare execute." *Winston Churchill?*

Pockets of laughter break loose throughout the audience. A little snicker, then a full-fledged laugh comes from under the red hat in the next row. The girl's right hand rises, open palm up, and then out of sight underneath the hat's brim. Tyler can imagine the delicate, white hand lightly touching her mouth. Then she laughs out loud again. Her laughter excites Tyler. How many women would have the nerve to come to a play alone? How many could laugh aloud alone without embarrassment?

Tyler's date nudges him with her elbow. "This is going to be good," she says. "I think you picked a good one." Tyler nods and pretends to return his attention to the stage. Instead, he watches the red hat in front of him bob up and down whenever one of the characters speaks a amusing line. Occasionally, she looks to the far-right end of the stage, and he is able to see a white cheek and small, smiling red lips.

Intermission brings the lights up.

"I'm enjoying myself," Candice says. "These actors really get into their parts. With such simple sets, they can't just blend in—the words and acting has to stand up, you know?"

"Yeah, they're not bad. I'm impressed." He had expected not-at-all-ready-for-prime-time players.

"I have to use the lady's room," she says in a loud whisper. "Do you have to go, too? Or do you want to wait in the lobby?"

"No, I'll stay here and watch our seats," Tyler says, as if somebody would take them if they both left. She looks at him oddly, but then says, "Okay, suit yourself. Be right back." Tyler stands to let her pass. Not quite believing his luck. He just might get a chance with the girl in the red hat.

When Candice is out of sight, he draws in a deep breath, wondering what he should say. If he thinks too long, he won't do it. The girl in the red dress and hat sits there still, an empty seat to either side of her. Tyler leans forward and taps her shoulder gently.

"Excuse me," he says softly.

The back of the hat turns away and that striking white face takes its place, grayish-blue eyes looking curiously at Tyler. "Yes?" she says.

"I'm sorry. I don't really know how to say this, but I just had to, uhm." *Don't get bogged down here. Be honest.* "I'm kind of stuck here on a blind date that isn't working out too well. I don't want to be rude to her, so I'm going along with it, but she really isn't my type and … I couldn't help noticing you. You're so pretty. I mean, you have *such* a pretty face. And I really like your hat. Such an *elegance* about you."

She smiles slightly, just enough to reveal the beginnings of large, gleaming white teeth, but her cocked eyebrows tell him she's sizing him up, unsure at best. She doesn't say anything.

"Anyway, my name's Tyler. I never do things like this, but I just felt I had to talk to you, to meet you. You really are pretty," he repeats.

Her smile grows warmer and she extends her hand to him. "I'm Lyvia." She pronounces her name *Liv-ee-uh*. He looks confused, so she spells it for him. "But you mustn't disappoint your date," she says with a bit of a country accent. Southern. Or small-town Midwestern, maybe.

He reaches to shake her hand, but comes up with only her small, warm fingers, more intimate somehow than the palm-to-palm handshake he expected. He feels her softness all about him. Then he lets go of her fingers and reaches for his back pants pocket for his wallet. He's able to free it from the pocket without a struggle. He finds one of his General Motors business cards, his proof of respectability, and shows it to the alluring young woman.

"My work number's about to change, but I can write my home number on it." He quickly pulls out a pen and writes out the number. "Give me a call. Please. I'd love to have a chance to talk with you, Lyvia. I'm not weird or anything. Really, I'm not. Promise me you'll at least call?" He likes the sound of her name. It rolled off his tongue easily, lyrically. So many syllables in such a short word.

She smiles, but won't give him the satisfaction of an answer. He sits back in his seat and pretends to read his program.

Soon Candice returns with two large Cokes. "Here you are," she says. "My treat."

The second act of the play goes by quickly. Saloon girl hookers, cattle rustlers and other lawless types join the brothers on the stage. Then a huckster from a traveling medicine show performs magic tricks, including one where he pulls a live white rabbit from underneath a saloon girl's hoop skirt. The younger brother points to all this activity as proof of the high state of culture in Oklahoma. Why should they return to New York? Tyler can watch the red hat while keeping his face pointed toward the stage. Wonder what Lyvia with her small-town accent thinks of this sly New York ridicule of life in the southwest?

The show ends. Everyone claps. The cast returns, bowing one by one. Lights come up. Tyler is confronted with his date. "That was really good," she says. "I think I would have liked to live in the old west."

"Oh, I don't know," Tyler responds, standing. "I bet it wasn't so great in those days. Think how dirty it was. No indoor plumbing." He looks over at Lyvia, catches her eye. She smiles warmly, tilting her head just a little, a shared secret. Then she walks down her empty row, over to a different aisle. Tyler and Candice get caught in the jam of their crowded aisle. Lyvia is gone.

"It's still early," Candice says as they walk out the theater's doors. "Why don't we get a bite to eat? Maybe a dessert."

Just when he thought he was home free. "I don't know. My babysitter…"

"Oh, come on," she insists. "It's a Saturday night. Live a little."

They spot a little diner half a block away. She walks close by his side, already feeling part of a couple. Tyler slides into the opposite side of the booth Candice has chosen. His red vinyl seat cushion is ripped, exposing dirtied yellow styrofoam innards. An attractive, dark-skinned waitress brings them waters. "Something to drink?" she asks.

"Just a Coke," Candice says. Tyler was about to order a beer, but decides to go with the flow. "Lemonade," he says.

"Listen, Candice," he begins when the waitress has left. "I'm not really sure I'm ready to be dating yet. Maybe it's too soon."

"Getting out is the best thing for you," she counters. "I have an aunt whose husband died a couple of years ago. Cancer. She's older, of course, about forty-five. But that's still way too young to be a hermit. We've tried to get her to do things socially, but she won't."

"How many in your family?" Tyler asks. Keep her talking about her family, so she'll quit probing into his life.

"I have four brothers. No sisters." She's the oldest, she says. Her family's from… *somewhere*. He missed it. They moved fifteen years ago, when she was eleven. Her father's some kind of manager with Chrysler. She said what department, but he didn't catch that, either. He looks at her and nods, encouraging her to carry the ball, their conversation, and run with it. He winds up, in his mind, and throws a split-finger fastball, his imaginary specialty, to jump ahead in the count against the Athletics' Jose Canseco. The big slugger from Cuba stands in again, crowding the plate. Tyler lets loose with one-hundred-and-five-mile-an-hour chin music, high and tight. Canseco lunges out of the way, kicking up a dust cloud. The catcher reaches up to snatch the pitch without rising from his crouch, making it look as innocent as possible, and flicks the ball back to Tyler. Canseco stares at him, fuming, then picks himself up from the ground. Tyler throws another split-fingered pitch, hard and knee high. It drops off at the last instant and the catcher has to make a nice play to scoop it off the plate. Canseco misses badly. One and two. Tyler has him set up.

"…better than in Flint, that's for sure." She pauses to take a sip from her Coke. Flint is where they shot a lot of that low-budget movie that came out last year making fun of GM's top executive, *Roger and Me*, by that fat, sloppy filmmaker who wears a red baseball cap all the time and a stupid smirk on his face. Like he thinks he's somebody because he made GM's Roger Smith come off as a coward and showed Flint to be a hell-hole of a city made worse by GM's cutbacks, one of the women in town skinning rabbits for some white-trash dinner party. *Wonder where Lyvia lives?*

God whispers to us in our pleasures, speaks to us in our conscience, but shouts in our pains; it is his megaphone to rouse a deaf world.

C.S. LEWIS

II. IN THE WHITE ROOM

9

Tyler's first car, a green Maverick, spins its tires on wet pavement somewhere inside his head, behind cobwebs of disuse. Tired and spent, he reaches back for that car with its pinstripes and add-on fiberglass rear spoiler, not so long ago, really. But he can't stay with it, can't concentrate, as if he's ninety years old with Alzheimer's. And a hernia. Or a broken hip maybe.

Drip

Trying to prove something with those underpowered cars, loaded down with lousy, ineffective pollution controls. All his friends drove lame little four-bangers, Pintos and Vegas, that couldn't squeal their tires unless it had just rained.

He bought a six-year-old pale green Ford Maverick when he turned sixteen, sophomore year, painted inch-wide purple pinstripes on it that must have been pretty ugly, now that he thinks about it. He'd wanted to buy one of those big V-8-powered muscle sleds, like his cousin's Pontiac GTO—*Get Turned On, baby*—but he'd been born too late. Buy something practical, his father said. "Gas is going to a buck-fifty a gallon if things keep up like this;

you better get something small." By this time, his father wasn't around much, so when he had something to say, it seemed best to listen. *Small.* No power; no guts; no glory. That was the Class of '81—no glory left for them. No glory at all.

Drip

The old heroes were all gone by then and there weren't any new ones waiting on the sidelines. Unless you counted Reagan, the old prune, conning the country into feeling good enough to pawn its problems off to the next generation. My generation, Tyler thinks. *Why don't you all ffffade away.* No heroes left.

Drip

But this is now, so it's the Sunbird he must be driving. An improvement on those first-generation Detroit economy cars of the Seventies. Better science. Still, you lost something with front-wheel drive; there was no *I-can-feel-the-tires-spinning-behind-me-but-I'm-in-complete-control* feeling when you peeled out. No glory. Instead, a whimpering, shuddering, halting, sliding, *excuse-me* sensation as Tyler spins the Sunbird's front tires on the rain-slicked asphalt. *Wet burn outs don't count.*

Drip

Not even musical heroes. They were gone, most of them, even if they hadn't all died before they got old. Leaving a great void, standards too high for the *jury-is-still-out* rock stars that have followed, except maybe Bruce. Tyler watches his hand reach out of the dream mist into the real clear and push a cassette into the Sunbird's tape deck, unleashing Springsteen's New Jersey voice mid-song into the cool, wet night air, mournful but not compromising, "... *some folks are born into a good life. Other folks get it anyway, anyhow...*"

Drip

Old lady in a yellow Buick land yacht. She leans forward against the steering wheel, a wrinkled statue with red lip gloss. Clutching that wheel so hard he can almost see the blue veins pop from her tiny forearms. Tyler keeps looking at her as he passes the Buick, again and again, he remembers it so clearly it must be etched on to the inside of his forehead, this scene. When he closes his eyes he can read it like a book, every detail. Trying to see what she's thinking, but she won't take her eyes off the center of straight ahead. God knows where she's headed in this rain. This dark.

Drip

Hard to see the lines anymore. Need more streetlights out here. Never enough light when you need it. Never was.

Drip

The car lurches as Tyler hits another pothole, splashing steel-black water everywhere. Road commissioner must be a dentist. That's why there aren't streetlights. They don't want you to see how bad it is. Somebody might complain and get the sheep stirred up. None of us got too much energy anymore. Anymore don't have much. Energy.

Drip

Light up ahead's still yellow, Tyler sees through the rain. On through. There oughta be a late game on cable. There oughta be

Drip

10

Tyler's eyes open to a hazy heaven. Whiteness, blurry whiteness. But something's not right in the music he can barely hear…

…find myself in times of trouble, Mother Mary comes to me…

It's too slow and in a sleepy woman's voice, not McCartney's, not the Beatles…

Drip

Speaking words of wisdom, let it be…

Muzak from somewhere above, so it must not be heaven at all; the music there would be *real*. His eyes focus on distant ceiling panels, fluorescent lights and, closer, an inverted bottle on a hat rack, a tube bending in odd turns if you follow it down, it curves around and disappears beneath a bandage on his left arm. *Drip… Drip… Drip*

"It's nice to see you awake again, Tyler."

His eyes shift to the right and refocus. A young, sandy-haired woman towers above, her pale skin and immaculate uniform nearly invisible against the all-white backdrop. Her immense height is an illusion, of course, it's the angle. Tyler's head is halfway buried in a pillow; she can't be that tall.

The nurse walks closer to Tyler's bed. He keeps studying this medical Amazon. No illusion; she is tall. Real tall. Her badge says simply, "R.M. Bindell."

"How do you feel?" the nurse asks. She stands with a bit of a slouch, one knee bent, a hand resting on her hip so her back turns and bends a bit not fully upright, as one who grew up tall through self-conscious teenage years and continues in the habit, slouching, unthinkingly lowering her height to the more normal and expected.

He's not sure if her question is rhetorical. How does he begin to answer? What is truth? What is beauty? How *does* he feel? A vague sense of pain, of that he can be sure.

Tyler coughs and swallows a phlegm clot. "I … don't … know …"

She appears to hear his nearly inaudible answer.

"Don't try to move much yet," she tells him. "We have you connected to a couple of tubes. You just tell me what you feel as I … can you feel this?" She squeezes the big toe on his right foot, underneath the bed sheet. He can and he tells her, more clearly this time. She touches his other foot and each of his fingers. With each touch, he grunts, *yes*. He feels it.

The nurse looks too young. And if she's going to squeeze his body parts, he ought to at least know what to call her. "What's your name, nurse?"

"I'm sorry," she answers. "I guess you don't remember. You gained consciousness yesterday for a time and met me and Doctor Browning. It's silly of me to expect you to. I'm Rachel Bindell. I'll be your primary nurse while you're with us in Intensive Care."

She pulls back the bed sheet and asks him to turn his head to the right. *Silly*, she said. How strange, that word. Nothing silly about all this *intensive care* whiteness. Two days he's been here. *At least. She said "yesterday," right?* Tyler turns his head slowly, but then a white-hot sledgehammer crashes down against the whole of his head. An electric shock from a cattle prod between his eyes bounces off the inside of the back of his skull. A flash of light, fire; darkness. He tastes milky mustard sawdust as he slips into the dark, where it's safe and warm. And quiet. No more fake Beatles muzak.

* * *

"Well, you probably shouldn't try to move your head again for a while." The tall, sandy-haired nurse holds a wet washcloth on Tyler's forehead. Her smock is stained brown and yellow. "You blacked out again, Tyler?"

"Yeah, I guess so." Then an attempt at a joke. "What happened to you?" he asks, looking at the vomit stain on her uniform.

She smiles and offers him a Dixie cup. He drinks the water slowly, rereading her badge: RN Bindell. After he swallows the last drop, he sees the bedpan she's holding for him to spit into.

"Now, where were we? Do you feel pain in any part of your body right now?"

She asks too many questions. If he wasn't so tired Tyler would have a few questions of his own. Like: *Why the hell am I lying in this hospital bed? What happened after I went through that traffic light? And where's Robbie?*

"No. Not really. Just tired, all over." He guesses the nurse to be about twenty-four, not very long out of college. Despite her manly height, she has a fragile, soothing feeling about her. Innocence maybe. Perhaps her cute little nose. Too small for her longish head, and slightly upturned, the nose livens up an otherwise drab face. Her tiny, dark nostrils seem to smile at him.

"You've been through a lot. And you men are *such* babies," the nurse says, making a joke, too, he supposes. "Now, do you mind if I take a look at your catheter?"

"My what?"

"Your catheter," she repeats. "That tube we've hooked up to drain the urine from your bladder. How did you think you've been urinating all this time you've been here?" She pulls the sheet back a little further. Sure enough, a clear rubber tube, taped to Tyler's right thigh, goes right into the end of his penis. It should hurt, but he feels nothing down there.

"Don't worry about the catheter," she says. "Just don't think about it. It's nothing."

Yeah, right, Tyler thinks. Easy for her to say. How is he *not* to think about it now that she's shown it to him?

"It won't bother you as long as you don't make any sudden moves," she says. Not that he was planning any. "We'll take it off real soon," she promises. "As soon as you're over these blackouts."

She sticks a thermometer under his tongue. "The doctor's keeping a close eye on you. We've already run two CT scans and taken some blood samples. You probably don't remember." He doesn't. She continues to explain, though it's a strain for him to listen: "The doctor will probably want to do more tests. So, you should expect some more blood draws. And some urine samples. You don't seem to be in too bad of shape, all things considered. But we have to be sure."

The nurse pulls a thermometer from Tyler's mouth. He doesn't even remember her putting it in there. She looks at it for a moment and writes something on her clipboard. Then she hangs the clipboard on the footboard of Tyler's bed. Must be a hook down there or something. She pours an orange liquid into a little clear plastic shot glass and hands it to him.

"Let's see if you can keep this down. It would be better if we don't have to do it all through the *eye-vee…*" *All what?* He's fading and she's not making sense. Tyler drinks it. Not as bad tasting as he'd expected, like peach schnapps. "Before I go get the doctor," Rachel Bindell asks, "is there anything you want to ask me?"

"Two things, yeah," Tyler says, his voice still raspy and faltering. "Where's Robbie?"

"Your son?" He nods his head only just slightly, but she gets it. "He's staying with your babysitter's mother. The police notified your parents in Florida about the accident. They're on their way up. The doctor can tell you more."

Parents? Florida? She's got it wrong. His father died five years ago, when Tyler was at college, and his mother lives in Ohio. The nurse must be mixing up some of the details with somebody else's story. Just his mom must be who's on her way here. She's really worried, no doubt. To make the trip. Traveling is hard on Tyler's mother. She's become a recluse since his father died—or really before that, when he disappeared for several years—afraid to venture out where she might run into people, anyone, people she knows or strangers. It's all frightening to her. Something's not right in her head. It's a struggle for her even to go to the grocery. Tyler has been meaning to drive down to Akron to visit her, but keeps putting it off. He spent a week at her house back in early March after Christie died and the funeral. A week extra was all the time he could take off from work. He hasn't seen her since. Some phone calls, a couple of letters back and forth. She probably needs him more than he needs her now, but he hasn't been able to be much of a giver lately.

The nurse edges toward the curtain that marks the end of his room and the beginning of something unknown. Then she hesitates, "You said there were two things? What was your other question?"

Tyler draws in a deep breath, then exhales. Probably rude but what the heck? "I was just wondering. How tall are you?"

Nearly out the room, she stops and turns back, maybe a tiny smile underneath the cute nose. "Six-foot-two. And a half," she says. Taller than him, but just.

11

Growing up in Akron, Tyler and his older sister, Celia, had just enough of everything to not realize how little they had. At least while they attended St. Michael the Archangel grade school and wore the same uniforms as everyone else. Then came public high school and the beginning of brand-name consciousness, particularly for Celia, who suddenly became ashamed of her parents and their modest, little three-bedroom ranch home with its unfinished basement. No elaborate family room down there like her friends' families had with their big color TV consoles and a pool table maybe. Just an old pull-out couch and a little black-and-white set with crappy reception. Tyler hardly noticed his sister's snubs to the family; he was too busy playing football, then basketball and then baseball as the seasons turned. In primary school through eighth grade, Tyler was a three-sport standout. He continued to hold his own as a freshman in the much larger public high school. But the better kids were getting bigger and stronger while Tyler waited for a growth spurt that didn't come in time. He hit six foot as a freshman but grew just another half inch the next four years. Then sometime during his first two years of college he added another one-and-a-half inches, too late for his fledgling athletic career. Height wasn't really the issue, though, except in basketball. He was too skinny and too slow to crack the starting lineup in football, as a receiver and defensive back. Every day in practice it was made clear. The only kids he could beat in the forty-yard wind sprints were the heavy-set plodders who played on the line. Quickness. There was no way to learn to be quicker, to work out harder to build on whatever God-given speed you had, same as jumping ability. What came in your genes was pretty much all you would ever get. He rode the bench in football while the same eleven kids played both offense and defense, the lazy coaches rarely subbing at all, concentrating all their coaching effort on the best eleven kids. The others rarely got their uniforms dirty on Friday nights. Weren't at least some of the kids on the bench as good as a nearly exhausted starter, at least for a few plays? He did get to play some on the special teams, rewarded with this bit of a bone from the coaches for his incessant hustle all week long in practice, blocking as an up-back, occasionally fielding a short punt but never running one back to glory. He quit football after his sophomore year.

In basketball, he fared better; his high-arching shots finding the bottom of the net with that satisfying *swoosh* often enough to make him valuable despite his lack of everything else a basketball player needs: height, speed and hops. Tyler wasn't quick enough to properly defend the other team's guards and he wasn't nearly tall or strong enough to play in the front-court with the bigs. He came off the bench as a shooting guard who could provide some instant offense, but would only stay in the game as long as the other team's starting two-guard was getting a rest, the back-up generally not having enough self-confidence to beat Tyler with raw quickness. Basketball was non-stop running, without breaks between plays like football; you needed three or four reliable subs. So, Tyler saw quite a bit of meaningful playing time. He even thought he might break the starting lineup as a senior, but in the end, he was just too slow.

In the spring he played baseball. Since grade school, it had been his favorite sport. By the time he reached high school, he had been made into a third baseman with a decent glove and enough arm strength to snap off the throws to first, sidewinding as he came up with a grounder. He started on the freshman team and the next year on JV. His hitting wasn't anything special, but enough liners ricocheted off his bat and landed in between fielders to keep him in the lineup, batting seventh or eighth but at least ahead of whoever was hitting ninth. Then, the summer before Tyler's junior year, a kid named Gil Verona moved with his family to Akron from New York City. He, too, was a junior who played third base, and he was a better player than Tyler in just about every way. He ate up ground balls like a vacuum sweeper, had an effortlessly smooth, side-arm motion when he came up with the ball, a blur of his wrist and an instant later you heard a sharp *pop* coming from the first baseman's leather glove. Verona was the best hitter on the team, too. His beautiful, compact swing connecting with relentless precision and surprising power—the kid was rather small, at least three inches shorter than Tyler; you didn't need to be tall to play baseball. And he was a demon on the base paths, getting under the opposing pitcher's skin with ridiculously long leads, easily jumping back to first with cat-like reflexes to beat a pickoff attempt, and stealing bases with equally caustic abandon. Gil Verona was the perfect leadoff man and third baseman. He earned All-District honors—while Tyler rode the bench—their junior and senior years. Both of those teams advanced in the regional playoffs to the state championship game due in no small part to Verona's stellar play, though they lost the big game both years. Tyler did not begrudge his teammate's success. It was just too bad he had to play third base.

Little old Akron. The more populous but perhaps lesser known of the pair of cities served by the Akron-Canton Airport. Rival Canton being known far and wide for its Pro Football Hall of Fame. Canton had one of the original NFL franchises, the Bulldogs, back in the day. An early powerhouse, along with another neighboring town and rival, even more obscure today, Massillon with its Tigers. Other early teams included the Pottsville Maroons, Decatur Staleys and, yes, the Akron Pros. A bit of a mystery today, why these little burgs became football meccas in the 1920s when much bigger cities went without football—you could see that Los Angeles and San Francisco were simply too remote for teams that traveled by train, but what about Cincinnati or Detroit or Baltimore or even Indianapolis? Some of that small-timeness happened in the NBA, too, though the birth of professional basketball had been a much more recent phenomenon. The Detroit Pistons had been the Fort Wayne Pistons back in the Fifties. Remarkable that their perfect-for-the-Motor-City name, Pistons, predated their playing in Detroit. If that rumored women's pro basketball league puts a team in Detroit, Tyler thinks they should be called the *Cylinders*, Freudian yang to the Pistons' yin, auto erotica.

His sister, Celia, outshone Tyler in school, earning a steady succession of A's without showing much effort. Tyler bagged a decent number of A's himself, but more B's, along with an occasional C. He didn't get much grief about the pedestrian marks from his often-critical father, as long as he was playing well on the teams. But by his junior year it was clear that Tyler's best sporting accomplishments were already behind him and Dennis became increasingly less patient in his son's lack-luster academic performance, especially when the older Manion had a few drinks in him.

Drinking also tended to make Dennis politically conscious. A dyed-in-the-wool conservative, he complained bitterly about what he saw as the moral failings of the Democrats. One of Tyler's last clear memories of his father is him gloating the day after his hero Ronald Reagan, *the Gipper*, won the election in 1980 over a dour Jimmy Carter, saddled with stag-flation and that admitted lust in his heart. A few weeks later, Dennis Manion had disappeared. Months after that, he called from New Orleans, to ask Dorothy to forward some mail – with no apology, no explanation, no "I'll be coming home soon." And then, he apparently had developed testicular cancer. A pair of Akron cops came by the house to let Dorothy know her husband had died, down in Louisiana, alone. Though her marriage to Dennis had been loveless for who knows how many years, Dorothy Manion grieved his passing and let it leave a void in her very being she never would attempt to fill.

Meanwhile, no one had seemed to notice that Tyler's older sister was drinking and carrying on at late-night parties, a habit she continued when she went off to Kent State. The college best known for an ugly Vietnam War-era clash ten years earlier that had turned deadly when National Guardsmen lost their cool and fired into an angry throng of protesting students, leaving *four dead in O-hi-o*. The black and white photo that appeared everywhere of an anguished girl on one knee, above a fallen fellow student, her hands raised outwards, and her mouth, frozen in time but clearly screaming *Why?!* Tyler's father had sneered each time he saw that photo, in the newspaper, magazines and TV, even. The rioting students had brought it upon themselves, he said.

Kent State was quite the party school when Celia arrived there. With an undeclared major, she dabbled in courses in art history and philosophy, just as she dabbled in various recreational drugs and boyfriends. But it became hard for her to justify why she returned home so seldom from a college only thirty-six miles away. After one year, she transferred to Valparaiso, a small, liberal arts school in northern Indiana, just as Tyler was enrolling at Ohio State. Sometime before she graduated as a fifth-year senior, with a degree finally in anthropology, Celia took up with a rather cultish evangelical church off campus led by a young, charismatic minister. Celia would tell Tyler in a departing phone conversation that this church leader seemed to her more profoundly self-confident, *cocky* even, in his conviction in an assured place in the afterlife than any priest or minister she'd ever heard preach. She had gone all-in. Celia became born-again, buying into the trinity of fundamentalist Protestant doctrine: *sola fide*, guaranteed salvation based on faith alone; *sola scriptura*, a reliance on the bible alone; and *babylon et fornicata es*, the spectacularly errant Roman Catholic church. Right after her graduation, she left for a new life as a missionary on a Pacific island. She has largely disappeared from the lives of Tyler and their mother. Occasionally, a postcard arrives with a pleasant, touristy photo on the front, and on the back, just a short note, revealing nothing much at all of what Celia is doing or thinking.

Tyler's mother has become more introverted with each abandonment in her life, first her dying marriage, then her dying husband, Celia's increasing estrangement, finally disappearing into cultish isolation in the Pacific, and then even Tyler, who had begun to chart the course of a life that will not revolve around Akron. Quiet and shy to begin with, she has become a hypochondriac and a hermit, rarely venturing out of her house, which has become cluttered with newspapers and magazines saved for no good reason, along with medicine bottles and canning jars, and dishes to feed the cats.

* * *

He waits for Dr. Browning. From what the nurse said, Tyler has been in the hospital for at least two or three days. Must be Monday night. Or maybe Tuesday. No windows to provide a clue as to the time of day. What seems like hours go by, staring at the white ceiling. Tyler's heavy eyes begin to blink, then close. He slides down the tunnel again into a quiet calm. Lying on his back in a bathtub big enough for him to stretch out his legs. A steady stream of hot water flows out of the faucet at his feet. The water level reaches his ears, then his cheeks. Deeper and deeper.

Then he feels a presence peering into his tub. He opens his eyes. A middle-aged doctor, dark but more brown than black, Indian maybe, all smiles and random energy about him, circles his bed. He glances at Tyler's chart. Then, noticing Tyler's open eyes, he walks closer to the head of the hospital bed.

"Good to see you awake again," he says, looking down at Tyler. He glances away, then stares back down, quizzical and waiting. "You do not remember me, do you?"

Tyler starts to shake his head, but that makes the room spin and his chest hurt. Instead, he tries to speak, but the grunt he hears from himself is not recognizable.

"I am not surprised. I am Dr. Haran Gupta. This is the third time I have introduced myself to you since you first regained consciousness yesterday. You have been fading in and out. Do not try to move your head yet," he says, in a thick, Indian accent that is warm and soothing despite its jumpy cadence.

Tyler clears his throat. "Where's Doctor … Browning?" he mumbles.

"Who is that, Tyler? There is no Brownie here. Perhaps you are thinking of Dr. Bauna who looked in on you some. Sarah Bauna. She is a lady doctor," he explains.

"Dr. Browning. That's who the nurse, Rachel, said would be here." Tyler feels the words come up from his chest and out into the white room, understandable now though not his usual voice. Someone else's voice, younger, childlike and cautious.

"Rachel. A nurse here?" Dr. Gupta asks in that up-and-down accented voice.

"Yeah. The tall one. Six-foot-two-and-a-half, she said she was."

"Six-foot and two inches or more tall?" the doctor says with surprise in his voice. "I suppose I would remember if one of our nurses was so tall."

"She was here … with a thermometer, for my temperature, and…" Tyler says haltingly.

Dr. Gupta smiles, looking down on him, then says softly, "I can assure you, we are monitoring all your body signals with the equipment we have attached to you. There is no need to take your temperature manually."

Tyler closes his eyes, taking this in. *What was dream, what was real?*

"Be careful not to try to move too much today," Dr. Gupta says. "We have you hooked up in several places."

Several? Tyler opens his eyes. A clear plastic IV tube runs from the inverted bottle into his right wrist. A cluster of tubes and wires sprout out of a large bandage on his left arm. He reaches under the sheet to his groin with his mostly free right hand. He's connected to a catheter, just like he remembers. He lifts the sheet just enough that he can take a look down there. The drainage tube seems to run down alongside his right leg, connected with white tape, perhaps in several places.

"Do you want to be in a more upright position?" the doctor asks. The top half of the bed bends on a slight incline. His head rests on a pillow, maybe two pillows. He can look out across the room if he gets tired of staring up at the white, acoustical tile ceiling.

"Yeah. I guess so."

The doctor looks away and makes a hand gesture. An orderly turns a crank at the bottom of the bed. *When did he come into the room?* Tyler feels the head of his bed begin to rise. Folding him like a sandwich made with a single piece of bread.

Meanwhile, Dr. Gupta is shoving another pillow under his neck and back. Tyler feels dizzy.

"Your blood pressure is normal," the doctor says, an answer to a question no one has asked. "Heartbeat is steady and there is no sign of any internal injuries. No broken bones. You are running a slight fever, ninety-nine-point-eight degrees. Very normal. Except for a few external contusions—bruises—and quite a number of cuts, you seem to be doing remarkably well."

"Then why," Tyler asks, "do I feel like warmed-over crap?"

"An excellent question," Dr. Gupta says. "It appears that your forehead struck your car's steering wheel quite hard, resulting in a significant concussion. There seems to have been a small amount of hemorrhage—*bleeding*—inside your skull. That is what we are most concerned with. But the bleeding appears to have stopped very soon after the accident. Good news for you."

Tyler rubs his forehead with his right hand. It feels raw.

"Quite a contusion there," the doctor says. "We will keep a close eye on you for a little while to make sure there is no further hemorrhaging. And we will continue to run tests, work to better understand how your body is recovering from the trauma it endured. Medicine, like all science, is driven by the spirit of inquiry."

He says this last bit triumphantly. The faith of the scientist that there is always more that can be known, whether in a patient or a petri dish. An extroverted and endless appetite for questioning. "There does not seem to be any lasting injury," he continues.

Tyler notices that the doctor's belt loops bunch all around his waistline, evidence both of a substantial, successful weight loss and a hesitation to buy new pants with a smaller waistline to fit his new self, not quite believing in this transformation having any lasting permanence, his disbelief holding him back. Holding him down.

"To a certain degree, your body is still in shock. It does not realize yet how well you survived the accident. And that probably explains any apparitions of very tall nurses who do not actually work here."

The doctor puts his hands on Tyler's face. With his two index fingers, he lifts Tyler's upper eyelids, looking back and forth into each of the younger man's wide-open eyes. Then the doctor releases Tyler's right eyelid and finds with his left hand a black rubber instrument, like a bent flashlight, from a pocket in his white smock. He peers through it. First Tyler's left eye, then his right. He doesn't comment on what he sees there. The bright light makes Tyler see purple and green blurs, then veins like on a psychedelic leaf. Dr. Gupta scrawls something on the paper on his clipboard.

12

The plant is strangely quiet. Tyler rides his ten-speed bike past row after row of idle presses: grimy, green and quiet. Five or six men in orange coveralls sit sprawled in a little circle, throwing dice and swearing softly. Tyler keeps pedaling.

Up ahead, Schulous stands in the middle of the aisle, arms out, fingers spread wide. He's wearing a deep blue, expensive-looking three-piece suit. White shirt, blood-red tie, gold-colored tie bar. Smoke rises from the cigarette hanging from his mouth. He says nothing. Tyler stops the bike a few feet in front of him. Now it's a single-speed bike, like it should have been all along.

Tyler dismounts the bike and lets it fall to the floor. It doesn't make a sound. He stands in front of his old boss, looking down into the eyes of the shorter man. Neither speaks. Schulous strokes his gray mustache with the bony fingers of his right hand. He raises his left hand above his head and snaps his fingers. A huge bald eagle swoops down from the rafters high above, screeching. Its talons extend like landing gear. Tyler's forehead is the landing strip.

***

The dream gives way to an unsettled and fuzzy awakening. In the quiet, he feels the losses, deeply. Without the distractions that guide his motions, he is stuck. He knows he has lost his bearings. Hopeless and alone, except for Robbie.

Tyler opens his eyes to the white room and Nurse Rachel Bindell. She comes over to the top of the bed and peers past his pupils, his irises, at something inside that he's never seen, even looking into Christie's magnifying mirror when he shaves each morning, his electric razor cutting the growth down to stubble and, finally, to softness. She's older than he remembers, the face is different, not so long and there's not the cute little nose. She is tall, but perhaps not quite so tall as before. Her name badge says, "R.N. Binder."

"How are you feeling, Tyler?" she asks.

"Better, I think, Rachel," he says, testing the name.

"It's Emma. Emma Binder."

She looks him over. "You look better; you're getting some color back in your face. That's a good sign," the nurse says. "Where did you come up with Rachel?" she adds.

"Is there a really tall nurse here, named Rachel Bindell?" Tyler asks, not quite ready to give up on this. Though it does seem an odd question to ask a nurse who herself might be just two inches short of six feet tall.

"No, haven't seen her," she says. "You've been in and out of consciousness. You've had a traumatic injury. It's not unusual for you to be a little mixed up. I've been taking care of you mostly."

Tyler's still not sure, but what's the use? This new nurse seems perfectly real. She's evidently in the here and now, as much as he can tell.

"If you continue to feel better, I'll take that catheter off for you," she promises as she leaves.

Tyler stares around the empty room, trying to remember any of it. How did all this happen, the accident? And where's Robbie?

He forgot to ask this new nurse the question the imaginary nurse had answered earlier, about Robbie.

She'll be back soon, he thinks, closing his eyes, already so tired just from looking and thinking, trying to remember. The pain is all over but not anywhere specifically. Not really pain actually, just a generally blah-yuck feeling. All over. He leans back in his mind, pivots on his right foot against the rubber and he uncoils, his right arm moving out and over his shoulder and letting go, his hand continuing to rotate until his thumb is almost straight down, his body thrust forward. Another wicked fastball right at the catcher's mitt target. He lets it go, lets it go.

* * *

The nurse is back. She inspects the array of tubes and wires coming from Tyler's right arm, makes some adjustments. She wheels a clumsy-looking computer-on-a-TV-stand across the room, and connects it to the machine beside Tyler's bed. The computer seems to be extracting data, but it might just as well be pushing information out to the bedside machine, teaching it something it needs to learn. Who can tell?

"How are you feeling, Tyler?" she asks. That seems to be the favorite question around here.

"Okay. Better actually. A little more rested than the last time you asked."

"Yes, you're getting stronger. We need to keep you under observation a bit longer, but we're hopeful that you won't slip into unconsciousness again. That was a nasty concussion."

"There's a lot I don't remember," he says.

She nods but doesn't comment. "Do you have to urinate?" she asks. "Do you think you can use a bedpan?"

"Yes. And yes," Tyler answers.

"If you think you can, I'll take your catheter off. Or, if you'd prefer, I can call a male nurse to do it. Whatever would be more comfortable for you."

Tyler doesn't take long to consider this. "You can do it," he says, anxious to have the thing removed. It doesn't hurt exactly, but it itches and it burns just a bit. Especially when he pulls the sheet back and looks at it. Not *comfortable*. Not at all.

The nurse pulls a thin, cream-colored latex glove over the long, skinny fingers on each of her hands. Then her cold, rubberized fingers begin working down there. "You may want to turn your head for this part," she warns him.

Tyler turns, but looks back out of the corner of his eye.

She holds his most private part in one hand and slowly pulls on the catheter tube with the other, surprising him how much tube was hidden inside him. As the end of the tube slides out, he feels a sharp pain, like a pin prick, in the very tip. Then it's over.

He tries to clear his mind of the pain so that he will be able to urinate. He has to prove to her he can use the bedpan, so she won't skewer him again. He rises up and she slides the shiny steel pan under him. It's not as cold as he feared it would be. "Give me a second," he says.

"Of course." She ducks behind the curtain.

After several minutes of disappointing nothingness, the tinkling sound and salty smell come as sweet relief. And he is able to raise himself up just enough to remove the bedpan from underneath him. He proudly hands the pan to Emma the nurse when she returns.

"Fine," she says. "Then we'll just put the catheter away for good. All right?" She begins to rip at the tape that held the tube against his leg.

"Far away," Tyler says, wincing as the tape removes a patch of blondish leg hairs from his inner thigh. He never really had noticed that he even had hair there until now that they are being ripped out down to the root with the section of tape. The innocence Tyler imagined in this nurse, or in her earlier incarnation as Rachel, has long gone.

"Do you feel up to a visitor?" she asks, pulling the sheet back over his body.

"Yeah, sure," Tyler replies. He stretches his left foot under the sheets, then his right. All clear below.

"There are several people here to see you when you're ready. But first you're supposed to talk to an inspector from the Livonia police. Detective Teddington's his name."

"What's the problem?" Tyler wants to know. *The police?*

"I'm sure he just has some routine questions for you about the accident. Not to worry."

The nurse leaves the room. Tyler's mind races over the last memories in its files like the bedside computer hunting through its RAM, waiting for the next command. Before he woke up in the white room … *what happened* … Saturday night? It's coming back to him, getting clearer by the instant. He remembers walking Candice from the little diner to her car in the parking lot across from the Attic Theater. A few raindrops began to fall. She was going on about some trouble in her family—he wasn't really paying attention, hoping for the rain to pick up so he could bolt off to the solitude of his own car. He needed an exit line, but couldn't think of one. She moved closer in the dark silence. Could she actually be expecting a kiss? She sees him perhaps as some ugly equal and imagines the two of them a fitting pair, each making the other beautiful in their own minds. Like the old Johnny Carson line, *When turkeys mate, they think of swans.*

And then the drops did quicken, into a delicious cool drizzle. "I better be getting home," he said suddenly, "to my boy." Then he turned around and just started walking.

This must have caught Candice by surprise; for the first time all night, she was speechless. He felt like a jerk, but he kept walking.

"Tyler," she called to him when he was almost to his car. "Give me a call when you need to talk. I know it's hard for you."

He turned around and looked at her in the shiny, wet blackness: a pathetic believer, still thinking she was right for him. "Okay," he called back. "Goodnight, Candice."

She must have said goodnight to him, too, but he was already climbing into the Sunbird, scanning the parking lot for the exit, wary of those street punks he'd seen earlier.

He took Woodward Avenue to the I-96 "Jeffries" freeway and headed west, home, out of the city. The rain came harder. It was about midnight, still early for a Saturday night. Lots of cars out; haloes circling the approaching headlights on the opposite side of the freeway. He popped in a Springsteen tape, the live album. His thoughts turned to the girl in the red hat. Would she call? Or had she already dismissed him as a mysterious jerk, betraying his date so callously?

He exits at Farmington Road, same as always. Less than four miles from home. He thinks of Nicki, wondering what she would think of his disastrous blind date. Maybe he'll tell the babysitter everything: about the ad in the "Companion Column;" how he made the selection among the four letters; how instead of being a young Sally Field, she had turned out to be more of a Rosanne Barr. Maybe even tell Nicki about the girl in the red hat, Lyvia. What would Nicki think of all this, he wonders. Probably best to keep it to himself.

He moves into the left lane of north-bound Farmington Road and slowly passes a woman driving a huge old Buick. It should be hard to see in this dark rain, but Tyler in his memory can clearly see the old lady hunched up against the steering wheel. She's got her inside dome light on, the old bat! How can she see the road? Tyler gasses it just a little to put some distance between him and the crazy old lady; no telling what she'll do. The light at Seven Mile Road is yellow, but he can make it. The Sunbird's wipers stroke another gush of water from his windshield and … there's nothing more. Just white after that. And an odd buzzing or chirping, maybe, like crickets but coming from deep inside his head.

"Tyler Manion, I'm Detective Randall Teddington," announces a man in his late forties, wearing an inexpensive-looking brown, three-piece suit and a narrow, bright yellow tie. An odd color match. He stands at the foot of Tyler's bed. "Do you mind if I ask a few questions? Don't worry. I'll keep it short."

The cop's hoarse voice, probably a smoker's, makes Tyler edgy. "Sure. Go ahead."

"Okay, Tyler. Can you tell me what you remember about the accident on August fourth?" Teddington has pulled a salmon-colored reporter's pad out of his inside suit pocket and a pen from who-knows-where. He's writing before Tyler begins to answer.

Speaking in short fragments, conserving his breath, Tyler tells the police detective that he was driving west on the Jeffries Freeway, coming home from a date downtown.

Teddington interrupts. "Did you have anything at all to drink that evening?"

"No. Nothing. Just soda." Tyler mentions the rain, the traffic, the old woman in the yellow Buick on Farmington with her dome light on. "So, I passed her. She was going real slow. I kept going on, into the intersection at Seven Mile." He stops talking.

"Then what happened?"

"I don't know. That's where it ends."

"You don't remember anything else?"

"No, sir," Tyler says. *What's this cop after?* "Next thing I remember is being in this hospital room."

"What color was the light at Seven Mile when you went through?" Teddington asks. This is it: the $64,000 question.

"It had just turned yellow," Tyler answers. But the truth is, Tyler's not sure anymore. He remembers seeing yellow, but had it lapsed into red?

"Yellow," Teddington repeats, writing on his reporter's pad.

"What's this all about?" Tyler asks. Finally, his turn to ask a question.

Teddington closes the spiral pad. He clicks his pen and slides it into his shirt pocket. "Your car collided with a late-model Toyota Corolla, driven by a seventeen-year-old girl. The crash put you in the hospital. You were unconscious for most of two days, but you don't seem to have any lasting injuries. As I'm sure your doctor has told you. Unfortunately, the girl wasn't so lucky. She was killed. Instantly."

He lets this sink in for a moment. A seventeen-year-old girl. Killed instantly. *Holy crap*; killed.

"The coroner's autopsy found the girl's blood-alcohol content to be considerably over the legal limit for adults. Your blood showed you alcohol-free." He pauses, then adds. "I had to ask you anyway—if you'd been drinking. For the report."

Tyler feels his body stiffen. He feels chilled and a sharp pain bites across his left arm. His eyes follow the tube from the inverted bottle on the hat rack down to the messy gauze wad fastened with white strips of tape to the pale flesh just below his bicep. *Drip.* Not much slack. *Drip.* Suddenly, despite the chill and the pain and the pounding inside his head since he heard the words *killed … instantly*, his stomach hungers for a Big Mac and a large order of fries, sprinkled heavily with salt. The crickets are louder, too.

"There weren't any eyewitnesses, but we'll make an effort to find this elderly woman in the yellow Buick. She might have seen the whole thing," the police officer is saying. "For now, I can tell you, the department is proceeding under the assumption that it was the girl's fault. DUI. She apparently disregarded the red traffic light on west-bound Seven Mile and proceeded through the intersection at a high rate of speed, striking your vehicle."

"Was anybody else in her car?"

"No, she was alone," Teddington answers, shaking his head. "You got to wonder what it will take for these high school kids to learn you can't drive when you're plastered." He steps backward, watching Tyler lie there motionless. "Sorry about your accident," he says. "And thanks for your cooperation."

"No problem," Tyler says, not sure he has cooperated.

But Teddington's words, *high rate of speed*, do provide some comfort. If the girl struck him at a pretty good clip, she must have run her light, right? Unless … she saw the glow of the light facing Farmington Road, Tyler's traffic light turning yellow in the haze as she approached the intersection and knew, even in her drunken stupor, that her own light was about to turn green. She timed it, maybe, just as Tyler had done countless times himself at night, seeing the yellow glow of the light perpendicular to his, coasting just long enough to make sure no maniac was stretching that yellow well into red. But she hadn't checked to make sure; she anticipated the green perfectly, maybe, and accelerated just in time to T-bone Tyler who should never have been in that intersection on a miserable, rainy night. *Was it red?* The light isn't red in his memory, so why can't he just let it drop?

***

The nurse, Emma, returns with another woman, much shorter, dressed in white, but not a nurse. The shorter woman carries a clipboard dangling a little, plastic spiral cord, a cheerful pastel green, connected to a matching pen.

"Now that you're feeling a little more like yourself," Emma says warmly, "the hospital needs to know how you plan to pay for your stay with us." The short woman is from the Administration office, she explains, and will need to know the details of his health insurance.

"No problem," Tyler says to the nurse. "But first, can you tell me where my son is? I'd really like to see him."

"He's with your babysitter and her family. We talked about that earlier and you seemed okay with that arrangement," she says. "They've been asking about you, of course, and were glad to hear how much better you're doing. You'll get a chance to see your son soon."

Tyler is pleased to hear this. He turns his head slightly to address the short, silent woman. "HPP," he says. *Health Protection Plan*, the HMO of choice among his circle of GM friends. Then he remembers: he's not a GM employee anymore. His mind retreats back to that last meeting with Schulous and those forms he signed for the pregnant secretary, pushing his signature through the carbons. His health benefits continue at least until his severance pay period ends, right?

"Now then, who is your primary physician?" the woman from Administration wants to know. Emma has moved to the other side of the little room and busies herself with some equipment that hangs from the ceiling.

"Doctor Klirow, I think," Tyler says, trying to remember.

"Doctor Mohammed Klira?" the woman guesses for him. Tyler's not sure. He remembers it was a foreign name, but that's about it. Hasn't had a reason to see him for quite a while.

"Have you been a patient with us at St. Mary's before?" she asks him.

"I haven't, no." he says. "I can't remember the last time I had to see a doctor. But my wife came here a lot. My son was born at this hospital. Two years ago, this fall."

"But you are a single parent now?" Emma asks, walking over to his bed.

He doesn't wear his wedding band anymore. He wore it for three and a half months after Christie died. Then he took it off one night and laid it on his dresser in front of their wedding picture. He hasn't touched it since. What's it to this nurse anyway?

"My wife died six months or so ago," he tells her. The lack of precision in his answer seems disrespectful, as if he doesn't even remember the date anymore when Christie was taken from him, February 19th. But it's too late; the callous words have left his mouth to bounce all around the sterile white room.

"Oh, I'm so sorry, I didn't know. I guess I didn't see that in your paperwork. How long were you married?"

"Almost five years. We got married the summer before our senior year at college. The Ohio State University."

His voice trails off after this small bit of collegiate pretentiousness he sometimes allows to creep into his spoken thoughts. There are so few things about his history that seem elite or even special. So, he embraces OSU's stubborn inclusion of the article "*the.*" It goes back to the university's earliest days and is now as much a part of the proudly scarlet-and-gray tradition as Brutus Buckeye, the school mascot. "What about you, Nurse Emma. Where'd you go to school?"

The clerk from Administration, shut out from this conversation, flips a page noisily on her clipboard and writes something.

"Me? Northern Iowa," the nurse says. "I'd like to hear more about your wife and we can trade college war stories if you like, but, as it turns out, you have some visitors waiting to see you. Is there anything else you need, Debbie?"

"I just need his medical record number and insurance card," the clerk whispers.

"That would be in my wallet." He instinctively reaches down to the right half of his buttocks, but of course it's not there.

"In the drawer beside your bed," Emma says. "Let me get it for you." She retrieves his wallet and hands it to him. The first thing he notices is that there's no money in the wallet's fold. No charge cards, either.

"Hey, somebody ripped me off," he says, not really surprised.

"Your money? Not to worry. Nobody took it," Emma says, smiling. "It's locked up in the Administration office."

"Oh, okay. Thanks." He fishes out two plastic cards with magnetic strips on the back, like credit cards but not. "Hey, let me ask you something, Nurse Emma. Somebody looked in my wallet to identify me when I came in, right?"

"Yes, of course."

"And somebody took out my money and credit cards for safe keeping?"

"Yes."

"So how come they didn't go ahead and pull my medical record number and HPP card then?" he asks.

"We did. That's why you're in this nice room instead of the musty basement where we throw dead-beat emergency patients who come in with no insurance," she says flatly.

His forehead scrunches up as he looks back up at her.

"I'm kidding, of course," she says. "We can't just go rifling through your personal information, Tyler. That would be an invasion of your privacy." This from a woman who has held his penis in her cold, latex-covered hands.

* * *

The visitors turn out to be Nicki and a woman who must be her mother. The nurse had kept them waiting because she knew Tyler wouldn't want to focus on the insurance information if he learned his son was nearby. Tyler smiles and motions for them with his right hand, his free arm.

"Come over close. It's still hard for me to sit up. Hi, Nicki."

"Mr. Manion, this is my mother, Colette Saliba," Nicki says stiffly. "Mom, this is Tyler Manion, Robbie's father." Her mother knows all that by now, surely.

"How are you feeling, Mr. ..." the mother starts, but Tyler cuts her off.

"Just Tyler, please. Both of you," he adds, looking into Nicki's green eyes. "As long as I don't move, I feel okay. But real tired. A lot." That comes out a bit garbled, but they seem to understand.

Colette Saliba looks to be in her mid-forties. There's a touch of gray in her thin straight hair, pulled back into a bun, but her face is smooth and youthful-looking. She has a much lighter-toned complexion than her daughter. Round black glasses all but hide little dark eyes. Her yellow pants and white, long-sleeved blouse reveals most of her pale, white neck, but nothing below. An Amish-like outfit but with a little color.

"Your son is with my husband in the waiting room," she says. "They only allow two visitors at once. My daughter will go get him in a minute. We just wanted to see if you were awake."

Nicki doesn't wait. She pulls at the curtain and disappears.

Tyler smiles at the girl's mother. "Thank you for taking care of Robbie until my mother gets here."

"Oh, it's the least we could do. He's been no problem. But he's missed you. He got all excited when we told him we were going to see you." Her eyes never quite meet Tyler's.

Nicki emerges from behind the curtain, carrying the little boy. "Hi, Robbie," Tyler says softly. "Great to see you. Did you miss me?"

The boy peers out at Tyler unsure, undoubtedly frightened by the monitors, the IV tubing and his father's bruised, beaten look. "Okay, Dad-dy," Robbie stutters.

"Come over here," Tyler says, reaching out his hands. The little boy runs over and climbs onto the hospital bed, legs and arms churning to propel him up onto the white sheets.

Nicki's mother takes two steps backward, feeling for the curtain behind her. Only two visitors allowed; she's one to follow the rules exactly. "We'll wait for you in the lounge," she says to her daughter. "And we'll keep praying that you feel better soon, Tyler."

"Thanks for coming," he says to the closing curtain.

Nicki moves Robbie on the bed sheet to be closer to Tyler. With his left arm, Tyler draws his son against his gowned chest. The boy's arms open in an instinctive hug. Tyler strokes his curly brown hair. It smells like Johnson's baby shampoo. *No more tears.*

"I missed you, Robbie. Did you wonder where I went?"

Christie's blue eyes in miniature look up at Tyler. The boy says nothing.

"My mom told us not to tell him what happened, to just say that you had to get some rest," Nicki says. "But I know Robbie. I had to tell him something. He was afraid you weren't going to come back." *Like his mom hasn't come back.* "So I told him you fell down and got a few little boo-boos and that we'd visit you real soon."

The boy reaches for the IV tube connecting Tyler's left arm to the dangling bottle. "No, Robbie. Don't grab that," Tyler says, holding his son back with his right arm. "You'll hurt Daddy." Robbie buries his head against his father's chest and starts to whimper.

"I think he's freaked out by all this, you know?" Nicki says.

"Yeah, I don't blame him," Tyler says as he rubs the boy's back. "I'm kind of freaked out by it, too."

"Do you know about the girl in the other car?"

"A cop was just in here," Tyler begins, moving Robbie a little to the side so he can breathe easier. "He asked me some questions, what I remembered. I never saw the other car. He said, the cop, that a girl … a seventeen-year-old, hit me. In the rain. I couldn't see very well." He tries to tell it straight, but it comes out all jumpy. So tired again, already. "She was drunk, he said."

"It's been in the paper," Nicki tells him.

"Hey, bring me that newspaper when you come back, with my accident story. I mean the story written about the accident. You'll come back? Tomorrow?"

"For sure."

"What time is it anyway?"

"About eleven," she says. Then seeing his blank look, adds: "In the morning. Tuesday."

"Why aren't you in school?"

"My mom will write them a note. I have a pretty good reason to miss a morning of class."

"So, tell me about the girl. In the other car."

"She was a junior at Livonia High. I didn't really know her. I mean, I didn't know her at all. But I know a guy who went out with her a few times. And I know some people who were at the party she was coming from."

"They were drinking," Tyler says, meaning it as a question but somehow forgetting to raise up the tone of his voice at the end.

"Sure," the girl says, understanding what he meant. "The guys were drinking beer, and the girls were drinking those wine cooler things."

"I guess you're missing out on all that, since I've got you babysitting every night."

"Missing out on my own funeral, you mean. No thanks," she says. "Besides, at this rate, you're going to be putting me through college, you know?"

"Jeez, I forgot. You've been watching Robbie all this time." Tyler clears some brain cells for a quick calculation. "Must be going on, what? Sixty-five hours or something. At three bucks an hour… *crap*, I owe you two hundred bucks already. I'm going to be broke if my mother doesn't get here quick. Hope you take VISA."

"Cash only, *pull-eese*," Nicki says, white teeth shining in a broad grin. "No, seriously, don't worry about it. Just pay me for Saturday night, like you planned. I wouldn't want to take advantage of you while you're in the hospital."

Tyler's eyelids blink, feeling heavy. He shuts them, resting, just for a moment. *Take advantage of me?* He laughs at the thought, just slightly, but that sends a sharp twinge of pain through the back of his head, and he winces noticeably.

"Hey, can I ask you one thing?" she asks in a hushed voice. "Had you, you know, been drinking that night?"

"Not at all. Just soda. They musta checked a blood sample when they brought me in, but that police detective asked me anyway. Luckily, you set me straight the other night, right?"

* * *

Tyler opens his eyes and sees Nicki leaving. "Hey, you goin' already?" he asks.

"You were sleeping. You should get your rest."

"Where's Robbie?"

"I brought him out to my parents. In the waiting room. But I came back for a second to bring you today's newspaper in case you want to read it later. My Dad bought it to read, but he's, you know, done with it. It's not even the *Free Press*. It's a *USA Today*. That's all they had down there. Tomorrow, I'll bring you the paper with the story about the accident. You should get some sleep."

"Thanks. But hang on. I'm awake. I just closed my eyes for a minute."

"Okay, a little longer, but my folks are probably ready to go. I know my Dad is. He took off work today."

"Yeah, hanging around a hospital's not much fun. I wish I could get out of here, too. But tell me about how you heard about the accident? Who told you?"

"You said you'd be home around midnight or so. Robbie was sleeping, of course. I was watching TV. I made popcorn, you know, in the microwave. It was getting pretty late, but I didn't think much about it. I kept watching TV, kinda falling in and out of sleep, nothing too exciting was on. And then the doorbell rang. It kinda startled me."

Tyler listens intently.

"It was a police officer, a woman cop," Nicki says. "She asked if this was Tyler Manion's house and I said it was. I told her I was your babysitter, watching your son. She asked if I knew where your wife was. She didn't know, of course, so I told her that your wife had died back in February. Then she said that there'd like, you know, been an accident, that you'd been hurt pretty bad and were taken away by ambulance. To the hospital."

"What did you do then?"

"I didn't know what to do. The police officer wanted my name and phone number and that kind of stuff. She asked about your son, who would watch him while you were in the hospital? I said I would, but she said I was too young for her to leave Robbie with me, *indefinitely*, you know? So, I called my mother and the cop waited for her. I let her come into your house to wait. She asked to see Robbie and we poked our heads into his room without waking him. She was like looking around at everything, without touching anything, as we moved through the house to the kitchen, you know, to wait. I'm sure that's just her doing her job, being alert but it still seemed kind of nosy," Nicki says, catching her breath.

"Anyway, my mom came pretty quick. We decided to let Robbie sleep, that I would spend the night at your house, and then we'd move him to our house when he woke up. And that my dad would help us move his baby bed to our house. The policewoman agreed to this, but she made my mom write out on a paper that she would take temporary responsibility for the boy, and sign it. After she left, my mom went back home and got me a toothbrush and a night shirt, and I just found a pillow and went to sleep on your couch."

"What did Robbie think when he woke up and I wasn't there?"

"He asked about you but didn't seem too worried when I said you weren't home yet. I was there, so I guess it seemed normal enough. He started asking more and more as the morning went on. We found out what we could from the hospital, which wasn't much because, like, we aren't relatives. Finally, my mom got through to somebody who listened long enough for her to say that she was looking after your little son, so she was asking, you know, on behalf of your direct relative. I think that musta been confusing; it sounds confusing as I tell it now. Anyways, she told my mom that you were still unconscious. We came down here Sunday afternoon while Robbie was napping. My dad stayed back. Luckily, Robbie didn't wake up. He's not too good with little kids and Robbie doesn't know him."

"I'm sorry you had to go through all that," Tyler says.

"It wasn't anything. But we were worried, you know? We came back again Monday and they said you had come out of it for a bit, were going to be okay probably. But like you slept the whole time we were here. They had you hooked up to all this stuff and you didn't look too good."

"Do I still look pretty banged up?"

"Yeah, your face is bruised and swollen. It's kinda, well, startling at first. I guess not too bad. When you were sleeping or unconscious, what's the difference really? You did look pretty messed up. You look better now."

"Yeah, I'm sure," Tyler says. He needs a mirror to see how bad he really looks. "Robbie didn't seem too shocked, I guess, when he saw me. Maybe a little."

"Today, you do look better. Really. We got the word this afternoon that you were awake now, and we asked if Robbie could come. I'm glad they said yes. He was really, like starting to wonder, even though we kept saying you weren't far, that you'd be home soon."

Home soon. Yes, looking forward to going home. Not soon enough.

13

Christie sits on the recliner reading from some old-looking, hard-covered book. Tyler walks toward her, picking his way through the toys on the floor, looking for patches of carpet to plant his bare feet. Robbie plays quietly with a Mickey Mouse dress-up doll on the floor, buttoning and unbuttoning its shirt, zipping and unzipping its pants. The room is strangely silent; the TV is off.

Tyler's dead, of course, a ghost. They can't see him, can't hear him. He's on leave from wherever ghosts live, checking out his family, seeing how they're getting along without him.

"Honey, pick up your toys," Christie says to Robbie. "Mommy's going to have company tonight. You remember that nice man who was here the other night?"

"Okay, Mommy," Robbie says obediently. He puts Mickey on the bottom shelf of the entertainment center. His plastic army men go in the green bucket. The picture books go back on their shelves.

Tyler moves in front of Christie. So, she's dating now. Good for her; Tyler hopes she finds somebody who'll be nice to her. And

Robbie's going to need a man around. Not that Christie couldn't raise Robbie on her own, but there'd inevitably be gaps in his upbringing. Things only a father could teach him. Like how to pee standing up without getting it on the floor; how's Christie going to show him that? Or how to throw a ball? She can't throw worth a crap.

She has let her wavy, reddish hair grow longer. It's a different look for her, but he likes it. She sets down the book and looks straight ahead, right through Tyler.

"I just remembered something," she says aloud, probably to herself. "I told Aaron I'd iron a shirt for him, so he'll have one for work in the morning. I better get to it."

Aaron Foster? Neticut? Sleeping with Christie? Tyler hopes it isn't so. Maybe he misunderstood. Still, how many Aarons can there be?

He follows her downstairs to the laundry room, hoping she'll say something else out loud. Instead, she silently heats up the iron and places a white, long-sleeved shirt on her ironing board. It's not one of his shirts, but is it Aaron Foster's? Christie says nothing more. Too bad; ghosts can't read minds any better than anyone else, even in a dream.

* * *

The doctor and nurse are back, studying the machine that he's hooked up to, some sort of computer monitoring his inner workings. They talk in hushed breaths, trying not to wake him, or perhaps trying to keep some terrible secret from him.

So, he asks: "What's the good word?"

"Good evening, Tyler," the doctor says. "All your vitals check out. Everything's as normal as could be expected. You seem to be making a quite adequate recovery." That sounds like barely passing, if this had been a test from college, but maybe the doctor means it in a good way. Better than the alternative.

"So, I can go home soon?"

"Not so fast. You have been through a very traumatic incident. We need to watch you closely for a bit longer. Maybe two more days."

Tyler sighs. He's already restless and bored.

"We need to see that you can get up, go to the bathroom by yourself," the doctor says. "And eat something light. Then we can transfer you from Intensive Care to a normal recovery room. Hopefully tonight. If so, you may be able to go home by the end of the week."

If the end of the week is Friday, that would be three more days. Discharge seems to be a sliding promise.

The nurse, Emma, asks Tyler if he needs to urinate; he does. She helps him sit up completely and to slowly, carefully, swing his two legs out off the side of the bed. "Does that make you dizzy?" she asks. The doctor stands a few steps back, watching.

"I'm okay, I guess," Tyler says, not really ready to commit.

"Just a minute while I disconnect you." The nurse unplugs a set of wires from the computer machine behind the bed. They plug in and out like the jacks in the back of a stereo. The tube from his left arm stays fully connected to the bottle hanging from the hat rack. She sees him staring at it and says, "We'll keep the IV hooked up. I'll help you wheel it along as you walk." They walk together slowly to a small side door that opens to reveal a little bathroom. "Can you walk on your own those last few steps and pull the IV stand with you?" she asks.

Somehow, he manages to do it, then closes the door behind him for privacy. He pulls up the light green cotton hospital gown he's wearing, sits down on the toilet and relieves himself, everything working like normal. When he emerges from the bathroom, Emma helps him back to his bed. "A little dizzy, are we?" the nurse asks.

"Yeah, we're a little dizzy. But not too bad. It felt good to get up and out of this bed."

The nurse is already plugging in the stereo jacks into the computer and watching the various screens respond to having him back on board. She doesn't say anything more, so everything must be about what it should be. "Now rest up a bit and they'll bring you a little dinner. Eat that okay and we'll move you to the Recovery Ward. You'll have a TV in your room down there."

Now you're talking, he thinks, shutting his eyes in careful obedience. *Now you're talking.*

* * *

Dinner is bland, about what he expected. A little thing of chicken salad. He spreads it with a plastic butter knife onto a couple of saltine crackers. No mayonnaise in the chicken salad. It's dry and sticks to the inside of his mouth. A small plastic bottle of apple juice. And pudding for dessert, butterscotch. Seems more like a meal for Robbie. He eats it all and, strangely, he's not really dissatisfied. Thought he'd still be hungry.

It must be late into the night when they come to move him. A fairly involved production. The nurse and an orderly unplug him and help him into a wheelchair. They hook the IV bottle to a metal hook extending up from the chair into the air behind him. He'll keep the IV for a bit longer, the nurse says, even though he's shown he can eat without throwing up. Must be medicine in there, drugs; not just nutrients. They wheel him down to an elevator that doesn't seem to respond for the longest time after the orderly pushes the call button. Tyler fights the urge to reach out and push the button again. Just when he's about to scream, the lift comes and they get onboard. Slowly the door shuts, then nothing. Finally, Tyler feels the slightest shift as the elevator begins to descend, slowly, slowly. No wonder it took so long to arrive.

The elevator door opens, ponderously, and he's wheeled down the unit to his new room. They help him walk into a new bathroom, going again for the night, then into his new bed, hanging the IV from a new stand and reconnecting the wires to a new computer, smaller than before. And it doesn't seem like they connect all the wires this time. There is a little cube of a TV hanging from a cantilevered contraption from the ceiling over the foot of his bed and off to the right. The nurse gives him a remote with only a few big buttons.

"It's late," she whispers. "Keep the volume down real low if you watch anything."

Nurse and orderly leave. Tyler fires up the TV. The color on the little set is too vibrant, exaggerated and blurred. Can't find a button on the remote to adjust the color intensity. Late-night reruns. He flips until he finds a station playing old episodes of the *Cosby Show*. The top-rated show in prime time and already in rerun rotation for mothers nursing babies and whoever else isn't sleeping at whatever insane hour it must be. Dr. Cliff Huxtable, in a purple and brown and gold sweater that looks particularly loud on Tyler's little TV set with its crazy amped-up colors, is getting a lecture from Claire, his wife, Felicia Rashād in real life who is married to Ahmad Rashād, the retired football player, used to be a wide receiver with the Vikings but he was called Bobby Moore before that when he was on the Cardinals. One of those black guys who convert to being a Muslim and change their names, like Muhammad Ali and Kareem Abdul Jabbar. Tyler remembers him because the Vikings are in the NFC Central, the same as the Detroit Lions, so they play twice every year. And Rashād was always a Lion killer. Back when Tyler was in junior high and high school in Akron, and cared, really cared, about football. A Lions fan when all of his friends liked the Browns or Steelers, or even the Bengals. It was always the Lions for Tyler. His first memory of pro football is watching the Lions beat up on the Browns and their Leroy Kelly, who his friends all pretended to be when they played in the park, and he made his choice right then. Tyler would be Mel Farr, and the Lions would be his team.

Over the years, Detroit never seemed to have an answer for Rashād. A *lady-killer*, too, no doubt. Tyler remembers five or so years ago watching the Lions' annual Thanksgiving Day game, a football holiday in Detroit, when Rashād, by then a TV announcer, a pretty good one actually, proposed to this nice-looking Felicia in the pre-game. Now Cliff, who is Bill Cosby, of course, tries to explain why he did whatever had gotten him in trouble with Claire, but she won't have any of it. She gives him a pseudo-stern dressing-down, index finger wagging, but it's pretty clear it's all in fun because they're both cracking smiles. Studio audience laughter erupts and Tyler instinctually jabs at the remote to lower the volume. *Keep it quiet*, he was told.

He didn't catch the joke but it's just as well, he's getting tired now and clicks it off. Remembering Ahmad Rashād in that purple and white uniform, white horns painted on that garish purple helmet. Running smooth as a stag through the Lions' secondary, reaching up with long arms and soft hands, picking the spinning football out of the sky. Detroit never could stop him.

14

Early morning sunlight streaks through the Venetian blinds to his left. Wednesday morning, it must be. What difference does it make, what day it is, now that he's unemployed and stuck in a hospital bed?

Like a tall, heavy icicle warming in the sun that finally lets go of the gutter along the roof line and drops to the ground below, a thought filed away in a distant corner of his brain suddenly breaks loose in his consciousness: baby Robbie. It was early in the morning on the first of November nearly two years ago, when Christie and Tyler brought their son into the world, in this same hospital.

Her due date hadn't been until November 7, but to Christie's great relief, her contractions began a week earlier. It was the afternoon of October 31 that he drove her to this hospital. Halloween. He worried about leaving their house unattended, but what could they do? There was no time to ask someone to watch the place. At least her contractions hadn't begun the night before. In Detroit, the night before Halloween is *Devil's Night*—a night of mischief and vandalism, and in recent years, arson. Some of these fires undoubtedly set by slumlords who'd rather pocket the money off an insurance policy than rehab a building and then try to attract working tenants who might actually pay their rent. In the city, black people come out on the streets to watch the buildings burn on Devil's Night. In the suburbs immediately surrounding Detroit, white homeowners supposedly hide in bushes with shotguns, protecting their homesteads. In the somewhat more distant ring of suburbs, like Tyler's Livonia, more trusting in the power of prayer or the police, people lock their doors and turn on lights, inside and out. Thank God it wasn't Devil's Night.

Tyler sat in a chair next to Christie in the Labor and Delivery room, reading out loud from a *Parents* magazine and keeping an eye on her monitor. Looking at the digital readout on the machine, he could tell before she could when a contraction was beginning. Then she would feel it. Her body would wrench in pain. All Tyler could do was squeeze her hand and rub her back and help her remember the breathing routines they'd practiced in birthing class. It didn't seem like much, but at least he was there for her. *Hee, hee, hee, who.*

Christie had been crestfallen when she learned that her regular doctor would be unavailable to deliver her baby. He was out of the country—having told her that he would be back well before her due date. But now the baby wasn't waiting any longer. Tyler figured the next doctor in line at this top-notch hospital was probably just as experienced and qualified; what difference did it make, really?

"You don't understand," she moaned, "I have a relationship with him." Tyler had thought his was the only *relationship* she had, but by this point in their young marriage he'd learned when to keep his mouth shut.

Wave after wave; the contractions came quicker, more intense, barely a minute of relief before another, even worse than before, started up again. Tyler no longer mentioned to Christie when he saw the first signs of a contraction building. She already knew, she said she knew all along before he did and didn't need to hear it from him looking at the machine's monitor they kept behind her so she couldn't see it. She had no patience for him then and he didn't want her to connect the pain to him, but she already did. He could see anger in her tensed face as she fought another jagged wave of the pain. Hatred? No, that was too strong. But her love for him seemed pretty distant.

Every ten or fifteen minutes, the nurse would check on the paper tape slowly emerging from the machine under the monitor, like an old stock ticker tape you saw in the black-and-white movies from before the big market crash in '29. Black Tuesday. Then she'd leave them on their own again. Tyler had expected there to be a nurse with them the whole time. If he'd known they were going to leave him in charge, he would have paid closer attention in Lamaze class. *Hee, hee, hee. Who, who, who.* Was this the right breathing pattern for heavy labor? What would happen if they got it wrong?

Every half hour or so, the doctor who was not her regular doctor would pop in the room, asking how things were going and checking Christie's cervix with his gloved fingers. "Still only five centimeters," he said to Christie with a frown, as if he was disappointed in her. "You've got to get to ten before you can push. Make sure you don't push too early."

Nightfall came. Tyler could hear the hospital staff laughing down the hall at the nursing station. Somebody had dressed up as a gorilla for Halloween. Tyler poked his head out of the room to see, but Christie already was going into another contraction, crying out for him, her coach. Did she really need his help to breathe? Or did she just want to make sure he participated in whatever discomfort she could share, a strange, desperate bond between them, her pain?

The two of them struggled alone through the on-again, off-again-on waves of agony. The tape from Christie's monitor now reached the floor and had begun to coil like a snake. Just after midnight, the stand-in doctor checked Christie again. "Six centimeters," he announced.

"That's progress," Tyler said cheerfully. "You're doing great, honey."

"Still a long way to go. I'm going to give you a little Pitocin to speed things up a bit." The doctor popped out of the room.

A few minutes later, he appeared with a nurse pushing a cart full of colorful little vials. "Ten units," he told the nurse. Then he squeezed the bag of clear liquid above the bed, dripping into Christie's arm. "But first, give her a new bag of Ringer's. She's almost through this one."

Tyler remembers every detail. While the intensity of Christie's pain numbed her to the flurry of activity about her and she later could not recall much of anything except the pain and her own screaming, Tyler's brain responded by latching on to every sensation in the room. The nurse replaced the IV bag hanging above Christie's bed. She opened one of the vials on the cart and drew its contents up into a needle. Then she stabbed the needle through a little black rubber diaphragm on the bottom of the bag. Like the little black rubber seal where you inflate a football or basketball. The Pitocin joined the saline solution, slowly dripping down a clear rubber tube into Christie's left arm. When the nurse withdrew the needle, the diaphragm sealed cleanly around the hole.

The contractions came quicker, lasted longer and hurt more. Christie whimpered and bit against a wet washcloth, while Tyler used another washcloth to wipe the sweat from her forehead. "Still six," the doctor who was just a replacement said the next time he checked her.

"Are you sure?" Christie and Tyler cried out together.

Then he had taken Tyler aside and told him, "If she doesn't open up soon, we'll have to do a C-section."

Christie heard the words clearly; perhaps he'd meant her to hear. The threat spurred her on, where the chemical had failed. The next time he checked, her cervix had dilated to eight centimeters, a little more than three inches, Tyler calculated.

"Now there, that's better," the substitute doctor said. "Eight centimeters is the start of *transition*."

Christie managed a smile, sensing a light at the end of the tunnel, her womb.

"Now, remember, don't push yet. The contractions may start to hurt more, but don't push."

She looked helplessly into Tyler's eyes. "Did he say they're going to get worse?"

When Christie's cervix had dilated to nine and a half centimeters—almost four inches—the doctor told her she could start pushing. The nurse cranked the bed to raise Christie to a nearly seated position.

"Now, the next contraction is about to start," the doctor said calmly. He seemed to say *now* a lot; evidently delivering babies kept you focused on the present. "When you feel that contraction begin, I want you to take a deep breath in and hold it. Hold it in while you push. Dad, you count to ten while she pushes. Then tell her to exhale."

"Ohhh," Christie moaned.

"Okay. Here we go," the nurse said. "Inhale."

Christie sucked in a deep breath and held it. The nurse pushed Christie's head forward. "Push, woman. Push!"

Tyler counted to ten while the doctor held his fingers between Christie's legs. Christie exhaled with a sweaty rush. "Again," the nurse said.

"One, two, three…"

"I can feel the baby's hairy little head now," the doctor said with seemingly genuine excitement, though surely he had delivered dozens, maybe hundreds of babies. A full-fledged doctor after all. Christie pushed again and then Tyler could see the top half of the baby's head. Its straight black hair was greased back flat with blood and water from the placenta.

Another push and its whole purple head popped out, bigger than seemed possible emerging from the stretched hole of Christie's vagina. "Now, *stop*. Don't push," the doctor ordered.

Christie caught her breath, sweat streaming down her face. The doctor dabbed at the baby's mouth and nose with a cloth, then sucked fluid from its nose with a tiny vacuum hose. "All clear. Push with the next contraction, Mom."

And then they had their boy. Dark purple and wet with blood and slime, looking more like the creature in *Alien* than a pink, freshly powdered newborn in a diaper commercial. His head was misshaped into almost a pear shape from the trauma of the long labor. The doctor who was not Christie's regular doctor but was still quite skilled and experienced nonetheless assured mother and father that their baby was fine. He would get his color in a couple of hours and his head would look normal in a few days as the soft bones of the skull came into proper shape.

Christie held Robbie against her chest, smiling, laughing. All was forgiven. After sixteen hours of labor, he finally had arrived. Not on Halloween but a couple of hours into All Saints' Day. Of course, to be a Catholic born on November 1 was kind of like having your mail permanently addressed *Occupant*. Robbie would have to share his day with every saint under heaven, but it was all right. He was theirs.

* * *

A short black man wheels a cart into Tyler's room. Without saying a word, he takes a bowl of hot cereal from the cart and sets it on the bed stand. Next to it he places a little plastic cup of juice covered with an aluminum foil seal, a little carton of milk, a square plastic platter with scrambled eggs and two pieces of soggy-looking toast. A napkin is tightly wound around plastic utensils with a paper strap circled around the center like a cigar band.

"How about some coffee?" Tyler asks. "Please," he adds, remembering his manners.

"I don't believe you're allowed to have coffee, sir," the man tells him. Before Tyler can protest further, the man wheels the cart around and passes through the curtain out of sight.

Tyler eyes his breakfast without excitement. Then he pokes his plastic fork into the eggs, a uniform color of light yellow, perhaps Eggbeaters; they don't look real. His stomach groans in empty anticipation. He's been living off IV nutrients for two and half days, except for that mini meal the night before. About time he had something to fill the void in his belly. Not much taste, but at least it will take up some space. Boredom already has become the worst thing about this hospital stay, Tyler decides. And who knows how long he'll have to remain here? He needs to find his bearings; the world has continued to move while he lie unconscious.

He reaches for the *USA Today* that Nicki had left him yesterday. He hadn't felt like reading it before. Now it's old news, but not really to him. He holds off on rushing to the Sports section. He ought to at least glance through the real news first to get up to speed with what he's been missing.

Nothing too interesting on the front page. Iraq still seems to be a big deal:

USA Begins UN-Sanctioned Embargo against Iraq

He glances around at the rest of the front page. There's a heat wave in the southwest, something about mosquitoes and disease, and something about a space probe to be launched next week from the Space Shuttle Discovery, an 800-pound unmanned spacecraft, Ulysses, that will meet up with the planet Jupiter on Feb. 8, 1992, a year and a half from now—how can they be sure of the exact date already? Tyler turns over the front section and looks at its back page, the multi-colored weather map of the USA, all orange and red in the southwest states like the front page had mentioned.

In a different box, the big cities get their own forecasts for the next few days. It's going to be hot and sunny in Detroit the whole time. Without a window out to the world, he hasn't been aware if they've had any rain. Did he leave his lawn sprinklers set to come on each day?

Then he flips backward through this front section of the newspaper. The *Opinion* pages are next from the back. Usually something interesting here, more in the form of an argument than a straight news story, so it's easier to know what you should think about it. A big cartoon of a mean-looking Saddam Hussein standing over the country of Iraq, kicking sand into little Kuwait, with overspray carrying far beyond, into Saudi Arabia and other parts of the Middle East, countries Tyler is only vaguely aware of, Bahrain, Qatar—spelled with no *u*, Oman, the UAE, whatever that is. And Iran. That one he knows. The *Opinion* piece that goes with the cartoon makes it clear that something must be done to stop the bully dictator in Iraq:

> Iraq's invasion of Kuwait leaves the USA vulnerable once again to an outlaw on a rampage in the Middle East. The United States must respond clearly and forcefully. Iraq's Saddam Hussein is a terrorist, warlord and murderer who hopes Thursday's invasion will raise oil prices now and help him rule the Arab world later.... The last thing the USA or the world needs is a power-hungry dictator capable of wrecking the economy or launching nuclear weapons. The time to take a stand is now.

Continuing to flip backward through the front section, Tyler comes upon this short item, not connected to anything:

Three of four call USA's role in Vietnam War a 'mistake'

He skims the article. Seventy-four percent of those polled this month say that USA's involvement in the Vietnam War was a "mistake." That's up from the sixty percent polled in January 1973.

An odd span of time since that first poll. Is Vietnam something people will get asked every seventeen-and-a-half years?

Having done his civic duty to stay informed, Tyler reaches for the red section, *Sports*. A big feature from Cooperstown, New York, where Jim Palmer and Joe Morgan are to be inducted in the Baseball Hall of Fame. Palmer, a twenty-game winner eight times in a nine-year span, could have been nine-in-a-row but an elbow injury limited his play one year. The dominant pitcher of his generation, the story says, along with Steve Carlton and Tom Seaver. Now he's doing those underwear commercials, Palmer is. And Morgan, the slugging second baseman for the great Big Red Machine teams, standing intently in the batter's box, Tyler can see him, staring down a pitcher, his black bat twitching as if Morgan is having back spasms or a nicotine fit like that neighbor of his, Nora Johnston. *Must have driven pitchers nuts.* Then Morgan's hands flash and the black bat slashes out. The pitched ball in Tyler's memory has no chance.

* * *

Tyler carefully inches his way over to the bathroom and does his business. Then he takes a hot shower in the tiny space behind a plastic shower curtain. He peers out the bathroom door. No one there. He walks out slowly, naked, and dresses in the new hospital gown the morning nurse has left him. Dizziness floods his brain. He feels weak and flushed. He climbs back into bed and lays his head back onto the pillow. *Got to remember to ask Nicki to bring some real clothes.*

* * *

A nurse he hasn't seen before checks his blood pressure and asks if he needs anything besides rest. Lying in the bed, Tyler has been fighting an urge to scratch the inside of each of his ears with his index finger. "Some Q-tips, please. My ears are itchy."

"Oh, I'm sure we can arrange that," she says. "You know not to stick them into your ear canal, right, hon?"

Tyler doesn't want to jeopardize his fix of Q-tips. "Of course," he says, looking straight into her dark, brown eyes. Then he switches the subject. "Also, nurse? Where are my contact lenses? It's kind of a pain to read without them."

"I'm sorry, didn't anyone tell ya? They're in the bathroom, soakin' in a sterile saline." The bathroom door, to Tyler, looks a hundred miles away. "Don't worry, hon. I'll bring 'em to you."

She holds a tray over his lap while he rinses the lenses and pops them into his eyes.

"My vision really isn't too bad," he says. "Just a little far-sighted. Without my contacts, I end up holding whatever I'm reading out away from my face. It gets tiring."

She nods and draws a Kleenex from a box on the bed stand and wipes a saline tear off his cheek. "Your parents are waiting to see ya," she says.

Parents? Now this nurse is making the same mistake Rachel the apparition had made. What's going on?

"No, that's not right," he says. "My father's dead and my mother is afraid to travel more than a couple of miles from her house. She's what you call a *recluse*."

"We're kinda flexible with our visitin' hours at the first," the nurse continues, not seeming to hear him. "But enjoy it while it lasts. We gonna move ya to a different recovery room later today or tonight. And they gonna be stricter with the visitors, hon."

"When can I go home? I'm feeling pretty good. Can't I just go home now?"

"We'll see what the doctor says. We don't want to rush ya outta here just yet," she says, smiling a perfect set of white teeth.

The nurse pushes the curtain out of her way and disappears. Maybe his mother found someone to drive her. One of his uncles or cousins, probably. Somebody he hasn't kept in touch with and won't recognize. He's not good with names, and with relatives it can be embarrassing when you don't remember. Got a pretty good excuse, though, having been unconscious and all.

* * *

His mother-in-law's shrill voice reaches him before she does. "Tyler, how are you?" Then the short, red-haired woman bursts through the curtain. "We came as soon as we heard."

Her husband trails a few steps behind. Tyler, sitting on his bed against a mass of pillows, sets down the *USA Today* he was reading.

"A lot better, Rhonda. You didn't have to come all the way here. I'm sure I'll be going home soon."

Tyler hasn't seen his in-laws since Christie's funeral. They had said they wanted to stay in touch, especially for Robbie's sake. But with them in Florida, how much could they really stay in touch? A phone call once in a while and a present in the mail twice a year, probably. Robbie's birthday and Christmas.

"The police called us, so we called your mother, and when she couldn't come, well, we knew we had to."

Rhonda Lattering puts her hand on Tyler's shoulder. Her other hand pats the copper red mass of perm surrounding her milk-white face. Florida must be a tough place to live for someone with such pale skin.

"You're feeling better," she says, repeating his words as if to test their sincerity. Then, nodding her head, she says, "You look pretty good. We didn't know what to expect."

"Thanks. They're taking good care of me."

Rhonda lowers her voice to a whisper. "We told the nurse we're your parents, so she wouldn't tell us we had to wait to visit you. We knew your mother wouldn't be able to make the trip, so we figured, why not?"

"That was good thinking," Tyler says flatly.

Over the years, he has maintained a fragile peace with this woman. From the beginning of his relationship with Christie, he saw the only way to keep her mother from coming between them was to make Rhonda like him. So, Tyler sucked up to her, Dale Carnegied her to death, giving her no reason to dislike him. With Christie gone, he shouldn't have to butter her up anymore, to be so agreeable. But Tyler doesn't have the energy to shake off the comfort zone they've developed in their relationship, a comfort based on him sucking up.

"Well, it's good of you to come all this way," he says. "It's nice to see some familiar faces. Being cooped up in this room is driving me crazy."

"You don't have much of a TV in here," Tyler's father-in-law observes sympathetically.

Quiet and even-tempered, like Christie, George Lattering is easy to like. Tyler has never argued with him, mostly because George has no deep-seated convictions. And neither does Tyler, really. At least not in any subjects the two have ever discussed. Apathy is the antidote to anger and dissension.

"You probably missed it, but they're saying the PGA Championship will go on at Shoal Creek this week after all. They made a big show of accepting their first black member a few days ago. But, get this—the membership is *honorary*, so it could just be temporary. They'll probably bounce the guy out as soon as the TV trucks pull out Sunday night."

As this subject could be controversial, George does not take a clear position on it, and naturally, neither does Tyler. "No, I missed all that."

"Should be good golf. And the weather's supposed to be great for it."

George doesn't seem to notice the disapproving look Rhonda has for him as he babbles on about the weather forecast in Alabama.

"They say I'm going to be moved to a different room later today. So then maybe I'll get a bigger TV," Tyler says, changing the subject, while still staying connected to George's prattle.

"Where's my little grandson?" Rhonda asks abruptly.

"My babysitter and her mother are watching him. Over at their house," Tyler says. "They're good with him."

"But I'm sure he'd rather be with his grandparents," she says. "We'll go get him as soon as we leave you. We're going to check into the Holiday Inn…"

Her voice trails off as she looks away, slipping into her martyr role. He hates it when Rhonda pulls this act. They make a motel reservation, then wait for Christie to insist they stay at the house. They've gone through this same routine every visit since that first year of their marriage when Christie invited her parents to visit for eight long, trying days. Like caged tigers, Tyler and Rhonda got on each other's nerves, although neither would acknowledge it in their happy talk. He resented the way his mother-in-law took charge of every detail while she visited. Rhonda disapproved of Tyler's different way of doing things. At first, she corrected him—didn't he know that salt wasn't good for him, that the fork went on the left side of the plate and the spoon and the knife on the right, that he should use his turn signals before changing lanes on the highway? He tried not to show how much her nagging annoyed him. Then she seemed to change her strategy with him: she would only talk to him if he asked her a direct question. Otherwise, she talked to Christie and George as if Tyler wasn't there. So, naturally, he asked her an inordinate number of questions. Christie tried to warn him not to take Rhonda's coldness personally. Her mother, she said, made a point of ignoring the loved ones in her life from time to time.

At the dinner table on the evening of the sixth night of their visit, tensions finally boiled over. As Tyler rolled his corn-on-the-cob over a stick of butter, Rhonda lashed out at him. His table manners were barbaric, she said. It was only proper to use a knife to apply butter to your corn. Tyler held his tongue, waiting for Christie to come to his defense. But she pretended not to hear, irritating both husband and mother. Each resented Christie's stubborn non-alliance in the escalating tension.

And then, nothing. A few heated words were exchanged, strangely, between Christie and her father, the two neutral parties. Rhonda and Tyler talked around each other, but otherwise acted civilly. On the last day, Rhonda and George packed quietly and left, with only the briefest of goodbyes.

Every visit since, Christie's parents have made motel reservations they never use. Tyler has made nice to Rhonda, and she has mostly responded in kind. Each must have suspected the other's insincerity, but the peace between them made life easier for everyone, so it was not challenged.

"Oh, come on. Don't be ridiculous," Tyler says. "You'll stay at my house." As soon as the word *my* is out of his mouth, it feels wrong. It was always *our* house and even with Christie dead and buried, it is jarring to exclude her from a discussion with her parents about their house.

"You sure you won't mind?" Rhonda wants to make certain that Tyler won't forget she didn't invite herself. *What does she want, a contract?*

Tyler looks to George Lattering for help. But his father-in-law pretends not to hear. He stands, fidgeting with the curtain, his back turned to them.

Tyler forces a smile. "Of course, I don't mind. Go take my house key off the ring there," he tells his mother-in-law, pointing to the little table beside his bed. "In fact, take my whole key ring. I won't be needing them. I guess nobody'll need those car keys anymore."

Rhonda reaches for the keys and slips them into her purse. Sensing the negotiations have drawn to a close, George turns toward Tyler's bed. "Where *is* your car?" he asks.

"I have no idea. It'd be great if you could check on that for me. I'm sure it's totaled, but I had some things in it I'd like back. Cassette tapes, mostly."

"Give me the name of this babysitter and her telephone number," Rhonda says, derailing the men's conversation. She pulls out a pen and small pad of paper from her purse.

"Nicki Saliba. 646-4633." An easy number for Tyler to remember, just enough repetition to have a bouncy rhythm.

"We'll go pick Robbie up and bring him home, feed him supper," Rhonda says, outlining her plan for all to follow. "Then we'll come back with him for a visit this evening. You'll be in your new room by then?"

"Yeah, I think so." He feels tired. And glad they seem to be leaving. They stand over his bed for an uncomfortable several seconds. Sitting pathetically against a wall of pillows, Tyler readies for some kind of awkward embrace. Rhonda and George have never been very touchy-feely, even with their own daughter. Now, no one seems to know how to initiate their exit. Finally, George extends his right hand. Their handshake feels a little too business-like until George brings his left hand to cover Tyler's hand from the other side. The younger man's hand is swallowed inside his father-in-law's two big, sweaty palms.

Rhonda takes a step backward, then seems to reconsider. She leans toward Tyler's bed and says in a hushed but still shrill tone: "We heard a girl was killed in the accident. A drunken little slut, apparently."

Tyler feels Rhonda's eyes probe his blank face for some response. Every so often, she says something shocking, just to see how people handle it. He used to make the mistake of reacting with a look of surprise, or worse, by blurting out some rebuttal. *It just eggs her on*, Christie kept telling him; *just ignore her*. So, he says nothing. His face the blank screen of an unplugged television.

She waits for his reply and when it does not come, she turns and walks away from his bed. "Goodbye, Tyler," Rhonda says just before she pushes past the curtain. "Get some rest."

"George?" Tyler calls to his father-in-law before he reaches the curtain. "Don't let them scrap my car yet. I want to see it when I get out of here."

"Okay, Tyler," the older man promises. "Sure."

"It's just not all clear in my mind. The accident. I think seeing my car, maybe even sitting in it again, if I can. It might help me remember."

"What's to remember?" George asks, clutching at the curtain. "You worried about your insurance settlement? Don't you have no-fault up here in Michigan?"

That's just the problem, Tyler thinks. Everyone keeps telling him it's not his fault. Whose fault is it that a fresh-faced seventeen-year-old girl won't graduate, won't dance at her senior prom, won't be around to dump some guy who thinks he's in love with her?

"Yeah, it's a no-fault state," Tyler says.

* * *

The tallish nurse, Emma, is back when Tyler opens his eyes again. "Sorry to wake you, but I need to take your temperature and blood pressure again," she says. "Now that you're not hooked up to all the equipment, we have to do this the old-fashioned way."

He opens his mouth so she can slide the white plastic probe under his tongue. A little wire extends to a box with a digital readout. The nurse taps on his chin for him to close his lips around the probe. She sets the box on his bed beside him and then wraps a gray strap of rubber around his left arm. She pulls it tight over its own velcro, then inflates it with a little bladder pump. It squeezes his arm, makes him feel small. He tightens his left hand into a fist. His bicep expands only a little. His body has become soft, bloated and tired, his muscles withering away in this hospital bed. Truth be told, Tyler was already getting out of shape before the accident.

The nurse holds a stethoscope against the hollow of his arm on the inside of his elbow. She presses the cold, silver-dollar-sized head of the instrument against an unseen blood vessel beneath his skin and slowly releases the air from the strap, listening for a gush of his blood suddenly flowing. The cells in his forearm and his clenched fist must wonder what has happened: *Who turned off the flow; has his heart stopped working; are we all going to die?* But then the flow of blood returns and the cells can get back to doing whatever they do.

The nurse writes on her clipboard and plucks the thermometer from Tyler's mouth "Good," she says simply.

"I didn't think I'd see you again, after I got moved into this room," Tyler says.

"I work both wards. You really aren't that far from Intensive Care," she says. "We need to make sure you're stabilizing, not going to have another spell of unconsciousness, before we move you to a regular recovery room."

She removes the strap from his arm and sets the equipment on a stand she's wheeled into his little room. There's more than just an efficient smoothness to her movement. She has an athletic gracefulness he recognizes that's impressive for a woman of her height.

Tyler crumples up a piece of hospital stationery on his lap: a letter to his mother he'd begun before he dozed off. "Toss this out for me, will you, please," he asks the nurse.

She takes it from his hand and twists at the waist toward the small trash can a few feet away. She flicks it with an easy release of her long fingers. It rims off and falls to the floor. Her frown betrays suppressed competitiveness.

"You played basketball?"

She laughs. "Four years of high school and one at college. But I was never a shooter."

"What position did you play?"

"In high school, I was a defensive wing. You probably never heard of such a thing, did you? It's how they play girls' basketball in Iowa."

Tyler shakes his head.

"Careful. Don't twist your head like that. It wasn't too long ago you were blacking out on me," she says. "In Iowa, girls play a six-man game. Two forwards and a center on offense, two wings and a center on defense. The defensive players can't advance past the half-court line and the offensive players stay in their front court. It's kind of old-fashioned."

"You were on defense all the time? That doesn't sound like much fun."

She folds her long arms in front of her and shakes her head. "It was *a lot* of fun. I was pretty good, too. I made our all-district team as a senior and got a partial ride to play in college. But a knee injury ended all that after my freshman year."

"Wait, in high school, you never got a chance to shoot the ball?"

"I never took a shot until our last game my senior year. We were losing pretty decisively, so the coach let each of the defensive players who were seniors take a turn on offense. I took three shots before I made one, but it still felt good."

She sets the clipboard down on the table. "So, in four years I scored two points," she says as she sits on a chair she has slid over next to the bed. "How 'bout you? You must of played some kind of ball in school."

"Yeah, a little football, some basketball and baseball, too," Tyler replies. "I wasn't fast enough or big enough to be very good at any of those sports. I was kind of skinny, believe it or not." He pats the soft ring of flab around his belly. "My junior and senior years, in basketball, I was usually the second guy off the bench, so I got some decent minutes. I wasn't tall enough to play forward or center. But as a guard I wasn't quick enough and I wasn't a great ball handler, either. About the only thing I could really do well was shoot."

He wads a page from the newspaper, and rolls it between his hands until it's a tight ball. Then he lifts both hands over his head, cocks his right hand, flicks his wrist and fires the paper wad at the waste can. He gets good rotation on the little ball and though it, too, strikes the can's rim and bounces up, it falls back down into the bucket.

"Shooter's bounce," he says. "Boy, I wish we had a three-point shot when I played. I could've had some fun."

The nurse leans back in the chair. "You were starting to tell me about your wife yesterday."

Tyler sinks back against the pillow. "Well, I don't know what you're interested in."

"How did you meet her?"

Tyler draws in a deep breath. Might as well humor her. What harm can come of it?

"We both went to Ohio State," he says, dropping the *the* this time. "We met at a party in somebody's dorm room. There probably were fifteen people in this little room, just standing around a beer keg or sitting on the lower bunk."

"We had the same kind of parties at my college."

"It sounds pretty stupid now, but that was how we spent our Friday and Saturday nights. Somebody would sneak a keg into their room. Word would get out and everybody would come, taking turns filing through the room because it was so small."

"How did you actually meet?" the nurse persists.

"There's not much to tell, Nurse Emma." He likes calling her that for some reason. So formal and old-fashioned sounding, like her first name itself, it comes off as his own nickname for her. "I went to this party with a buddy and two minutes after I made my way over to the keg, I looked around and he was gone. I guess he had caught sight of some girl he didn't want to talk to." Tyler smiles, thinking of that night. He stretches his arms, exhaling deeply. "Well, I didn't know anybody at this party, so I just walked over to this cute red-headed girl and started talking to her. She looked kind of lost herself, you know, shy. Approachable."

"Do you remember your first words to her?" Emma asks.

"Something dumb probably. I don't know." He tries to remember, closing his eyes. *Not so long ago, really.* "I think she was wearing a sweater, yeah, a blue sweater. She had these really bright blue eyes. I probably said something about how I liked her sweater and that it brought out the blue in her eyes. I don't know."

But Tyler *does* know. He remembers now; that's *exactly* what he had said. And he remembers how Christie had smiled, that bright, toothy smile of hers. But it's like he's reading these descriptions of Christie from some words he has written about her, words etched into his brain. He can't *see* her in his memory; she is already fading away from him. He keeps his eyes shut tight and tries again to conjure her image. *Why can't I see her?* he implores his inner self; *Where has she gone?* He opens his eyes, without showing his frustration to this nurse who seems intent on bringing him back to places he will return to if he must, but alone.

"That sounds sweet," the nurse says.

"Turns out she was a freshman and was glad to have someone to talk to and take an interest in her. I'd never have the nerve to say all that now to some girl I didn't know. It was easier in college somehow. You could get away with being direct like that, because everybody was, you know. On the make. I suppose I'll have to get into that way of thinking again."

The nurse leans forward in her chair. "When did you get married?"

"We graduated together in '86. She was two years younger than me, but it took me five years to graduate because I switched my major a couple of times. And she was young for her class. We were married in June that year. After our honeymoon—we went to the Florida Keys, didn't have the money to go somewhere really exotic—we moved up here to Michigan. I'd lined up a job with GM. Does that cover your questions?"

He blurts out that last bit, not meaning it to sound quite as sharp and cold as it does, hanging in the air between them, like a wet umbrella held sideways, a slippery circular wall with a little metal tip extended out from the center, defensive with a hint of offense. He doesn't mean to give her a hard time. Her questions are innocent enough.

"Yes, thank you," she answers. "Two more, though, if you'll put up with your curious nurse for just another minute. How did you ask her to marry you? And what do you do for General Motors?"

"I took her to the Golden Mushroom, in Columbus, and had the waiter bring her the diamond ring after he brought our drinks," Tyler says matter-of-factly.

He was pretty proud of himself at the time for pulling off something fairly romantic. Christie certainly had gone for it. They were just kids still in college and it had seemed like a grown-up thing to do, the ring and the waiter, like something on TV. But he doesn't feel like getting too gushy, not here in this sterile room with this Emma. He wonders why she has so much time to chat. Doesn't she have to get back to the nurse's station or something?

Before she has a chance to ask about the ring, or what words he had used to ask Christie or how Christie had reacted to all this, he gives her the answer to her second question.

"I was in HR at a GM stamping plant in Garden City. I studied that in college—human resources management. But they laid me off last week. It's been kind of a rough few months, actually."

"I guess so," she says, extending a hand as if to touch his shoulder, but not quite reaching all the way. Instead, she rests her hand on his bed. Then she jumps up suddenly. "Hold on a minute," she says, walking quickly from his room. Like he was going somewhere.

She returns a few minutes later with a tiny, older woman in a black habit and gown with white trim, an aged female penguin, like the nuns back in his primary school.

"Tyler, this is Sister Harriet Worthy," Emma says. "She's a chaplain here at the hospital. In what we call 'Spiritual Care.' I think it would be a good idea if you talked with her. If you don't mind."

"No, I don't mind," he says, although it certainly wouldn't have been his idea. Kind of talked out. "Nice to meet you, Sister."

Emma gets the little nun up to speed with the recent tragedies in his life: his wife's sudden death, the car accident, his lost job. The nun nods but remains silent. She's perhaps not as old as she first looked to Tyler. Mid-sixties, maybe. Little wrinkles radiate from the corners of her eyes, adding to their quiet intensity. She looks like she's about to speak, but does not.

"Do you mind my asking," Emma says softly to Tyler, "how your wife died?"

"She had an aneurysm burst in her head. I guess it had been there for a while and nobody knew it and one day it just burst. She was dead when the ambulance arrived." He says this in one breath and without blinking.

"That's horrible. Were you there?" Emma asks him.

"Yeah," he says, locking eyes with the nurse and keeping his voice steady. "We were at a state park. It was a warm day for winter. February nineteenth. No snow on the ground or anything. So, we took our little son, Robbie, for a walk in the woods. I was carrying him piggy-back and he got too heavy. I set him down, just to rest a minute. But he got cranky. I let him climb on me again and off we went."

The nurse looks down at the floor, breaking eye contact.

Tyler feels his voice crack a bit, but he continues. "After a while, he got heavy again. So, I asked Christie to carry him. Just for a little while. Here I am telling my wife who doesn't weigh much more than a hundred pounds to carry our kid because I'm tired and he's being a brat. I was going to take him right back, but as soon as he was on her back, she takes off running."

Emma's eyes connect with his again and his voice levels.

"She started running up this little hill and all of a sudden fell down. I thought she had tripped. I ran over and picked Robbie up because he was crying really hard. Then I saw that Christie wasn't moving. She was laying there face down."

Tyler dabs his eyes with the sleeve of the gown over his one free arm.

"There wasn't anybody at the park to yell to for help. I had to pick Christie up and get her to the car. Robbie was crying and wouldn't listen to me. I had to carry them both, sort of one over each shoulder back to the car. I laid her down in the back seat and drove to the nearest house. They called 911. An ambulance got there in just a few minutes. They did CPR, but couldn't bring her back. Later, they told me she was dead when they got there. I hadn't even known there was anything wrong with her. *She* didn't know."

The nurse reaches for a Kleenex and hands it to him. He wipes at his eyes, then blows his nose. He wads it in his one hand, his right hand, and throws it toward the wastebasket, but it's too light, and it unwads in the air, fluttering to the floor.

The old nun, this Sister Harriet, finally speaks. "You can't blame yourself, Tyler," she tells him. "How could you have known?"

This question doesn't call for an answer, so Tyler doesn't give one. The silence lingers over them. Then he notices the nun's eyes have shut and he sees her mouth moving slightly, tiny movements as she silently speaks. She continues on, mouthing holy thoughts, oblivious to the other two. Not much of a chaplain, Tyler thinks. Shouldn't she have something more to say?

"Had your wife been having headaches before this happened?" Emma asks.

"Not really. At least she didn't complain of any. She stood up to pain better than me."

"An aneurysm is just a weak spot in an artery in the brain tissue, Tyler," Emma explains. "It got stretched out like a tiny balloon by the blood pressure, but Christie might not have felt anything wrong. All of a sudden, that balloon burst. It could have happened at any time. It can happen during lovemaking. Isn't that sad?"

"Yeah, that would be." He knows all about aneurysms now. The doctors had said pretty much what this nurse was saying: often there was no warning. But Tyler had to read up on it for himself. The day after Christie's funeral, he found a medical textbook in the library, trying to understand what had taken his wife away. While it was true an aneurysm could burst at any time, it was more likely to happen when the person's blood pressure was raised, when the heart was pumping hard. It was not unheard of for an aneurysm to rupture during intense sex. At least he didn't have to live with that. He hadn't killed Christie directly. He and Robbie shared the blame.

*　*　*

Emma sticks her head through Tyler's curtain. "You have another visitor. We've been letting you take visitors when they come and you're up to it. But once you get moved to a room on the main recovery floor, they're going to have to come during regular visiting hours."

"No problem. Thanks." Same thing that other, shorter nurse had told him, restricted visiting hours. They must really mean it.

A minute later, Nicki appears carrying Robbie.

"You two? I can't believe it," Tyler says.

"What?"

"My in-laws were just in here. They flew up from Florida. I gave my mother-in-law your phone number so she could bring Robbie home."

"Daddy," the boy says, climbing up on the bed with Nicki's help.

"Hey, kid. Give me a big hug. I missed you."

Robbie steps on Tyler's lap and puts his arms around his father's neck.

"Don't worry," Tyler tells him softly. "I'll be coming home soon."

Tyler looks up at Nicki. "They're going to move me to a different room this afternoon. I think they'll let me walk around some. I'm sick of being stuck in this bed."

"Sick?" Robbie asks.

"Yeah, Robbie. Daddy's still sick. But I'm feeling a lot better. You been a good boy for Nicki?"

"Okay, Daddy," he answers, smiling. "Good boy."

"Are you ready to go home to your house?" Nicki asks the boy. He seems confused at this and does not answer.

"Grandma and Grandpa have come to see you," Tyler explains. "Do you remember them?"

Robbie looks up at the ceiling as he tries to remember. "Gramma red hair. Like Mommy," he says finally.

"That's right," Tyler says, squeezing the boy's shoulder.

"Mommy come, Daddy?"

Tyler rubs his son's back. "No, Robbie. Mommy's still gone. She loves you very much. But she can't come back. We'll have to wait to see her in heaven. But that won't be for a long time."

Time here as we know it, that is. Heaven, supposedly, is timeless. In our world, *time is just nature's way of keeping everything from happening all at once*, as Woody Allen said. How confusing would that be, a world without time? In heaven, somehow, it's not a problem. All those people up there living eternally, never even pausing to sleep. What do they do up there with all that time?

Nicki sits on the edge of the bed and taps Robbie on the shoulder. "Why don't you show your Dad what we brought him from your house."

She opens her big purse, more of a beach bag, really, and Robbie pulls out a paperback spy novel, *The Master Cure*. Then he pulls out a box of Tampax.

"Not that, silly," she says, blushing. She takes the tampon box from his hand and stuffs it back in her bag.

"I bought that book in an airport last year," Tyler says, holding the paperback his son has handed him. "I started reading it, but didn't get very far. I guess you found it laying around somewhere?"

"Yeah, it was in the TV room. I was straightening up a bit. I saw that it had a bookmark sticking out, not too far into it. So, I figured it was something you had just started reading."

"Thanks. Might as well start reading it again. It's pretty boring here."

Nicki leans over to Robbie and whispers into his ear, loud enough that Tyler can easily hear. *"What else do we have for your dad?"*

Robbie looks unsure. He turns to the babysitter and replies in a whispered burst: *"What?"*

"Look in here," she says, opening the bag again. "Remember?"

Robbie smiles happily and pulls out a wrinkled piece of blue construction paper. It's scribbled with red and brown crayon. In the middle, neat cursive letters spell out the words: "Get well soon, Daddy. I love you, Robbie."

Tyler pulls his boy close for another hug. "Thank you, Robbie. That's real nice. You did a good job."

As the boy bounds off the bed, Nicki opens the bag again and reaches in for a square piece of something tiny, wrapped in newspaper. Or rather, a page of a newspaper, folded over a few times.

"I brought you part of the paper from Monday," Nicki says quietly, so Robbie won't hear, "with the story of your accident."

Tyler unfolds the little bundle. The *Free Press* "Local" section. Just three paragraphs; no photo.

LIVONIA TEEN KILLED IN CAR CRASH

Seventeen-year-old Linda McNeary, set to begin her senior year at Livonia High School, was killed in an automobile accident Saturday night near midnight. The under-age girl was found to be over the legal blood-alcohol limit for adults, according to Livonia police. An investigation is underway to determine how she obtained the alcohol and under what circumstances.

McNeary was alone in a Toyota Corolla when she struck a Pontiac Sunbird, driven by 26-year-old Tyler Manion, also of Livonia, at the intersection of Farmington Road and Seven Mile. Manion is in serious condition at St. Mary's Hospital, but is expected to recover. Rain and fog may have been contributing causes for the accident, police say.

McNeary was the daughter of Roger and Sue McNeary. She is also survived by a brother, Peter, who is 12. Funeral arrangements are not yet available.

"Didn't say too much about me, did it?" Tyler says after silently reading the article. His words come out sounding uncaring and self-centered, so he adds: "It's awful for this girl's family, the Mc-Nearys."

Now the girl has a name and a family in Tyler's consciousness, which makes it more awful. No longer an abstraction in his foggy memory, driving through the rainy night all liquored up. This Livonia family's sweet-faced daughter, their lost treasure, dead and maybe buried by now.

Tyler hands the newspaper back to Nicki. He doesn't want it anymore. As she goes to stash it back in her bag, he notices a hard-covered book in there, one of his old college textbooks. Psychology.

"Why're you carrying around that old psych textbook?" A welcome change in subject.

"Oh, it just looked interesting. I came across it while I was straightening up. You don't mind me borrowing it if I'm careful?"

"Sure," Tyler says. "Keep it as long as you like. Knock yourself out. It *was* kind of interesting as I remember. Psychology was my original major before I changed my mind. Couple of times, actually."

"I can't wait to go to college. High school is *so* boring, you know? And most of the other kids are so obnoxious."

"How are they obnoxious?"

"They're just *so* immature. They think they're like independent and, you know, *rebellious* to their parents. But they're really such pathetic conformists."

"What do you mean?" Tyler persists.

Nicki rolls her eyes up toward the ceiling.

"Like one day last year I wore a Michigan State football sweatshirt to school. These two girls who think they're just so cool made a point to tell me that only freshmen wear Spartan stuff. Sophomores and up wear Michigan."

"That is pretty pathetic. Who decides what everybody wears? The fashion police?"

"See how dumb it sounds," she says. "And girls who I know are real smart get so stupid giggly when boys are around. Some girls, you know, won't speak up in class even when they know the answer because they're like intimidated by the boys. That's why my Mom and Dad have me going to an all-girls high school."

"Why are they intimidated?" Tyler remembers himself ten years ago, a skinny shy kid with acne. Hard to believe any girl was ever intimidated by him.

"Girls don't want to look smart in front of the boys. And they sure don't want to go against what a boy has said, even if they know it's wrong."

"I guess it can be an awkward time," Tyler says. "For both the boys and the girls." After a moment, he adds a bit of fatherly advice: "Try not to let it hold you back. Being shy is the worst waste of time in the world."

"I bet when I get to college, I'm going to have better things to worry about than what other girls are wearing."

"Then you better not join a sorority. Hey, don't be in too big a hurry to grow up, Nicki. You still got two great years ahead of you before you ship off to college. Enjoy being a kid."

"I'm not thirteen, you know," she says, turning her back to him and looking down at the floor. "Do you still think of me as a kid?"

The dark brown skin on the back of her neck glistens under the fluorescent lights in the white room. Around the middle of her neck, the skin is just a little bit lighter brown, mostly untouched by the sun. Then he notices she's trimmed her wild, thick hair back a little. Where the darker skin meets the untanned brown is not a sharp line but blurry, as if melting together.

"I mean, not a little kid like Robbie." Tyler glances over at his son, pulling on a curtain, trying to pull himself up to look out the window. All boy, that one. "You're mature, but still a kid. Yeah, you are. This is your only shot at being sweet sixteen. What's the rush?"

In other lands, she'd already have been married off without romance or any pretense of love. That's not a deal she'd want to sign up for.

"I'm going to be seventeen in a couple of months," she says, arguing, then cuts herself off. "There's no rush. I just feel older than sixteen."

The power girls that age have over the boys with awkward, cracking voices and zitty faces, their burgeoning breasts and all that softness that can seem so untouchable, so far away. Yet, most of them don't realize they have it, the power. The girls who do know it, rule the roost and make life miserable for everyone else.

"That's normal as I remember," he says. "Every sixteen-year-old thinks she's twenty-one. And the girls are the worst."

She giggles and the young woman sitting on his bed is a girl again.

"Summer's almost over. Once I get back in school, I'll be okay. I'm just not looking forward to it right now."

"Why not? Just wait 'til basketball season starts and you start canning those long jumpers. Then we'll see who likes school," he says. "Hey, there's somebody I want you to meet."

Tyler reaches for the buzzer dangling from a chord behind his head. He grabs it in his fist and squeezes the button with his thumb. Robbie wants to play with it, but Nicki is able to distract him with a tiny plastic giraffe she pulls from her bag.

"This nurse who's been taking care of me played basketball in high school. She was all-district and got a partial college scholarship before she hurt her knee. And you know how many points she scored in her four years in high school? Two."

"No way," Nicki says.

"Yes way," Tyler replies. "She was a defensive specialist."

"I feel my ears burning." The tall nurse pops through the curtain.

"Nicki, this is Nurse Emma Binder. Nurse Emma, this is my babysitter, and very mature friend, Nicki Saliba."

"Just Emma, Nicki. Tyler keeps calling me *Nurse Emma* just to pull my chain." She turns to Tyler. "Did you call me for something?"

"I just wanted you two to meet each other. Nicki plays b-ball for Divine Mercy High. You should see the range she's got on her shot."

"Glad to meet you, Nicki. Mercy always has good teams. You must be quite the athlete."

"Oh, I practice a lot. I think I've got a chance to start on varsity this year. I'll be a junior. Tyler said you were a defensive specialist?"

"Yep, I played defense the whole game. I grew up in Iowa…"

The tall nurse briefly describes Iowa girls basketball for the babysitter. Tyler sits back against the pillows, holding Robbie, while the two jockettes describe their games and favorite moves to each other.

Finally, Emma excuses herself to take care of another patient.

"Don't forget, Nicki," she says. "Shutting down your opponent is just as important as scoring yourself. Coaches love good defenders. Shooters are streaky." She glances at Tyler. "They get cold, then what good are they? But defense is a constant. If you can stop your man, you'll play a lot of minutes and be valuable to your team."

Nicki gathers Robbie in her arms to take him home. The boy has grown fidgety and pulls at her hair. "Stop it, Robbie. That hurts," she tells him.

Tyler gives his boy a playful swat on his bottom, well-padded with a Huggies diaper. "You be good now, kid." Robbie lets go of the girl's hair.

"Call my house as soon as you get home and let my mother-in-law know you're coming," Tyler tells her. "Her name's Rhonda. Actually, you better call her Mrs. Lattering. Be nice to her. She can be a bear." This woman who bullies those closest to her, beginning with George. How beautiful, caring Christie emerged from her womb unscarred, he'll never know.

"Really?"

"Oh, don't worry. She'll be nice to you. But she's probably worried about Robbie, so hurry home and give her a call. Thanks for stopping by. And thanks a million for taking care of the little guy."

"He was no problem. He never is." Just to make a liar out of her, the boy squirms in her arms and breaks free. "I better get going. I'll come back tomorrow maybe."

"If you want, that'd be great. I hope you didn't take it the wrong way when I said I think of you as a kid. I like talking with you better than most adults. Being a kid's not so bad."

She smiles back at him. Not bad at all.

15

There's a better TV in this room; at least the picture is better. The programming still leaves something to be desired. Last night, he watched two incredibly stupid Tuesday evening sit-coms, *A Different World* and *The Golden Girls*. Plus, *America's Funniest Home Videos*, most clearly staged. Then he partially made amends by falling asleep to something a little more substantial: *Nightline*. A pretty dull piece on the Savings & Loan scandal. What can you say about these senators playing around with all our money? The economy was already just sputtering along and now we have this S&L mess that's going to cost tens, maybe hundreds of billions of dollars to fix. Then there's that crazy dictator invading Kuwait, driving up oil prices, just daring Bush to come get him. Kicking up sand and shaking his fists, Saddam Hussein is a petulant child who badly needs a shave. *All these Arab men seem to have perpetual dark stubble*, he thinks. Not only do they make their women wear those awful *burqas* in the stifling heat that make them look like sinister space aliens when they're just women underneath all that cloth. Maybe not so much in Iraq, but still the *hijabs* covering their heads and hair so not to set off even a spark of desire among their volatile men, ready to erupt at any provocation. But then these men don't even shave properly, not bothering to clean up like Westerners do when women are around.

He reaches now for the thick cord that leads to the remote control. There's a tiny, tinny speaker in the gray channel changer box. The speaker inside the TV has been disconnected or removed. The *Today* show is on, the original of the network television morning news-entertainment programs and still the ratings king. Jane Pauley's gone, having a baby. Her replacement, Deborah Something, is cold and humorless, aloof perhaps, though a lot more sexy than old Jane was, in a flirty-librarian kind of way. Bryant Gumbel's wearing glasses, too, looking professorial. He tries to keep the viewers watching through the commercial break by teasing with hints of an interesting segment coming up: a Washington economist will address the burning question: *Are we already in a recession?* It's hard for Tyler to take Gumbel seriously doing news, expecting to see him in a locker room interviewing football players. Now Gumbel's younger brother is doing NFL games, and he's pretty good, Tyler must admit. Too bad everybody doesn't have an older brother to pave his way into some sweet career.

Then that obnoxious Willard Scott comes on, yucking it up with Bryant. Tyler read somewhere that Gumbel secretly hates Willard and tried to get him dumped, but the chubby sidekick used his connections to hold on to his cherished position as America's most ridiculous weatherman. And what an easy job. The National Weather Bureau does all the forecasting. All he has to do is read off a teleprompter and point at a blue screen. Wonder what Willard does the rest of the day? People must like him, though—he's got his own commercials now. Tyler half expects Willard to interrupt his weather spiel and start pitching True Value wrenches or fly swatters.

He switches to *Good Morning America*. Barbara Bush—God, she looks old—sits in a formal living room somewhere, chuckling. She's talking to Charlie Gibson about her book, which was ghost-written by her dog. Or something like that. Tyler must have heard it wrong. Then Barbara turns into an even-older-looking woman and Willard's back, talking about old ladies in Georgia and Idaho celebrating their one hundredth birthdays. Something's wrong with the channel changer. Tyler must be leaning against it. He hits the button to bring back Channel 7, ABC, and the Barbara Bush interview. She's there only an instant before she is replaced by Willard again.

A deep voice from the other side of the curtain startles Tyler: "Leave it on the weather."

Tyler has a roommate. And apparently just the one TV between them, just past the end of the short curtain that must separate their beds.

"Oh, sorry," he says. "I didn't know anybody else was here."

The curtain does not reply.

"My name's Tyler and I …"

The deep voice cuts him off. "I'm trying to hear the weather, okay?"

Tyler waits for Willard to run through a series of satellite photos of storm systems. Then a map of the United States shows the expected high temperatures of the day. After a ten-second gap of silence during which the local weatherman was supposed to give the Detroit forecast, but didn't, Willard cuts up some more with Bryant, who pretends to enjoy the mindless banter.

Just to be safe, Tyler waits for the commercial. Then he slowly swings his feet off the bed. He pulls back the curtain, doubling the size of the room and revealing his roommate. A black man with gray, almost-white hair, seventy years old at least, maybe older, covered up to his neck with blankets.

"Good morning," Tyler says. "My name's Tyler Manion."

The man turns his head slowly to look up at Tyler. Deep wrinkles line his forehead, but the rest of his face is smooth. "John Henry Cuhlman," he says.

"When did you get here?" Tyler asks.

"Early this morning. You was sleeping. What you in here for?"

"I got in a car accident. Saturday night. They had me in intensive care for a while, then another room. Moved me here last night. How 'bout you?"

"Liver problems," the older man says, rubbing his nose with a thick, black hand. "Don't go jumpin' to conclusions. I ain't an alcoholic. I just got me a bad liver is all."

"Sure, okay," Tyler says.

He climbs back into his bed, leaving the curtain open. Bryant is back with his serious but sexy sidekick. She politely introduces the economist and then gets right down to brass tacks: "Dr. Parker, are we in a recession?" Parker's answer is a qualified *no*. It's not an official recession, he says, until there's two consecutive quarters of negative growth. The economy has slowed down, no question, but not to the point of negative growth, not yet. Even though the last three months of the year should be miserable, he says, and early '91 even worse, you won't hear anyone in the Administration use the *R-word* for at least six months.

"These economists don't know what they're talking about," Cuhlman says, still looking straight ahead. "Anybody can see the country's headin' straight down the dumper. You don't need all these official numbers to see that."

"Tell me about it. I lost my job last week," he says. The economy is a temperamental woman, prone to mood swings, Tyler thinks. Right now, she's got PMS, but the real bleeding's still to come.

The old man looks at the television, at Bryant and the economist and says nothing. The segment ends. Next comes an ad for a denture cleaner. Then one for laundry soap. You can tell by the commercials it's past eight-thirty. The TV sponsors have the viewing demographics figured out—all the people with jobs have left for work, leaving only housewives and retired folks at home to watch. Tyler can guess what the *Geraldo* and *Donahue* commercials will be—feminine hygiene products and Ed McMahon hawking life insurance.

"Where'd you work?" Cuhlman asks suddenly, still staring straight ahead. Tyler had nearly forgotten his roommate.

"GM," Tyler answers quickly. "At the Garden City plant. I'm in human resources."

Cuhlman turns his face slowly toward Tyler. His dark brown eyeballs float on sad yellow ponds. "What's *human resources*? That like *Personnel*?"

"Exactly," Tyler says. "Or it can be called *Employee Relations*."

"And you got laid off? How's that? I thought you guys wrote the rules."

Cuhlman rubs his massive hands together on his lap. The skin on each hand is dry and cracked. Deep, crooked lines radiate from each of his knuckles. Tyler has seen these same rough-skinned hands on the hourly men on the floor of the plant. Squat, muscular fingers hardened day after day by the same punishing movements.

"Nah, HR people are overhead cost just waiting to be trimmed," Tyler says. "All the companies are cutting costs."

"Why? They ain't lowering prices, that for sure."

Tyler doesn't answer. Why get into a business discussion with this old man? What does he know about cost-containment actions, corporate competitiveness and level playing fields?

"I bet it's the Japanese," Cuhlman says, smiling.

"Yeah, the Japanese companies are tough, but it's more than that. The government's handing us new regulations right and left. Clean air, fuel economy standards…"

"It's the Japanese," Cuhlman repeats firmly. "And I know why you ain't ever going to compete heads up with them."

"Why's that?" Tyler asks. The old codger must have read something in *Reader's Digest*, got some simplistic answer that he thinks nobody at GM has ever thought of. Next thing he'll be talking about that hundred-miles-per-gallon carburetor GM supposedly has hidden away in some engineering lab, conspiring with the oil companies to keep it off the market. Might as well hear him out. Better than listening to Willard Scott.

"Everybody knows the Japanese got smarts and lots of education, but that ain't all. They sacrifice. They dedicated, you understand? Givin' up everything to work for the company."

Cuhlman's voice does not rise and fall as he says these words. There is an evenness about him, a solidness, that Tyler did not notice at first. Though half-shut, his sad eyes do not blink. But the cloudy yellow ponds provide no window to the man's soul, not yet at least to this newcomer. Tyler nods.

"You got to like that in a person, willin'ness to sacrifice. Lot of people in this country forgot how to work hard. You even know what hard work is?"

Tyler looks down at his own puffy white hands. Except for the slightly calloused tips of his two index fingers, hardened by countless pecks on an electronic keyboard, his hands are soft and unblemished. But soft skin does not necessarily mean easy work. If Cuhlman could look at the inner lining of Tyler's stomach, would he see the same deep lines that pock the old man's hands? How many nights did Tyler wake to churn over the previous day's work, running over confrontations and disappointments, trying to overcome some sticking point before the next deadline? For a while he was tormented by a recurring dream: He'd be sitting back in his recliner watching a game on TV, when he'd suddenly realize he was supposed to be at work. He'd punch at his remote control and the game on the screen would be replaced by rows of text, row after row of raw computer data interspersed with incomplete commands written in something that seemed to be a combination of Pascal and Fortran, languages he had learned in college, thinking at one point he was going to become a computer programmer, then opting for social science and business while still putting together enough credits to earn a minor in computer science. At least he had that to show for his five years in college. The channel zapper would transform in his hand into a computer *mouse*, a small device for moving a cursor on a computer screen. With the mouse, he would scroll through the strange text. But he could find neither the beginning nor the end. It was endless, yet incomplete. It needed his input to run, yet there was no point of entry. He'd wake up in a sweat. Then he'd try to escape into his baseball pitcher fantasy and sometimes that would be enough to get himself to fall back asleep. Other times he'd feel so hot and gassy in his stomach he'd have to get up and chew a couple of Tums. Then he'd lay in bed staring at the ceiling, waiting for sleep to possess his reluctant body. Anybody who thought his job was soft didn't know much about stress. He doesn't have to apologize for his soft hands.

"I worked long hours at my job," Tyler says. "It might not be hard work physically, but it's hard. We don't work up a sweat, but we sure work up some stress."

"So, if there was enough work to keep you that busy, working long hours and all," Cuhlman asks, "why'd you lose your job?"

"Like I said, the company is on a cost-cutting kick," Tyler says. "The salaried worker is an easy target. They lay off a bunch of people and scare the ones still there into working like mad. They tell you: *You ought to be glad you have a job.* Like it's a real privilege to work your butt off doing what they used to pay two people to do."

"Sounds like you guys oughta to get a union," Cuhlman says.

Tyler ignores this. "If you want to be a manager someday, you're supposed to act like a manager even though you aren't making half a manager's salary. You got to walk their walk and talk their talk."

Cuhlman nods. "Your management says you got to compete with the Japanese companies, right?"

"We've got to compete with everybody. But the Japanese are the ones to beat, sure," Tyler says, trying to be agreeable. No use getting the old guy all worked up.

"But they ever tell you that your competition ain't Toyota, it's the Toyota worker? The Toyota worker doing the same job you do?"

Tyler's intrigued by the old man. Where does he come up with this stuff?

"No, not exactly."

"As long as that Toyota worker's willing to work his tail off, to sacrifice, his company's gonna have an edge on your company. Unless *you* sacrifice just as much. But you don't want to sacrifice."

Tyler says nothing. The word *sacrifice* echoes in his head. He pictures ancient Aztecs in loincloths, burning a dark-skinned virgin with long hair and terrified eyes to appease unseen, angry gods. The Japanese must be like that. Sacrifice. Another image flashes in his mind, like those new ten-second TV commercials: Abraham, with a long, white beard and brown terry cloth robe, clutches a knife preparing to slaughter his only son to prove his obedience to his own unseen God. You don't see that kind of blind faith anymore.

Cuhlman turns his head away, draws his right hand into a loose fist and coughs into it. His nappy gray hair isn't so thick in the back. Tyler can see a purplish stain about the diameter of a baseball on the top of Cuhlman's skull. Then the old man turns back to face Tyler. His eyes look sleepy, his body drained. "But you know what don't make sense?" he asks, his voice lower than before and a little raspy.

"What?"

"If these Japanese so smart, why do they work so hard? The companies they work for must be makin' big, big money."

"Billions of dollars, sure. Hundreds of billions of yen." Tyler feels tired, too. He doesn't have the energy to guess where Cuhlman's headed with this.

"Billions. Okay. But what do their people have to show for it? I'm talkin' about a guy with a suit-and-tie job like yours, a computer guy, say. Everything I read say they work like crazy over there. For what? For squat, that's what."

Cuhlman shuts his eyes and rubs them. He continues to talk with his fists pressed against his eyes.

"He works nine or ten hours a day, this *salaryman* they call him, six days a week, then gets on some train packed tighter than a sardine can for an hour-and-a-half ride home to his shit hole of a little apartment. He ain't got no *leisure* time, no time to spend with the family. No backyard to play ball with the kids. If that Japanese fellow so smart, why he's busting his ass his whole life for *nothin'*?"

Tyler leans back against his pillow and smiles. "I guess he's too busy working to figure it all out."

"But you ain't got that excuse, do you? Don't you see it's all those under-paid Japanese working stiffs that's your problem?" Cuhlman's eyes open slightly.

Tyler leans forward on the bed. "You're saying that if all those workers in Japan would demand to work less hours and to get a fair share of those big profits, my company wouldn't have to go through all this cost-cutting and job elimination?"

"That's it," Cuhlman says, "'til then, you got to sacrifice."

* * *

Tyler finishes the chapter and folds down the corner of the page to mark his spot. Fifty pages into the paperback and he's just starting to figure out who's who. Why don't they make these books simpler? He glances at the clock. Six minutes to eleven, nearly the morning visiting hour. Who will come to see him today?

Before he can guess, his mother-in-law appears in the room with Robbie. The clock isn't fast; his mother-in-law has managed once again to skirt the rules others mindlessly obey. She lives above the law, and no one calls her on it. She's got the whole world intimidated.

"Good morning, Tyler," she says. "Our grandson keeps asking for you. Look at him. You didn't tell us how much he's grown. I can't believe how well he talks."

It's a wonder he's gotten a word in edgewise, Tyler thinks. "He's a talker, all right."

Robbie leaps onto the bed, into Tyler's arms. The paperback Tyler had been reading falls on the floor.

"How you been, Rockin' Robbie?" Tyler says, pulling his son tight against his chest. Then he loosens the hug and rubs the top of the boy's head. Robbie looks up into his father's brown eyes.

"Daddy, daddy, daddy," he repeats happily.

"Last night, I read him three or four of his picture books. He has so many," Rhonda says. Her mouth spits out the words rapid-fire. She never slows down; must be all that coffee she drinks. "I'd point to a picture and he'd tell me its name. He knows all his animals and his colors. He's just like Christie was at that age, sharp as a whip."

"A tack," Tyler begins to correct, but stops himself. "Yeah, he takes after his mother. He loves books."

Tyler smiles at this. Christie was a world-class reader, fond of stuffy, old literature that Tyler found completely impenetrable. She'd read books by those long-dead Russian heavy-hitters—Tolstoy, Dostoevsky, Chekhov—while he'd read *Sports Illustrated*. And she'd actually remember what she read. Of course, Tyler is pleased to see his son take to books like Christie must have when she was a little girl. But the truth is, he sees a lot of himself in Robbie, too. Half of the boy's chromosomes are his; shouldn't he get some of the credit for Robbie's brains? Besides, Christie wasn't the only one to read to Robbie when he was just an infant—and who does Rhonda think has been reading to the boy for the last six months?

"It took us the longest time yesterday before we finally met up with little Robbie," she says. The words come quickly, like before, but her tone is noticeably chillier. "Why didn't you call us when your babysitter brought him here?"

"She must have just missed you coming in. I couldn't have called you. You wouldn't have been back at my house yet. I told Nicki to call you as soon as she got home."

"Well, you could have waited a few minutes and then called," she persists. And she has a point. "We tried calling the girl's home over and over and couldn't get an answer. We were beginning to worry that something had happened to him. You shouldn't have put us through that."

But you toughed it out, Tyler thinks.

"I'm sorry," he says. "I wasn't thinking. I'm glad you were able to get it straightened out." Where is George for all this? He would sense the tension and helpfully change the subject to sports or the weather.

With one point scored, Rhonda comes at him from a new direction.

"We went to the market and stocked you up with some food that'll actually be good for you and Robbie."

Here it comes: the nutrition lecture. Rhonda Lattering has the same trim figure Christie had, minus Christie's pleasant businessness. None of the women in Christie's family have any extra fat on their bones. It's genetic, like mother's and daughter's red hair and smooth, creamy complexions. Rhonda never has had to watch her weight a day in her life, but that doesn't keep her from crediting her lean figure to her puritanical eating habits. Tyler has to admit she looks good for her age, if only she'd smile a little more. And talk less.

"I threw out all that junk food you had," she says. "You know better than to stock up on potato chips and candy. It's not good at all for Robbie."

Sidestepping her assault, he says: "Anything will be better than this bland hospital stuff I've been eating."

"Good food," Robbie says. "Hot dogs. Ice cream. Pop."

"Shhh," Tyler says, "you're making me look bad."

Then he turns to Rhonda to make amends: "We eat balanced meals, really we do. Lots of fruit and meat. Vegetables, too, sometimes. I just like to have a few snacks around for a treat once in a while."

Rhonda smells easy prey. "I'm afraid my grandson's nutritional needs are being neglected," she says sadly. "You're feeding him too much junk."

"No, really. You're getting the wrong impression. I haven't been to the store for a while, so we might be low on some of the vegetables and fruit and stuff. Robbie, tell Grandma Lattering. Don't you love corn? Don't you love applesauce?"

"Corn. Applesaws," Robbie says agreeably.

"How about broccoli, Robbie?" the boy's grandmother asks. "Do you like broccoli?"

"Yuck," the boy says.

"He's just a kid," Tyler says, trying to keep from flaring out at this woman. "But, hey, he knows what broccoli is. That shows I've tried cooking it for him. I can't help it if he doesn't like it."

Rhonda smirks a self-satisfied smile and says nothing, this round clearly going to her as well. Robbie fidgets with the television remote control. Tyler searches for some safe topic of conversation.

"Looking out this window, I'd say we've been having some nice weather since you got here," he says.

"Hot and humid," she counters. Strange complaint coming from someone who lives in Florida.

But Tyler doesn't call her on it. "Well, summer's almost over. We might as well enjoy it while it lasts." Hard to argue with that.

"I took some phone messages off your answering machine for you."

Rhonda unzips her purse and hands Tyler three slips of paper. On each slip, Rhonda's wildly cursive handwriting documents a different call: from Webb, from Tyler's auto insurance agent and from someone at an investment service wanting to talk about mutual funds for retirement savings. He balls up the investment salesman's phone message, even though it's the most detailed of the three, and flicks it into the wastebasket. The other two he'll call when his mother-in-law leaves.

"Thanks, Rhonda," he says. "Were there any others?" You'd think he'd get more calls than that. He hasn't been home since Saturday night and here it is, what, Tuesday? No, Wednesday. Tomorrow he can go home, maybe, if the doctor thinks he's fully out of the woods. Or Friday. He hasn't really heard any firm commitments.

"Oh, there was one other call," she says slowly, playing this card carefully, watching him as she speaks. "Last night a woman called for you. She said her name was ... what was it? Linda or something. No, it was more unusual than that.... Liv-vi-a. That's it."

Tyler feels his eyebrows rise. *Lyvia.* The girl with the red hat. At the play. Those soft white cheekbones and that cute small-townie accent. She had actually called him. Amazing. But he hadn't been there to talk with her.

"What did she say?" Tyler asks, straining not to show much interest, though he's probably already given himself away.

"She just asked for you. I told her you had been in an automobile accident." A pause. "And that you'd been in the hospital. For several days."

"Well, what did she say to that?" Tyler asks, fighting an urge to lean forward and grasp his mother-in-law's thin, pale neck in his hands until she sputtered and coughed up every last detail about the girl in the red hat. Robbie scoots off the bed and picks up the fallen paperback.

"Oh, she asked how you were. I told her that you seemed to be doing better, but that the doctors just wanted to be sure. Lots of tests still before they would let you come home. She asked for your room number. She'll probably call you here."

Rhonda looks into his eyes and manages a smile, a peace offering perhaps. "Are you dating now?" she asks.

"Lyvia? No, not really. She's somebody I just met. I mean we haven't actually dated."

He looks at Rhonda's round, white face. Christie's face thirty years from now if she'd lived. "It's hard. I feel like it's time to start getting out again, but I'm not sure I'm ready. So soon."

The miss-starts and false hopes, like that dreadful experience with Candice, leading only to thoughts of escape. He's not ready for that, not at all. But he'd risk all that awkwardness for the chance to hold the smooth, soft warmth of Lyvia, all red and creamy white, against his own disquieted chest, or to have her sit happily on his lap while he stroked the back of her neck underneath her auburn hair with one hand and held his other hand on one on one of her knees or perhaps just below, cupping the curvy pliancy of the underside of her leg at the calf.

"You must be lonely," his mother-in-law says. Her face still shows warmth, but Tyler knows how quickly this woman can turn on you.

"At times, sure," he says. "I'm lucky to have Robbie. He's kind of become my social life."

"I'm sure it isn't easy for you to talk with me about the women in your life," Rhonda says.

He laughs at that, in spite of himself. What can she want him to say? Surely, she'll let it drop. But she continues to look straight at him, her eyes never soften and seldom even blink. They never lose that edge, that caffeinated alertness.

"It's hard to accept that Christie's gone, but you have to move on with your life. Christie wouldn't want you to stop being a man."

Stop being a man? "It's only been six months," Tyler says, forcing a smile.

Robbie has crawled under the bed. He begins scraping the book against the bed's metal frame.

"Robbie! Get out from under there!" Tyler scolds. "You know better than that."

"Come along, Robbie. We should be going back home," the boy's grandmother says. "Your father needs his rest. He gets cranky like you do when you get over-tired."

"I'm not being cranky," Tyler mutters.

"Come on, Robbie," Rhonda says again, grabbing the boy's wrist. "Let's go. I'm going to cook you up some good, healthy food at home."

Robbie looks up at his father, then breaks free of his grandmother's grasp. He runs over to the bed, holding his hands above his head. Tyler pulls the boy up into a tight hug. Then he kisses Robbie's forehead.

"Be good for your grandma. Show her what a good boy you can be."

"Bye-bye, daddy," Robbie says.

* * *

"Hello, Mom? It's Tyler."

The voice at the other end of the telephone line seems weak and distant. "Tyler? Where are you? They told me you were in an accident. Why didn't you call me?"

Tyler has dreaded making this call. Now that he has put it off so long, it's even worse. Much worse. "I started writing you a letter, but I didn't like the way it sounded. I didn't want you to worry about me over something that's really not that big a deal."

"Not a big deal? How long were you in the hospital?"

"Well, actually, I'm still in the hospital. But it's just while they run some tests. You know how doctors are. They just want to be sure everything's perfect before they let me go home. Tomorrow, maybe."

"You don't know how worried I've been. I almost called my neighbor—you remember Glenda Evans?—to ask her to drive me up to Detroit to see you. But I couldn't bother her. She has a sick aunt in Massillon she has to see to."

Tyler can picture his mother speaking into the heavy black phone hanging from the kitchen wall in the little house where he grew up. The only phone in the house, his mother's only connection to the world beyond Stark County, Ohio.

"Mom, I'm sorry I didn't call you 'til now. I knew you wouldn't be able to come up here, so…"

"I'd be up there in a minute if I could. But you know how those highways make me feel. Especially around the big cities. I don't know how you stand it. And now you've been in a car wreck. It was bound to have happened. So much traffic where you are."

"It's really not that bad…" he starts to say.

"Now that you're not working, Ty, why won't you come back to Akron? You had your last day at GM by now, didn't you? What's keeping you in Detroit?"

"Nothing, Mom, to tell you the truth. I'm looking all over for a new job. That could take me anywhere. Wherever I find the best job, that's where we'll go. Robbie's at an age that he'd be easy to move. I wouldn't want to do that to him once he gets into school, you know?"

He's rambling a bit, but what does it matter? A mother cannot hear too much talk from a child who has moved far from home. "But chances are," he says, "it won't be Akron. Let's be serious—there's not a whole lot of opportunity back home."

"But this *is* your home," she pleads. "It's where you grew up. And it's where I'm going to live until they cart me away to my final resting place. Doesn't that mean anything to you, Tyler Gregory?"

He rolls his eyes, unseen on her end of the line.

"Of course, it does, Mom." Looking for a way to steer out of this guilt trip, Tyler goes on the offensive. "Dad always said he was proud of me going to work for such a big company, working with important people, you know he always said so. I'm not going to find another job like that in a small town."

"Well, look where it got you," she replies. You've got to hand it to mothers; they know how to counter punch. "That company you worked for didn't seem to care much about you. Now where can you turn to for help in that big city? Maybe you'd do better working in a place like Akron where people aren't so heartless.

And where they don't drive like crazy people. To think of you, in a hospital still as we talk, after all these days."

"Mom, listen," he says. "Robbie and I will come down and see you as soon as I get out of here. We'll stay for a nice long visit. You'd like that, wouldn't you? You haven't seen Robbie in more than three months. You should hear him talk now."

"Oh, that would be nice. Since your sister moved halfway across the world, I'm left here all by myself. It gets lonely. But you haven't told me about this accident you got yourself into."

"It was last Saturday night," Tyler begins. "I was coming home, in the rain, when I came up to this intersection and this high school girl ran a light and plowed into my car. It must have been pretty bad. The girl was killed, and I got knocked out cold for a day and a half." No use holding back at this point; she probably knows all this anyway from Rhonda.

"The girl died? They didn't tell me anyone died. You must feel awful."

"She'd been drinking, Mom," he says. That was good enough for that police detective, Teddington. It ought to be good enough for his mother. "But, yeah, I feel bad about it."

"That's terrible. How old was she?"

"Seventeen. She was coming home from a party where they'd been drinking."

"Just seventeen years old and she's dead. Just like that. It's terrible," she repeats. "Just terrible."

***

Noise somewhere, a strange ringing noise. Tyler opens his eyes. Tries to focus. Still ringing. Reaches. The phone. On the bed stand.

"Hello?"

"Hi, Tyler, It's Nicki. How're you feeling?"

He tries to pull his brain out of the sleep fog. "Pretty good, I guess. I just … fell asleep."

"Oh, I'm sorry. Should I call back? I thought you might be bored, like you said."

"No, that's okay. Thanks for thinking of me. I *am* bored. What's up?"

He stretches his arms and tilts his head from side to side to unkink his neck. Then he runs his free hand through his tangled hair. *How long has it been since I showered?*

"Oh, I don't know. I guess I'm kind of mad at my mom."

"What for?" Tyler spots a spider on the white wall past the foot of the bed. It's moving up toward the ceiling. How does a bug like that get in here; isn't it supposed to be sterile?

"She won't let me go to a concert next week. We already bought the tickets and everything. She thinks all rock groups are, you know, Satan worshippers or something."

"Wow. That's a bit of a generalization, don't you think?"

The spider stops moving, perhaps feeling Tyler's gaze.

"Totally. But that's what she says. A friend of hers has her convinced that like if I listen to rock music, I'm going to start going to devil services, or whatever."

"Well, is it true? You thinking of becoming a devil worshipper?" He laughs out loud at the thought. He's never even seen her wear nail polish. She's not really the bad-ass type.

"Oh, yeah. It's real tempting. Got this urge right now to find a goat and slit its throat so I can drink its blood. And chant songs backwards. Is that what they do?"

"Beats me," Tyler says. Wasn't it all just a marketing con, Black Sabbath's whole act and all that play-it-backward stuff on Led Zeppelin records, and even the Beatles with that *Paul-is-a-dead-man, miss-him, miss-him* backward cut on the so-called *White Album*? "I'm not really up on my satanic rituals. What band were you gonna see?"

"That's the thing. It's not just any concert. It's U2. At Tiger Stadium."

"Wow, really? That'll be the biggest concert of the year round here. I saw U2 in Columbus my junior year. College. They were just starting to make it big in the U.S. From Ireland. Hey, I survived it. As far as I know, I haven't become a slave to the devil."

He reaches for a section of the newspaper on the bed stand, pulls off a page and crumples it into a tight ball. Then he fires the ball at the spider, but misses badly. It doesn't flinch.

Even after going to the concert, and even after they've grown into global superstardom these past few years, Tyler has never been completely bowled over by U2. The music is transcendent, to be sure, but the singer Bono seems a little too caught up in his own one-name awesomeness and in the lasting deepness of his often cryptic lyrics. Helping to fight world hunger and bring about peace, though; you have to give him credit for all that. Rock stars used to be known for busting up hotel rooms and carrying on with young groupies; now here's one who wants to save the world. It does seem a step in the right direction.

"But funny that your mom's worried about U2, of all the crazy rock groups out there," he says. "They started out, I think, as sort of a Christian rock band. And there's still a lot of God and worship stuff in their songs even now."

That early hit, "Gloria", has a flurry of Latin: *In Te Domine*. "In you Lord." *Bono Vox*, as he used to be known, belting out, in the English parts, "Oh Lord, loosen my lips." And that one about Jerusalem: "To the side of a hill, blood was spilt." Some songs where it's obvious: "you carried the cross and my shame" or "one man betrayed with a kiss." Others just plain mysterious. "Your eyes make a circle. I see you when I go in there. Your eyes." So much on the inside, can you hear it?

"My mom's pretty ridiculous sometimes," the girl says through the phone line.

Colette Saliba's tense face behind those black glasses forms momentarily in Tyler's mind. The woman needs to loosen up. Still, there's something likable there, he imagines, somewhere underneath the severe, hardened shell. He could talk reason into her. Telling her, maybe, about Bono running around the concert stage with a white flag, railing against "the Troubles" in Northern Ireland, agitating for peace, and still bringing it back to impassioned prayer: *The real battle just begun, to claim the victory Jesus won—on Sunday, Bloody Sunday.* Not a satanist; not at all.

"You want me to talk to her?" he asks.

"No!" Nicki responds immediately, sensing immeasurable embarrassment. "It wouldn't do any good anyway. She's pretty set in her ways. And, really, why should she listen to you?"

Tyler takes no offense at this. Why indeed would she listen to him?

"What about your dad?" he asks. Tyler has never met the man. Though now he vaguely remembers something about the babysitter's father possibly being Arab. Maybe something Christie had mentioned once.

"Oh, he's pretty mellow, actually. I mean, he wants me to act right and all, but I don't think he sees much harm in me going to a concert. If it was up to him, it wouldn't be a problem, you know?"

"But he's an Arab, right? A Muslim, is he?" No point in beating around the bush at this point, he thinks.

"He's Christian, Tyler. He's from Lebanon, but he moved here years ago. Why?"

"I don't know. I was thinking he might be the one to crack down hard on you."

"People seem to just assume that, even my friends. You know, the whole Arab thing. But like I said, he's pretty easy-going. It's my mom who's kinda uptight."

Tyler is mildly curious about the girl's father and about her mixed blood and upbringing, but he's getting talked out. Lying there on the bed with the phone pressed against his head is taxing somehow. He thanks Nicki for calling, and adds: "When I get out of here, I want a rematch of *HORSE*."

"I'll take on you *and* your nurse, anytime," she replies good-naturedly.

Just after he hangs up, the little gray-haired nun, Sister Harriet, pokes her head into Tyler's room without warning. A rainbow-colored crucifix hangs on a silver chain below her neck, standing out against her black-and-white habit.

"Care if I visit with you for a few minutes, Tyler?" she asks. Did she somehow overhear his mention of satanic worship rituals and is here to conduct an intervention?

"Sure, come on in." What else can he say to this unexpected guest? Sitting up makes him feel itchy to move around.

"I just wanted to see how you were doing," the little nun explains, perhaps in answer to some mild annoyance she heard in his response. She'd hardly said a word when she was here earlier with Emma, but now she wants to talk.

"Getting a little restless. I'm ready to go home."

"I know. The time moves so slowly here. Such a drag, it is. But you'll be home soon enough. How's your boy? I saw him in here yesterday, but didn't want to interrupt your visit."

"Great," Tyler says. "Hey, can we walk somewhere while we talk? I'm really ready to get up and move around."

"Then that's just what we'll do."

He puts on the socks and shoes he was wearing the night of his accident. Not as comfortable as his sneakers, but they'll do. Standing up feels good; no dizziness. They take the slow-motion elevator to the ground floor, and walk down the length of one hallway and back to the lobby, the hub, then down the next hallway and back again. Spokes in a wheel, just like the main streets that extend from the heart of downtown Detroit, spokes in a giant wheel: Fort Street, Michigan Avenue, Woodward, Grand River, Gratiot and Jefferson. Not a complete wheel, though. More like a flat tire, the Detroit River preventing any spokes from heading to the south. Beyond the river, by way of the Ambassador Bridge, is Windsor, Ontario. A geographical curiosity: the only place in continental United States where you can head due south and get to Canada. That's why every Detroiter snickers knowingly when hearing that song by Journey they still play all the time on the radio—"Don't Stop Believin'": ...*Just a city boy / Born and raised in South Detroit*. The thing of it is, there's no such thing as *South Detroit*. Unless you count Canada.

They dare not venture outside even though the weather is agreeable. The little nun hasn't secured any formal release for Tyler. They're free-lancing this bit of exercise. But the walk is just what Tyler needed, stir-crazy in that bed for so long. Stretching his legs with long, slow strides, feels good, liberating. He seems to grow stronger with each successive hallway jaunt, back and forth.

This short, gray-haired sister reminds him in appearance, if not demeanor, of a stern old nun he had long ago as a teacher, back in sixth grade. Sister Dolores. He was a reasonably bright kid, especially in the subjects she taught—math and science—so he should have found it easy to get along with her. He never had any trouble with any of the other nuns at school. But something about Sister Dolores rubbed him the wrong way. And vice versa. One day, in punishment for some trivial offense he can no longer remember, she made him stand in front of the class with his hands behind his back, leaning so that his forehead would hold an eraser pinned against the blackboard. Angry and humiliated, he turned his eyes sideways to study his tormentor, sitting behind her teacher's desk while his classmates silently worked math problems. Then he noticed one of Sister Dolores' hands. His brown eyes widened as he watched the hard, dry nails on her bony fingers scratch black folds of cloth in her lap. Tyler couldn't wait to tell his friends at recess. *Sister Scratch*. The cruel nickname quickly spread throughout the school. Then, strangely, nothing happened. With each passing day that did not bring some awesome punishment, Tyler began to wonder if God was so all-knowing after all. In any event, he seemed farther away.

Tyler and his walking companion say very little to each other, just small talk free of complications. And free of physical complaints from Tyler, providing the nun reassurance that they aren't overdoing it with this walk. So perhaps that emboldens her.

"You've been confronted with death, Tyler," she says as they get to the end of a quiet hallway. A strange conversational opening. "How are you dealing with it?"

"You mean the girl in the car that hit me?" he asks. "I'm bothered by it. I mean, it's awful. And I guess I wonder if there is anything I could have done to avoid her car. I mean, it was raining bad. Hard to see in the dark and all."

"She made a poor choice to drive after she'd been drinking," the nun says. "Do you forgive her for that and how it hurt you?"

"Forgive her? Sure. I hadn't even really thought to be mad at her. I mean, she was just a kid, and now she's dead. Her family must really be hurting. I'll be out of here soon enough. I'll get another car and move on. But she's gone and isn't coming back."

"If you hold no anger in your heart, take the next step. Pray for her."

"Okay," he says, not really sure what he's agreed to. Thinking about it, he adds: "But I don't really know that she needs my prayers. As you said, she made a bad *choice*. There were probably other kids drinking and maybe she just got caught up in all that. And if she hadn't ever had much to drink before, maybe she didn't even know that she was way past being safe to drive."

The nun looks at him with quiet eyes framed with crooked lines revealing not just age but some wear and tear along the way. Perhaps years of sun or wind, taking its toll. Maybe an outdoorsy life, assigned somewhere as a missionary nun in Africa or Asia where the sun really beats down.

"I mean, it was a mistake, a stupid mistake. Tragic, really. And she's the one who died. I guess I don't see that as sinning or anything. Just a waste." He pauses, but she says nothing. "Do you think it's necessary, me forgiving her, for her soul to move on up to heaven? Do I have some power to keep her out? Because I don't want that."

She looks at him and smiles. "No, I don't think it works that way at all," the nun says finally. "Forgiving her is important for *you*. We mustn't cling to any ill will toward anyone. We have to let go of it. None of us have any say in who is granted salvation and who isn't. At least not the way I understand it. But I'm sure I'll be surprised by a lot of things when they're finally made clear."

Tyler looks for a way to switch the subject. "Let me ask *you* something, Sister. Why did you become a nun? Did you always know that it was your, you know, calling?"

"Not at all. I'm a late-in-life convert."

She tells him how she'd been a rebellious child during the awful years of the Great Depression, growing up in Baltimore. Her father was a doctor, and their family lived quite well, but she always thought they should have had more.

"Such a bratty little girl I was!" she exclaims. "To get me out of their hair, my parents sent me to a girl's boarding school in Virginia, and then to William and Mary, where I studied philosophy."

She sees Tyler roll his eyes slightly. "Not very practical, right? But I discovered something about myself. I loved to learn, to immerse myself in all this *thinking*."

The old nun pauses in telling her story as they near and then overtake an elderly patient in a wheelchair alone in the corridor, boney white arms straining against the wheels but remaining motionless like an island. His mouth perpetually agape; the demons he's seen. A nurse hurries down the hall toward them, then takes charge of the wheelchair patient, so they continue on.

When she was in tenth grade at the prep school, just before the Christmas break, she says, news came that a navy base in Hawaii had been attacked. Pearl Harbor. The terrible, far-off war had been brought home to America.

"But the war's only impact on my life seemed to be that fewer boys would be around when I went off to college. I hated the war because it threatened my social life, if you can believe that. The whole world destroying itself, and I just became more selfish and inward-looking. I wasn't just indifferent to the destruction of these unseen countries, I resented them for it. Not very nun-like, I know."

"What turned you around?" he asks.

"Nothing, for quite a while," she responds. Four years of college led to two years of graduate school. Then she had made her way to New York City, "taking up with other educated outcasts in a dirty little apartment in lower Manhattan. Soho." She worked as a waitress until she got bored and quit and had to find another job in some other restaurant or bar. "Until it all became nothing but a drag."

There it is again, *a drag*. Odd for a nun to say.

"I got in with some Beats, became one of the Beat Generation, as we didn't mind being called. As if we expected to soon take over our whole generation with self-indulgent living and resistance to the whole success-striving thing. Or *Beatniks*, as we were scornfully called by those who thought we must be Communist troublemakers. We were all so *rebellious*, challenging the *unexamined life* of the consumer society. But our discontent didn't lead us anywhere. I had no interest in marrying, having children. It didn't fit the scene, you know?"

Hard for Tyler to imagine this old nun so many years ago in a smoke-filled lounge, getting bombed on hard liquor, clicking her fingers to the beat as a scruffy-bearded man in a beret sits on a stool reading bad poetry, like they made fun of in an episode of *Happy Days* when he was a kid, he remembers.

"I know I'm rambling, but this walk seems to be doing you good. I'll pick up the pace of my little life story, so I don't bore you," she says to him. "The drab Eisenhower years gave way to *Camelot* in America. A young, dashing president challenging us to get involved. *Ask not what your country can do for you*, he said. Found myself inspired for the first time in my life. And, eventually,

I decided to go all in on an idealistic Kennedy invention, the Peace Corps. To somehow make a difference in the world. But before I'd even left New York, I heard that Jack Kennedy had been murdered. And everything changed for me, turned on a dime."

She set off for San Francisco, she says. "California called to me. Something was going on there. Not very different from what I'd been doing in New York but with more vibrant colors, you know? Another escape from responsibility. I gave it a go, but after a year and a half, the whole scene was becoming too weird, even for me back then. And this was '65, a couple of years before things really got tripped out. I was older than nearly all of the 'Flower Power' college kids and drop-outs, so maybe I was quicker to realize that we were all still pawns in a cynical game. The leading voices of the counterculture talked a lot about liberation and freedom. But they were really all about *control*. They saw the masses as *sheep* that could be easily led astray, to fight in some kind of revolution. I wanted no part of that. So, I moved in with friends living away from it all in Santa Rosa and just cooled my jets for a while. Of course, as it turned out, those masses of hippies were much less interested in revolution than in trying to satisfy their own unrestrained appetites."

It's hard to tell what to make of all this beatnik-hippie talk from the old nun. She looks at him, expectantly, that way women do when they're not sure he's paying attention. He nods and that seems to suffice.

"Then as I was about to turn forty, it hit me. *My life is more than half over, probably, and what do I have to show for it?* It was 1967, the *Summer of Love*. I guess I decided I was too old for all that. It was finally time to grow up."

"A little too *groovy*, eh?" Tyler says.

"Yes, exactly. I needed to put all this pointless hedonism behind me and stop thinking only of myself. So, I finally did join the Peace Corps. They sent me to Costa Rica, a beautiful land where people live with far less than we're used to. But they have each other and their faith. And you know what? Somehow in what we'd consider meager living, they have hope and a real sense of *joy*. It changed me. Working for the good of others can do wonders for you."

"How long were you in Costa Rica?" Tyler asks.

She smiles. So, he *is* listening.

"Three years. In 1970, I came home, determined to commit my life to the Lord. I knew by then that he wanted me to serve and that I would never find anything resembling peace or happiness if I ignored the call."

She tried to join a cloister of Carmelites, a strict order, she says.

"They were skeptical. The Carmelites' spiritual focus—their *charism* as we call it in the business—is contemplative prayer. It's amazingly fulfilling, I'm sure, for those who are called. But the good sisters could tell it wasn't really right for me."

After much discernment, she says, she joined the Sisters of Mercy in Michigan. "My vocation allows me to be immersed in daily prayer but also to serve the sick, the injured and the dying in hospitals and nursing homes. A wonderful combination, actually. The past twenty years I've tried to make up for all the lost time and selfishness earlier in my life."

Tyler looks down at the carpet ahead of him as he walks. Can lost time ever be made up, really? Isn't it gone forever once it's lost? He stops, and abruptly changes the subject.

"Sister, do you think we meet up with our loved ones in heaven?"

She seems relieved to be done with the story of her wayward youth.

"Yes, I'm sure of it. But I don't think it matters the way we might expect," she says mysteriously. "Think about it. You'll want to be with your parents, your son, your wife. If you marry another woman, you'll want to be with her, too. But each of them will have close associations that won't mean as much to you. Some of those you love may not love others in your sphere. They may not even like them. How can any of these imperfections be reconciled in a state of perfect love and grace?"

"So, I'll meet up with Christie in heaven, be happy for her that she's there and all, but we won't really hang out much together?"

But the old nun just shrugs. The unknowable finally wins out.

16

Somehow, he lost track of a day. It's Thursday, not Wednesday. He's supposed to be going home soon. He realizes it's Thursday because it says so on the top of the newspaper that's sitting on his bed when he returns from the walk with the nun. It's folded and creased, clearly having been read by someone. But it's a new newspaper to him, marking a day that a moment ago he'd forgotten had already arrived.

"I left you the paper," Cuhlman says in his deeply resonant voice.

The curtain is open. Cuhlman is under layers of covers, his head nearly encaved in the large, flaccid hospital pillow. His eyes are almost completely shut.

Tyler picks up the cheerfully colorful *USA Today*:

Iraq's Hussein Promises Cheap Oil if USA Allows Occupation
BAGHDAD: The dictator of Iraq, Saddam Hussein, proposed to the ranking USA diplomat in Baghdad a solution to the Iraq-Kuwait conflict: If the USA gives its blessing to Iraq's annexation of Kuwait, Hussein's gov-

ernment will in return provide cheap oil to the USA from Iraqi and Kuwaiti oil fields.

Tyler smirks as he reads this. Hussein can't really believe he can just buy American support with promises of discounted oil, can he? If we wanted the oil, we could just go in and take it, right? How's this stubble-faced creep and his Iraqi army going to stop the American military machine if we get it cranked up?

And, in fact, it already has been cranked up. The U.S. has launched "Operation Desert Shield," described as a wholly defensive operation to protect neighboring countries against further Iraqi aggression. Cuhlman has tuned the television they share to CNN, which is carrying a live report from Saudi Arabia. No pictures yet, just a map and a far-off, disembodied voice: a correspondent with a fake-sounding name, Wolf Blitzer. Even the news reporters are going Hollywood now. He pronounces the place e*hr-ock* not *eye-rack*, and that other troubled country over there *ehr-rahn* not *eye-ran*, showing he's got a superior education. The same way Dan Rather says *hair-is-ment* instead of *huh-rass-ment*, like it's supposed to be, missing the whole onomatopoeia of the harsh-sounding *huh-rass-ment*. How can you have *sexual harassment* without *rass*, which rhymes with *ass*, got it, Dan?

Cuhlman hits his channel changer, bouncing about, lingering when a well-endowed brunette in a bikini leans into the camera and says something Tyler can't quite hear. It's a beer commercial, Miller Lite, where life is one long fiesta about to break out into an R-rated movie, just off camera. Women's bodies are everywhere in America, selling us cars and candy and everything in between. Breasts and legs and derrieres are our most treasured decorations, our most powerful selling aids, our biggest distractions. How can you keep from looking? It's addictive. Those in the know take offense to all this *objectification*, as they call it. And Arabs find it scandalous for an entirely different reason. They consider a woman's body to be a treasure to be hidden, jealously guarded and exploited in private, he thinks. They understand the destructive power of all that passion when women's bodies aren't kept under wraps.

* * *

The drumbeat of restless warriors, incessant and insatiable. Somebody else's kids sent into harm's way. Things had been mostly quiet since Reagan's quick little adventure in Grenada, hardly a fair fight, like the Yankees taking on somebody's Little League team. This smells bigger. Totally winnable, for sure, but at some cost that will prove immeasurable to the parents getting that knock on the door, that neatly folded flag. And what beef do we have against the Iraqi people, anyway? Couldn't we just have the CIA put the hit on Saddam Hussein and call it a day?

The shared television has brought the roommates together. Tyler sits in a chair beside Cuhlman's bed. The overseas conflict, the looming showdown in the desert; it makes for easy, natural conversation. Both are leery of a messy entanglement for the U.S., yet both would like to see Saddam cut down before he can make real trouble. Mostly they just sit there, long pauses in their unrushed conversation, pleasantly oblivious to the roar which lies on the other side of silence. At some point, Cuhlman had muted the television and never restored the babble. Perhaps ten minutes goes by before Tyler looks into the cloudy eyes of the old man and asks: "You ever serve? In the military?"

Cuhlman exhales through his nostrils, an almost inaudible snort, then grimaces in pain. "The Army. I was *involved*, you could say, in the fight to free Europe," he says. "You might of heard of it? Started on a ugly stretch of beach in northern France."

"You were in the D-Day invasion?"

"Yessir. My company landed at Cherbourg. With two other negro companies, as they called us back then. Some white soldiers, too. Higher ups didn't think we could get the job done without 'em."

He stops there, and it seems that he will have no more to say. Tyler looks at him with wide eyes, prodding the old man to go on. But Cuhlman just scratches his head.

"So long ago, I don't want…" he says trailing off.

"C'mon, man. Don't tell me you don't remember something so big in your life."

"I can remember all right, if I want to," Cuhlman mutters. "Maybe not today."

Tyler nods. Unleashing an old memory can open an unwelcome new wound you're not ready for, and for what?

But this little unspoken understanding between them then grows a life of its own, seeming to spark Cuhlman to a new place. Here but not here. He coughs. Eyes close. Slowly, he begins to let it out.

Cherbourg was on a jagged point of France reaching up toward Britain across the cold, dark English Channel, he begins, like a travelogue narrator setting the stage. Just to the east, to the right if you were looking at a map, were the now more-famous Normandy beaches—Utah, Omaha, Sword, Juno and other sections of rugged shoreline code-named for the Allied invasion. "We never had a code name as far as I ever knew. We had no idea where we was landing. I guess they figured a bunch of negroes couldn't be trusted even with a code name. Wasn't until later that we figured out Cherbourg is where we came in."

Cuhlman breathes deeply, then continues. "Tens of thousands of black soldiers fought for the U.S. in the war. Two thousand of us there on D-Day. Bet you didn't know that, huh? And a whole lot died. A whole hell of a lot. To liberate Europe from the worst racist the world has ever known, fighting in a segregated American army."

German machine gun nests on high ground above the coastal cliffs, he says, cut down so many of the on-rushing G.I.s who had jumped from their troop boats into the cold, shallow water, black bodies falling all around him into the salty foam. Each man carrying seventy pounds of gun and gear. A terrible rainstorm of bullets striking the foaming sea water all around him with a sound he can still hear in his mind today: *thuckt, thuckt, thuckt.* He forced himself to continue sloshing through the waves crashing against the shore, the spray making it hard to see. *Thuckt, thuckt, thuckt.* Stepping over dead bodies of soldiers who'd been ahead of him in the same near-suicidal dash.

He reached shore and climbed up onto the rocks, ignoring the wailing cries all about him. Hours it must have been, climbing, crawling, running, diving for cover, then continuing on right into the source of the barrage. Finally, the sheer number of determined American negro raiders proved too much even for the coldly efficient machine guns. They climbed behind crags of rocks until they were near enough to throw grenades into the two concrete bunkers protruding from the top of the cliffs. Then rushing in to shoot the few Nazis who'd survived the blasts. Shutting them up forever. Bullets into chests and faces. No mercy asked for; none given.

"There was only a dozen or so Germans, combined, in the two machine gun nests, as it turned out," Cuhlman says slowly, eyes closed. As if in some kind of trance of hallowed remembrance. Lines of tension overwhelm the wrinkles on his face. A bead of sweat rolls down his neck.

"The tattered bunch of us negro G.I.s pitched them Nazi bodies over the concrete walls. Tumblin' down the steep, rocky hill that we'd climbed up. To let the others in our invasion party know it was safe to come on up. And, I guess, 'cause we needed to feel the satisfaction of violence against their unholy, dead bodies."

At last, the American soldiers could stop and rest, Cuhlman continues. Only then did he feel the pain of wrenched muscles and a hundred small bruises and cuts he had blotted out of his consciousness in the mad dash to survive the hellish rain of machine gun bullets, to reach the enemy and kill him. He wiped the hot barrel of his rifle with a muddy sleeve, gratefully. The clouds above released a cold drizzle, then gave way to a wet fog of not-quite rain.

"And then, finally, God bless it, all was quiet. Quiet at last."

Tyler listens intently. The old man had been a cold-blooded killer and a hero, who would have known? Does he still have that killer inside him?

"How did you keep moving forward in the water—into the bullets—when the others were getting cut down?" Tyler asks. "Didn't you want to turn and run the other way?"

"We'd been told sort of what to expect when we'd come out of them landing boats—Higgins boats, they called 'em. Like a railroad box car without the wheels, stuffed with men. The front opening up when it reached shallow water near the shore. We'd trained for it, much as we could. We knew we just had to jump into the water and keep going forward. There was no turnin' around. And no place any safer behind us."

"Were you scared?"

"Of course. Terrified. If you stopped to think about what the hell was happenin', you'd just freeze. No doubt many good men did. It happened to me for a instant in the water, but I shook free of it and just pushed ahead. So many were being cut down all around us—maybe the only sane thing was to try to hide. To just wish yourself away from there. But it wasn't about who was sane. It was about movin' on, goin' forward. Just movin' on, you understand?"

"How'd you get through that?"

"We knew they couldn't get all of us, so we just had to believe some of us would make it. Might as well be me. That's what each of us thought, I guess."

Quiet for a time, then a whisper. "I ain't talked about any of this in… don't know how long." His face marked with shiny vertical tracks where sweat droplets roll down from his forehead. "Years."

Tyler tries to picture himself running up a bloody beach through such hell, but he cannot. Nothing in his life would have prepared him for that.

Cuhlman takes a drink from a plastic cup on his bed stand. "As we started marching toward Germany, we passed right through all those other landing places and saw the remains of these awful, brutal fights like we was just in ourselves. On and on like that."

Tyler listens wide-eyed to Cuhlman's stories of an epic conflict that he has only read about or seen in Hollywood reenactments. He's never heard a first-hand account of the horrors of combat. His father had been too young to join the service during the world war, and old enough to skip Korea. Two of Tyler's uncles, older brothers of his father and his mother, had fought in WWII—one in Europe, one in the Pacific. Both had survived the fighting and returned home, but Tyler had never talked to either of them about their war experiences. Now both are dead and forever silent. Why hadn't he taken the time to seek them out and listen to their stories?

"What'd you do after the war?"

But Cuhlman has grown tired of talking. Silence again sits there neatly between the two patients, and neither feels the need to break loose of it.

Finally, Tyler gets up to retreat to his part of the room. But first he reaches out his right hand without thinking, as if something momentous has happened between them that calls for the formality of a handshake. Without a word, Cuhlman reaches out and Tyler grasps his hand, which is somehow smaller than the younger man expected. As Tyler lets go, he sees why. Cuhlman's beefy right hand is missing a finger, the pinkie.

* * *

After a lengthy spell, resting on his bed, Tyler is back with Cuhlman. Silently watching the little hospital TV together. The mental siege of four or five consecutive commercials proves too much for Tyler to bear. "So, when you joined the Army at twenty-six, you must of been older than most of the others coming in, right?"

"Older than some, yeah. But it wasn't just the kids out of high school going off to fight, like you think, like it was for Vietnam. The Japs' sneak attack on Pearl Harbor shook us all out of whatever we was doing. All of a sudden, we was at war. On two continents. If you was an able-bodied man, you enlisted. Teenagers, men in their twenties and thirties, white and black. You just did."

"Did having to serve in a black part of the army make you seem, I don't know, less appreciated?"

Cuhlman shakes his head. *"Appreciated?* You got a funny way of speakin'. Hell, we knew our place. That's just the way it was. The officers expected us to fight and kill, or be shot and be killed, just like any other soldiers. To them, you all just replaceable parts anyway. There ain't no appreciating nobody."

Cuhlman takes another swig of water. "But yeah, to what you said before, I *was* older than a lot of the others in my platoon. I'd been working, growing up a bit, into a man. And I'd played six years of professional baseball."

"What? Really? In the major leagues?"

"In the Negro major leagues, yeah. That was a separate deal, too, back then. I played for a couple of years with the Pittsburgh Crawfords and three for the Newark Eagles. In the Negro National League. First base."

"I had no idea. That seems like such a different time, so long ago, blacks having their own league."

"We would of been happy to play with the white major leaguers, let me tell you. Still, we played at a high level and had our own stars. My rookie year, the great Satchel Paige was on my team. He could throw harder than any man alive, black or white. I went up against him in several games over the next few years, after he left the Crawfords. Only got one hit, a weak little single, in all those at-bats. And for two years, I played with Josh Gibson, a fearsome hitter. He could drive a ball out of the park like no one on Earth. They say Mickey Mantle hit the farthest home run ever recorded, but that's only 'cause they never measured Gibson's shots."

Tyler shakes his head in amazement. *The old man has lived quite a life.*

Cuhlman talks a bit about these star players who never had the chance to showcase their greatness against the prevailing stars in the "real" major leagues, and about some of the everyday ups and downs in his short baseball career.

"Then it was time to go off to war. Wasn't my idea, of course. The Japanese had forced the issue. But I never answered your question."

Tyler looks confused. He doesn't remember what question he'd asked.

"What I done after the war," Cuhlman adds helpfully. "Went to work at a tool-and-die shop in Newark, my hometown."

"Why didn't you go back to playing ball? That injury to your hand?"

"This little thing?" Cuhlman holds up his right hand with the pinkie stub. "No, this ain't nothin'. Just a little reminder of some shrapnel from an explosion that knocked me out cold for a couple of days in France. Kinda like you with your car crash. Hell, this is my glove hand. I'm a lefty, you know? Playin' first base, you remember me sayin'?"

First base is most often fielded by left-handers, Tyler knows. Lefties have a natural advantage playing at first, running toward the bag with the glove hand facing the field, or putting the tag on a runner on a pickoff throw from the pitcher.

"Playin' first base is sweet justice for lefties," Cuhlman says. "Missin' part of my little finger inside my glove wouldn't of mattered at all."

"I didn't know you're left-handed. You shook hands with your right."

"Lefties got to make accommodations in a right-handed-world. Just the way it is."

"So why didn't you try to play ball again, when you came home?"

"It was just the toll of it all. The war. The killing all around. All the noise. And the never knowin' that you was ever safe where you was. It just wore out my insides. No way I was gone ever be able to stand up at the plate again with a pitcher throwin' his meanest stuff at me. You got to be fearless to play ball at that level. And I knew I didn't have it in me no more, you understand?"

Tyler presses Cuhlman. "But didn't you want to at least give it a try, to see if you could still play?"

"Once you been in the killing of war, there ain't no going back to the times before. It's in your mind's eye and you can't unsee it. You got to be pure inside your mind to play baseball against the best. I wouldn't of had a chance hittin' the ball."

"What about Ted Williams?" Tyler persists. "He came back and had a lot of great years after the war."

"I ain't sure how much actual battle action he was ever in. But that man was different anyways, from what I understand. An *angry killer* at the plate. He found his energy from being mean. Now, I was no Ted Williams, mind you. I was pretty good in my day, but he was an immortal if ever there was one. Me, I played for the joy of the game. I could never of done that after the war."

Tyler nods, listening to this old man who must have been so imposing, on the baseball field and on the battlefield, but now is withering away before his eyes.

"So, I came back to New Jersey, and went to work in that machine shop."

But playing baseball around the country and then serving in the army had opened up Cuhlman's mind to a bigger world, he says.

"By and by, I knew I wasn't long for livin' there. I seen a lot of ugliness in the world, but also bigger possibilities than I had in Newark."

He moved to Detroit, where two of his cousins were working. "They got me on at Ford's at one of the Rouge River plants, making windshields for the '48s. It was a good job for raising a family. Worked there until I retired. Thirty-two years in that old glass plant."

He looks off mournfully, the glass plant days now just as gone as those he had spent fighting Germans in France or playing pro baseball.

"Yeah, that kind of work is hard. I worked in a stamping plant. Administrative job," Tyler adds, sheepishly. "When I'd go out on the floor, I could appreciate what it'd be like to be out there all day. Sweaty, dirty. And really, really loud."

"What was this Human Relations work you done for GM?" Cuhlman asks, a little out of breath and seemingly pleased to move the conversation over to Tyler.

"*Human Resources*. A lot of stupid, busy work, really. GM has all these processes to follow. The HR people are like the police, making sure each process is followed. Busting people's chops for not following arbitrary rules. The job isn't at all what I had thought it would be when I picked human resource management as a major in business school."

"What did you think it should be?"

"HR people should be change agents. They should be about creating change, helping people adapt," Tyler explains. "Not stopping change from happening. HR people should help the organization grow and develop, should understand what changes would be good for the company. And they should help individuals grow and develop, too."

"Give me a for-instance," Cuhlman says, big, sad brown eyes studying his younger, white roommate.

"Well, computers. They're going to change everything in the workplace. With computers, employees could take care of managing their own benefits, which would free up the benefits people to do other things."

"Or the company could get rid of those people."

"Sure, they could and they will do some of that. But most of the HR people could be working to help make the company change for the better, instead of resisting change like they've always done."

"Do any of the HR people act like you think they should—as 'change agents' you called 'em?"

"A few. I tried to be one," Tyler trails off. "To a degree, I guess. But it's like good cholesterol and bad cholesterol, you're either one or the other. And there's not enough good cholesterol going around."

* * *

Late in the evening, the doctor stops by. Looks deeply into a computer behind him and down at Tyler's charts. Everything's in order, evidently, because he confirms that Tyler can go home the next day, probably by late morning. It takes a while to complete the discharge, he says. Tyler calls his house and relays the news to George. They'll come around ten o'clock and drive him home when he is released. Tyler asks to talk to Robbie, but the boy is already asleep.

* * *

The TV news reader tells of a horrific crime: a violent sexual assault of a five-year-old child, tortured and murdered. There's disturbing video from the crime scene, the newsman warns, knowing that most viewers will pay attention all the more. Blood stains throughout a child's bedroom, including on a teddy bear lying on the floor, its head bent sharply to the left as if its neck had been broken. Tyler clicks off the television and shuts his eyes.

An hour later, the bloody crime becomes all too real, played out in front of him—a sweet little girl abused, tortured and killed. Tyler shakes himself awake from the abhorrent vision, burned into his brain. Sweating, tingling all over, ears buzzing. He sits straight up and is engulfed in nausea but does not vomit. Catching his breath, he studies the quiet hospital room under the soft glow of various lighted instruments and the hallway's fluorescent haze coming in a bit from under the closed door. In the darkness, he sees the length of curtain, hiding his sleeping roommate from him. He cannot bear to close his eyes, worried that the vile, sadistic images will return. He smells it, an evil somewhere in the room. Unseen and surely not there, he tells himself. Yet, the absolute ugliness is so palpably *here*, with him in the room. His stomach tightens again, ready to retch. *What is it, this evil?* Banished from our modern, sophisticated thinking, a quaint notion, replaced now by *psychosis*. Something to be diagnosed and treated. But then perhaps we sell true evil short, and let it hide in plain sight.

Tyler swings his legs over the bed. He sits upright and attentive, scouring the dark room with his contact-less eyes, seeking some visual confirmation of the detestable presence. Nothing. Keeping his eyes open to prevent the murderous images from reappearing in his brain, even for an instant, he silently prays one Our Father after another, five or six …. *deliver us from evil. Amen. … Our Father …* His unspoken words produce nothing, no connection, just a fuzziness inside his head. Like listening to music on his car stereo tuned to a distant AM station; the signal may be strong enough, but the sound that reaches his ear lacks definition and depth: tinny and unsatisfying. Just a hollow chirping monologue, his own rote prayers. But at least the smell is gone and with it the feeling of having to vomit. He lies back down and closes his eyes. Becoming that pitcher with the wicked fastball so that sleep will come for him once again without the nightmares. Like a stuck toilet resisting the repeated attacks of a too-cheap plunger, the dark thoughts remain, fouling the works of his mind, until finally letting go with a slurping mental release into the night.

When Tyler wakes up again, it's nearly seven. Light is streaming in all the places where the shade doesn't quite cover the window. His eyes shut again, his head still too heavy to lift just yet. *A baby.* Something about a baby he was just dreaming. No nightmare this time. A good dream, he thinks it was, if he can remember, but it's gone.

Instead, his foggy mind returns to another happy memory, when Christie came to him with that little sliver of paper and a kind of a test tube, like the tiny pieces of litmus paper back in high school chemistry class testing pH: acid or alkaline. But the slip of paper Christie holds tells of a far greater mystery: a baby, sure enough. Christie throws her arms around Tyler's neck and draws him in for a wet kiss, held longer than just hello or goodbye, then snapping back her head so suddenly their lips actually make a popping sound, and she's laughing and crying all at once. They've been officially trying to have a baby just these past three months or so; didn't take long at all. Tyler hadn't had time to even consider the possibility that they might not be able to have a child. It never had occurred to him that when he let his great navy of swimming sperms loose, none might be able to get the job done, piercing that big ovum and planting his genome inside, tail still wagging outside the egg like the flag on Iwo Jima. Christie is crying real tears of sweet relief. The thought *has* occurred to her, of course, but it's all right now. She's going to be a mom and him a dad, just like that, their lives changed forever. For the good, yes, even if it's a bitch financially; you know that going in.

Those cells split and split, and then he can see life shaping together in the grainy, black-and-white ultrasound when she's in with the ob-gyn. The doc has put a cloudy jelly all over her belly and is moving through the goop with a little sonar device with a coiled cord like a telephone has, the cord running into a little computer on a wheeled cart and there's his kid-to-be on the monitor, hard to see much detail but the doctor can tell. *No, we don't want to know* if it's a boy or girl, so the doc won't say whether he can make out a tiny penis in all the graininess.

It hadn't been all that different for Tyler's parents back in Akron in 1964. Before ultrasounds, of course, just a doctor with a stethoscope hearing a heartbeat inside his mother's belly. She was happy to be expecting this second blessing in their married lives, and his father full of resolve, feeling his obligations increasing but determined to deliver, so that this new little one would grow up secure in his place and able eventually to stand on his own two feet and make it in this world, a productive member of society, a net positive, producing at least a little more than he uses up. As if a life could be measured like that.

And then little Tyler was born, screaming at the doctor and his mother for making him endure such an unpleasant, crushing journey through the birth canal into harsh white lights and a spank on his rear, such humiliation, when he had been perfectly content inside the warm, sloshing amniotic waterbed he had always known. Diapered and breast-fed, pampering hugs and cooing sounds from his mother as he found his bearings over the next fourteen months until finally getting up on his legs and taking his first fearful steps, a late walker. But then he got the hang of it quickly, plodding along arms out, a toddler robot. Somehow his knees learned to bend a bit and the running began. Then off to school and though his birthday is in October and his parents could have easily kept him home another year, he starts kindergarten at four; he's bright and ready to learn the secrets of the numbers and the alphabet. That early start would forever be his disadvantage in sports, always one of the youngest, going against bigger, duller kids each grade through high school. Who knows if he'd been held back, red-shirted by his parents until he was five, how much more playing time and coaches' primary attention might he have received over the years, developing a little more athletically along the way.

Maybe he could have been a star on his high school baseball and basketball teams. No way to ever know.

Then he was off to college to learn something useful enough to make a solid living and finding his way to General Motors in Detroit, the largest industrial corporation the world has ever known, where he will work his entire career, thirty-five years or more and retire, with a gray-haired but still-good-looking, smiling wife with all her teeth, and the kids and grandkids, each playing a bit of sports, even the girls though it's just mostly soccer for them, applying themselves at their schoolwork and at college, keeping the productive cycle going, earning their own keep. And then he would be retired and living off his GM pension and a little Social Security if there was anything still there to pay out to Tyler and the others his age, the tail-end of the baby boomers after their older brothers and sisters have sucked the life out of the program and all those FICA dollars stolen out of his paycheck have been spent. But he's set on his pension anyway, plus his *IRA*, a new type of savings account the beanies have come up with to keep you from losing so much to taxes. He's got a motorboat in retirement to take the grandkids fishing or water-skiing and tubing on fine, hot summer days. His whole life a perfect arc launched from way back inside his mother to his own happy landings, but now it's mostly been lost. His father's downward slide was the first augury that Tyler's wheels might someday lose grip of the pavement, but it was that shocking loss of his beautiful Christie that bit him so suddenly, like unseen teeth of angry piranha in murky water tearing at the hands of one trying to lift what looked to be such sure, easy treasure. And then his job, again, stolen from him with no warning. There will be no thirty-five-year GM career, no pension. Tyler's wheels have spun off the road, his life trajectory no longer on a happy path but careening into a dark tunnel of the unknown, *where the streets have no name,* as U2's Bono sings. And where exactly are the streets unnamed? In the desert, faint tracks hinting at some oasis? On the moon, perhaps, he thinks hazily. Or heaven?

He slowly gets up to pee and then he peeks around the curtain. Cuhlman is awake, reading. Tyler walks over to the chair beside his roommate's bed and sits without saying a word.

Finally, the old man looks up from his book. "Did I hear 'em say you going home today?"

"Yeah, that's right," Tyler answers.

"About time they let you go. Never did seem like nothin' was wrong with you."

"Easy for you to say."

"Not really. I got more than my share of problems," Cuhlman says.

The *Today* show starts into its second hour. The Jane Pauley replacement, Deborah Norville is her name as it turns out, sits between Bryant Gumbel and Joe Garagiola, the long-time baseball announcer somehow doing morning newsertainment now. She tries to fit in between the two sportscasters; this is *Today*'s crazy new lineup. She's awkward even if she is kind of hot, in that studious way of hers, droning on about Mormons and polygamy. Gumbel and Gargiola look like they'd rather be at Giants Stadium or maybe Shea. Music wafts in occasionally audible bleat-bleats from a tinny radio playing in some nearby hospital corridor, classic rock, Supertramp: "…*oh, what you might have been. If you'd of had … more … time. Oh!*"

"Thanks for sharing your stories, you know, yesterday," Tyler finally says. "It's really something. You've been part of so much history."

"Tell you what," Cuhlman says. "You come back to see me some time when we both out of this place and I'll pick it up from there."

"That'd be great," Tyler says, knowing it'll never happen.

17

Tyler is finally going home. He sits on the bed, waiting for one final meeting with his doctor and then, assuming the doctor okays his release, a bit of an exit interview with the nurse on duty. Meanwhile, the TV jumps about in spasms, nothing good on this late in the morning, Cuhlman flipping back and forth restlessly between CNN *Headline News* and ESPN *SportsCenter*, each repeating segments they've already seen this morning: NASA's *Magellan* spacecraft nears a landing on Venus; Carlton Fisk has tied Johnny Bench for most homers by a catcher, 327, the two connected already by that fantastic World Series back in 1975—remember?—when Fisk, so young, hopped up and down the first base line, waving his hands frantically to will his line shot fair, a walk-off winner in Game Six, but then the Reds won Game Seven anyway; another character from that unstoppable Big Red Machine, Pete Rose, is a cross-over news story from the sports world: he begins his five-month prison sentence today in Texas, nailed for tax evasion, like Al Capone; they couldn't put him away for betting on baseball though that's what will keep him out of the Hall of Fame. The all-time hits leader, mostly all singles but still, and not going to Cooperstown. So sure that he was above it all, the ultimate sucker's bet.

The short, gray-haired, former hippie nun pulls back the curtain just a bit and pokes her head into Tyler's world.

"I wondered if you want to talk some more before you go home."

Tyler nods. "Sure." Not really, though.

When Tyler doesn't move to get up, she shuffles over to his bedside. Pulls over a chair. "The other day when I was here with your nurse, Emma, you told us how your wife died," she reminds him. "Then, when we went down for a walk, we talked some about the girl in the other car. But nothing more about Christie. I don't mean to pry, but I sense there is more you didn't mention, about when she died."

A pause hangs in the air between them. She waits him out. He sighs. She waits.

"Yeah, I guess so," Tyler says finally.

Why does the old nun want him to open this dispiriting box he's kept sealed for half a year? Her earnestness draws it out of him like a long-in-coming bowel movement.

"The paramedics arrived in their EMS van and tried to revive her, with oxygen and with those electro-shock paddles. But she wouldn't come back. She was already dead, like I said before."

He closes his eyes, and he can see them working frantically over her, but his mind can't seem to bring back her face, and then the picture shuts down. He stops, but the old nun keeps sitting there, silently demanding more. He opens his eyes and begins again, like that cassette player, auto-reverse.

"One of them asked me if she'd wanted to be an organ donor. At first, I looked at him like, *I can't believe you're asking me that right now.*"

But then he remembered that, yes, she had. They had talked about it once. Of course, death had seemed so remote. Something that happened to others, so much older.

"He asked me if Christie's driver's license had an organ donor sticker. I fished it out of the little purse, like a fanny-pack, she brought along sometimes when she didn't want to lug around her usual purse."

Tyler was always scolding her to clean out all the unnecessary stuff in her purse, receipts from who knows where, pens that sometimes didn't even work, loose change, including piles of pennies so heavy but practically worthless. This little purse of hers was better. Inside he found her wallet with her Michigan driver's license, donor sticker on the back.

"The EMS guys had already put the oxygen mask back over her nose and mouth." One of them explained repeatedly to Tyler that they couldn't bring her back—her brain activity had stopped completely—but they needed to keep her organs preserved.

The chaplain nun nods slightly, seemingly understanding where this is going.

"I couldn't believe it. How would a ventilator do any good if she was really dead?"

The paramedic told him that often it was possible to resuscitate the heart of a brain-dead patient, allowing other organs to stay in a healthy state so they could be transplanted later.

The nun finally speaks: "What did you think of all this?"

"I didn't know what to think. In shock, of course, having just lost her. So sudden, you know, everything…" He trails off and then starts again. "Good that part of her might help someone else. But that should of been *way* down the road. Years and years before she was giving any organs away."

He looks at the nun's sad, understanding eyes and goes on: "After the funeral, I looked up how all this works. It turns out that organ harvesting—well, they don't call it that in the hospital world. *Organ retrieval*, I should say—is a big business. It works best from these *beating-heart cadavers*, as they're called. That's what my Christie had become. I mean, really?"

Tyler hasn't been down this road with anyone—never told his mother; never told Christie's parents. Rhonda would have flipped out. Even now it feels wrong to talk about his wife this way, behind her back.

"The EMS guy asked if Christie might be pregnant. I said no, I didn't think so; but, sure, it was possible. He said they would check before they removed any of her organs. It didn't make any sense. I mean, what the hell?"

Later, when he was digging into all this, he'd read from a medical journal that fetuses can continue to grow in a mother's womb even after she's medically dead. He tells the nun that he had read about a case of a *beating-heart cadaver* giving birth to a healthy baby more than a hundred days after the woman's brain activity had stopped, delivered with a Cesarean.

"Isn't that just crazy?" he says, shaking his head. "The baby kept growing inside her all that time."

The nun's colorless face brightens as Tyler relates this bizarre story and she nods. "Yes, God's miracles so often are. Crazy, if we try to understand."

Tyler nods silently, skipping ahead in his mind. Unseen medical teams would soon enough confirm that Christie was indeed not pregnant, and that the organ retrieval could commence. But no one had bothered to provide this final update to Tyler. And no apology had been forthcoming when he finally reached the right people on the phone a week later and been told matter-of-factly that it all had gone forward as he had agreed. In whose bodies these bits of Christie had ended up, he would never know.

"She's helping some others live on," he mumbles. "That ought to mean something to me. Maybe someday it will, you know?"

Later, reading up about organ retrieval, Tyler became aware that Christie's organs had not just been invaluable—of course, they were priceless to those receiving the organs—but were worth big money. A single intact major organ could be valued at three hundred thousand dollars, one of the articles had said; a typical beating-heart cadaver had one-and-a-half million dollars' worth of functioning tissue to give. And organs from an otherwise perfectly healthy twenty-six-year-old body would be far from average. Christie's liver, kidneys and heart, as well as some lesser organs, would fetch top dollar in some invisible economy that operated far from Tyler's world. Not that he would have taken any money for Christie's gift. That would be unthinkable.

He returns his focus to his frantic conversation with the EMS team. "I kept asking if there was any chance to get her brain to function again and they kept saying 'no.' There was no activity in her *brain stem*, they said. They could tell this by the machines they had her hooked up to, I guess. So, I signed off on a bunch of forms. It's what she wanted."

"How was Christie in her faith life?" the nun asks.

"We went to church most every Sunday," Tyler answers. "To mass." Then, thinking that this basic information doesn't do justice to his wife's faithfulness, he adds: "Actually, she connected with God. Deeper than me. Or farther along, I guess."

"How did you know?" she asks.

"We didn't talk too much about it, really. But she seemed more focused than me at church, you know? Lots of times I can't remember the readings right after they're finished. And in her praying, at night. I think she felt like God was listening and that she could sometimes feel an answer coming back. I never get that, you know, *connection*. How do I even know he's there?"

Tyler hadn't really pressed Christie about it. She wouldn't have been able to explain it anyway, this closeness to someone you couldn't see or hear.

"*Faith is a knowledge within the heart, beyond the reach of proof*," the nun says, probably quoting someone.

"I guess I wish God was like the moon," he blurts out. "Up there where we can see him, but still far away. Above it all."

The TV continues to review the sports highlights of the previous day, mostly baseball, but the volume seems lower. Maybe Cuhlman turned it down.

"How do you pray, Tyler?" the nun asks, bringing the conversation back within her wheelhouse, and calling him by name for the first time.

"I say the usual ones. But it seems kind of forced, really."

"Do you ever just talk to God? Just tell him what's on your mind?"

"Sure, but not out loud or anything. I might think something like 'Please look after my little boy. Keep him safe.' Like that."

With Christie gone, Tyler needs some help getting it right, raising his son alone. He doesn't think too often to ask God to step in, to help him out. Just once in a while, maybe.

"That's good. But do you ever simply talk to God about what you are afraid of, or what makes you happy or sad? Or blows your mind?"

Another odd hippie expression, and it strikes him as funny. But he doesn't let on.

"Sure. Well, not really. I figure he knows it already, right?"

"It's still good to tell him. It makes for a stronger *connection*, to use your word. A personal connection, mind and soul. To him."

"Not sure I know much about that."

"Just talk to him like someone in the same room with you. Someone very important, that is, but also a friend."

"So, like, respectful? But friendly, too?"

Tyler imagines this sweet spot, where prayer will actually work, bridging the impossible gap between his stupid little human life and some all-powerful Divine One. An awfully small sweet spot, if it's there at all.

"*Omnia in bonum*," she whispers, eyes closed. Just before she turns away and ducks back around the curtain, leaving Tyler completely alone, she adds, a little louder: "It's all good, Tyler. Find peace knowing Christie is already with God in his garden. Or will be very soon, in our way of time."

* * *

He steps out of his little bathroom after one last use of the toilet before he's discharged. A colorful arrangement of flowers—yellow, orange, pink, white and purple daisies—in a little peach-colored clay vase sits on the table by his bed, delivered while he was taking a dump. He finds a small white envelope tucked in the flowers. Inside is a simple white card printed with a generic: GET WELL SOON! But it's the one-word signature, all curves and feminine charm, that ignites within him a feeling of hope and anticipation: *Lyvia*.

The grapes of the vine will never become wine unless they are crushed. So, too, we will never become what we are meant to be unless we are first crushed by suffering.

BISHOP FULTON SHEEN

III. KODACHROME

18

October 9

Tyler pulls down the box from the shelf inside the closet off his front entrance way, above the jackets and coats on hangers. An odd assortment of gloves and hats, his and Robbie's and Christie's. He still doesn't know what to do with her clothes and other belongings. He gave some of them to Goodwill a couple of months ago, but he couldn't go about it with the cold indifference to her memory that the job required. So, he's mostly avoided her things, putting off the sorting and giving away for another day. She never wore much jewelry, so he'll keep most of what she had. Her wedding and engagement rings, of course. A few necklaces and bracelets. And maybe a dress or two. But why? He and Robbie won't have any use for a dress, and if he gets remarried someday and maybe has a daughter, a dress from some dead woman who never was her mother won't mean much, will it? Still, he's reluctant to let go just yet of things so completely hers, tellingly Christie in style and scent, bringing him back to that time they had together, yet not bringing *her* back, so it soon hurts too much to stay there.

He's looking for the camera. Already he has looked in the two junk drawers, in the kitchen and in the front room, without finding it. It's not that big for an SLR camera, but much more substantial than one of those little cheap instamatics. The Nikon had been a gift from Christie on his birthday the first year they were married. Shooting photos—not snapshots, but real photos—takes a good eye, which he has, and patience, which never has been his strong suit. He's taken plenty of lousy photos but some good ones, too, and has learned to take pleasure in it, in setting off to capture something and seeing later that you did, in fact, get it. But it's been at least a couple of months, probably longer, since he has used the camera. Something Robbie did this morning, the look of bewilderment on his face, had made Tyler wish he was looking through his viewfinder and clicking off exposures, capturing that expression on film before it evaporated away forever. The boy is growing up fast and you have to remember to take pictures along the way. Christie and Tyler never had been good about organizing their photos, and since she's been gone they've just ended up in a couple of shoeboxes in the basement. But they can always be organized later. If you don't take pictures as they happen, you can't go back in time and get a do-over, much as he would like one, now and then. The boy is growing up so fast.

Tyler thinks of another place the camera might be hiding, behind a little hinged door on one of the compartments of the entertainment center which houses his TV and VCR, and the stereo and tape deck, and a CD player now, too. All their wires and cables coming together and fanning back out, most of it hidden from sight. The TV is on, as it usually is in Tyler's house when he's home—mostly sports but some CNN, too, so he can keep up with the things they tell you are important. They're talking again about Bush's speech to Congress last month and what this *new world order* will bring; he meant it as a good thing, but others aren't too sure.

"Out of these troubling times," Bush says again in a clip from the speech they keep playing, "a new world order can emerge, freer from the threat of terror, stronger in the pursuit of justice, and more secure in the quest for peace." He's talking about getting a coalition of countries to join the U.S. to force Iraq to back out of Kuwait, out of lawlessness, or face terrible consequences, and this will teach criminal rulers everywhere not to mess with truth, justice and the American way—says the White House correspondent, more or less.

But Saddam Hussein, the crazy dictator of Iraq, is not rolling over. Today, he made a promise to unleash a new missile to strike Israel, which he calls the "Little Satan," a younger brother or son perhaps to the U.S., aka the "Great Satan." Hussein's new threat, today, evidently is the reason the Bush speech has come up again in the news. But the Iraqi ruler's threats apparently are not new news in Israel; CNN shows video from a week ago of gas masks being passed out to people throughout the little country of the Jews. Yesterday, Israeli police shot and killed seventeen Palestinian rioters, setting off more riots in Gaza and the West Bank; seventeen more reasons for revenge killings. The cycle continues, on and on.

With the Mideast items exhausted, the anchor woman—a busty brunette who looks like she would rather be talking about something a little more fun—moves to the next story: radio stations around the world are playing the song *Imagine* to honor John Lennon, who would have turned fifty today. Tyler himself just had a birthday three days ago, but it came and went without so much as a cake and candles, no one here to remember it. Robbie's too young. He did get a card from his mother; it arrived a day early. She's good about getting ahead of the mail. One of those cards that is meant to be funny and also sentimental, and ends up somehow being neither. The Hallmark copywriter trying too hard to make a guilt trip seem reasonable and pleasant, shaming a wandering son to return to his frail old parents: *To a special son… No matter how far or near you are, we always wish you nearer. No matter how fuzzy our memories get, we'll always hold you dearer. Happy Birthday, son!* There's no more "we," of course, his father gone and then dead, but she doesn't cross out the plural pronouns and replace them with singular ones; that would be disrespectful. His mom wrote some of her own thoughts on the card, spilling over to the back, wishing Tyler well, glad that he has recovered from the accident, and ending with the guilt-provoking question, "When are you and Robbie coming back to Ohio to visit like you promised?" John Lennon, gunned down in New York ten years ago it will be in December, but they decided, the world, to honor him on his birthday rather than marking the day of the killing, trying not to give his assassin any more power, any more negative control. Imagine. The Beatles at fifty.

The Nikon is there, behind that little door, and so is the video camera, a Sony. Everything electronic is Japanese now. Tyler should have remembered; he would have seen the camera when he put away the camcorder. He used it a few weeks ago, recording Robbie eating chocolate ice cream, a sticky mess all over his face and bib and highchair, still chatting away happy and content. He has Christie's love of ice cream. And of chocolate, evidently. Tyler has learned to keep the video segments short. When they first got the camcorder, they videoed everything—Robbie getting a bath, learning to stand up, eating his breakfast—often in ten- and twelve-minute pieces with hardly any talking, terrible television to play back and watch, just death. Better to film two or three minutes tops, or shorter still. The camera is a bit awkward and heavy to carry around, it records onto a full-size VHS tape inside it. Some of the new ones record on a much smaller tape, 8 mm, like an audio cassette, but then how do you ever play it back on your TV and VCR? And the battery pack, so heavy, and hot when it's running. Now that he's a single dad and responsible himself for all of the support gear for a toddler, he's less able to cart along the camcorder. He *has* used it around the house here and there, though, the boy growing up and talking so much now. *The time goes by so fast* all the older parents say wistfully, as if offering sage and original advice. *Enjoy them now; before you know it, twenty years has zipped by and they're off to college.* But the single parent is thinking: *How do I just get through this day?*

Four pictures left. On the Nikon. When Robbie wakes up from his nap, Tyler will bring him down to his workshop in the basement, show him some of the things he's been working on and see if he can arrange something interesting for a photo, Robbie with one of the less dangerous tools or a piece of sanded wood maybe.

***

The unobstructed sun creates a deep blue sky above a blaze of red and orange and yellow leaves wafting high on maple and oak and ash trees, a gentle wind's cool and crisp refreshing gift, the kind of autumn day when Michigan can credibly claim to have the finest weather in the nation. The colors are spectacular this year; several days of an unusually cold snap in late September shocked the trees into an early preparation for winter. So cold that just about all the trees, all at once, let go of their chlorophyll and embraced their autumn complexions. And then, just as the leaves turned color, the weather turned mild, dry and calm—no cold rains and high winds to knock the leaves off the trees. So, Tyler decided to take Robbie to the park with the Nikon tucked in the diaper bag. A way better photo opp than in the basement workshop.

The mid-afternoon sunlight is still a bit too strong. Twilight orangey hue, like the early morning dawn without the fog, is the *magic light* photographers talk about in the magazines, perfect for some added warmth on your subjects, the imprint of a divine finger, though you have to be careful about long shadows. October brings an early sunset. Tyler won't have long to wait. He's already scoping out locations and backdrops.

217

As usual on a weekday outing to just about anywhere, Tyler is the only dad among many moms, chatting to each other or doting on their precious little ones, while keeping a cautious eye on the suspicious man with a toddler who may or may not be his. Have to watch out for these pedophiles who sneak about park playscapes and malls, looking for a chance to lure an unattended child into a dark bathroom stall or kidnap away to their lonely homes and unspeakable actions. Tyler can feel the unwanted heat of their inspecting eyes, these moms on high alert, so he makes an extra effort to act natural and relaxed with his son. It would be nice if Robbie would call him *Daddy* loud enough that the moms could hear, signaling his legitimacy.

"C'mon, Robbie. Let's try the swings."

He leads the boy over to the end of the swing set where little yellow plastic buckets, with two holes at the bottom for a kid's legs to stick through, hang from chains, much more protective than the regular swings made from a strip of black rubber that wraps around an older kid's hips and butt when he sits on it, but requires some holding on by the kid, hands clenched around the chains. Tyler lowers Robbie down into the bucket, guiding his little legs through the holes. He fits perfectly and chirps with enjoyment as his father pulls him backward, then lets him go, flying through the air but still secure, then reaching the end of the little arc, heading backward toward Tyler again. The boy does not tire of this new game. When Tyler lets the little bucket's arcs grow shorter until it settles, chains straight down, Robbie turns his head around. "Again," he says, and Tyler complies, pulling the yellow bucket with his son inside back toward him. Then, lifting his arms above his head, he casts the bucket down from the steepest drop yet, not too fast; it'll scare the boy.

But Robbie's shrieks are outbursts of pleasure, of unfiltered joy. In the world a little one lives in, everything is in the now. Nevertheless, little ones grow up; they can't stop it. To the youngster, each day is possibility and adventure, sometimes a burden; time passing slowly or faster depending on the enjoyment or worry of the day. Either way, the days ahead seem endless to the young. Much later, to the old-timer, they become a precious commodity, rapidly fading, yet each day made up of the same twenty-four hours, one rotation of the Earth. In the life of the Earth, our seventy or eighty years is a nothing. Can it be all we are given?

"Again, Daddy," Robbie says when the bucket begins to settle.

So it goes, on and on. Tyler is in no hurry, and Robbie never gets his fill. The sun still burns brightly, the magic light still a ways off, so Tyler revels in their own magic time, soaking it in like the boy does, absorbed only in the happy moment's abundant purity and grace, entirely sufficient, undistracted by thoughts of responsibilities or mounting bills or faraway invasions and crazy dictators and another war. Imagine, indeed.

* * *

The light breeze now brings a bit of a shiver, the sun lazily lowering toward the flat Michigan horizon, settling in behind the thin flakes and feathers of distant cirrus clouds now glowing orange and red to match the leaves, and purple on the fringes. A quick check of Robbie's diaper, laying him on his back on a suitably dry if not entirely clean picnic table. It's soaked. Velcro tabs let go, and Tyler slides the Huggie with its Sesame Street characters off his tiny bottom, feeling the diaper's satisfying heft. Dry diaper affixed, pants raised back up and little jacket zipped, hoodie at rest, not cold enough to need it yet and better to see Robbie's thickening and curly brown hair; the hood would mat it down even if he slipped it off for the photo. Then it's off to the location Tyler has selected, the top of a fort made of greenish wood, pressure-treated with some mysterious chemical to withstand the elements instead of rotting. He places Robbie in just the spot, asking him to stay there and look back at his dad. Tyler then retreats to ground level, crouching down on the wood chips on the ground so that his camera is looking up at the boy with reddish orange leaves and clouds of a similar hue behind him underneath that glorious, blessed blue. The timeless beauty of a public park in autumn stands out even in a suburb like Livonia, full of shrubs and well-tended lawns; how much more so in largely treeless Manhattan or Chicago or Detroit. The locals living in those concrete deserts must especially relish the verdant oasis of a well-developed green space. A welcome diversion from the sterile, entrapping cityscape.

He turns on the flash, at its lowest setting, to make sure Robbie's features are distinctly lit, not silhouetted into grainy darkness by the still bright backdrop. The fill-flash will make Robbie pop out in the photo with hyper-clarity, he knows. No need to bracket the exposure, he's sure of the setting and wants all four clicks left on the roll to ensure he gets one with an expression suitably happy or cute or inquisitive, whatever Robbie is feeling. The expression on Robbie's face is what will make this work or fail.

"C'mon, Robbie; look this way," he begs, trying to make it sound inviting, not a command to be stubbornly disobeyed, those Terrible Two outbreaks of willful independence already appearing at times, though Robbie's second birthday is still nearly a full month away. They'll go to the zoo to celebrate, he's already decided—the boy is too young to have real friends to invite over. Another great chance for photos and memories. *Got to remember to buy another roll of film*, ASA 200 at least, maybe 400, November notoriously gray, dark to the camera, details obscured if your film isn't fast enough.

Then, for an instant, Robbie is transfixed, staring off at something wonderful, a butterfly? a squirrel? Tyler gently squeezes the shutter release, the camera held steady by his cradling hands, elbows tucked into his chest. Again, with steady aim he fires, then twisting the zoom lens to bring Robbie a bit closer against the fiery background that grows softer, slightly out of focus with this shortened field of view, firing the shutter again, then twisting some more to bring the boy closer still, the wonderment on his face still there, firing for the last time just before Robbie turns away, the moment forever ended. Christmas for camera-wielding parents comes every time they pick up their film from the drugstore and open the envelope to see what turned out and what eluded them, one of the few mysteries left in the adult world.

***

I had a vision of love / And it was all that you've given me…

 He drives home seemingly victorious from the playground photo shoot, the radio playing that Mariah Carey song again, kind of catchy but tiresome because it's on all the time. Why does he listen to that dumb pop station? The one that used to be found at preset button number five on the in-dash stereo he'd installed in Christie's Sunbird three or four years ago, now part of the mangled mess of sheet metal from what had once been stamped into pieces just the right shape and size by a monstrous press in that same plant where Tyler had worked, back when he took employment for granted, just something you did between twenty-two and sixty-five, something you're stuck with, not something to be appreciated or valued.

 When he'd found this new used car, a deep green '85 Chevy Cavalier, from a classified ad in the *Free Press* promising a "near-mint" condition that was surprisingly accurate on a car with nearly sixty thousand miles, one of the radio buttons had been set to this station, 107.8 FM. He'd changed the other buttons to stations he listens to—classic rock and sports talk mostly, plus one "alternative rock" station he rarely selects but keeps set because it's a lifeline to younger, cooler versions of himself, and the Detroit affiliate of National Public Radio, WDET. This pop music station, again button number five since it's the highest frequency of his chosen stations, the farthest to the right if the car still had the old analog radio frequency gauge, like a sideways thermometer with a red horizontal line indicating where you were on the dial, plays whatever songs are currently hot, popular. The same songs again and again throughout the day. He prefers tunes from ten or twelve years ago, when he was a teenager in high school and more in touch with songs as they came out. Maybe they were better in the late Seventies or early Eighties or maybe he was just the right age to feel a connection to the music. It mattered more back then, to him, just as these new songs must matter intensely to the teens of today, which is sad because these songs have such little intensity. Like this pathetic Mariah Carey song, now winding down. Kids today must have enough intensity in their lives already, without the music.

The song is over, and the radio DJ mentions this, ominously: World oil prices, driven up by the tense situation in Kuwait and Iraq, have hit an all-time high of over forty dollars a barrel, and will surely drive gas prices up higher from today's average price of $1.34 a gallon, he says. Which is pretty reasonable compared with Europe or Japan, he feels compelled to remind his listeners. And the price really hasn't come up much since the Oil Embargo of 1974, when Americans first heard of OPEC and the price of gas first broke over a buck a gallon. Prices here in southeast Michigan are lower than the national average, the DJ says, trying to ease the worry a bit, now that he's brought it up. This station's usually so upbeat and enthusiastic and now he's caught himself being a downer.

*　*　*

Divine Mercy's varsity basketball team opens the season with a road victory, 42-38, led by Nicki's twelve points (5 of 7 shooting, 2 for 2 free throws). No other starter on either team shoots even fifty percent. Mercy's coach, Virginia Myers, makes a mental note to put in some more plays for the off-guard. Nicki's going to get the opportunity to put some points up. The next game will be at home.

19

Robbie and Tyler walk mitten-in-hand into the daycare center, an early morning frost serving as a reminder that winter in Michigan is not far off. Robbie's wearing a knit wool cap, insulated boots, winter coat zipped up over the top of the sweatsuit outfit, blue with an orange basketball and the words, "World's Greatest" in white letters, nothing else. The officially licensed *NBA Champions: Detroit Pistons* merchandise is ridiculously expensive, although Robbie does have one tee shirt—and Tyler has two—that he broke down and bought last spring after they beat the Trailblazers for a second straight world championship, something to remember, to hold on to. Tyler takes off his son's winter hat, his mittens and his coat, while unzipping his own down jacket. It feels hot inside after coming in from the morning chill.

As soon as he gives his father a hug, Robbie spins away and bounces off to join his day-care friends, little boys and girls playing together in harmony, until two of them want the same colorful object. The loser of the ensuing tug-a-war inhales noisily as tears well up, prelude to a crying fit that the daycare ladies will take in stride with soothing words and the appearance of an alternate toy more desirable than the one the two kids were fighting over.

Tyler slides into the Cavalier, his seat all the way back but he still goes through that wiggly body motion to get comfortable, like he had to with Christie's Sunbird. Really the same car, the Sunbird and Cavalier, brought to the market by seperate divisions within the GM empire. The same four-cylinder, push-rod engine, same platform, just a different body style and slightly different interior. He got the Cavalier from a guy selling it through the newspaper, asking $3,800. Tyler got him down to $3,500, exactly the amount he'd received from the insurance company for the totaled Sunbird—$4,000 minus the $500 deductible. One thing he likes better about the "new" car is its manual transmission. He prefers driving a stick to the automatics that have largely taken over the American market these days. It's a little more economical on the gas and helps the little I-4 engine feel almost peppy. The Sunbird with its automatic was pretty slow to get moving. Soon after he lands his next job, he's already decided, he will trade this Cavalier in for a new car, not a wimpy economy car like this one or the girlie Sunbird, though not a land yacht either. Maybe an Olds Cutlass Cierra, smaller than the Cutlass Supreme, the one that's in the TV ads all the time, *not your father's Oldsmobile*. Or maybe one of the new Saturns, the car that is supposed to remake General Motors, though the standard Saturn engine, a little four-banger, puts out only eighty-five horsepower, like something from Eastern Europe, a Yugo or Trabant, wimpy as can be. He'd certainly opt for the more powerful optional engine. He'd really prefer something more like a Camaro, of course, but it'd be ridiculous to horse around with Robbie's car seat in a two-door coupe, have to remember that. A quarter tank of fuel left, he notices. No need yet to stop for gas. Though it's easier when he doesn't have the boy with him, so maybe he will if he sees a good price.

He heads down Eight Mile Road toward his doctor for the two-month follow-up to his release from the hospital. He feels fine, mostly, but it seems best to comply with the medical advice coming off a closed-head injury that left him out cold for two days. No one ever called it a "coma" but isn't that what it was, that period of unconsciousness, two whole days and then some? If you follow Eight-Mile toward the east for ten or so miles, it changes from a suburban thoroughfare bisecting Livonia and becomes instead the border of the badlands of the city of Detroit to the south and a series of mostly civilized suburbs to the north, a virtual DMZ with hookers and drug dealers, day and night. You don't see any of that in staid Livonia. He passes up another gas station.

On the news talk-show station the conversation is all about the new Germany, officially reunited a few days ago, East and West no more. It's the *end of the Cold War*, one of radio voices is saying. We can get on with the *peace dividend* now and Eastern Europe can rebuild and prosper. A sunny vision of Russia just letting go, content to see the Soviet empire recede into the night. Another guest on the show is skeptical. "They still have all those nukes. And Russia knows that without the belligerence of atomic muscle, they're a third-world country with a wrecked economy," he says. *Don't be too quick to check off this box on the to-do list for democracy and peace.*

Tyler's Cavalier pulls into the parking lot of a bland brick and glass building with a sign reading "Livonia Internists" where a couple of dozen doctors, labs and little medical supply companies share office space. He signs in on the sheet in front of a chubby receptionist who doesn't look up to greet him, and takes a seat in the waiting room with three others: two men, an Asian and a black guy, and a woman in a veil and a shapeless, full-body covering of dark fabric, at least he assumes it's a woman; how would you know? A virtual United Nations, here in Livonia.

He picks up a *Sports Illustrated* from mid-June with Nolan Ryan on the cover after he had thrown his sixth career no-hitter, a record, at the age of 43. Tyler opens the magazine to the cover story. Ryan already had held the mark for no-hitters when he threw his fifth back in 1981, breaking the long-standing record of the great Sandy Koufax. Ryan, the article says, also has the record for most total strikeouts in a career, far more than any other pitcher in history. But it is this sixth no-hitter, thrown by a certified baseball geriatric, that may be his most amazing feat. The story details just how Ryan mowed down each of the Oakland A's for his latest no-no, mostly with his blazing fastball, of course, but a surprising number of curveballs, too. One of those unlucky, hitless A's was lead-off man Rickey Henderson, a lock for the Hall of Fame, who also had happened to be Ryan's 5,000th career strikeout victim, last year, and had said afterward, "If he ain't struck you out, you ain't nobody."

Eventually, Tyler is ushered into a little room where a nurse checks his blood pressure and lets him know that the doctor will see him soon. Fifteen minutes later, Dr. Mohammed Klira knocks on the door and steps inside the room before Tyler has a chance to respond to the knock. The doctor looks through the patient file in a manila folder while asking Tyler how he has been feeling since he came home from the hospital. Has he been sleeping and eating well? Satisfied with Tyler's responses, he then asks: "How are you doing without Christina?"

Tyler is unprepared for such a question from this man he hardly knows. Of course, Klira would remember Christie as a regular patient; he knows Tyler mostly as her husband.

"I miss her, of course," he says. "I thought I was starting to get over it, the loss. Then the accident, you know, and maybe I had too much time in the hospital just thinking about everything. And it didn't help that I lost my job, too. With GM."

Dr. Klira listens to this and makes a few notes on a paper inside the folder.

"That is a lot for anyone to deal with. How are you handling it all?"

"I don't really let things get to me. I know I'll be all right."

The doc nods and writes out orders for blood and urine samples for routine tests. "And I want to have an MRI scan of your head. It will give us a thorough look at your brain tissue to help us be sure you have fully recovered from your injury. Every indication is that you are much better but sometimes trauma can remain hidden. And we need to be mindful of the stress you are under. You might think about meeting with someone who you can talk through all of this."

Tyler's blank expression prompts the doctor to add: "A psychologist."

Before he leaves for his next patient, Klira asks Tyler how his son is doing. His forehead creases with mild irritation at his patient's automatic non-answer: "Fine." He tells Tyler not to be overly concerned if the boy regresses a bit over the next few months as his mother's continuing absence may take a toll on his little spirit. This echoes what Robbie's pediatrician had said a couple of months ago, just before the accident that put him in the hospital. Then Klira reminds Tyler to keep up with Robbie's immunization schedule, though the boy is not this doc's patient. He shakes Tyler's hand warmly and disappears out the door.

A nurse steps into the room and draws blood from Tyler's left arm, enough to fill four little test tube vials, then covers the wound with a Band-Aid. She hands him a little Dixie cup and tells him to step into the toilet room and fill it. In a few days, they'll call him with the test results. That is, unless they are abnormal—then he'll have to come back in and meet again with his doctor. The MRI will be done in a different office building and will have to be scheduled, two or more weeks out.

***

Next, Tyler drives back across town to the public library. On the two days a week when Robbie is in daycare, Tyler spends at least a couple of hours hunting for job leads. Two days a week is about right. It allows Tyler to get serious about his job search while keeping his daycare bill somewhat manageable. It's expensive but it's good for Robbie to be around other kids his age, so he can continue to develop his social skills. Tuesdays and Thursdays usually. This week is different because Monday was Columbus Day, a holiday for those with jobs. So, it's Wednesday and Friday this week.

In any event, this leaves five days out of every seven that Tyler can be with his son all day long. If he was working, they'd only have the weekends together. *I'm the one raising Robbie*, he thinks with pride, not some collection of daycare ladies watching a whole herd of kids, yet entrusted to make all the right impressions in each of their pliable, unformed brains. Future adult personalities determined by experiences they will never remember: astronauts, ministers and serial-killers alike. Tyler knows it's on him if he wants the boy to grow up with his head on straight.

But not working gnaws at Tyler, and there are plenty of times when he's no good to be around anybody, even his son. Each week of unemployment further dulls his sharpness and erodes a bit of his self-confidence, which he needs in spades if he's going to interview well. No one wants to hire someone unsure of himself. It has only been two months since he was let go by GM, but it feels longer, probably because of the foggy time he spent in the hospital.

In the library's reference room, a wooden rack holds the latest editions of local and out-of-town newspapers, each strung over a long wooden dowel, as if they are wet and hanging to dry. He takes one stick at a time from the rack and scans the classifieds and the business sections of the national newspapers—*USA Today*, the *Wall Street Journal* and the *New York Times*—then some of the papers from relatively nearby but out-of-state cities—the *Toledo Blade*, *Cleveland Plain Dealer*, *Columbus Dispatch*, the *Akron Beacon-Journal* and, finally, the *Chicago Tribune*. Always the *Trib* last, because Chicago is not where a Detroit sports fan would ever want to move. The Windy City is home to the rivals of each of the Detroit pro teams—the Bulls to the Pistons, Bears to Lions,

White Sox to Tigers, Black Hawks to Red Wings—each pairing in the same division of its sport's league. For the right job, of course, he'd get over it. But he looks through the other cities' papers first.

Occasionally, there is in the HELP WANTED section a human resources job listing that interests him. He carefully writes down the pertinent information, or if it is particularly detailed, reluctantly takes the paper over to the library's Xerox machine, holds the page against the glass and pays a dime for a photocopy. It's not the ten cents that's the problem; it's the hassle of fumbling with the newspaper's wooden staff and the copy machine's cover that only opens just so far. Later, at home, he will carefully compose a cover letter to specifically address the needs of the hiring company as best he can discern them from the ad and from any supplemental research he has been able to do at the library. Sitting in front of his personal computer, a "clone" of an IBM AT made by a company in Texas called "Dell Computer Corporation," he is able to call up a cover letter he had written to another company and edit it right on his screen, manipulating it until he is convinced it is perfect, or at least ready to print. He signs the letter and puts it in an envelope with a copy of his résumé and sends it off in the mail, knowing he will likely never hear a word back in response. But somebody must get hired to fill each of these jobs and eventually it will be him, he figures. And, *seriously*, he has worked for the world's largest corporation; that has to count for a lot. Not everybody realizes just how moribund GM's human resources group has become. That experience will look good to a smaller company aiming to grow bigger.

Just one promising item in the want ads of all those newspapers today, a listing in the *Toledo Blade* for a human resources professional "with up-to-date skills"—that's code for *not too old*; no problem for Tyler. The company is Lockery Manufacturing ("formerly Lockery Screw Products") with a new "100,000 square foot state-of-the art manufacturing facility." That will seem big to most people—the size of two or three typical K-Mart stores—but to Tyler, it's one-twentieth or so the size of GM's Garden City Stamping, just one of the hundreds of plants in GM's global empire.

Maybe a smaller company *would be* better; perhaps he could make a difference at this Lockery company. Tyler takes the newspaper-on-a-stick over to the reference room and a waiting Xerox machine, and makes a copy of the ad, fumbling with the stiff pole's awkwardness. The copy is all crooked on the page but that doesn't matter to him. Before he leaves the library, he will come back to this reference room and look up what he can find about Lockery Manufacturing … or Screw Products … if the reference book is not completely *up to date*. A company that manufactures screws doesn't sound too exciting, but his profession is all about managing people and people processes regardless of what the company does, one not much more or less exciting than the next. Besides, a job is a job at this point.

None of the rest of the newspapers he peruses yield any more job leads, so his work today will be limited to Lockery. The company's name is oddly familiar—because, he realizes, it makes him think of the town in Scotland where that Pan Am flight went down a couple of years ago, bombed from within by some suicidal lunatic thinking he was a hero or martyr. *Lockerbie.* A routine take-off, passengers just settling in, trying to get comfortable, exhaling deeply now that they were safely onboard, maybe after they had to run to the gate, relaxing now. Then a sudden ear-splitting noise, the explosion that rips apart the thin sheet metal separating the cabin's warm, calm air from the freezing, non-air outside, and they're ejected into the atmosphere, still alive momentarily, arms and legs flailing as they fall, unable to breathe, only a frozen nothingness rushing into their lungs. Below it's quiet on a Scottish golf course, the birthplace of the sport, its ancestral home suddenly defiled by a deluge of bodies from the heavens that minutes ago were alive and chatty, waiting for the drink order.

Tyler knows how this will go. He'll do his best to get his cover letter and résumé off in tomorrow's mail. Being quick in response is essential. In this economy, a job posting in even a small market newspaper like the *Blade* will generate many more responses than the company will want to process—his peers in HR combing through perhaps the first dozen or fifteen letters they receive to cull down to six or eight résumés from candidates who actually possess the required skill set and experience. Over the next couple of weeks, those résumés will be bandied about within HR until it is decided which are the four or five most promising. Then some HR functionary will call these four or five candidates as soon as it can be arranged—preliminary telephone interviews that will place enormous pressure on the candidates to foster a positive impression with the disconnected voice, no visual cues to help steer the interview toward a promising assessment. But, as it turns out, the functionary doing the screening won't have much authority anyway, perhaps whittling away just one of the candidates as poorly suited for the role for some capricious and arbitrary reason. Then the remaining three or four remaining candidates will be given the opportunity of in-person interviews, each candidate undergoing several back-to-back meetings with some of the decision-makers, if they can be scheduled in a reasonable time. When the interviews are complete, each of the managers who did the questioning will have to meet to compare assessments. Perhaps two weeks will go by before such a meeting can be arranged. Then they will look over their notes to try to remember something that distinguishes one candidate from the others. If one candidate emerges as the clear consensus choice, the company may move forward with a job offer. More likely, two candidates will be invited back as "finalists" for another round of interviews, leading to one being selected as the winner. Unless an internal candidate has since emerged. Or a hiring freeze has been put in place. Or the job description has been changed. But, putting all that aside, it is clear that the key to even getting the initial opportunity to be considered for this game of corporate roulette is to have your letter arrive and be opened among the first twelve or so. After that, HR will simply not be bothered to look at another application; they will have enough intriguing potential candidates already. Tyler's résumé and killer cover letter may indicate assuredly that he is the next Barry Sanders or Michael Jordan of HR and no one at the company would ever know it.

* * *

Home from the library, he glances at his telephone's answering machine. Its little red light is flashing. Maybe one of the companies he sent his résumé last week or the week before has left a message that will begin the long, slow dance of follow-up calls and telephone interviews, then a visit to corporate headquarters for a nerve-racking battery of in-person interviews, followed by *The Wait*. Nope, it's an agent from a life insurance company, Allstate, leaving a long and rambling message, an annoyance, but it does remind him that when his little severance period is up, GM will no longer be popping for his term life policy. He can't leave Robbie destitute if something should happen to him. So, he writes down the number but makes a mental note that he is not sold on this agent, whose distant, disembodied voice on the answering machine sounds detached to the point of apathy. The voice is at odds with the TV commercial Tyler has seen in some variation a hundred times, usually during college football games but sometime the NFL. He doesn't feel like he'd be in *good hands*—those warm, comforting hands, extended and open, touching at the pinkies to form a chalice of loving protection. Maybe it would be better to just open the Yellow Pages and start from scratch when he's ready to think about life insurance. But not today.

 The clear glass dish over by the microwave catches his eye and he remembers he needs to return it to Nora Johnston, the nosy neighbor who brought him that pie thing which wasn't half bad even though it sat for almost a week in his fridge, covered with plastic wrap, while he was in the hospital. He'll walk the dish over to her house and then it will be time to go fetch Robbie from daycare. But he ought to stop and get gas on the way, before the boy is onboard; the fumes can't be good for him. *Fill your tank before the price goes up,* the guy on the radio warned. Once they start talking up the prices, the gas stations are sure to follow suit, and next thing you know it's $1.69 and 9/10ths and climbing.

He strides with purpose up the brick walkway to the front door of the ranch house across the street from his, nearly identical in size but with much more elaborate landscaping. *Let's make this quick.* He sees a little motion through the glare of the front window and before he can even ring the bell, Nora opens the door wide and beckons him in. Tyler explains that he is just returning the dish, thanks her for the pie and mentions that he needs to run off to get Robbie. But even as he fights the urge to turn and run, he sees that he's already most of the way in the doorway and she is talking a mile a minute as she leads him through the neat-as-a-pin living room over a plush white carpet. He catches the distinct stink of cigarette smoke hanging in the air from some time ago—though the air is not cloudy and there isn't even an ashtray in sight. She offers him coffee.

"Real coffee. You'll taste the difference and never drink that instant again," she says enthusiastically.

A mostly finished glass of red wine sits on the coffee table next to an issue of *People*, cover and back cover and spine making a low-rising tent as it lies there spread-eagle, hastily marking the page left off, somewhere in the middle of the magazine. Nora sees that Tyler has noticed the wine glass.

"Would you rather have a glass of merlot? I have a bottle open from a good little batch Stan brought back from his last trip to northern California. You'll like it. I'll pour you a little while we wait for the coffee to brew. Actually, it goes well with coffee. It has just enough body to hold its own, even with a rich, hearty coffee. I hope you like it strong; is there any other way? I can put out some cheese and crackers, if you like, too."

Tyler begs off the cheese and crackers, and explains again that he has to go get Robbie soon. If she hears him, she makes no sign of it. Once she has her stainless steel Cuisinart coffee machine fired up, she leads Tyler back into the living room and motions for him to take a seat on the couch. She fills a wine glass for him and refills her own practically to the brim. He takes a sniff like he knows he's supposed to do, but the glass is filled too high to give it a swirl, so he takes a little slurp into his mouth and rolls it over his tongue a few satisfying seconds before gulping it down. It's warm, dry and a bit oaky, in a good way, he imagines.

"That's good," is all he can think to say, not real sure about the oaky part.

"Yes, it's from a great year, 1984. We were just coming out of the last recession, remember? The grapes seemed to bounce back, too, that year. It has a taste of plum and a hint of currant in its body," she says before taking another hearty swig of the dark red wine.

1984. That was the year we were all going to be slaves to a totalitarian Big Brother, Tyler is thinking. It was seemingly so far off in the distant future when Orwell wrote it, must have been hard to imagine ever arriving, and now so quickly receding into the rearview mirror of time. The year, too, of Michael Jackson's *Thriller* and, of course, those Detroit Tigers with their incredible start that they kept going all the way to the World Series.

"Even with its healthy body it has a softness to it, a *fleshiness* the vineyard calls it, especially compared with their stouter cabernets." She lowers her voice just a notch, leans in a bit toward him, crowding his comfort zone and adds knowingly, "The cabs get that from a higher concentration of tannin."

A long, slender leg still sporting a luxuriant summer tan extends from a short, frilly white skirt and rests at the ankle over her other knee. The place where the lower side of her thigh on the underneath leg disappears under her skirt is dimly lit in the shadow of her foot and ankle, but he can see it well enough to imagine the softness of the flesh just at the point where leg and buttocks merge in exquisite feminine harmony.

She catches him noticing and says, "I must look the fright. I had my tennis lesson and even in the crisp air this morning, worked up a good sweat, as usual. I was just about to take my shower when I saw you coming up the walk. I'm so glad I didn't miss you. I've been meaning to see how you were doing. We read about the accident but thought it best to give you some privacy."

Nora's hair is drawn back, and he can faintly see the impression of where a hat or visor lay tight against her forehead and above her ears. Her hair is creased there, just a bit. Tiny lines form in her skin at the outside corner of each eye, especially when she says something particularly expressive, the beginnings of crow's feet, the only concession to age on an otherwise well-preserved body. She's wearing a little less make-up than usual, and he can see that her mascara and blush are a little uneven, dabbed away on one side with some tennis-practice facial sweat, but it serves to soften her a bit, make her more human and less the abstract, obnoxious neighbor he has always thought her to be.

"Where are all these photos from? They look like Ansel Adams' work. Are they?" Tyler asks, showing off his knowledge of photography as he eyes three matted and framed black-and-white prints of rocky, western landscapes hanging on the opposite wall. She's clearly out-classed him in wine sophistication; now it's his turn to take the lead.

"Oh, no," she says, lightly laughing. "Stan will love to hear you thought so. He shot each of those. He loves to go out west and capture the roughness of it all, the rock formations, the big fir trees and waterfalls, always in black-and-white. He says you notice the texture and contrast so much more when your eyes aren't distracted by the colors, and he's right. I'll have to tell him you admired his prints when he gets home. He's out of town until tomorrow."

This last bit of information turns their wine-sharing, couch-sitting closeness into conspiracy. She has regained the upper hand, having bested him again in conversational mastery, even when they were talking about photography, a strong suit for him.

He sips his wine and mutters approvingly, "Yes, they're beautiful. He has quite an eye." This would give him the opportunity to get off the couch and walk over closer to the prints, getting some space and distance from Nora's glowing presence. But he hesitates, needing to finish his sip, and the moment is gone as she steers the flow back to his accident two months ago.

"The paper didn't go into too much detail other than to say you were in the hospital. We saw that you had an older couple taking care of your son. Your parents?"

"No, my wife's parents." Bringing up Christie should help counter the talk of Stan, but only seems to deepen the conspiracy.

"Oh, where do they live?" Nora asks.

"Florida. They came right up when they heard about it. The accident."

"Oh, that's nice that you're still keeping up a relationship with them. I'm sure they still consider you part of their family."

"Yeah," Tyler says, finishing another little swig. "Or at least Robbie. He's their only grandson."

Nora wants to know about his injuries and his stay at the hospital. Tyler covers the high points—unconscious for a couple of days and then they kept him there several more days, mostly for observation, as he seemed to have sustained no lasting damage. No talk of the teenage girl killed in the other car; that was in the newspapers she has surely read.

"But you've been home a lot since then. Aren't you cleared to go back to work?"

"I'm kind of in transition," he says delicately. But she doesn't seem to understand that, so he just comes out with it. "I lost my job at GM right before the accident."

Nora straightens up in some sort of involuntary recoil, creating a little more space between them, which helps Tyler breathe.

"I had no idea," she says in the way of someone who expects to know most everything about a neighbor. "That's terrible. You've had so much *difficulty* to go through all at once." She leans back in, closer even than before. "Just let me know if there's anything I can do for you."

"Oh, I have a little severance from GM to tide me over and I'm hot on the tail…trail, I mean…of some pretty good job leads. Lots of irons in the fire. I'm not too worried."

Nora smiles, relieved of the burden of further exploring the depressing topic of Tyler's joblessness, and takes another gulp of wine, nearly emptying her glass. She looks up at the ceiling, lost for a moment in the fine taste of the merlot and the warm buzz of its afterglow. This provides Tyler with the opportunity to gaze at her generous cleavage, the top blouse button helpfully undone. Smooth, tanned skin wraps tightly around each breast as big and solid as a six-ounce softball, rising up as she leans back gazing at a still higher point on the ceiling, no sag at all. They have to be fake, enlarged and yet firmer than the compact breasts of a twenty-year-old gymnast, the wonders of modern silicone science. Still, they are something to behold. Her gaze lowers; a satisfied smile has taken residence on her graceful face. For a moment, Tyler sees within her a hidden personality, a lazy poet perhaps or maybe a latent killer, living inside the normalcy of another tennis-playing, suburban housewife.

Then she snaps out of her little reverie. "Our coffee! I almost forgot. You'll love the rich taste of this bean I've discovered at the market, Kenya Double-A, very high-grade. And buying this coffee helps those poor, starving people in central Africa. They've always got a drought going, as I'm sure you know."

She's already up and about the kitchen, filling two mugs. "You take anything in it?" she asks, bringing a little tray that she sits before them with their mugs steaming and a little porcelain pitcher with cream, a sugar bowl and another little bowl, all matching, with several pink packages of artificial sweetener.

She lifts her mug to her lips, undefiled black coffee from those double-A-rated Kenya beans, and eyes him through the steam over the gently angled mug, cautiously sipping the hot brew. The tease must be a game for her, confident in her attractiveness but lonely. Surely, she doesn't have anything more in mind for him than this high-octane flirt. Neither does he; it would be nothing but trouble.

Tyler pours a little creamer into his coffee. He would have added more but Nora didn't leave him much room; even in this, she's crowding him. He stirs it gently with a spoon from the tray, but it still looks too hot. *Just a sip of scalding liquid will burn your tongue,* he's thinking. Then you have that irritating numbness for a couple days that cripples your taste and can even cause you to bite your tongue; it gets in the way suddenly as if the burn has blinded it or made it sloppy in pulling back from the teeth that form its home. He finishes his wine instead. Nora pours a little more in his glass, perhaps from a second bottle.

"Did you hear what verdict came down today from the jury in that Mapplethorpe case in Cincinnati?" Nora asks, taking charge again of their conversation. She's a talker, a pro. You have to hand it to her. "That artist with the photos that upset everybody down there."

"Yeah. He put a crucifix in a jar of pee and we're supposed to call that art and be glad he's getting an endowment for it, our tax dollars at work."

"Well, actually that was another so-called artist, Andres Serrano, with the crucifix. But it happened about the same time, and everybody gets them mixed up," she says gently. "Mapplethorpe exhibited a series of black-and-white photos of himself and other men in, you know, homo-erotic poses. With whips and what not. It was all meant to shock and get attention."

"Not what the art museum goers were expecting, I'm sure," Tyler says, wanting no further details. "So, what happened with the jury?"

"Not guilty. They found it was all free speech and not covered by any obscenity law. I'm not one for censorship, mind you, but I have to say that these weren't any images I would want hanging in my art gallery."

"So maybe he didn't break the law, but the museum isn't being forced to show his pictures again, is it?"

"No, and I wouldn't expect the good people of Cincinnati to welcome them back any time soon," she says, now looking for a chance to end this conversation and move to another topic. She must feel the sexiness of the room being sucked away as thoughts of the Mapplethorpe photos unsettle Tyler's mind, even though she had stopped short of a full description.

Tyler clearly is looking to escape. He sips at his coffee, still hot but drinkable, and looks at his watch. "I better go," he says. "Gotta get over to the daycare."

"Well, you can finish your coffee first," Nora says in a tone that fails to conceal her irritation. "It'll help clear your head before you get in the car to drive anywhere."

Maybe from this suggestion put into his mind, Tyler now does feel just the start of a buzz. He has only had one glass, but a pretty big one filled all the way up and maybe just a bit of a refill, or did she top it off twice? Perhaps mixed with unseen toxins he's unwittingly inhaled—still floating in the air from cigarettes consumed earlier in the day, plus the perfume he gets a whiff of whenever Nora leans in. It all adds up to a slight fogginess. Surely not a problem to drive on one glass of wine, but just to be sure he'll work on his coffee some more.

"How's your boy?" Nora asks, smiling, sensing another round won.

"He's great. But I do think it shook him up when I was away in the hospital. With his mom gone, you know…" he trails off.

"It has to have been hard on him," Nora says, tapping with two fingers on Tyler's leg, just above the knee. "We don't really understand what's going on in a young child's mind…" But then the master conversationalist trails off, realizing too late she has led them to a place where she has no experience that can compare to his own.

"We're really close, and he knows I'm there for him. He's a great kid. He's bright and active and usually pretty cheerful. He doesn't give me a hard time, really."

Tyler takes one last gulp of coffee and sets the mug down, still half-full, as he begins to rise off the couch, all in one motion. "Thanks, again, Nora. For everything—the pie, the glass of wine and the coffee. But I really do have to get going."

She doesn't fight him this time but walks him to the door.

"Take care of yourself," she says and leans forward and up on her toes to give him a hug, a squeeze through his back that draws her lean, perfumed firmness up against his chest and thighs and slightly twitching crotch, holding there long enough that it doesn't feel like he is leaving at all. But then she lets go and he has the door open and the space between them grows again like any two neighbors with lives that never quite intersect.

* * *

Robbie is in bed now and Tyler flips through the channels. Nothing much on. A CNN anchor details the latest school shooting in lawless America, this time by two women. You don't see that too often, so Tyler hovers on this channel. At Adamson High School in Dallas late this afternoon, two females "of undetermined age" drove up to a group of students waiting for rides home and opened fire on them. A girl was hit and taken to a nearby hospital. The students didn't recognize the women, and they are still at large. This latest incident makes five school shootings nationwide in the past six weeks, including an earlier one at this same Dallas high school. Officials are at a loss to explain the surge in shootings in American schools, the newsman says.

* * *

Something stirs inside him and he awakes in the dark, vaguely unsettled. By a dream already forgotten? Or some stray worry; he has enough surely. His waking hours are full of plenty of time to concentrate on his problems, his job now to get a good night's sleep so he has the energy, the focus, to do what he can to move forward during the day. Time now is for sleep. He turns to the image inside his darkened mind of the smoke-throwing pitcher he becomes when he needs to, throwing harder even than Nolan Ryan, mowing opposing batters down one by one. Rickey Henderson now at the plate, in a soiled Oakland A's green-and yellow uniform, dirty from sliding into second and third earlier in the game, two more stolen bases for the tally on his plaque someday in Cooperstown. "You ain't nobody," Tyler says to himself as he blows it by the batter; Henderson has no chance.

20

Thursday morning. Tyler should be sleeping in. No daycare today; no job searching at the library. But it's just another morning to Robbie; no calendar in his head or hanging over his crib. So, the boy wakes up at six-fifteen, pretty much the same as any morning. He fusses a bit, then starts talking out loud to the *Sesame Street* characters on the mobile above his head. Tyler has raised them high enough over the crib that he can't reach them standing up on his tippy toes, hanging onto the side rails. It won't be long before the boy will be able to get out of the crib. He tries to climb out, to swing a leg up over the rail. It's still too high. But he can almost pull himself up. He's getting stronger and his grip is impressive. It's time for Tyler to look for a new bed, low to the floor and without bars, the opposite of a crib's philosophy of imprisonment—a bed that will let the boy come and go as he pleases without tumbling out of a high perch and hurting himself. Of course, the kid still can't turn a doorknob, so he won't have reign over the whole house when he wakes up and decides he should be somewhere else, but that day's coming soon.

Tyler turns his head all the way around to look back at his clock, and that sets the room spinning as he lays there. It continues to spin. He hasn't felt this sensation since the last time he drank way too much and went to bed before sobering up, probably back in college. Back then this feeling was a normal part of a weekend, but he doesn't associate it with his post-graduate adulthood. The room begins to steady and then everything feels fine. He slowly, deliberately swings his feet out of the bed, a queen-size Serta that, of course, got more of a workout when Christie slept there, too. He still sleeps on his side, the left, and probably should flip the mattress soon or it will become noticeably flatter there. Even before Robbie thinks to cry, Tyler has had his first-thing-in-the-morning whiz, washed his hands and brushed his teeth, even spun a Q-tip luxuriously inside each ear canal, silently relishing the sensation of spinning cotton fibers against the tiny hairs deep inside his ear, but not the micro hairs that inhabit even deeper, unseen reaches, performing the mysterious task of translating waves of sound into nerve impulses, each sound wave causing vibrations of the eardrum to activate those three tiny bones—hammer, anvil and stirrup—whose twitches in turn are picked up by the nearly microscopic hairs called cilia in a snail-shaped cochlea, the inner ear. It is the cilia that generate the nerve signals that go straight to the brain, interpreted as various differentiated sounds, though no one yet knows exactly how a vibrating hair follicle creates an electrical signal in the nerve. Scientists can identify every step in a complicated process like human hearing, but they are at a loss to tell us how those crazy hairs swaying one way for a Mozart symphony and another way for a screaming baby generate discernible electric impulses in the nerve endings to create the sensation of those sounds in our brains.

Tyler opens the door. Robbie looks up with a smile full of joy and surprise as if he never expected it to be his father opening the door just like every other morning, at least since Tyler came home from the hospital. Yet, the boy holds up his arms expectantly, clearly familiar with this routine. A fatherly embrace is its own reward, but also leads directly to liftoff out of the crib's jail-like confines.

Tyler sets Robbie down on his back on the changing table and removes the heavy, wet diaper and tosses it cleanly into the nearby pail. The boy will soon be getting old enough to start introducing him to the idea of peeing into a toilet, a little blue-and-white plastic version with a deflector shield to direct any errant spray back down into its bucket until he gets the hang of holding his little penis down to shoot the spray where it ought to go. But Tyler has decided he will not rush things, plenty of time for toilet-training; best to make sure that Robbie's good and ready. Reminded by Klira last week, Tyler can see now that Robbie may in fact be regressing. He has seemed at times lost without his mother. He never really had a chance to mourn her leaving as Tyler has, too young to understand at first that she was really gone and not coming back. Now, finally she has vanished from his day-to-day consciousness though surely not from his memory, not yet. A void is harder to know, to identify, than a physical pain but can maim all the same. It's all somehow now taking a toll inside Robbie, an array of unseen electric impulses firing inside his nervous system in ways no one can begin to fathom. Yesterday, after he had made his escape from Nora Johnston's lair, Tyler at the daycare had talked quietly to one of the higher-ups about his son's reverting to mostly one- or two-word thoughts these days. She had noticed it, too, but reassured him that some *regression* was completely normal and temporary. That word again, as if it is tattooed on Robbie's forehead. If it persists, he should discuss it with the pediatrician, of course. In the meantime, Tyler will give his boy extra hugs and make a point to speak to him in clear, complete sentences. And to listen to Robbie even when it's the same thing over and over. Who else will listen if not a father?

"You ready for some breakfast?" Tyler asks his son. Then, realizing he has chopped off the first part of the question like his friend Neticut, Tyler repeats it in full. "Robbie, are you ready for some breakfast?" The redundancy seemingly goes unnoticed by his son. "Okay, Daddy," he says agreeably.

After they finish their cereal—Captain Crunch with Crunchberries for Robbie, Raisin Bran for Tyler—the boy lets his father brush his teeth, wash off his face and pull a brush through his wavy hair. Then Tyler grabs a little Ninja Turtle figurine that will hold his boy's attention for a five-minute car-ride to the grocery store and in the store, riding in the cart, little legs hanging down from the child's perch, father and son sharing the same handlebar from opposite sides. Tyler pushes the cart methodically down each aisle, skipping only the one with dog and cat food and one that's mostly sanitary napkins and other such female supplies. The grocery excursion is the highlight of their morning and they both enjoy taking in the sights and smells all around them. They linger in the cereal aisle; both need to add to their dwindling stash of morning sustenance. As they pass a particularly colorful box adorned with those ubiquitous Care Bears, Robbie lights up. "Wanna try?" he asks his father. "Wanna try dat? Wanna, daddy?"

"Do I want to try that one, you mean?" Tyler repeats, filling out the thought for his son.

"Okay!" Robbie exclaims.

Tyler does not hesitate to grant his son's implied request, though this sugary cereal is by no means the healthiest choice he could make for his son, and he—Tyler—does not have any desire to try it. But all that's beside the point. Robbie is happy, staring at the little Care Bears on the cereal box, imagining the adventures he will have with them when they're reunited by the television in the living room.

* * *

The garage door receives the invisible command from the remote control attached to the passenger-side sun visor and obediently rises. Tyler draws his right hand back onto the steering wheel and aims the Cavalier into the garage. He carries three paper bags full of groceries into his kitchen and then returns to free his son from his car seat just as Robbie begins to get squirmy.

They wrestle a bit in the living room, then Tyler reads him a book, *Clifford the Big Red Dog*, that many years ago had been read to him, by Tyler's mom probably more so than his dad. Fathers were less involved with their kids in those days, except for sports and teaching them to drive. They linger over a lunch of chicken noodle soup and crackers with peanut butter, extra crunchy, of course. What is the point of *creamy* peanut butter, anyway? Good to get the boy started on crunchy so he doesn't have to buy both kinds like Christie would have insisted. Then it's time for Robbie's nap, and Tyler's pretty bushed, too, maybe he'll just watch a little something on TV while relaxing in the recliner. Good to have spent some quality time with the boy today. He has Nicki coming over to babysit later, when he goes out with Lyvia. ESPN has a report on Herschel Walker, on break from the NFL and working out with the U.S. bobsled team, nearly breaking a record while training for the Olympics. It used to be good enough to excel in one sport. Shipped last year from the Cowboys to the Vikings in a blockbuster trade for the insane package of five players and six draft picks, Herschel Walker is *Superman*. But he must feel the pressure from Bo Jackson and that flashy new kid, Deion "Prime Time" Sanders, playing both pro football and big-league baseball. What will Herschel do with his spare time after the Winter Olympics—become a NASCAR driver or split atoms?

Tyler had been thrilled when he'd first heard Lyvia had called him, though he tried to low-key it with his nosy mother-in-law. Rhonda had taken the call, told Lyvia that Tyler had been in an accident and was still in the hospital, slowly recovering. Lyvia would later tell Tyler that she had meant to visit him in the hospital, but her schedule had been crazy at her part-time job at the Borders bookstore that is helping to pay her tuition as a graduate student.

She couldn't get off during visiting hours, so she'd sent the flowers. She had thought about writing her phone number on the little card with the flowers, but decided to hold off just yet. He might have turned out to be a stalker, a male Glenn Close with a *Fatal Attraction,* she must have been thinking. All she really knew about him was the little bit he had told her when he surprised her at the theater while on a date with someone else. Seeking her out when the other girl wasn't around had been caddish, if that was a word, and the fact that within hours he'd been in a serious car accident was just another strike against him, adding to the strangeness of it all. If she'd known then that the other driver had been killed in the wreck, she probably wouldn't have had further contact with him, she would admit to him later.

But there was something about what she remembered from that first brief encounter with this earnest, good-looking young man at the theater, so wanting to meet her but still somewhat *collected* and not too desperate, that intrigued her just enough for her to call him again. She waited a few more days and tried him at home. They had talked for nearly an hour—about the accident and the hospital. And about Rhonda, his mother-in-law. Lyvia had asked him if the woman who had first answered her call was his mother, and Tyler had come clean, that she was in fact his mother-in-law. He hadn't meant to drop all this on her the first phone call, but that led him to add that Rhonda was "actually my late wife's mother who came up to help with my son." Having blurted all that out, he then explained how his young wife had died suddenly seven months earlier—okay, that was a minor distortion; Christie had been dead not quite six full months—and that they had a little boy, Robbie. He was amazed how well she took all this new information about him. She told him a little about herself. She was pursuing a Master's degree in English Literature at the University of Detroit. *Odd. Christie had been an English major, too.* Lyvia mentions that she was born in the Missouri town of Eureka. *What a weird name for a place. It should end with an exclamation point*. But she is already going on about having moved away from Eureka when she was just a little girl. To a far-flung suburb of St. Louis, St. Charles, where her parents still live.

He asked if she would have dinner with him. She hesitated and asked that they keep it to a phone call one more time before meeting. She was quite direct in admitting that she was being cautious until she knew him better, though she did give him her phone number. And her last name, Lamont. Tyler was happy to accept these terms. He'd thrown a lot at her—especially the bit about his wife and kid. Of course, he hadn't quite got around to mentioning how he'd lost his job at GM, or about the girl killed in the accident. Or, for that matter, his father passing away seven years earlier. The telling of all these other tragedies in Tyler's life would have to wait; no point in piling on.

A few days later he called her and again they spoke at length, far longer than Tyler normally talks on the phone. They chatted easily, catching each other's jokes and exaggerations, enjoying the other's aural company like long-time friends but without the disappointments and irritations that invariably build up over time. The sounds of the other's voice register as pleasant, desirable and enticing, full of possibilities. Like a tiny sampler portion, an appetizer, the warm and lush-sweet aroma inhaled discreetly by one who does not let on how hungry he is from an extended fast. Forty days in the desert with nothing but sand and fleas they used to do back in the Bible, even harder perhaps than six months without the companionship of a woman.

* * *

Finally, she agreed to dinner, at a casual-but-fine-dining place Tyler had suggested, the Oak City Grille in Royal Oak, though she made it clear that she would meet him there, so he still wouldn't have her address yet. Yes, she was being cautious with someone she'd just met and hardly knew, she reminds herself. *The wolf and the crane; the fox and the cock*. And even now, after two months, she continues to keep their relationship from progressing too quickly, knowing that she must move slowly because he might not. On the rebound from the disastrous, shattering loss of his wife, he would be susceptible to this new attraction, reckless, until waking up one morning angry at his own betrayal of her, the wife, too soon. And then forever their magic would be lost, her pairing with Tyler poisoned by haste, too late once recognized. But now she wonders how he may be interpreting her hesitation. Will he find her less interesting? Or will he suspect that something had happened in that expanse of time before they'd met, living a life invisible to him. Something deeply scarring, reverberating: *the broken wall, the burning roof and tower*. Maybe not suspecting violence but unloosed passion, deep with regret now, passions awakened and stirred before the time was right, Solomon's Song ignored: *Promise me, O women of Jerusalem, by the swift gazelles and the deer of the wild, not to awaken love until the time is right.*

Or maybe he will see her as just another *paint-stained art student* like Yeats' heart-breaking, would-be lover, constant in rejecting her infatuated but determined suitor, just a game she plays with him, endlessly.

In any event, she has not slept with him. After that first dinner date when he showed no signs of being a psychopath, she let her guard down a bit and let him pick her up at her house for their next date, ending with an open-mouthed kiss that lingered but didn't lead to him being invited inside. A few days passed before they went out again, just drinks this time in a quiet bar in want of customers where they talked easily and without the hesitation of wondering what to say, just saying it, and the other responding in kind, just easy. Then they were on the phone each evening that they weren't together; they'd become a couple without declaring it.

Though he is fragile and confused from all the loss that has come his way, she is the one who is lost, Lyvia thinks. Literature has been her beacon, but also a welcome distraction, she knows, as she has put off the deepening of a spiritual awareness she had sought when she returned home, broken, from a love affair gone terribly wrong.

* * *

She has charisma and a sharpness about her that draws them forward together, he thinks, and Tyler is happy to be swept up in her wake. Yet she also seems to be following him, drawn by some unseen power he'd forgotten he had, or maybe never had before at all, even with Christie, if he can bear the thought. And physical chemistry, too, they have in abundance. She blends easily with him, curving smoothly against his tall, straight form, like a silk scarf around a store mannequin that makes them both seem more appealing; she laughs at his stories and looks at him admiringly with the gaze of one content with what she has in this other self, for now anyway. Lately, they kiss long and deep like sea creatures not needing to come up for air. Twice last week in her townhouse she let him touch and squeeze her, his hands running freely under her blouse while she dug her clear-coated nails into his back through the thin fabric of his shirt. When their lips finally would break apart, she'd tilt her head backward and breathe in little startled puffs as he kissed with restrained fury the soft, white fragile skin along her neck up to her cheeks and ears. And then, the hot current running through her abruptly stops, an imperceptible circuit breaker blown, and she pulls away, smiling still and not displeased with him it seems, but no longer giving anything away. Both times last week ended pretty much like this; no explanation given.

Tyler waits expectantly for tonight. He will push gently on the door to their sexual completeness. If she resists again, he will ask her about it directly. They do talk easily and without traps, so perhaps he can navigate even this tricky course. Maybe there's just a progression in her mind, a requisite number of dates they must complete before advancing to the next base. Maybe tonight won't end so suddenly.

The doorbell rings. Nicki. Had to come here directly from her basketball practice after school. Tyler is meeting up with Lyvia a little later than he would have wanted to accommodate her schedule. Robbie slides off the couch in the living room, leaving his cartoon friends for now, and runs excitedly to the front door, arriving the same time as his father. The door opens, and the boy squirts through it, colliding with the teenage girl's legs, throwing his arms around the back of jeans just above her knees, like a caterpillar with sticky appendages wrapping itself around a dewy leaf, gripping it with unthinking strength, inseparable from its host.

"Hey there, big guy. I'm glad to see you, too."

The boy says nothing but looks up at the babysitter and continues his tight grip on her legs.

"How 'bout we let Nicki come inside and show her what you're watching on TV."

Still Robbie hangs on. He stands with each of his tiny sneakers on the girl's tennis shoes, so Nicki walks forward with stiff legs like Frankenstein's monster, carrying Robbie along into the middle of the front room, then spinning suddenly and they fall on the carpet in a heap, setting off peals of laughter from both of them.

"So glad you're able to watch him, Nicki. You're just great with him."

"No problem. You know I like spending time with him," she says, mussing up his hair "even when he's being a silly pain."

After going through the usual updates—how long it's been since his diaper's been checked, his last meal, what's available for supper and a snack later—Tyler puts his arms through a brown sports coat. Along with a blue button-down collared shirt, khaki Dockers and brown loafers, it's a dressier look for him.

"Must be a big date, huh?" she asks tentatively.

"Same girl I've been going out with the last few weeks," he says, before realizing he hasn't said anything about Lyvia to Nicki.

She's got to be curious even if she hasn't asked. He has unthinkingly betrayed their bonded, adult-like alliance and returned to a relationship of parent to sitter, nothing confided between them, strictly a transaction of needs.

"Her name's Lyvia," he tells her, trying to make it right again between them. "She's a grad student at the U of D, studying English. I met her just before my accident, but didn't go out with her until last month. Well, the end of August, I guess. She's the first girl I've been out with since Christie died." That one blind date with Big Candice doesn't count.

"How'd ya meet?" Nicki wants to know.

"Actually, it's a funny story, but a little involved. I'm kinda running late, so let me tell you about it when I get back tonight, okay?"

"Deal," Nicki says, and then shuffles off to catch up with Robbie who has pulled out a bunch of Hot Wheel cars and dragged them into the kitchen. The linoleum floor makes a much better track than the carpet in the other rooms.

***

Tyler picks up Lyvia and they head for a movie and then dinner. They were going to do it the other way around, dinner first, but the show times weren't cooperating. They decided on *Ghost*, which has been out since the middle of the summer but is still playing in lots of theaters and has become one of the highest grossing films of the year. He's always thought of Patrick Swayze as a bit of a doof, though Christie thought he was pretty great in *Dirty Dancing*, which she saw with some friends when it came out, a chick-flick Tyler never had interest in seeing. Demi Moore is hot in a wholesome way.

The two sit close together in the theater, sharing a Big-Gulp-sized diet Coke. No popcorn; it would just get their hands and faces greasy and spoil their appetite for dinner, seafood tonight, they've agreed. They both like the movie. There's a scene where

Swayze's character sits behind Demi Moore, while they work a mound of spinning clay, their four hands caressing it suggestively, the Righteous Brothers singing from an old record player. Tyler squeezes Lyvia's shoulders and she lets him draw her closer, neither taking their eyes off the screen, but the armrests get in the way, and it soon becomes uncomfortable.

They were both over-dressed for the movies but just right for the restaurant, the Halifax House in Troy. She's wearing a deep blue dress with sheer lace on the top of her shoulders and her neckline down to just above her bosom, revealing through the lace a mysterious, enchanted valley outlined by blue fabric like the sky. The sleek dress smoothly covers Lyvia's carefully toned waist, running to mid-thigh, shimmering hose more silver than nude down shapely legs to blue pumps with a bit of a heel but not too high. She wore a white shawl over her shoulders when they were out in the cool October night, but has it folded beside her now, knowing that it subtracts from her sexiness, even though it's a bit chilly in the restaurant. A pewter necklace and matching earrings set off against her fair white skin, soft and delicate, her shoulder-length reddish-brown hair feathered neatly. Picking up the blue hue of the dress, her gray-blue eyes deepen with intensity.

He orders Chilean sea bass, expensive but a favorite of his; she has mahi-mahi, which is really dolphin fish but nobody would order it if properly labeled because they would think of dolphin, of cute chirping Flipper, even though a dolphin fish is anything but cute, a droopy-faced swordfish without the sword, an ugly high forehead instead. Their conversation turns to his job search. At first, Tyler avoided the subject with Lyvia; it made him feel like a loser. But he saw that not talking about it made it all the more awkward. When he has allowed their conversation to dance around, upon and even squat for a few minutes on the loss of and the searching for a job, on a fall from the expected career arc that can be quickly righted but hasn't yet, Lyvia listens wide-eyed and quiet, respectful. She doesn't judge or think him less than he is because of it, and that has brought him closer to her.

"A couple of leads I've unearthed in the newspapers," Tyler is saying, "but none around here." They are still way too early in their being a couple for either to acknowledge any consideration of their relationship when Tyler mentions the pursuit of an out-of-state job opportunity, but each of them thinks about it. Lyvia has another year of grad school at the University of Detroit before she can become mobile. Unless their relationship continues to deepen over the next weeks and months, they wouldn't even try to long-distance it if a job takes Tyler away, would they?

"What companies are you investigating?" Lyvia asks, a safer way to inquire, *Which cities are you considering?*

"I saw one yesterday for a small auto supplier, Lockerbie Manufacturing or something, in Toledo. No, Lockery. They used to be called Lockery Screw Works. But I suppose somebody told them that people might not want to work for a *screw works* or buy from somebody that may want to screw them over." *Screw them over* sounds less crude and overtly sexual than *screw them*, Tyler decides, thinking quickly enough to say it that way without backtracking. "I bet they had to pay a high-priced consultant to tell them that, and to come up with the new name."

They each take another bite of fish. Then Tyler adds, "I've got my résumé pretty well perfected and can come up with a cover note pretty quick. You have to do a little research into the company and find out where they're headed or what challenges they might face and mention that in the cover letter. That gives them the idea that some candidate for a junior HR job has the know-how to come in and be part of the team that can lead them forward. But you have to say all that without it sounding braggy, or like a know-it-all."

"Toledo wouldn't be bad," Lyvia allows herself to say out loud. It's an hour's drive away, a straight shot down I-75.

"It's kind of a pit, actually. Like Detroit without major league sports. But it wouldn't be too far away, and a little closer to my mom."

"How's she doing?" Lyvia asks. She only knows the basics—widowed mother, very much a recluse, living alone in Akron.

"Oh, about the same, I guess. Robbie and I are gonna drive down there Saturday, I should tell you that, and stay a few days, maybe a week. It's been too long since we've visited. The little guy has grown up so much." Lyvia has met Robbie; they all went to a park last Sunday, Robbie climbing all over the playscape and pretty much ignoring her. "When we get back, the three of us should do something together again," Tyler adds.

"I'd like that," she says, lifting a glass of chardonnay to her lips. And then the conversation turns to Lyvia's master's thesis, a topic she attacks with vigor, making up for the last several minutes of short answers and respectful listening while they had navigated subjects Tyler finds troublesome. Now she becomes animated and enthusiastic, happy to be back in the driver's seat.

"T.S. Eliot considered a work of art a living thing, created but then released into the world by the writer or painter or other artist. He wasn't alone in this idea, but he took it much further. It's perfectly valid, he would say, for a reader living many years after the creation of a poem or novel to bring new experiences to bear on the understanding of its meaning. The work is alive, constantly growing from new meanings that reflect the changing human condition, even though the artist likely never anticipated those developments."

"Give me a for-instance," Tyler says, being helpful.

"Well, in my thesis work, I'll be looking at some of Eliot's own poems with an understanding of someone living twenty-five years after Eliot died. Take *The Waste Land*, a brilliant epic poem he wrote in 1922 as a relatively young man—just a little older than you, actually—in the aftermath of The Great War, what we know as World War I. Europe had been ravaged, and Eliot was deeply affected. He also was going through terrible personal worries—his marriage failing as both he and his wife suffered from depression, or what was known at the time as a *nervous disorder*. So, the poem can be understood on multiple levels—the story of the destruction wrought by modern war or the harrowing wasteland that is daily life for the chronically depressed. It is the great cities of Europe in rubble; it is Eliot's marriage on the rocks. But after the Second World War, after Auschwitz and Dresden, Hiroshima and Nagasaki, *The Waste Land* takes on new levels of horrific meaning of mankind's ability to annihilate, and the inhuman brutality of ever-more-modern warfare—none of which Eliot could have foreseen when he wrote the poem. The Rape of Belgium in 1914 shaped the poem Eliot wrote; the Rape of Nanking in 1937 shapes our further understanding of it."

She takes another sip of dry white wine, catching up to Tyler who is on his second glass, smiling as he takes in Lyvia's lecture, picking up most of the historical references, more than the average Joe or Jane today, so ignorant of anything outside their own time and place. History has always interested him because it records what was *real*, not like the made-up stories in a novel. But books on historical subjects tend to be so thick and dense; he rarely even starts one anymore. Instead, he watches The History Channel with shows like *Biography*—even those old ones with Mike Wallace narrating, Hitler and Churchill and Mussolini with grainy black-and-white footage. There must have been someone carting along one of those heavy movie-reel cameras right into battle; what a crazy job that would be.

"Either way, *April is the cruelest month*," Lyvia is saying. "That's a line from *The Waste Land* that most everyone has heard."

"I always thought *April is the cruelest month* was a Michiganism, talking about the cold, wet weather that keeps coming when you feel like it ought to be warming up; it's always so disappointing," he says.

Lyvia smiles, then continues. "In a way that's exactly the point; you're applying your own experience to the words. But listen: *April is the cruelest month, breeding Lilacs out of the dead land, mixing Memory and desire, stirring Dull roots with spring rain.* Isn't that a beautiful but harrowing depiction of nature and mankind trying to pick up and live again after a devastating winter or a horrific war? Or a bitter divorce?"

"Yeah, I can see all that in it."

"On a much lighter note, take Eliot's playful poem *Old Possum's Book of Practical Cats*. It's been reinterpreted in a fanciful way in the Broadway play, *Cats*. Have you seen it?"

"I've never actually been to New York," Tyler confesses, an admission that makes him feel small and sheltered, naïve. He pictures Lyvia in that form-fitting blue dress walking hand-in-hand with him through Times Square that he has seen in so many movies and TV shows. They ignore the bums and head for the bright lights flashing before them. Broadway beckons.

"Oh, we must go! To New York, I mean. There are so many other plays to see, of course. *Cats* is traveling now; it had a run here at the Fox last year. You should have gone. So many great plays—musicals, dramas—most of them so much better than that silly farce where we first met, when you ditched your blind date to hit on me." She laughs at the memory, the same laugh that impressed him at the theater, confident and unashamedly out loud.

"I didn't ditch her. I just let her go off to the bathroom by herself. And I wouldn't call it *hitting on* you exactly. I was just looking to *upgrade*." Like a frequent flyer bumped up to first class where he rightfully belongs.

"That's not any way to act on a date," she says, furrowing her brows in the same disapproving way she had when she'd sized him up those first moments there at the Attic Theater.

"I'm sure I wasn't too smooth, but I just couldn't let the moment pass and then never see you again. You were just gorgeous and cute and ... maybe even *available*. I just knew I wanted to somehow be with you. I'd never done anything like that before. I'm just glad you didn't throw away my number."

"And I'm glad you didn't turn out to be a psychotic stalker. Or at least you don't appear to be one. But the jury's still out; I'm keeping my eye on you," she says as the waitress clears away their dinner plates. They decide to split a dessert, a New York cheesecake. "But back to Eliot. Another seemingly somber poem, *Ash Wednesday*, is really full of hope. It's about spiritual conversion, *the pearl of great price*. Human salvation can come from an awakening of individual souls…"

The restaurant is buzzing, waiters and waitresses moving fluidly to clear tables, seating an even later crowd, though it's almost ten-thirty. It's going to be a late night for Nicki, a school night; tomorrow's Friday. Tyler calculates the time it will all take, more than an hour, surely—he needs to find a way to wrap things up here without rushing Lyvia, get the check, have the valet fetch the car, seems silly to have valeted a Chevy Cavalier but he did, then drive out to Hazel Park to Lyvia's townhouse, and then he'll still have a good thirty-minute drive back to his house in Livonia. He'll have to cut it off for the night with Lyvia at her door, give her a good rousing kiss and get back in his car and get going or Nicki's mother will never let her babysit for him again. Maybe burn all her CDs, too, while she's at it. Actually, this will be a good move on his part, cutting the date off with just a quick, good-night kiss. Takes the pressure off Lyvia and whatever's going on inside her head. And proves that he's in this for more than just a chance at all that awaits underneath the blue dress and silvery hose. There'll be another night for that.

"…those people in Australia remember well, the *Ash Wednesday fire* of 1983 was the worst in the continent's history, raging for three days, killing over seventy people, destroying two thousand homes and tens of millions of acres of bush. But there were also miraculous stories of survival, including eighty people who survived the terrible fires near Melbourne by stuffing themselves into a sewer pipe for more than twenty-four hours. The poem read anew by those who lived through these fires has a whole new layer of meaning quite apart from anything Eliot himself intended. We think only of our American experience and maybe Europe, but there are, of course, plenty of Eliot readers in Australia, too."

Tyler grows fidgety waiting for the bill, so they can begin their exit. Why do waitresses always hover around when you don't need them, Tyler thinks, inevitably popping over to ask if we like the food just as he is coming to the punch line of a joke or the good part of a story? But then when you're ready for the bill and in a bit of a hurry, nowhere to be found.

"And, of course, there is Eliot's first major poetic work, published in 1915, *The Love Song of J. Alfred Prufrock*…"

Alfred was Batman's butler, Bruce Wayne's butler, really. Bruce Wayne being one of the few millionaire superheroes. Normally, the very rich are the bad guys, or at least completely indifferent to the poor, the every-man, and it's up to some Robin Hood to take their money to help the huddled masses. Lyvia doesn't seem to notice Tyler's inattentiveness. He's a master at maintaining eye contact and nodding just often enough, while thinking about whatever invades his mind under the guise of being more interesting than whatever words float about in the air above and around him.

"The protagonist, J. Alfred Prufrock, seems to be middle-aged, old enough to have profound regrets…" His mind jumps to J. R. Ewing. One of those rich guys we love to hate. Who shot J.R.? And then Patrick Ewing. The dominating center from Georgetown who magically went to the New York Knicks—just when the franchise in the nation's number one media market most needed a savior, they drew the lottery ball with the biggest prize; the fix clearly in. But still the Knicks aren't as good as the Pistons, who have built their two-time championship team without cheating. The team that fans in every other city hate with a passion. The *Bad Boys*, especially Bill Laimbeer and Rick Mahorn, playing basketball like it's hockey, lock-down defense and physical intimidation.

And even little Isaiah Thomas, with such an angelic baby face and that lightning quickness, has matured into the role of head mobster, just like Michael Corleone in *The Godfather* films.

Lyvia is still talking about this Prufrock guy. There seems to be some sexual overtones; Tyler tried to tune in for that but couldn't stay focused. If he had one of those pocket cassette recorders he could have taped this monologue and Lyvia would have her dissertation done, only it would be too long; she'd have to edit it down. And then it hits him; the flaw in this perfectly gorgeous, smart and lively woman who seems enthralled with him: she talks too much. He's already been on some phone calls with her that lasted half an eternity, but he had been along for the ride, captivated by everything about her and not minding the lengthy conversations. Now that he realizes that she really can be a motor mouth when she gets going, will he ever see her the same way again?

* * *

Having dropped Robbie off at daycare on this Friday morning, Tyler drives the Cavalier east on I-96 toward the Redford nursing home where Cuhlman told him he could be found after he was released from the hospital. Cuhlman was surprised when Tyler had called the other day. Like Tyler, he had figured they'd never see each other again. But Tyler has been restless lately, less purpose to his days. So, he decided to see the old man again. His stories of black and white soldiers fighting in the war against Hitler, and playing professional, blacks-only baseball, have a certain *vastness* found only at the intersection of history and personal experience, and are a welcome diversion from the frustrating monotony of his job search that shows zero sign so far of hitting pay dirt.

Meanwhile, the severance pay is all but gone. Daycare is so expensive on top of the mortgage payment, and pretty soon the gas bills for heating his house will grow immense again as the Michigan winter sets in. He hadn't wanted to take any government handouts, but last week he swallowed his pride and walked into the state unemployment agency, a dreadfully depressing place that makes the DMV seem a model of efficiency and pleasantness. They must put the meanest, most bitter survivors they can find to work at the unemployment office to make sure it's a dispiriting experience for all involved, so the recipients don't get complacent and stop looking for work. Tyler doesn't need the extra motivation. Some equal measure of self-respect and dwindling bank account ensures that he will be on the meager unemployment dole as short of a time as possible. A lot of his savings went to pay for Christie's funeral. He should have had some life insurance on her, but they hadn't thought they needed it, him being the bread-winner and all. GM sprung for his life insurance policy, but covering Christie would have been extra. He really needs to look into some life insurance on himself now, for Robbie just in case, now that his GM-provided term policy will run out any time. Where did he put the number of that guy who called the other day?

Tyler exits off the highway and turns left, north, on Beech Daly Road through a couple of lights and sees the nursing home, Great Oaks Senior Living, on the right, just like Cuhlman said it would be. He walks to the front desk, signs in as a visitor and makes his way back, past a nursing station and a surprisingly large dining room to a quiet, wood-paneled room off to the side, a conference room, perhaps for meetings but made to look more comfortable than that. There's a small glass table in the center surrounded by four plush chairs, and a couch under each of two rectangular windows, one looking out at green lawn and trees, the other overlooking part of the parking lot and a Chi Chi's Mexican restaurant.

John Henry Cuhlman sits in one of the chairs, arms resting on the table, opposite the window with the better view. Tyler reaches out and shakes his beefy but pinkiless hand and takes a seat on the side of the little table facing the other window.

"Good to see you, Tyler," Cuhlman says. "How're you doing?"

"Like new," he says, before inquiring about Cuhlman's health. This sets off the litany of complaints you get from an elderly person, but especially a nursing home resident whose daily dosages of pain medication and special attention depend on a regularly updated catalogue of ailments.

Before Tyler can regret asking, Cuhlman cuts himself off. "But I won't bore you with all that. How's your job search goin'?"

"I keep plugging away, but nothing yet. Turns out it isn't so easy to land a good job these days."

"You mean with that recession the fellows in D.C. and New York still ain't ownin' up to yet?"

"Yeah, seems like companies are getting pretty cautious about headcount. Even when they're just looking to replace somebody. Next will be freezes on hiring, and then I might be really shut out."

Tyler takes out the little mini-cassette recorder he brought with him from home, a remnant from his college days. He's going to use it to go with his notetaking, so that Cuhlman will have some start at a collection of memories to pass on to his adult children, who apparently haven't bothered to listen to these stories much themselves. For his grandkids' sake and maybe even further down the line. The old man had readily agreed to all this.

"Well, don't hesitate to reach out to your friends if things really get tight. I might be able to loan you a few hundred if you're gonna need it to get by."

Tyler doesn't know what to say. This old black man is now Tyler's *friend*, ready to trust him with a sizable loan, he says, after they have spent just a few days together as hospital roommates.

"I wouldn't think of it," he blurts out. No way he's taking money from someone living in a nursing home. Cuhlman's relatives would come after Tyler, thinking he was trying to steal from the old man. "You got your own bills to pay, I'm sure."

"I got some money stashed away; don't you worry about me. Just remember you got a friend here."

That word again, *friend*, seemingly freely extended. Strangely, Tyler doesn't feel crowded by this unexpected closeness. He smiles. "Thanks, man. I appreciate your friendship. I'll let you know if I need a loan. Right now, I'm still in decent shape."

"Okay, fine. No problem. But the offer's still good. Our talks back in the hospital got me thinkin' again about the war, first time in ages. Trudgin' through France again in my mind. Maybe I didn't want to think about it. Or just no one axed me about it in a long time."

Tyler picks up the feeling that their privacy is being compromised. He looks over his shoulder quickly, but that sets his world spinning like he has just come off The Octopus at Cedar Point. He likes riding the big roller coasters, but not those spinning rides that turn his stomach. He ignores the motion now, just looks past the spin. An emaciated, old white woman in a wheelchair ten feet or so outside the conference room leans forward, straining her thin, wrinkled neck, covered with dark liver spots and vein lines, to see through glasses thick as a bottle bottom, curious and lonely, frightened and disoriented with Alzheimer's, like a bug-eyed goldfish in a little bowl looking out through water made cloudy by its own excrement. So much more to see even at the end of life, but we just can't make it out.

Cuhlman sees that he's lost Tyler's attention. "What you suffer from is a terminal loss of focus," he says with clear annoyance.

"So I've heard," Tyler says musingly. "Okay, I'm back now. *Really*."

They sit there silent for a few minutes until the quiet becomes unbearable for the younger man's fidgety brain. Something else has invaded his consciousness that he feels compelled to share with his former roommate.

"You know, back in the hospital one night I had a strange experience I didn't get the chance to tell you about. I woke up from a nightmare, one of those that leave you still having the creeps even after you wake up. About some psycho-killer and a little girl.

They'd talked about a violent rape on the evening news, and I guess when I fell asleep my brain was still thinking about it. But when I woke up from the dream, I couldn't shake it. And here's the thing…"

He pauses to let Cuhlman catch up, for the old man to give him some signal that he's following all this. Cuhlman's eyebrows rise expectantly, so Tyler continues.

"I could feel something in the room with me, with us. You were asleep on the other side of the curtain, and I wasn't going to wake you. But it was like I felt—it sounds weird now—but the presence of *evil* right there. And there was this awful smell that I somehow knew was connected to it. It wasn't just the hangover of a bad dream. Something was in the room with me." This provides an all-too-easy set-up for Cuhlman to zing Tyler: *Probably was a smelly fart, cut loose in your sleep.* But that's not how he responds.

"Somethin' like the devil, you mean?"

"That's what I was thinking, yeah. And I didn't want anything to do with it. So I, you know, said a couple of little prayers while I just lay there, my eyes wide open. I didn't want to shut my eyes, like maybe with eyes closed I would see something I didn't want to see. That doesn't make sense, does it?"

"A lot of this world don't make sense," Cuhlman says, his own eyelids dropping shut, "let alone things of the next world. We generally don't think too much about 'em. But we probably should."

Evil in the air, another carcinogen we breathe in unknowingly so that it enters our bloodstream, becoming part of us. Not dissipating over time, deadly as ever. Cunningly invisible, blending in quietly with all the vapid rapidity in this harried life.

"Yeah, exactly. In fact, later when I was thinking about this whole thing in the room, the smell of evil, I sort of wished that I would of seen the devil there right in front of me. Wished that he would of showed himself to me. It would of been the scariest thing, I know, and I didn't want that, not then. But I've been thinking. If the devil would come out and show himself, he'd lose a lot of power over us, wouldn't he? Because if we knew for sure he existed, we'd know for sure that God exists, too, right? It would remove all doubt." Tyler stops, but Cuhlman waits for him to go on, so he does. "And if you really believed, without any doubt, you would live your life different, wouldn't you? I mean, wouldn't you?"

All this comes out of his mouth in bursts. He lets it out before the uncomfortableness of it all has the chance to stop him. Whenever Tyler has been around people wearing their religion on their sleeves too much, *Bible-thumping*, he's run from it. He certainly doesn't want to be the one thumping and making others run from him, even this old man who has shared some of his life's story with him in the hospital and now has promised to tell more in this old folks home that smells like Listerine and where half the residents sit in their wheelchairs with their mouths hanging open and a bewildered look in their eyes, dazed by the speed at which their lives have passed them by, no longer remembering much. If you can't talk about the devil and God in a place so close to death, where can you?

"That would be something," the old man says, stroking the gray stubble on his chin and neck. You don't have to shave every day when you live in a nursing home. Amazing that Cuhlman keeps himself up as well as he does here. "Runnin' into the devil in person. That'd be something, sure. But I don't think it'd remove your doubt for good."

"Don't you think if you saw him right in front of you, horns and pitchfork and all, you'd know it was all real, all the church stuff, too?"

"Well, I don't know if he'd look exactly like that, like a devil cartoon, you know?" the old man is saying. "He's smart enough to disguise hisself."

Tyler fidgets with his hands, wondering why he brought all this up. Easier to talk about war and old-time baseball.

"But maybe not so smart," Cuhlman continues. "He might reveal hisself in a different way. The devil tends to overplay his hand, I think. Remember the story of Job? Satan is just hangin' around heaven with a bunch of angels, chattin' it up with God, like they must of done, before Michael the Archangel knocked Satan right outta there. Anyways, God is braggin' on about Job, such a good and upright man. But Satan says that Job is only happy with God 'cause he never really had nothing go wrong in his life. So, God makes a bet with old Satan that he can't make Job curse the Lord, no matter what terrible things come along. Satan takes the bet, but he blows it. He has four separate calamities fall upon Job, all on the very same day. His oxes and mules gets stolen away by raiders. Another band of foreigners take his camels. And then his sheep and the shepherds are just vaporized by lightning, just like that. To top it all off, a great wind comes into the house where Job's sons and daughters are having a nice meal, and it smotes them all dead. Pretty subtle, right? Well, all that calamity shook Job up all right, but he don't curse God. 'The Lord giveth and the Lord taketh; blessed be the name of the Lord.' That's what Job says. But maybe Satan throwin' all that violence all at once at Job made it pretty damn obvious that something out of this world was happenin', and Job was smart enough to stay on God's side."

Cuhlman rubs the roughness on his neck again. His eyes focus unblinkingly into Tyler's eyes, through the floating contact lenses, cutting deeply.

"But whatever way the Devil might appear to us in this day and age, say it was horrible and frightening, and you knew exactly who he was. The damn devil hisself. It would be shocking, sure. And maybe a life-changin' thing, like you say. But maybe, if you follow me here, you'd pretty soon doubt what you seen. You'd think you'd been asleep in a nightmare again. And if you told anybody about it, they'd think you was nuts or dreamed it all up. They wouldn't believe you, and pretty soon you wouldn't believe it, either. He'd still be ahead and laughin' at you, the devil. So don't go wishing him here. I'm too old for that. Too fragile."

And he does look like he could easily be broken, this once strong, rugged man who has lived through a world war and racial bigotry, but doesn't want to meet the devil today.

* * *

Cuhlman talks at length about his baseball days, the Army and the war, before and after D-Day. And about returning home to his girlfriend, Jackie, and marrying her, starting a family. Making a new beginning with his wife and, soon, two children. A boy and a girl. Long, hard days working without complaint in the little tool and die in New Jersey and then the massive Ford glass plant in Michigan. Coming home to shower off the sweaty grime and enjoy another couple of hours with his family. His life not exactly a Norman Rockwell painting, he says unsmilingly, but deeply satisfying. He didn't have to remind himself each day to appreciate all that he had at home having lived through the terrors of a world war he could now happily forget.

Finally, Tyler says he's out of mini-cassettes and, anyway, needs to pick up his son at daycare.

"This has been amazing. I'm glad I could capture all this for your family to have."

"Yeah, it's a good thing you doin' and I appreciate it. But that don't absolve you, remember that."

"Absolve?" Tyler tries to think what he could have done, maybe back at the hospital, requiring forgiveness.

The old man looks back into Tyler's questioning eyes. "You don't get it, do you?"

Tyler shakes his head. "Not a clue," he admits.

"Whites on top of blacks, that's the way it's always been and still is. Unless you move off the top and tell the others up there to make way, you part of the problem."

"What are you talking about? I'm not on top of anybody. I don't even have a job. And, anyway, I don't see you as black, just my friend, like you said, you know? I'm not prejudiced or anything," Tyler insists.

"What do you mean you don't see me as black, after I been telling you all these things? Fighting the same enemy, or playing the same beautiful game, but not on the same level of respect, you know?" Cuhlman's mouth has turned down into a bit of a scowl and the wrinkles around his eyes are pulled taut.

"I just mean your skin color doesn't mean anything anymore. To me."

But Tyler's words don't have the desired effect. Cuhlman turns away, looking out the window.

"It means something to me," the old man mutters.

Tyler goes over this exchange in his head, over and over, as he drives to Robbie's daycare. What had set the old man off? They were having such an easy time together and then, what? Maybe Cuhlman's medication had worn off. *Just bizarre*, he thinks.

* * *

As they go through pre-game warm-ups, the Mercy girls seem preoccupied with the newness of it all: running out of their own locker rooms to the buzzing of family and friends, their first home game. As she waits her turn in line behind her teammates in one of the drills, Nicki looks up and finds her parents toward the top of the bleachers that pull out of the wall on two sides of the little gym, unfurling like an accordion. Prim and pale Colette Saliba sits stoically next to her darker husband with his jet-black hair and mustache. Nicki's father sees his daughter glance his way, and they lock eyes for an instant, exchanging bright smiles. Then it's her turn at the front of the line, and she sprints down to the block on the right side of the baseline and cleanly catches the passed ball, rising up in a fluid movement, her white sneakers kissing off the wood floor and propelling her upward. Just before she reaches the peak of her jump, she releases the ball held high above her head, her right hand following through like a little wave to the crowd. The ball flies on its rainbow arc with perfect backspin, but is well short of its intended target, missing even the rim. Air ball. Nicki glances over at her coach who is looking down at the clipboard she holds throughout the game. Hopefully she didn't see that.

The horn sounds, a wordless national anthem plays on a scratchy recording. The girls in their uniforms, the Divine Mercy Fillies in blue, Farmington Hills' St. Joan of Arc Marlins in red, continue to stand at attention as the announcer leads the small crowd in prayer. The starters on both teams fidget nervously, picking at their nails or pursing their lips, rising up on their toes, like racehorses anxious to be led to the starting gate; *let's run already*. Most of the other Fillies, the early subs and the benchwarmers, smile and stare ahead bright-eyed, taking in the majesty of the moment, the first home game.

The starters are announced and shake hands with their opponents at center court. Then they take their places for the opening jump. Finally. Nicki draws in a deep breath. *C'mon; let's go.*

Mercy's center, Shannon Murphy, a red-haired sophomore starting because of her ungainly height, wins the jump easily and taps the ball to a dark-haired sprite, the team's point guard and captain, Melissa Gilbert, who immediately sprints up court. The fastest player on the team and the only one besides Nicki who can dribble smoothly between her legs, she is a confident ball handler and passer who knows her role. Despite long hours of practice, the senior remains a lousy shooter. So, she's a pass-first playmaker, ready to reward an open teammate with the ball. She glides up the court with effortless speed, alarming the red-shirted opponents who move quickly into the paint to prevent an easy layup. Melissa stops suddenly, dribbling the ball in a rapid beat, waiting for Nicki to get open, to the right, a few feet off the baseline. She fires a sharp bounce pass that rises up off the floor into Nicki's expectant hands at chest level, so that she receives the ball and jumps up to shoot in one fluid motion. She cocks the ball over her head as she leaps upward, releasing the ball before an opposing player can get anywhere near her. The ball rides on an invisible arc high above the players, crests and descends cleanly inside the rim, snapping the net with its backspin like an exclamation point audible throughout the gym. Eight seconds into the game and Divine Mercy has a lead it will never relinquish.

For what seems an eternity to the Marlins and their supporters, Nicki continues to feel it, ripping off an assortment of jumpers from all around the basket. It's as if she's alone at a dance, hearing the music and moving mindlessly, just letting it go. *Making it rain.* No one on the opposing team can match her shooting. Nobody else in the gym hears the music, except Melissa maybe; she keeps putting the ball in Nicki's hands just as she arrives at the very spot where she's open and ready. Then she rises up in rhythm and sets the ball once again on its beautiful curving path toward its home below the center of the rim. It's obvious to even the casual observer in the stands that Nicki is the best player on the court, at least tonight. With five minutes to go in the first half, Mercy up 31-19, Joan of Arc's coach calls time out. Nicki slugs water from a plastic bottle and wipes her sweaty forehead with a towel. Coach Myers motions for the team to gather around her. Looking into Nicki's green eyes, she says: "Keep shooting the ball, just like you're doing, Nick. They'll have to double team you if you keep making 'em. Then, Melissa, get the ball to whoever they leave open."

After a Joan of Arc missed shot, Nicki comes off a well-set screen by the gangly red-haired center and receives another perfect pass that in one smooth motion gets sent on the familiar rainbow path to the center of the rim. Just as she releases the ball, Nicki is fouled hard by a late-arriving defender. Two of Nicki's teammates help her up off the floor and exchange high-fives with her. She cans the free throw for a three-point trip. That gives her 18 points and the Fillies a fifteen-point lead. Next time down the court, two defenders are all over Nicki. The pass goes to the other side of the floor, though the unguarded teammate's shot is an air ball. Just before the half ends, Nicki cuts sharply off another pick and loses both defenders. She darts to the far-right baseline, just outside the three-point line, catches another on-the-money pass and puts up a high-arching shot that seems to float above the girls on the floor before slowly descending cleanly through the goal; all net. Later, she will learn that her twenty-one-point half has tied a school record set back in the Seventies.

In the second half, Nicki is mostly a decoy drawing a constant double team. Her teammates make nearly half of the wide-open shots they put up. Divine Mercy cruises to a 64-47 win. Nicki finishes with 28 points.

21

Tyler and the rest of southeast Michigan awaken Saturday morning to the surprise of a covering of white all around them, an overnight snow, freakishly early, the second week of October. It's only a couple of inches, didn't stick at all on the roads and highways, and will probably be gone by mid-afternoon. But it shocks them, gazing out their windows, rubbing the sleep out of their eyes in disbelief, like the hungry Israelites must have been shocked that first morning they woke to a snowy covering of manna all around them in the desert, asking, *What is this?* Again, you hear: *If you don't like the weather here, wait ten minutes and it will change.* They say this in Michigan and just about everywhere in the country, except San Diego, where it's always perfect.

    Nicki is watching Robbie again this morning, just for two hours, so Tyler can make his appointment at a radiology lab, a routine follow-up his doctor ordered after the accident and hospital stay. He signs his name on the clipboard at the counter and takes a seat. None of the magazines look interesting, back issues of *Parenting*, *People* and *Redbook,* and a token issue of *Sports Afield*, a hunting magazine, the only concession to male patients. Though now he does see that there's an issue of the *Sporting News*, a kind of tabloid newspaper for baseball fans mostly, but also a fair bit of football, basketball and hockey, especially now, the sweetest time of year for the ecumenical sports fan, complete overlap—all four major sports in action. But it's over on a chair next to another patient, the only other person in the waiting room. Perhaps it was left by an unseen other already called up and beckoned into a patient room, but this early that seems unlikely. Tyler could go over and ask the guy nicely if he can read it, and chances are it would be no problem. He decides to wait until he is left there alone and can pick up the paper without any bother.

But Tyler's name is called next, and he is ushered into a lab room, no indication of why he has jumped ahead in priority; maybe this other guy was just early for his appointment. He sits down and waits for the technician, a short, thin woman with long, straight blonde hair, standing with her back to him, a white lab coat obscuring his view of her butt, leaving his eyes nowhere to go. She turns around toward him, still writing on a clipboard she holds, and walks over. Her expressionless face has been weathered by the sun, like dry, cracked leather, and perhaps cigarettes, though she doesn't have the tell-tale stale, smoky smell as she draws nearer.

The technician tells him she's going to take a scan of his brain. Something called an MRI—for *magnetic resonance imagery*. Similar to a "cat-scan," both producing somehow an image of a brain in 3D that can be carefully analyzed. She explains to him quickly how this test procedure will work, in a voice revealing little enthusiasm—he will lie down on his back on a narrow plank behind him, she calls it a *gurney*, letting his head sink into a cavity of hollowed-out styrofoam at the top of this plank. As if on a moving sidewalk, he'll be drawn into a tube-like machine that will take a series of scans of his brain. He needs to remain motionless for the duration of the test, nearly thirty minutes. The tube is rather confining—does he suffer from claustrophobia?

Tyler answers *no*, not sure if he has ever been in anything more restricting than an elevator full of people, which does give him a rather unpleasant feeling of being crowded. In fact, that same crowded feeling agitates him a bit now that he thinks about it—but too late, the blonde technician has already noted his answer and is continuing her explanation of the procedure. He will have a little ball to hold in one of his hands. It's actually a signaling device connected by wire to another room where the tech will be running the test, safely away from the radiation she should not be continually exposed to. If he feels so uncomfortable that he cannot continue, he is to squeeze the ball, and the tech will get the signal to stop the test. But then she goads him, "You won't have any trouble, I'm sure. You look pretty tough." Playing to his male ego, she short-circuits any hesitation from Tyler.

He lies down on his back on the narrow gurney and the tech draws three straps over his body, each fastened with velcro—over his ankles, over his wrists and waistline, and a thinner one over his temples and forehead. "It's very important that you don't move at all during this test, especially your head. Just try to relax."

Despite the restraints, Tyler is not uncomfortable. How bad can this be, lying down for a thirty-minute nap? Then the tech presses some buttons, and the gurney begins to move, slowly, backward so that Tyler is drawn head-first into a gleaming white tube, like the torpedo tubes he's seen on a World War II submarine on display near a lighthouse in Muskegon on Lake Michigan, only cleaner. It's not much bigger around than he is at his widest. His whole head goes into the tube, then his neck and chest. He can see the opening grow farther away as he peers down at his legs without moving his head. Head-first, he continues to penetrate the slender chamber of the machine. Like a giant, dark vagina it engulfs him, but without the pleasant sensation of rubbing against those *Sugar Walls* in that Sheena Easton song.

When Tyler is drawn fully into the torpedo tube, just his ankles and feet still outside—he could only see to about mid-thigh, but the gurney kept moving another two or two-and-a-half feet it seemed—the motion finally stops. He closes his eyes and tries to forget the tightness of the tubular wall and the straps keeping him trapped inside. The ball rests loosely in the palm of his right hand. He can do this; it's not so bad.

Then the tech must have activated the machine because it begins to make a loud shrieking noise—*EEEEEccch... EEEEEccch... EEEEEccch*—pulsing so strong it rips through his eardrums and tears at those three little bones in the middle ear, feverishly vibrating to the awful beat. After ten or twelve seconds, the frequency of the screeching changes—*ERRRRR... ERRRRR... ERRRRR*—deeper and even more disturbing, until just as he starts to get used to it, the noise changes again, just as loud—*AAAArrrgggh... AAAArrrggh... AAAArrrgggh*.

On and on, a new tortuous frequency every few seconds, no letup in volume. He feels sweat rolling down his cheeks, or are they tears? He resolves not to squeeze the ball, but it is too much. Just as he thinks he can't take it anymore, the screeching subsides and he hears the humorless voice of the blonde tech. Never thought he'd be so glad to hear her voice, the torture finally over.

"All right, hon," she says flatly. "We're half-way done. Just remember to keep your head perfectly still."

Then the noise fires up again, biting into his brain as if the tube was a giant stapler sending pairs of steel prongs into his head, again and again. His expectations of freedom cruelly dashed, the disappointment is crushing; he can't go on. The ball remains loosely gripped, his escape valve if only he squeezes it. But he knows that a reprieve will only forestall the torture; he'll have to endure the awful test from the beginning if he ends it now. Just count to ten, he tells himself; you can get through this.

At ten, he feels himself still hanging on, not dead yet. He begins another count to ten, just as the frequency changes again, an ear-splitting scream designed to crumble whatever unbroken pieces of bone are left inside his middle ears.

And then, mercifully, the bitter tube grows quiet. He hears the tech's voice mixed in with ringing noises he'll live with for days, saying, "That's it. We're done. I'll get you out of there now."

The gurney begins its slow ride out of the steel womb of the MRI machine. He opens his eyes to see the tube's opening around his waist, then his chest and then, finally, his head emerges, and he hears himself laughing, deliriously it seems, as the tech rips apart the velcro holding his head tight against the depression of styrofoam, and then the other two straps as well.

"That was awful," he says, spittle spewing from his mouth, even though it feels dry. "What do you do for people who tell you they're claustrophobic?" he asks.

"Oh, we have a different machine that is more of a big cube than a tube," the blonde torturer says.

"What? I didn't know there was a choice!"

She doesn't answer him, just writes down some numbers on her clipboard. "We'll get those results to your doctor in ten days or so, hon," she says.

* * *

He still is well ahead of the two hours he told Nicki he might be, so he heads over to the Perry Drug Store to pick up the film he'd dropped off Tuesday, four days ago. It must be ready to be picked up. You can get doubles of each exposure or oversized prints for the regular price, which is probably more expensive than it used to be before the promotion became standard fare, but it sounds good. He always goes for the big prints, 4x6s. You can see the detail so much better than with the standard size. Before he pays the cashier at the film counter, he opens the envelope and inspects the photos. You don't have to pay for ones that didn't turn out.

The photos are in the reverse order of when he took them. The shots from the park the other day come up first. Right on top is an amazing shot—the one he took of Robbie with red and orange leaves behind him, sunset clouds glowing red and pink and orange, topped off with deep blue sky, fill flash making Robbie pop, his eyes fully open above a brimming smile. He'll blow this one up, cropped slightly for an even tighter composition, and frame it. The rest of the photos from that day are all worth keeping, too. Then he comes to some other ones he took of Robbie earlier in the summer when they went with Webb Rucker to Metro Beach. Here's one that Rucker took of Tyler and Robbie together on the blanket, not very well composed but at least it's not blurry.

He keeps flipping through the photos, then stops, the look on his face changing so drastically the teenaged cashier asks him if anything is wrong.

"No, nothing. It's nothing," Tyler stammers, face-to-face with Christie, back with him again in razor-sharp living color, pictures he forgot he had taken; he would have had them developed long ago. A close-up of her face, all smile and smooth cheeks and brilliant blue eyes, her white skin not yet touched by the sun in midwinter, framed by reddish hair in curls and waves. He can't take his eyes off the picture, just stands there holding it. Then he looks at the remaining three of Christie, from a little further out, including one in which she's looking at him with a knowing grin and bright eyes, some secretly funny moment they had shared, now lost forever—can't remember what it could have been that made her look at him that way. There's only this photo which cannot talk. Someone is behind him now, rustling some papers impatiently, so he pays for the photos and leaves the store, his head as lost as it had been inside the torpedo tube, but the pain is so much worse. Christie bubbling up inside him. He feels the tears streaming down his face as he fumbles for the car keys and then slumps into the driver's seat. Lost to him and never coming back.

* * *

Tyler walks in the front door. Nicki is changing Robbie's diaper. "How was he?" he asks the sitter, the standard question.

"Kind of quiet and clingy, to be honest," she says. "He doesn't seem his usual self lately. He hardly talks and just wants me to hold him while we watch TV."

Tyler's already thinking ahead to what he needs to do to pack the car for the trip to Akron to visit his mother, but he pulls back into the present long enough to finish the conversation with Nicki.

"Yeah, sometimes lately he's like that. A couple a months ago, his doctor told me that I shouldn't be surprised if Robbie regresses a bit. Just normal as he works through the loss of his mother in his own way."

Lying on his back on a towel covering the carpeted floor, Robbie looks up at Tyler while the girl fastens the new diaper with the velcro straps and pulls a pair of little blue jeans over his legs and padded butt. When she lifts him up onto his feet, he looks lost, standing with the two people that take best care of him, but another is missing, the one who brought him into this world and then disappeared so many days and nights ago.

* * *

His legs and right hand mindlessly engage the car's gears in a steady progression of forward progress. Left foot presses the clutch down, the stick pushed forward to the left to find a nesting place in first gear, a little gas with his right foot, clutch slowly released, more gas now, then just two or three seconds later, the clutch down again as he lets up on the gas, stick pulled back toward him into the notch that is second gear, clutch released and engaged again and again, third and fourth gears, all smoothly done without any conscious brain activity. Robbie stares out the window contentedly, trusting his driver completely. Of course, the boy hasn't been told of his father's car accident, a story for when he is older; the part about the teenage girl dying makes it rough. As soon as the boy can understand a bit more will be the time to tell him, while Tyler still can do no wrong in his eyes, except for when saying *no* to a demand deemed no good for a small child. Then Robbie will sulk and pout like any little one, soon enough forgiving the dad who is everything to him.

The Cavalier accelerates onto the freeway onramp and merges into light traffic on west-bound I-96, the Jeffries Highway. Just two exits later, Tyler signals the right turn and eases into the far-right lane. He lets off the gas a bit to coast, slowing his momentum for the approaching curve that will bring him to a new highway, the southbound I-275. He steers into the curve and then corrects just a bit, a fraction less steering input, finding the exact position to match the curve's consistent arc, a perfect radius extending from an imaginary middle, a quarter of a clover-leaf, the on-ramp curve taking him three-quarters of a complete circle, two hundred seventy degrees. He holds the steering wheel to stay right in the middle of the onramp, left hand at the top, the ring finger still with a distinct depression marking where the wedding ring should be, but now resting on the top of his dresser. The Cavalier circles the big, flat round patch of snowy grass inside the freeway on-ramp like a massive full moon or a giant communion host; *See, I am making all things new.* Right in the middle of the curve, the *apex* to a racecar driver, Tyler begins to push down on the accelerator to hold the line around the curve better—as the car speeds up, its weight balance shifts a bit toward the rear tires that otherwise could lose traction if he had entered the curve too hot, or if the road is still slick from the melted snow. *Over-steer* it is called when the rear wheels slide out in a curve taken too fast. Not good. The worst thing you can do then is to hit the brakes, your natural instinct, which only forces more weight forward and makes the back wheels even lighter so that they lose grip of the road completely. He continues to accelerate steadily through the second half of the turn, feeling the Cavalier hug the road as if on rails, not bad for a little econobox; you just have to know how to drive it. By the time he is merging with the south-bound cars, minivans, pickups and semi-trailers, he's just up to their speed, sixty-five or so mph.

Down I-275 he goes until it splits. The side he follows will dump right into I-75 South. Across the interstate, he can see where the other split of the highway he was on circles around a humped-up patch of snowy grass. It disappears behind the massive, untanned breast of a hill as it merges into I-75 North.

Traffic is light on this Saturday, and Tyler relaxes into his driving-for-hours-in-light-traffic posture, reclining the seat back a bit more, adjusting the outboard mirrors with a little switch his left hand finds easily—nice that the original owner chose the power-locks/power-windows option; a little mechanical joystick on the inside of the door would have been easy enough as a manual control for the driver's side mirror but a real pain to reach for the passenger side mirror, even in this little car. Soon enough, the Cavalier carrying Tyler and Robbie has crossed the border into Ohio. Before he gets to Toledo, Tyler eases the car to the left-hand exit which is always tricky because of the speeders, then onto the Ohio Turnpike. You have to get a little computer punch card as you get on. The toll-booth operator silently hands out the cards like a humorless blackjack dealer. Tyler automatically says, "Thanks," but for what—the chance to pay several bucks just to drive on a highway already paid for long ago by his and everyone else's federal tax dollars? The attendant nods but still does not speak, saving his voice for people who matter more to him.

> *You got to cry without weeping, talk without speaking*
> *Scream without raising your voice*

You do have to give it up to Bono, Tyler thinks. Saving the world with all the causes he fronts and still has time to make this pretty great album, *Joshua Tree*. When the little digital clock that is part of the radio display indicates that it is nearly 1:00, he switches to AM and punches the third preset button, 950 WWJ out of Detroit, for the CBS News report at the top of the hour. He knows he'll be able to get this station for at least another hour of driving as the route he is following wraps around Lake Erie. The radio signal takes a more direct route, of course, right over the lake. *As the crow flies,* he'll not be too far away from Detroit.

The lead story at the top of the hour is about Iraq again. Saddam Hussein, the dictator over there, has threatened to use a new sort of missile he says can reach Israel and will be used in retaliation for the nineteen Palestinian protesters killed earlier this month by Israeli troops. The CBS report includes a sound bite from President Bush, making it apparent that he wishes Hussein would quit changing the subject away from Kuwait: "Saddam has tried to, from the beginning, justify the illegal invasion of Kuwait by trying to tie it into the Palestine question. And that is not working. The Arab world is almost united against him."

Bush pronounces the name *sad-um* so that it rhymes with "madam," not the way everyone else seems to pronounce it*: Suh-dahm*, rhyming with "bomb." Other times Bush seems to call the Iraqi leader *Sodom*, like the wicked city destroyed by God in the Old Testament. Though it's not exactly clear what sins were being committed there, it's where we get the word *sodomy*, so it gives you a pretty good idea what was going on, Tyler reasons. Is Bush trying to goad the Iraqi madman with these petty insults, get him to cross a line in the sand, so we can be justified in unleashing the wrath of America on him? It seems to be working. Hussein is clearly pissed at Bush, saying defiantly that any invasion *by the imperialists* will set off *the mother of all battles*. A curious phrase, Tyler thinks. He does not associate motherhood with tanks and bombs and weapons of mass destruction.

* * *

As the Cavalier continues south on I-77 past Bath and then the turn off to Cuyahoga Falls in central-east Ohio, the home stretch, Tyler slips in the Pretenders cassette, *Learning to Crawl.* Before he left home, he had cued up the tape to the track "My City Was

Gone." It opens with a waling bass riff that has become much more well-known than the song itself, co-opted by that entertaining blow-hard Rush Limbaugh as the opening to his national radio program. It's a strong beat, unique and memorable.

But what Tyler really wants to hear is tough, little Chrissie Hynde's pained, lamenting voice. *I went back to Ohio, but my family was gone.* Singing of the brutal winds of progress tearing through their shared home state, farmlands and countryside replaced by parking lots and shopping malls. *Like the wind through the trees. Ay, oh, way to go, Ohio.*

In another five or six minutes, they'll come up to Akron, birthplace to both Hynde and Tyler. She attended Firestone High, a rival of Garfield High where he went, but years earlier. He must have been in first grade when she graduated. Ten minutes to the east is Kent State, where she was a student in 1970 when those four kids were shot by the National Guard. Hynde dropped out of college and moved to London, where she gathered up some drifters and put together a band that became the Pretenders. A few years and a lot of drugs later, their song "Brass in Pocket" hit #1 in the U.K., launching the band to stardom on both sides of the Atlantic. Two of her original band mates over-dosed in 1982 but she replaced them like disposable parts and has soldiered on.

Now they're just minutes from his mother's house. Robbie's starting to wake up. That's good; he'll come out of the stupor of a motion-induced afternoon nap and be ready to get reacquainted with his grandma. It's been too long. He really should have come home sooner. Christie had been so good about writing a letter to his mother once a week, a little update on their lives, often with a photo or maybe a recipe or newspaper clipping. Tyler would add something to the bottom of her letters, but it was Christie who did most of the work. And she'd remind him to call his mother once a week, although something often came up and sometimes a week turned to two. Now his calls and letters have become even less frequent. He knows she is lonely and fearful. Why hasn't he made a better effort to take care of her?

Off the interstate now and west on State Road 764 for five blocks, turning to the south on Brown, not quite a mile, then west again on Woodsdale, another quick jog on Thornapple Avenue, then right on Ralston. The sixth house on the right is where Tyler grew up and his mother still lives. The modest cubical houses throughout this collection of neighborhoods south of Akron's city center, called Firestone Park, were built in the early Forties just as the U.S. was being dragged into the war. On the perimeter of Firestone Park and in adjoining areas, most of the homes were built in the Fifties, noticeably bigger and more elaborate, remnants of the post-war baby boom and newfound prosperity. Of course, even these ranches and bungalows are smaller than the Seventies- and Eighties-era houses in Tyler's neighborhood back in Livonia, and the lawns aren't kept up as well, the bushes overgrown, and the sidewalks cracked. What passed for prosperity in the Eisenhower years pales to today's standard of living, jacked up by eight years of supply-side Reaganomics and deficit spending and just now starting to crumble a bit in the recession George Bush will inevitably get the blame for, though it's probably cyclical and would have happened no matter who was president.

He pulls into the old driveway, right up next to the garage door. No need to worry about blocking the way out; Tyler's mother hardly ever drives her old Plymouth Volare, a car his father had proudly bought new back in 1978. Twelve years old now and probably less than forty thousand miles on it. The dark brown three-bedroom ranch seems smaller than in Tyler's memories. It had been big enough when Tyler and Celia were growing up. Each had their own bedroom and, in fact, still have their rooms kept up by their mother almost the way they left them, waiting for them to come home. The brown wood siding needs painting, Tyler observes, though maybe it's okay to get through another winter. He'll need to check the caulking around the windows. Robbie stretches his arms as Tyler frees him from the car seat's restraints and finds his land legs as his father sets him down on the driveway. They amble up the front walk to where Dorothy Manion is waiting, just inside the storm door. She undoubtedly had never changed it out in the spring for the screen door she should have had in place for warmer weather. She should let the cleansing breeze of outdoor air inside the house when the weather's good, but instead keeps in place the extra barrier, some added protection against unseen intrusive agents of disruption.

"How was your drive?" she asks Tyler as he opens the glass door. He gives his mother an unhurried hug, then steps aside so she can scoop Robbie up into her arms. The boy hesitates, a few feet away, before Tyler reaches around and scoots him over to his mother. Robbie flops lifelessly in her arms, like a stuffed animal but with warm, rubbery skin. As she leans over to kiss his cheeks, he turns his head away.

"Fine. No problems. Traffic wasn't too bad."

They all head into the kitchen, where Dorothy has a plate of warm chocolate chip cookies waiting for them. She pours Robbie into one of the chairs, with a booster seat. "How 'bout some milk with your cookies? Would you like that, Robbie?"

The boy looks up at his father who nods back. "Okay," he says softly.

"It's good to see you, Mom. I've been meaning to get back here sooner..." he trails off. He really doesn't have a good excuse, other than his extended stay in the hospital. But that was six weeks ago. He could have been working on his job search here, at the Akron library, just as well as back in Michigan.

"It's good to have you home, Tyler. It's been too long."

Dorothy Manion is fifty-eight. Her shoulder-length, brown-and-gray hair is straight and out-of-style by fifteen years. A drab, loose-fitting dress and house coat, pale blue and tan, covers her slightly stooped frame. At first impression, she seems older than her years, frail and weak. But when you look at the smooth complexion of her face, you can imagine you're seeing a much younger woman. If she would just get out of the house for some fresh air and exercise once in a while, dress a little flashier and take care of her hair, she might pass for a woman in her late forties.

"How is little Robbie?" she asks as they finish their cookies. "I don't believe he's said a word since he's been here."

"He's still waking up from the car ride. And taking in the new surroundings."

"Well, I have some things he might like. Let's go into the living room and see what we have there." She seems cheerful and together. *Maybe she's getting a bit better.*

Tyler sinks into her pale green sofa, the same couch she's had in this room since he can remember as a little boy. Robbie plunks down on the light brown carpet, which once was plush but has been matted down over the years, now flat and vaguely damp. The room is warm and humid, stuffy, though it's crisply cool outside and sunny. The blinds are mostly drawn but let in just enough light that they can see without turning on any of the lamps in the room.

Robbie's grandmother brings him a red, white and blue cardboard cylinder, like an old Quaker oatmeal container only taller, and pops its slightly tarnished steel lid. She dumps the contents of the tube on the floor by the boy.

"My Tinker Toys!" Tyler exclaims. "You saved them all this time."

Red, blue, yellow, orange and green wooden sticks of different lengths, and beige-colored wooden connectors, like sandwich cookies rimmed with holes to mate with the colored sticks, poured onto the floor right out of Tyler's memory.

"And I have your old Erector set and some of your model rockets," she says, "but Robbie's too young for them. There is one other thing I think you'll both like."

She walks around the side of the sofa, reaches under an end table, and pulls out a blue, soft plastic case—a little bigger than a lunch box. She sets the blue case in Tyler's lap. He knows what it is before he even opens it.

"Wow, my cars!" he says excitedly.

The open case reveals three levels of black plastic cages, each holding twelve cars, a combination of Matchbox miniatures of real cars from the Sixties—a Mustang, a Falcon, a big Cadillac, a milk truck, even a green-and-yellow John Deere tractor, and Hot Wheels race cars with much fatter wheels—racing slicks—hanging from tiny, wiry axles, some of them bent so the wheels protrude at cockeyed angles.

"Come over and see these, Robbie," Tyler says to his son, taking out a few of the cars and setting them on the wooden table in front of the sofa. "Is it okay if he plays with the cars on your coffee table, Mom?"

"Of course," she says, smiling. She never would have let Tyler risk scratching the table when he was a boy and she has only become more particular over the years, but the rules may be different for grandchildren. Or maybe something has broken through the webs of paranoia inside her brain, and she really does understand there's little reason to baby the table anymore. Who is ever going to see it except these three? Still, Tyler takes it as a good sign that she so readily agrees to this concession. Perhaps she's mellowing a bit.

"Tell me how your job search is going, Tyler."

He tells her about his process at the library of looking through newspapers, including the *Akron Beacon-Journal*, he is quick to mention. Not many job openings so far, except for one in Toledo, and with the recession there are plenty of job seekers competing for whatever jobs there are. Still, he's optimistic. He has, after all, worked for General Motors, which has to impress the hiring managers at other, smaller companies.

"Well, I hope you can get on with one of the companies around here. The big tire companies must need people."

Akron is still known as the "Rubber Capital of the World," but its grasp on this claim is loosening fast. Goodyear is still here but the others have been bought up by foreign companies in a flurry of takeovers—Goodrich had merged with Uniroyal, and then just this year was taken over by the French company Michelin; General Tire was bought three years ago by the Germans; and, of course, Firestone, where Tyler's father had worked, by Japan's Bridgestone two years ago. The takeover of Firestone is a particularly ironic insult to American pride because of the history between the two companies. A Japanese rubber and tire company rising out of the ashes of World War II had wanted a new non-Japanese name that would sound like a successful tire maker, so it had mimicked the name of the most famous American tire company, with the hardly original *Bridgestone*. Forty-some years later, Bridgestone has taken over the very company it had aped, Firestone, founded by Harvey Firestone in Akron way back in 1900. The copycat has devoured the original.

"Sure, but it only helps if they need people for what I do for a living—human resources. A lot of companies are shrinking their HR staffs. If they can get by with fewer staff people, they will." The taken-over tire companies have kept some operations in Akron, but nothing like it used to be.

"If you can get on in Akron or Canton, you could live here. Or even if you had your own house, it wouldn't be too far away, and I could watch Robbie for you. That daycare you have back in Michigan must be so expensive. I can give him better attention right here."

"That would be nice, Mom. It really would. But I have to look all over, at least in Michigan and Ohio, maybe Chicago. I've got to find a job soon. GM gave me a bit of a severance, but that's pretty well gone and I'm living off savings now. I'm not thrilled about it, but I even started to get unemployment…" He trails off. Taking money from the government for being out of work is humiliating, an admission of failure. That's what it's come to, his fall from his expected career trajectory into the big old government safety net. His father, a life-long Republican, must be rolling around in his grave. After the eight go-go years of the nearly senile Reagan, peeling away regulation and letting a little deficit spending prime the engines of free enterprise, George Bush has inherited the undesirable part of the inevitable economic cycle, a nasty recession. Doing his best to get the country off its back, like the listless heavy-weight fighter's skinny old manager behind the ropes pleading for him to get up off the mat one more time, Bush continues to pledge *no new taxes*. But the Democrats now play the role of righteous, fiscal hawks insisting on deficit reduction by means of a little added burden on the wealthy who can afford it. Their ulterior motive is not hard to decipher. Ginning up the tax rates will surely prolong the downturn through the end of '92, just long enough for their guy, Bill Bradley, Dick Gephardt or maybe Al Gore, to defeat recession-saddled Bush in the November election; wouldn't that be convenient? This whole Iraq issue is taking up all of the Bush Presidency's oxygen, but by the time it comes to vote, John Doe American is going to care most about how well things seem to be going right here in the U.S.A.

"Taking money for unemployment?" his mother exclaims. "Has it come to that? You must really be running out of money. How are you going to take care of Robbie?"

Dorothy Manion shakes her head, then gets up and walks over to the kitchen. Seeing that the coffee has finished brewing, she pours a mug for Tyler and for herself. She takes hers black and adds some skim milk to his. She sets the mugs on coasters and sits down on the sofa beside him again. Robbie has left a half dozen Matchbox cars lined up in a row on the coffee table and now plays again with the Tinker Toys on the floor. He's figured out that the ends of the sticks fit into the connector cookies, but hasn't made them into anything yet. Tyler will need to work with him to get him going.

He takes a sip of coffee, but it's still too hot.

"Speaking of money, are you doing okay here?"

It's a delicate subject. Finances were never discussed when his father was alive, and his mother certainly wouldn't ever bring it up herself. It's perfectly reasonable for a parent to ask a son about his money problems, but it is out-of-bounds for the son to ask his parent about such a sensitive topic.

But Dorothy allows it.

"Oh, I don't need much. The house has been paid off for a few years now and so is the car, of course. I get a little each month from Dennis' life insurance and pension. Eventually, there will be Social Security. I don't have many expenses anymore, really, just what it takes to heat the house, pay the taxes and buy a little food for me … and for Anastasia."

This last she adds as a solid-gray, almost silver, cat walks into the room and rubs up against Dorothy's legs. Twelve years old, the Russian Blue has been her closest companion since Tyler went away to college. Like many of this breed, Anastasia has an extra toe on each paw—*polydactyly*, it's called. Six on each of her front feet, double thumbs, so that they look from the underside like little gray catcher's mitts; five toes on each of the back feet instead of a cat's usual four, not including the little protruding bump on the ankle that was itself a toe in prehistoric times on an ancestor much more vicious than the modern house cat, before the toe shriveled up into almost nothingness in evolutionary progress, just as humans still have a hint of a tailbone.

"So, you're okay for money?" Tyler asks again, pushing it.

"Yes," she says simply, ending the subject. Anastasia has jumped up on the couch between them, gratefully accepting strokes of petting from both these adult humans. Her purring motor switches on and fills the room with a pleasant hum.

"Would you do me a favor, Tyler? Go down cellar and look in the old fridge down there. In the freezer drawer. Bring up a container of Cool Whip. Please. I'll make us some pudding we can have for dessert. Would you like that, Robbie?"

It always rankles a nerve inside Tyler when she adds that *Please* after the fact, just being polite, he knows, but the separateness of the word makes it more emphatic, like she's exasperated by his unwillingness to have already done whatever she had just thought to ask him. She pets the cat, protectively curling her hand around it, so it won't be disturbed and jump away when Tyler gets up.

Robbie looks up from the Tinker Toys momentarily when he hears his name, but not having been paying attention, he doesn't know what he had been asked, so he goes back to playing with the colorful sticks. The room spins briefly as Tyler gets up from the couch. He heads down the stairs to the basement his father renovated fifteen or so years ago. The cement floor is carpeted and acoustical tiles cover the rafters and pipes so that it is almost like another finished floor, but with a noticeable smell of mildew and harsh, uneven light that doesn't reach many of the corners. There's a couch and stuffed chairs huddled around a television that hasn't been turned on in ages. Dust-covered piles of old newspapers and magazines rise up from a wooden coffee table in front of the couch, and from two end tables, and another stack has been started on a TV tray stand. Even this relatively newer pile is covered by a thick layer of gray dust. Bookcases and shelves house paperbacks and hardcover children's books and a variety of games and puzzles. On the other side of the wooden stairwell, standing on green and yellow linoleum, is a refrigerator used for overflow when the house buzzed with activity and frequent guests. Farther around this side of the basement are his father's workbench and the few tools that remain after Tyler brought most of them to his house in Michigan, to his own workshop in his basement. Carrying on the way fathers do, working on projects, fixing the things that break so often in this life. His mother doesn't like coming down here anymore. She only uses the extra refrigerator because the friend who grocery shops for her as a favor doesn't like to do it every week, so she buys bigger quantities of some things that will last a while. He finds the Cool Whip and returns upstairs to his mother, his son and the cat still right there where he left them.

After dinner and the pudding dessert, they all settle down on the couch and turn on the television. But there's nothing interesting on any of the four channels she gets with the rabbit ears antenna protruding from the TV, and three of the four are annoyingly distorted with static. Tyler volunteers to go back "down cellar" and find a book or two they can read to Robbie.

He returns with two Disney picture books: *Bambi* and *Snow White*. Robbie sits between the two adults who take turns reading the story, pausing often to point out this or that in the pictures. Robbie follows along and seems to enjoy these old tales. Robbie at his house has newer Disney books that go with movie videotapes Tyler and Christie bought over the last two years—good ones like *The Great Mouse Detective*, *The Fox and the Hound*, *The Little Mermaid* and *Oliver and Company*, and some duds like *The Black Cauldron* and *The Journey of Natty Gann* that he bought from the discount bin at Target.

Then it's time for Robbie to go to bed. He does not fight it. Tyler's mother has set up a toddler bed, a short crib without the jail bars, in Celia's old room, still painted the lavender he remembers from his youth, plastic horses and elephants on the shelves, along with sets of books, Nancy Drew and Trixie Belden, all frozen in time from when Celia was in junior high. Whatever changes his sister made to her room when she attended high school and college have been stripped away, like the home of a President or poet, owned in later years by a non-descript family whose remodeling touches are studiously removed by the historian, restoring to a particularly favorite time period held in higher esteem than the more recent past.

Tyler's room has similarly been frozen—to his high school years, though he doesn't detect any overt stripping away of his latter-day furnishings. Evidently, his room didn't evolve much as his own identity came into shape during his college years—his musical tastes changing from Top Forty to what the music executives call Album-Oriented Rock, his hair becoming longer and more consciously free-form, his clothes a little less teenager-chic. He wonders what he would make of the earlier version of himself that he was as a senior in high school, thinking ahead with some blend of unease and feigned indifference to his college years, excited about leaving home for some measure of college independence, yet equally filled with trepidation as the just recently achieved feeling of mastery of the high school routine is about to evaporate into a new unknown. Was he just an unformed version of his later self, destined to become exactly this adult that he now is, or was he like a near-sighted explorer continually confronted with forks in the road, many of which would not become apparent until he was long past them, his choices hardened into the unyielding cement of advancing time, never an opportunity to go back and undo them, to change his mind, or even to learn from his mistakes since he would never again be presented with those particular choices? Against a backdrop of light blue walls, the shelves in his room hold several small trophies for his contributions to a number of winning teams, including those two state champion runner-up baseball squads his junior and senior years. Souvenirs from family vacations taken years before his father starting pulling back, then disappearing from their lives, leaving the three of them without a leader who would plan these annual pilgrimages to historic sites, sometimes combined with an excursion to the beach—Alamo-Galveston, Gettysburg-Washington-Williamsburg, Cape Kennedy-Disneyworld-Daytona Beach—glass globes and cannons, sea shells and a miniature Saturn V rocket complete with a tiny Apollo capsule ready to carry away three unseen astronauts who would have to be the size of ants. Two posters on the wall: George Brett, Kansas City's sweet-hitting third baseman, not because he liked the Royals but because Brett was the ultimate good guy playing Tyler's position, a Golden Boy like Steve Garvey but on the opposite side of the infield; and Gary Danielson, a rookie quarterback for the Lions in Tyler's freshman year at Garfield High, coming over from the defunct World Football League with so much promise who did deliver just enough over his eight years in Detroit to keep perennially hopeful Lions fans optimistic about their chances the next year, only to end his career in Cleveland of all places.

Dorothy goes to bed soon after Robbie, leaving Tyler to switch around among the unsatisfying four channels the rabbit-eared TV sort-of receives. Still nothing on. He turns the set off and goes into the kitchen to use the phone.

"Hey, Livvy, it's Tyler." This just blurted out, the first time he has called her anything but the full Lyvia. But it did sound right as he said it: *Livvy*. The three syllables in "Lyvia" beg to be shortened with familiarity, but "Liv" is too short and abrupt, not classy enough. It doesn't occur to him yet that this is exactly what he had done with Christie's name, who was *Christina* when he met her. *Chris* wasn't feminine enough; it had to be *Christie*.

"I was hoping it was you, Ty," she says without hesitation.

So that's how it's going to be, their new names for each other. He tells her about his drive, that his mother is well, and about the Tinker Toys and little cars. She tells him about her day, meeting up with friends on a carefree Saturday. Their talk is light and easy. A welcome adult reprieve from the childhood immersion of the last few hours—he's a boy again here in his old home, answering to his mother. Reading the old Disney books with Robbie brings him even deeper into the realm of a child, his first true self, able to think and act on his own but still so dependent on others, so many selves still to become.

***

He returns to his room to unpack the smallish suitcase he had earlier set on his old bed. George Brett stares back at him with cheerful confidence as if Tyler is the pitcher he sometimes imagines himself to be, when he needs to forget some stress that might ruin his sleep, with the one hundred five mph fastball that every other batter finds so unhittable but perhaps the great Brett could hit. Danielson stands frozen in a pocket that never leaks, forever protected by his linemen's perfect blocks, though in real life he seldom had enough time to properly let the play develop. Detroit's offensive line play has been a weakness as long as Tyler can remember.

He looks through some of his old books and chooses a novel by John Irving that he started once but didn't finish, *The Cider House Rules*. Tyler had liked that *Garp* book but this one never really grabbed him. He reads the first few pages with a vague recollection of why he didn't get very far the first time; he doesn't like the characters. He reaches for another paperback, *Gorky Park*. He remembers seeing the movie first. It was hard to follow but worth the effort. The book is even better. This Soviet investigator Renko sets off to find a murderer who has left three mutilated corpses in, of all places, a Moscow amusement park. Amazing to think of a Cedar Point or Six Flags in the humorless Soviet Union. Tyler doesn't get very far into the book before his eyelids feel heavy and he catches himself reading the same lines over and over. So, he gets ready for bed, taking out his contacts with some difficulty as they've grown dry with his sleepiness, adhering themselves to his corneas. He peals the artificial lenses off each eye like a Band-Aid stuck to sensitive skin.

22

Sunday morning. They all get up to go to the nine-thirty mass at St. Paul's on Brown Street less than a mile away. With some encouragement from Tyler, his mother agreed last night to go with them to the service, but now she is balking. She just doesn't feel up to it, she says, urging him to go on himself with Robbie. Tyler had anticipated this resistance and made sure they were up before eight, so there would be plenty of time to play this out. Tyler has made coffee and Dorothy drinks it at the kitchen table in her bathrobe. Tyler sees this as encouraging. He was afraid she would refuse to get out of bed claiming some malady or another. Instead, she is honest with him. The thought of being in the same hall with hundreds of people—strangers and people who know her are equally frightening for different reasons—is simply too much. Tyler listens and smiles back at her worried face, occasionally making a comment about how beautiful the church bells sound ringing up in the tower, the talented choir leader who has been at St. Paul's for years, the healing power of prayer. Then he plays the guilt card, something any good Catholic would have seen coming. He mentions her Sunday obligation to attend mass as well as her parental obligation to set a good example for her son and grandson. And just like that, she caves in and agrees to come along. Twice more, while they are getting ready, he will have to pry her with encouragement and guilt to prevent her from back-sliding from her promise. He says nothing when he sees how she dresses for the service—with an off-white shawl over her shoulders and a blue silk scarf on her head like a hairnet, pearl-rimmed glasses on a neck chain, she looks strikingly like funny Jane Curtain playing Mrs. Loopner on that old *Saturday Night Live* bit "The Nerds," with Gilda Radner as her daughter and Bill Murray as Gilda's goofy boyfriend, Todd.

Inside the old stone church, Robbie has shed his shyness and becomes talkative. Tyler and his mother hush him with whispered pleas and distract him with crackers and Matchbox cars, and he does grow quiet for significant periods of time. But he keeps forgetting. He points to the priest in his emerald green vestments and asks his father, "Why? He wear dat?" loud enough to elicit snickering from those around them. Later, as the priest raises the communion chalice in a solemn moment of quiet that allows Robbie's voice to carry for a dozen rows of pews, the boy asks, "What he do?"

Each time Robbie draws attention to their little trio, Dorothy Manion becomes increasingly uncomfortable. Skittish. Antsy. Lines appear in her neck; her eyes and hands fidget. Feeling the weight of a dark cloud enveloping her in anxiety, Tyler leans over and whispers in her ear: "Bring your purse up to communion and we'll head out of the church as soon as we receive. Robbie's getting a little stir-crazy."

She nods silently and he can see that the prospect that a reprieve will be coming soon relieves just enough of the crushing stress to allow her to stay in the pew until they can leave. And Robbie helps matters oddly by continuing to fuss, wiggling and sniffling, getting ready for an all-out cry. It will be understandable when they bolt before the last song. They take their place in the line slowly making its way toward the altar, the priest and the extraordinary ministers as they are called, lay-people from the parish who assist the priest giving out communion to the faithful. ...*one bread, one body be; through this blessed sacrament of unity...*

The communion song provides a little auditory cover for Robbie's sobbing, still coming in little fits; the dam yet to burst. Tyler leads them out of the stuffy confines of the church, into the open vestibule and out into the bright morning sun above the parking lot's sea of cars, the bracingly chilly, fresh autumn breeze cascading over the three of them like a rogue ocean wave on the hot sands of the beach, reaching higher than the other waves of that tide, breaking through to the dryness, blessedly.

When they are back in the car, Tyler tells his mother that he is proud of her that she was able to face her fears enough to attend the church service. They will celebrate by buying some pastries for brunch. Before Dorothy can object to the additional errand, Tyler suggests that he drop her and Robbie off at the house—again putting the blame on his son's restlessness—and he will run out to the donut store alone.

Later, Tyler settles into the couch to watch some football while his son and mother nap. Robbie had an epic meltdown before he finally fell asleep; Dorothy submitted quite willingly. Her venturing out into the world, sitting with so many others inside the church, feeling them all staring at her gasping for breath inside the crowdedness of it all, has exhausted her. For his part, Tyler welcomes a couple-hour reprieve from his neurotic mother and his suddenly terrible-two toddler son. She has become inconsolably infantile in her fears, which has oddly reversed the regression in the boy. Nature allows some to grow up while others grow childish in old age, maturity and senility paired in harmony so that there is never too much lunacy or wisdom in the world at once.

The Browns are playing away from home, which means Tyler is stuck watching them. When they play at home and don't sell out the stadium, the game is mercifully blacked out of the Cleveland area and a better game is televised. This game is particularly bad: the Browns versus the New Orleans Saints, two losing teams going nowhere. Weak on both offense and defense, the Saints nonetheless have more than enough against Cleveland. The Brown's erstwhile savior, quarterback Bernie Kosar—an Ohio native who won a national championship for the University of Miami, then stunned the world by declaring his desire to play for Cleveland, who conveniently had the first pick in a special supplemental draft held that year—is mediocre and the rest of the Browns are pathetic. Tyler watches the post-game show to find out how the Lions did. Last he heard they had jumped out to an early lead against the so-so Chiefs on two TDs from Barry Sanders, including a sweet 47-yard catch-and-run. Unfortunately, that was the high point for Detroit fans as Kansas City rolled to beat them handily.

The disappointment of the games has put Tyler in an irritable mood. Robbie and Dorothy are up and drawing pictures with crayons on scrap paper on the kitchen table. He resists the burning temptation to complain or criticize—they've slept the day away and now it's raining out; Robbie is holding the crayon wrong; his mother has let them run out of coffee for the percolator which he could have bought when he was out this morning on his danish run. Instead, he asks what he can do to help get supper together. He will team up with his mother to put a simple meal together, meatloaf from a mixture of ground beef and ground pork, with mashed potatoes from a box of flakes. When he was growing up, his mother would have used real potatoes. But just as he is no longer that school kid living at home, she is no longer the confident and accomplished housewife and mother she once was. Time marches our earlier selves off a plank. They plummet into the cold, dark, unforgiving sea never to resurface, existing only in our memories. The current-model self remains on the ship, content to mop the deck and do the other menial chores that make up our daily lives, until this new self, too, must walk the plank. Eventually, we run out of newer editions to inhabit, and as we tumble into the sea, we realize it is really us in that last self, sinking with utter finality into the salty blankness. Of course, we don't know how many editions we have in this life of ours. Some like Cuhlman have had many and might still have another yet to come. For that girl, Linda McNeary, killed in the crash with Tyler's car, her seventeen-year-old self was the end of the line, all life snuffed out of her before the next self could get properly into position. Christie, too, knocked off the path that should have carried her as a young mother raising two or maybe three children, into her middle age, seeing them get married and giving her grandchildren, slowing down a bit into her later life, content with all that had come to pass, the regrets too few to concern her. No fairness in this disparity of selves granted throughout the divine economy; fairness must lie beyond, where only our souls can venture. In our unknowing what future still awaits us, we can only live fully in the now. So how can his mother just waste away her days hiding from life? Isn't it selfish, or self-defeating, of her to live this way? He says nothing of these thoughts as they work together in silence to clean the kitchen after their early dinner so that they can catch *60 Minutes*. He really should buy her a VCR so she can tape the shows she wants to see no matter when they come on, but he knows she'd never learn how to use it. Technology today is designed by young Japanese math whizzes who can imagine anything, except that others may find all the complexity overwhelming.

Tyler leaves his mother and son in the living room to get a colorful cardboard envelope from his suitcase in his old bedroom. He sits down on the couch beside Dorothy.

"I want to show you some photos I just had developed," he says, handing her the little stack of prints. She moves slowly through them, admiring the pictures of Robbie in the park. "Pick out whichever ones you want. I'll make more copies from the negatives. In fact, I'll give you an eight-by-ten in a frame you can hang up."

She smiles and nods, finding it hard to choose among many similar shots of her darling, expressive grandson.

Then she comes to the first photo of Christie and stops, like he had back in the drugstore.

"Oh, my," she says, simply. "So lovely, your Christie."

He explains to her how he'd forgotten he'd taken the shots, discovering them only this week.

"Have you shown them to Robbie?" she asks.

No, he says. He's not sure if he should just now.

"Of course, you should," she says without hesitation.

Dorothy beckons her grandson to see what they are looking at. The little boy climbs up on the couch in the warmth between father and grandmother and stares into his own mother's sweet blue eyes there before him.

"Mommy!" he exclaims, reaching out with chubby fingers to touch her face. They sit there on the couch squeezed tight but oh so comfortably together, looking at the pictures of Christie, and then of happy Robbie in the warm autumn playground scene. Dorothy dabs tears streaming down her cheeks and her son, too, needs to reach for the tissue box. Then the quiet moment together is fractured as the child squirms free to return to the miniature cars on the coffee table.

23

It's still raining Monday morning when they wake up. They watch *Good Morning America* on the couch in the living room, but without coffee because they're out. Tyler will have to run to the grocery this afternoon. It would be better if he can talk his mother into coming, too—they could make an activity for the three of them out of it—but he won't push it if she balks.

GMA gives way to *Sesame Street,* and Robbie sits on the couch transfixed. Tyler and his mother have moved to the kitchen, cleaning up after a breakfast of cereal and toast. They're talking about Tyler's dad, a subject he brought up, determined that their last full day before he and Robbie drive home to Michigan contain some substantive conversation. It's not like him to initiate any kind of talk that may unlock inner feelings, unearth forgotten unpleasantries, unsettle the ease of light and banal banter between them. But he's still shrouded in the fuzzy-headed aftermath of foggy sleeplessness last night, conscious that there is something he should know from this other self that his mother has become. While there is still time left on the clock.

"He worked hard, your father. When he was at the factory, his mind was completely there. He didn't want me to call him during the day, it would distract him. So, I learned to shut him out of our world, whatever you and your sister and I were doing, until he came home. Over dinner, he would want to hear about the things we had going on, even though they weren't nearly as important as the work he did at Firestone."

Dennis Manion had been an "industrial chemist" at the tire company. His father's core responsibility, it seemed to Tyler, was making sure the tire glue was mixed correctly and found its way in the proper amounts between the plies of rubber and belted steel on each tire as it came down the assembly line.

Tyler mentions to his mother a dinner table conversation he recalls from long ago in which his father had railed against a particular manager from corporate headquarters who was on a vendetta to slash budgets and enforce the cuts. Making do with less at work left Dennis with no sympathy for politicians who could never live within their budgets, who would rather raise taxes on their constituents than look for ways to get leaner, and who talked their way out of supposedly *draconian budget cuts* that were actually slight reductions in anticipated future spending *increases*.

But Dorothy doesn't remember this. She seems distracted, looking away from Tyler as if a buzzing insect had captured all her attention.

"How would you describe Dad to somebody who didn't know him?" Tyler asks, trying to get her to refocus.

His father had died when Tyler was in college. He has fond but already cloudy memories of his boyhood days here in Akron. Dennis Manion was not one to show affection outwardly. He might tussle Tyler's hair or pat him on the shoulder when he was happy with his son. He took great interest in Tyler's athletic successes and truthfully deserved a lot of credit for developing the skills Tyler needed in each of the sports he would play. Together they worked and played in the neighborhood park, father teaching his son to get down on one knee to field grounders fearlessly, pitching batting practice to the boy just a little harder than what he'd see in games. Or showing Tyler how to shoot hoops with a smooth, upright motion and making him dribble with his left hand until it was as deftly skilled as his right hand. Making him run crisp routes with pin-point cuts and catch the football with his fingers and hands, overcoming the natural instinct to smother it against his chest. They would drill for an hour or more at a time, greatly exceeding the limits of Tyler's ability to concentrate, building an unrelieved tension inside him like a tea kettle on a hot burner with no release, inevitably leading to failures that unleashed his father's shouted fury. And then, in later years, angry or absent became his father's *modus operandi*.

"That's an odd question from you. I'm sure you remember him well, don't you?"

Tyler nods but doesn't answer. Silence draws out more from the other.

"Well, he was intense, I would say. He was extremely focused on whatever he was doing. If he was at work, he didn't want me to call his office," she says, repeating from just a few minutes earlier. "If he was working on a project in the basement, he didn't want to be disturbed. But if he was doing something with me or with us as a family, he gave us his full attention. I think Shannon Celia inherited that from him," she says, using his older sister's full given name, a mark of her disapproval.

His missionary sister, so focused on her work on some Pacific island that she can't be bothered with worrying about her mother. And, by omitting Tyler from this thought, his mother implies that he is not someone who suffers from single-minded focus.

"How was he as a husband? To you."

Tyler is determined to not let the topic stray from his father, even as he stares past his mother through the window behind her out to the front lawn. The rain is coming down harder now. Looks like he won't have a chance to caulk around the windows. He'll need to get back down here again before it gets too cold. November is an in-between month. You get some heavy frosts, even a light snow, but there are usually some warm days, too. Indian summer.

"Oh, he was always loyal to me. Always made me know that I was special to him. I wouldn't call him romantic. No, not really. But protective. And happy to be seen with me when we'd go out. Of course, I kept myself up better when I was younger. Everything seemed to grow out of sorts in the later days of our marriage."

"I've seen your pictures—you were quite the looker," he says without awkwardness, speaking of this earlier self of hers when he was just a baby and even before. But as soon as he brings it back to her present self, he stumbles. "You still look good, Mom, especially in your face. You look younger … I mean … than your age."

She blushes just a bit and looks away.

"Oh, I'm past worrying what I look like." Or so not past worrying about everything else that she can't be bothered with her looks. There's only so much worry inside each of us; it's how we spend it. "How are you doing without Christie?"

"I miss her, of course. And sometimes I half-expect to see her around the house, with Robbie, or to wake up with her beside me."

That's a little too intimate, it seems, to say to his mother. He takes a sip from the ice water she poured for him earlier.

"But I'm trying to carry on. It's hard but you can do it," he says, talking about himself but also about her, his mother, and she gets it, because she looks away. The silence builds between them like a small puffy cloud, more cotton than worry, and they don't mind it.

"I've started to see someone," he says after a while. "A nice girl named Lyvia I met at a play, at a little theater in Detroit. She's a graduate student at U-of-D. The University of Detroit," he adds to clarify since his mother isn't from up there. U-D could mean the University of Dayton. "A good Catholic girl. You'd like her."

A bit of silence again, then: "Oh, Tyler. Don't you think it's too soon? Shouldn't you just spend your time with Robbie, give both of you more time? And with you losing your job, too. It would be better if you moved back here and maybe I could help take care of you both." Once this son of hers finally got up on his own two feet, she thinks, he has always run when he should walk. He jumps ahead when he should stay a little while longer, impatient with the present moment. Now, he won't move home where he belongs.

"I don't think you're in much position to take care of anyone," he says quickly in retort, not really trying to be hurtful.

She sets down the dish towel she'd been holding. "Yes, you're right. I can't even take care of myself, can I? Well, then, let's make a list of the things I need to have on hand. You'll do me a favor, going out to the Giant Eagle and getting them for me? Please. Soon as you know it, you and Robbie will be pulling out of the drive and leaving me behind."

At the Giant Eagle, after lunch, Tyler pushes his shopping cart up one aisle and then the next. It's not laid out like the Kroger's near his home in Livonia, so he can't just hunt things down. He has to let it come to him as he methodically covers the whole store. The list is heavy on packaged goods that will last a while. As for fresh fruits and vegetables, he keeps the quantities small, so she won't waste them when he and Robbie have left. She has a good selection of Tupperware for keeping leftovers fresh, but he could see where a woman living alone, especially one prone to lack of appetite during long bouts of depression, would throw away a lot of food.

His eyes gravitate to two smooth, sinewy contours rising up from a pair of heels before disappearing into the roundness of a blue jean skirt, the rest of the presumably attractive woman mostly invisible as she bends over next to a display of apples and grapes. He becomes aware of numerous female shapes patrolling the fresh produce section, the pinks and teals and hunter greens of their blouses and rain slickers growing out of dark blue designer jeans stretched tight over hips of various sizes and shapes. If there are any other men here on a weekday afternoon he takes no notice of them; they add no color to the scene scrolling before him.

He comes to the pet food aisle and finds a large bag of the particular brand of cat food Dorothy has requested for Anastasia. In the meat department, he selects a couple of nice steaks. If Tyler cuts the meat into very small bites, Robbie can help eat part of his grandmother's steak. *Coffee, can't forget that.* And the creamer he knows she likes but was out of even before he and Robbie arrived.

He loads the cartload of brown paper bags of groceries into the Cavalier's trunk—bigger than you might think it would be in a compact. He pulls out of the parking lot for a side trip to the high school for old time's sake. On the way, he pulls up beside a maroon Buick Riviera from the early Seventies, one of the biggest two-door coupes ever made. Its hood is seemingly as long as Tyler's entire Cavalier. The beast is packing an ungodly 455 cubic-inch V-8 according to the insignia on the lower part of the front quarter panel; that would be about seven-and-a-half liters the way engines are measured today, he figures. The little four-banger in his Cavalier is just a 1.8 liter—less than one-quarter the displacement of the Riviera's massive engine. The light turns green. Tyler lets his clutch out all at once, while pushing down hard on the accelerator pedal. The front tires chirp loudly as they spin wild and free on the rain-slicked black-top pavement. *Wet burn outs don't count,* but so what?

The Riviera grunts and a second later rockets past Tyler and his sad little Cavalier. The car's driver, younger than Tyler by at least a few years, doesn't bother to make eye contact. When the Riviera is well ahead of him, Tyler can see its driver glance into his rear-view mirror, undoubtedly with a smug smile before he makes a left-hand turn and disappears from Tyler's life forever, a shadow inside his brain soon to be painted over with something more memorable and perhaps important.

He drives past the John F. Kennedy Memorial Fountain on Monument Road. A spray of water shoots up from inside and underneath a large stone ring. To one side a low, rectangular reflecting pool leads to a little black, smoldering cone, an eternal flame it's supposed to be. Under the surface of the shallow water, he remembers, tarnished images of Lincoln, Jefferson, Roosevelt and Washington look up from the bluish-green bottom, or the reverse sides of the discarded coins—monuments, torches and eagles. Each tossed there with a superstitious wish, sinking quickly underneath the disappearing ripple. But not a single Kennedy, at least that he's ever seen there, fifty cents too steep a price for a wish not likely to come true; you never see them in your change anyway. Chlorinated water recirculating in the fountain, going nowhere, unnaturally.

One quick stop before he returns to his mother's home, up Brown Street until it meets Archwood Avenue. And there's the decrepit old high school, Garfield High, named for the twentieth President of the United States, assassinated before he could accomplish anything. Home of the Golden Rams. Not too far from Bishop Hoban Catholic High School, where Celia had wanted to attend, following most of her friends. But money was tight. Once she started at Garfield, it was clear Tyler would, too.

He parks the car in one of the few empty spots behind the school and walks out onto the football field, alone. The last period of class must be still in session. Too early for football practice. He stares up across the field and into the light mist above him, imagining he is about to field a punt. His fingers extend in anticipation. He looks up at the towering flight of the punted football, end over end it sails toward him, all the while players from the opposing team are sprinting down the sides of the field, trying to time it right so they can launch their bodies full force at him to create a devastating impact just as he touches the ball. But he's a bit deeper than where the ball will come down, so he can begin a forward lunge to catch the ball in stride, already accelerating. The players on the other team misjudge his position and end up colliding with each other as he steps ahead and breaks into a wild tear, free and loose and now able to juke the scattered remaining tacklers in motions they cannot follow. Eighty yards later, he glides into the end zone untouched and flips the ball nonchalantly to the referee who arrives a few seconds behind him, panting hard. Tyler opens his eyes, the imagined scene broken off like another take in a Hollywood film shoot, and walks off the field.

Around the stands he walks, avoiding puddles of water here and there in the grass, to the baseball field, just as he left it nine-and-a-half years ago. He takes his familiar position six feet off the third base line, bending his knees, leaning forward, weight on the balls of his feet, imaginary leather glove on his left hand, ready to man the *hot corner* as if Gil Verona had never become a Garfield Golden Ram. This is where Tyler belongs, third base. In the softball league, back when he worked for GM, they played him in the outfield more than at third, because again there was a stud athlete who wanted to play there. It's a tough position, demanding quick reflexes to be able to field the shots a big right-handed hitter, turning on a pitch, can send screaming right at you, or bouncing just ahead of your glove, handcuffing you or taking an unexpected, nasty hop right for your nose or mouth. Then you have to come up with the ball after it has bounced off your body and gun it across the diamond in time to beat the batter to first. He's still got what it takes, he thinks, to field this most difficult of positions, fearlessly, as his father had taught him.

Back inside his car, Tyler flips on his wipers; it's drizzling again. He tunes the radio to an AM station with news and talk. The Space Shuttle Discovery has returned to Earth, successfully completing its mission—the launch of the European Space Agency's Ulysses satellite on a half-billion-mile journey, including a tricky "slingshot" swing around Jupiter. Scientists hope to learn just how much water vapor can be found in the atmosphere of the giant planet. If water, essential to all life as we know it, can be found in significant quantity outside of our Earth, perhaps some evidence of primitive life forms as well, though not on frozen Jupiter. Meanwhile, NASA still hasn't found the cause of the fuel-leak problems that have kept shuttles Columbia and Atlantis on the ground for five months. Ever since that Challenger disaster a few years ago, the space agency has been cautious to the point it's become embarrassing. But you can't blame them—who'd want to sit atop a mountain of explosive fuel on the launch pad, waiting for take-off, wondering about that pesky little leak they weren't able to ever quite fix?

After a station break and all the commercials, a blend of the national ones he's heard before and local spots for car dealers and a funeral home, they start up another topic. Soviet leader Mikhail Gorbachev has been awarded the Nobel Peace Prize for all his reforms and for reducing Cold War tensions. The radio program host is indignant. He thinks Reagan should have won the prize for forcing Gorby into a corner where the wall had to come down and they had to go through with all that *glasnost* and *perestroika*. Gorbachev is the one marked like Cain with that ugly red birthmark looking like a worm trying to wiggle off the top of his forehead. You'd think someone so powerful could get that taken care of; don't they have a laser for that over there in Russia?

He parks the Cavalier in his mother's driveway and walks quickly through the drizzle to the box to get her mail. He steps over and around several water-logged worms, gray and bloated, lying on the sidewalk. Then he opens the mailbox's little door and finds it completely jammed with letters and fliers. He takes them out a handful at a time and carries it all in cradled arms, then works the front door's handle awkwardly but gets it open. He's a wet mess by the time he steps inside.

"Geez, Mom. Don't you ever get your mail?"

She looks at him with sorry eyes.

"Sometimes it's too hard to leave the house. The front yard is so open since we had to take down the elm tree." An early victim of Dutch elm disease, like just about every other elm tree in the

Midwest now, the big tree was cut down from the front yard at least a dozen years ago, when his father was still here.

"You've got to face this thing, Mom. You got to be able to walk out to your own mailbox."

"I do sometimes. It's not too bad when I first step out the door. But then I get to the sidewalk and the devil strip, and I feel like I'm just out there, in the open, where everyone can see me," she confides to her son. "And I just want to turn and run back into the house."

Devil strip is a local expression for the band of grass between the sidewalk and the street. No one seems to have any idea where the term came from; everyone around here calls it that, but only to his mother is it a fearful thing.

Tyler sits down on the couch next to Dorothy and the purring cat. Robbie is playing with some new old toys that she has found somewhere in the house. Tyler hands her some of the mail, setting the rest down on the coffee table. She sees that he's done a quick sort and given her the ones that appear to be bills. It's an opening to return to the subject of her money situation.

But before he can bring it up again, she says, preemptively, "You know, Tyler, I've been meaning to tell you something. It's about the sadness, *the cloud.*"

That's what Dorothy Manion calls the depression and anxiety that has become such a central part of her life. She rarely talks about it but must find it an easier subject than further talk of her finances.

"I was remembering where it all began, and I thought you should know. Your father and I had been married several years and had been unable to have a baby. We wanted children, very much so. The doctors couldn't help us. There seemed no good reason I couldn't become pregnant, but it just wasn't happening for us. That's when it started. The *cloud.*"

It overwhelms her senses, Tyler knows from the years he lived here, makes everything colorless and remote.

"I became quite distraught," she continues, "convinced we would never have children. Your father stayed busy at his work, but I knew it bothered him, too. We stopped talking about it, but I continued to pray for a child and I'm sure he did, too. Just as I was beginning to accept that we needed to adopt a baby, it happened—I was pregnant with your sister. She was the most welcome, unexpected addition, and I couldn't have been happier. Shannon Celia was a blessed little baby, perfectly healthy and just a joy. She hardly cried and very quickly slept through the night."

Dorothy lifts a glass of ice water to her lips and fills her mouth with the cold, clear liquid, the essence of all life. Her use of his sister's full name this time not said in any disapproving way, but from a deep fondness for a long-ago, happier time.

"Then not even six months after Celia was born, I realized I was pregnant again—with you, of course. So soon after we had become resigned to not having any children and we were going to have our second one. Your father was stunned. I would be 31 when you were born, and Dennis was three years older than me. I think he imagined that we might begin conceiving a new child every year until we stopped it. So, he did, stopped it. Had an operation without even discussing it with me."

This is a lot of talking for her. She must have been thinking about all this while he was off at the grocery.

"He said we should be happy with two healthy children, a girl and a boy. And that having more would be irresponsible, with the *population explosion* everyone was starting to talk about. The world couldn't sustain too many more people. It all sounded so reasonable. With two young children, I had my hands full and didn't think about it much right away, but it ate at me, knowing I could never have another child. And I know that's what brought back *the cloud*."

Tyler's mother says all this with her usual distant, blank expression. But there is something behind the vacant look in her eyes, deeper within her head, that Tyler notices now. It's unsettling, disturbing, yet hopeful. He has always seen his mother as shallow and weak. For as long as he can remember she has shied away from life, and he has held it against her, been embarrassed by her. The pills dulled her feelings of anxiety and made her numb to most everything, finally driving away both her daughter and her son. Or so he has imagined. Perhaps there is more to his mother than a pill-popping coward, perhaps she deserves more than he has been willing to be for her. The peaceful distance he thought they both were maintaining through their small talk, her blank stares and his infrequent visits may have been more his invention than hers. Maybe there is a greater person inside her, a self, who deserves the one thing that is so hard for him to give anyone: his undivided attention.

"Are some days better than others?" Tyler asks her. "Do you ever feel a break in *the cloud*?"

"For years there wasn't any let up. I would hope for any sign that I was coming up for air, even for a moment. Can you imagine what it's like to not see the beauty in a sunset or the deep blue sky, or in your child's smile, to never taste a bite of food and really enjoy it? I so longed to experience a single moment of anything I could call delicious, because then I would know I had poked a hole in *the cloud*."

The worst thing about her *cloud*, she says, is that it extends unbroken from horizon to horizon.

"There are no happy moments when you're in it. No breaks. If I could just once really enjoy the taste of my food, or a smell or touch, *the cloud* would no longer be so menacing. Anyone can stand an awful day or a terrible week. Everybody goes through slumps. It's only when the sadness is unending that it gains real power over you. Can you understand all this?"

"I guess so. It's what I think makes the whole idea of hell so frightening—that it lasts forever," Tyler says. *Or even heaven. Hard to think of anything that never ends.*

"Living under *the cloud* is a hell. Far worse than any physical pain. But its real power is that it won't let up. Going through labor, twice, was terribly painful but it was all worth it," she says. "This is so much worse and there's nothing worthwhile at the end to look forward to. Except the hope that there might be an end."

24

Heading back home from his old home. Interstate 77 North toward the Ohio State Turnpike. Past a white Volvo going the speed limit or even slower. It has a yellow-and-black sign in the back window, a square turned up on its corners: *Baby On Board*. He remembers when it seemed every second or third car had one of those little plastic signs, as if to say: *Drive safely around me, please; got a kid in here*. A reasonable request except that it became so common-place—asking for special treatment just like everybody else. He reaches into the shoebox full of cassettes sitting on the front passenger seat and comes out with a Paul Simon tape with the hand-lettered title: *Greatest Hits, Etc.* Tyler taped it from one of the records he borrowed from Webb Rucker. The first song, "Slip Slidin' Away," begins to play. The words familiar but this time stinging, about a woman who had long ago "become a wife," speaking stoically about the life she now lives in her middle-aged years. She says that a good day "ain't got no rain," the songwriter sings, but on a bad day, she can't leave her bed, thinking only of "things that might have been."

Is that what brings on *the cloud* for his mother, feelings of regret, what might have been? Or is it purely chemical, her body not producing enough of some endorphin or another, a deficiency that can be treated if she would just get the right medicine, the right dose? What does she think about inside that house day after day? Why can't she break out of it and just live?

Some things are just unknowable, the singer songwriter advises: *God only knows; God makes his plan. The information's unavailable to the mortal man.*

Is it really so impossible to tune in to God—to hear his words, know what he wants of us? So much more than a job, or career even. There's a bigger plan in play, yes, but is it so invisible, unknowable? Maybe we know in our hearts exactly what God wants of each of us—to become the best self we can be. What are the alternatives? To live like his frightened mother, he thinks, hiding from imagined terrors and biding her time, or in the moment just for ourselves, grabbing whatever we can, whatever we want. Hard to believe he'd be happy either way. Maybe clear spots can be found in the opaque, if we'd just look a little harder.

***

Robbie stirs in his car seat as Tyler guides the Cavalier onto the Ohio Turnpike toward Toledo. They are barely onto the *limited access highway* when Tyler hears an eruption behind him, followed quickly by the tell-tale stench. Tyler lowers his window a few inches and begins looking for the next turn-off. Thirty-six miles later, he pulls into the highway rest stop. He finds the diaper bag and then carefully extracts Robbie from his seat. They make their way into the bathroom. Tyler pulls his boy's pants down, then removes the diaper, seeping with a syrupy brown liquid with yellow and brown chunks. Trying not to breathe through his nose, Tyler drops the disgusting diaper into the trash bin by the sinks, as other patrons scurry out of the men's room. He uses five or six of the moist toilettes in the plastic tub that he'd brought in the diaper bag and eventually Robbie's bottom and legs are clean once again.

As they walk back to their car, they approach an Amish girl, with that unmistakable white bonnet on her head, walking toward them alone, her eyes looking down to avoid theirs. She has flushed cheeks but no makeup on a pale, freckled face. Her body is wrapped in a woolen blue coat that reaches down to her ankles. She's maybe fifteen; it's hard to tell exactly in her severe clothes. Tyler looks for the girl's horse and black buggy, but doesn't see any, which makes sense because the only way to get to this rest stop is via the highway that has a minimum speed of forty miles an hour. So how did she get here?

He cleans up the car seat and soon the Cavalier re-enters the turnpike. Within minutes, Robbie is asleep and Tyler's lost in thoughts of his own childhood. His father side-arms another grounder to his boy, who dutifully drops down on his left knee, holding the tip of his glove against the ground so the rolling ball won't squirt underneath it. Time and again, the boy fields the ball cleanly, jumps up and fires a throw into the backstop that simulates first base. Every so often, his father bounces the ball to his son, who must judge the skips. If the ball on its first bounce is still well ahead of him, he charges toward it and tries to field it on the big hop. If the ball's bounce is nearer to him, he must get down low, ready if it then turns into a ground-hugging roller and equally ready if it should take a hop up into his chest. Then he will block the ball, keep it in front of him, grab it bare-handed and fire it over to first. Occasionally, the ball takes a big second hop and smacks him in the chin or nose. If he flinches and turns his head away, his father yells at him and makes him run two laps all the way around the ball field. And maybe some push-ups. When he was younger, kindergarten and first grade, they practiced with a tennis ball so that it wouldn't hurt when the ball kicked up and caught his face. He learned to keep his head down, just like he was told, and maintained the habit when they switched to soft-core youth baseballs and finally to the real thing.

Throughout his Little League years, Tyler was a reliable, sometimes spectacular, third baseman. In one game, back when he was in third or fourth grade, a sharply hit ball took a wicked bounce and caught him square on his nose, almost blacked him out, it hurt so bad, so sharp, like when your funny bone hits something hard and unrelenting. But he stayed with it and threw the runner out. His coach ran in from the dugout, bringing one of the kids on the bench with him to go in for Tyler, who was confused and didn't want to leave the game. Hadn't he done just what he was supposed to do? He didn't realize yet that his white uniform top was streaked with a crimson river that continued to flow from his nose. He looked over at the bleachers behind the foul line and saw the horrified looks on the parents' faces. His mother had her hands up over her mouth; his father alone clapping, smiling at Tyler. Funny, he has no other memory of his father smiling like that at him.

He shifts his weight in the cramped bucket seat. His wallet digs into his right butt cheek. So much like the Sunbird, now deceased. When he gets a new job, he's going to get a better car, more room and more power, he again tells himself. George made sure they didn't crush the Sunbird before he had a chance to see it. They both went over to the storage yard the day after he came home from the hospital, his mother-in-law staying back to watch Robbie, thankfully, so he didn't have to hear whatever biting commentary she would have to offer.

The car was a sight to behold. The front passenger side completely caved in—the A-pillar twisted in a crazy angle, glass completely missing from the door and half the windshield—where the teenager had barreled her car into the front right side of his. Tyler could still open the driver's door, though it creaked and groaned in protest. He had to squeeze in behind the wheel, the seat cocked forward and bent toward his door, but he was able to get into it. In front of him, the remaining glass in the windshield was a cloudy white-and-green spider web. He tried to picture the approaching intersection that rainy night of the accident. He could see the light turn yellow in the foggy spray ahead as he keeps on going, ready to arrive home. Then nothing. He looks to the right, through the hole in the windshield and door, trying to remember an image of the other car. But he can't. Not even a color. Nothing. Either he never saw the car until it hit him or the trauma of the accident wiped clean the last few seconds of his consciousness. His next memory is the radiant white of the hospital bed, his spinning head and throwing up on that one tall nurse. That's when the spinning sensation began, in the hospital. He should tell his doctor this; it may be important. He needs to get this thing under control. It would be disastrous if he had a bad dizzy spell while driving, especially if he had Robbie with him. *Baby On Board.*

And what of that girl Linda McNeary? Her life squashed like his Sunbird but cannot so easily be replaced. Had she, too, become a so-called *beating-heart cadaver* like his Christie, somehow partially living on in another's body that needed a transplant to survive or was her young body too horribly mutilated in the force of the crash, her organs exploding beyond harvesting, her insides just a bloody mess? Like a deer hit by a car, as his father who loved to hunt told him once. Tyler's dad had hit a doe coming home from his job at Firestone one evening, but had not gathered it up and brought it home to be dressed and smoked. Dennis Manion knew that the force of the collision would have caused massive internal bleeding destroying the fibers of the muscle tissues that we call meat. Roadkill isn't worth harvesting.

The tape plays on: *I know they say let it be / But it just don't work out that way.* Simon on "Mother and Child Reunion" apparently rebuking that other Paul for his upbeat tune, sung to the Mother of God, it seems to Tyler, without sarcasm or irony. Roadkill, aren't we all in the end? Run over, if not by our failures then by our own misguided ambitions. Not worth harvesting. *Hopefully not how the Lord sizes us up*, he muses.

So many people around him dying before their time was rightly up. First his dad, not even sixty, and dead to his family for years before that. Then Christie, shockingly, only a few years out of college, starting out on their married life together. And now this McNeary girl, seventeen, just discovering boys probably. So much life ahead of her. He is the only connection these three premature corpses have to each other, their common denominator. Death hangs over him like a persistent shadow. Or an unwanted house guest getting way too comfortable.

Tyler shakes free of the dark thoughts. When he came home from dinner with Livvy that one night last week—Thursday?—hurrying because he didn't want to keep Nicki out too late on a school night, the babysitter had insisted he keep his promise and tell her the story of how he'd met his new girlfriend. He told her that he'd been set up on a blind date, not bothering to mention his ad in the *Detroit News* "Companion Corner." Unfortunately, this blind date was none too attractive, he said, rolling his eyes. Nicki snickered, puffed up her cheeks and put her arms into the belly of her sweatshirt to pantomime fatness. Tyler nodded and told her how he'd seen this pretty and stylish young woman in a red dress and hat in the row ahead, and how he'd talked to her when his fat date had gone out during intermission.

"I can't believe you did that," Nicki had said, clearly impressed.

"Me, neither," Tyler said. "It was one of those once-in-a-million-years chance that when it happens, you're so stunned that you never act on it. And always regret not acting. But this time it was like playing out in slow motion—I could see that I was going to have a shot at talking to this girl. So, I just decided to go for it."

Tyler had finished the story quickly: that was the night he had the accident, so when Lyvia called him, he hadn't been home. His mother-in-law told her he was in the hospital, and the girl had sent him flowers. Against all odds, she had called him again and they had talked. And soon they were dating.

It's going to be tougher to schedule babysitting with Nicki now that her basketball season is in full gear. Lyvia said that she wanted to do more with Robbie, so he'll take her up on it. She can come over to his house and when it's time to put Robbie down for the night, then they'll have some alone time. Of course, he'll invite her to stay over. He pictures Livvy in a skimpy nightie reaching only as far down as the space where the insides of her bare thighs don't quite come together, the little gap filled with the bottom front of her panties and the mossy dampness that could be waiting there for him.

It's the top of the hour, so he flips the stereo to AM radio and hits the second preset that jumps the tuner to 950, WWJ. ... *Hussein is not backing down even as U.S. forces in the Persian Gulf reach 200,000...*

Then Tyler remembers that the World Series opens tonight and should have started by now. He hits the other presets until he hears the sounds of a cheering crowd. The heavily favored A's against the Cincinnati Reds, who get no respect despite leading their division continuously since opening day, *wire-to-wire*, as they say. Radio announcer Vin Scully, filling in some dead airtime, notes good-naturedly that Reds owner Marge Schott again had fumbled her words earlier tonight. Speaking to stadium throngs over the public address system before the first pitch, she dedicated the 1990 World Series "to our military women and men in the *Far East*."

* * *

Eric Davis drills a line drive toward left center but still climbing. *That's going to be long gone!* The game on the radio makes the remaining drive pass quickly. The Reds get two more runs in the third and by the time Tyler pulls into his driveway, it's the fifth inning and Cincy is up 7-0. Robbie is just waking up, which is a problem. With three-hours-plus of solid sleep in him, he's not going to want to go to bed any time soon. They walk out together to the end of the driveway, wet from an earlier rain here. Now the air is clear and cold. Stars in the moonless sky look down at them like a rock concert's stadium full of fans, each holding the flame of a cigarette lighter at the appointed time before the big finish. The sacred darkness beckons.

"Let's go see what's in the mailbox," Tyler says to his toddling son.

"Okay," the boy says cheerfully, glad to stretch his legs after the long car ride.

A few letters in white envelopes await him in the box, along with a colorful flier of twelve or so pages printed on that slick paper that you can't recycle, and a *Sports Illustrated*. There's not enough light out to know if any of the envelopes hold anything promising inside, but most of them have a clear plastic window to make visible his address printed on a pre-printed card inside, the hallmark of a bill. He gets too many of those. When he still had his job, they were easier to shrug off as the price to pay for being alive and well in Twentieth Century America—bills for gas to heat his home, electricity, water and sewer, mortgage, cable TV, insurance for the car and for the house, property tax, the telephone and newspaper, on and on for all the things we take for granted but didn't have to pay for back in the days of the pioneers. Of course, they had Indians to worry about and had to venture outside if they had to take a leak in the middle of the night. So maybe worth it. But it's not just the money. There's a stress to all this that isn't easily measured. It's not often that Tyler just walks out to the end of his driveway on a clear, crisp night, breathes in deeply the nippy air, looks up at the stars—at the Big Dipper that shows you where the North Star is if you're lost in the woods; Orion the Hunter with those three bright stars making up a belt; the Seven Sisters—and allows himself to slow down enough to take it all in, to feel alive in the moment, unconcerned about the next.

The dead tree in his front yard, its two stubby little arms silhouetted against the starry sky, catches his attention. He's got to cut it down before winter. Across the street, the blue glow of a television screen can be seen through the front curtains of the Johnston's house, the old man and his restless wife probably watching the boob tube together. She's thinking of adventure and those untapped dreams she still harbors, maybe about chance encounters with younger men and the things she might teach them about passion, mystery and romance. Old Stan Johnston may be feeling frisky tonight but he's not the lover she has in mind.

"It's cold, Daddy."

Tyler scoops up the greatest treasure in his life, his son, into his arms, his right hand grasping the mail, his left hand holding his set of keys. He'll need to switch hands to open the door. He might be able to dribble a basketball with his left hand, but he's never used it to work a key into a door lock.

In the light inside his house, he scans the mail. Nothing that looks like it's from an employer. Another diaper change, then Tyler moves the highchair into the living room so he can feed his son where they can watch the rest of the World Series game. The A's can't get anything going and continue to trail 7-0. During the seventh inning stretch, Tyler's boyhood hero George Brett, still with the Royals, comes into the broadcast booth to be recognized as the first player to lead his league in hitting in at least one season in three different decades. In this just-completed 1990 season, he got off to a terrible start and considered retirement. But he caught fire in July and hit nearly .400 the second half of the season, passing Rickey Henderson as the league leader in late September and never looking back.

Robbie's playing with Duploes now, clicking them together to make a stack. So much of everything is new for him. Each day, each hour, a new experience rolling onto the screen that seems suspended right in front of his eyes. It all flows together, continuously running. Something familiar, then something new again.

Unpleasant disruptions are blurred with randomness like sand that falls in the cracks of a sidewalk and helps smooth things out. No conscious reasoning yet to weave it all together, make sense of the patterns of life, just moving from one scene to the next like a TV with somebody else holding the clicker. He's a happy kid, mostly, rolling with the changes that come his way. Sometimes the channel gets changed suddenly and he watches what's on that one. A lot of what's happening out there in front of his eyes makes no sense, like when a VCR is playing on fast forward; it's a blur. But that just makes it interesting, funny. As long as no one expects him to make sense of what's going on, it's all for the good.

25

The next day, Robbie's back in daycare. Tyler is on his way to have coffee with that old hippie nun, the chaplain from the hospital, Sister Harriet Worthy. She had called his house while he was in Ohio, one of only three messages on his answering machine, asking to meet so they could continue the talk they'd started that last full day of his at the hospital. When Tyler called her back, he said he was doing fine, really, and also he wasn't sure when his health insurance would run out. He was trying not to rack up any extra medical bills. She replied that this wasn't part of any hospital treatment, that taking care of *souls* was always free of charge. He asked her what she meant by that, and she said again she just wanted to follow up on what they'd talked about in the hospital, which Tyler doesn't really remember exactly, and that there wouldn't be any bill. He agreed to meet her at a McDonald's for coffee. Maybe if he gets there early, he'll get a McMuffin, too.

But Sister Harriet is already there when he arrives, wearing a black-and-white habit and the rainbow crucifix; you can't miss her, she stands out among all the working stiffs, men and women alike dressed in suits for work, the only difference these days being the ties men wear. Women have even incorporated shoulder pads into their suits, trying to be seen as muscular as men, hardly ever wearing a skirt, thinking the men will treat them more seriously if they don't have the distraction of bare female legs. The odd couple of Tyler in his jeans and this nun in her penguin outfit go up to the counter to get their coffees. Tyler grabs a couple of sugars at the condiment stand because he forgot to ask for cream and needs to cut the bitter black taste with something. They sit down toward the back, next to the locked door to the McPlayland, empty of kids in the still early morning. He tries to relax as much as he can with this nun reminding him of his grade school days with all the rules the sisters were always enforcing. Punishments for trivial offenses that somehow violated the order they cherished. Sister Scratch and the others.

After inquiring how he is feeling, Sister Harriet whispers a little prayer, quietly kicking off their meeting without drawing too much attention from the other McPatrons: "Send forth your spirit and they shall be created. And you shall renew the face of the Earth."

That's it! Tyler thinks, remembering in a flash that truck he had passed on the way to Metro Beach. *Renew the Face of the Earth.* That should become the slogan of the Sherwin-Williams Paint company, replacing *Cover the Earth* and that awful logo of the red-dipped Earth dripping paint down through the hole in the ozone layer under Antarctica, into outer space; the red goo won't stop with simply destroying the Earth. Even Bush now calling himself *the environmental President* after eight years of Reagan dismantling the EPA and letting polluters run amok. Time to change, Sherwin-Williams. Time to change.

The hippie nun has already jumped to the reason she called for this meeting. "I wanted to talk to you just a bit about your faith life," she says. *So here we go*, he thinks.

"Yeah, okay. But let me ask you something first," he says. A stalling tactic he had picked up in his short marriage, when Christie wanted to talk about something that he was sure didn't have any right answers. "When we went for that walk at the hospital, you talked about what led you to become a nun. You said something about being in Costa Rica with the Peace Corps. About poor people there being happy."

"Yes, that's right. Although, I think *joyful* might be a better word."

"Okay. What made them joyful?"

"Well, poor is a relative term, we have to start there," she says, stalling as well, it seems. "If somebody doesn't have enough to eat, or can't get medical attention, or is without access to clean water, their misery naturally overshadows everything else. We have to help bring these basic things to people in need. But the people I worked with in Costa Rica weren't lacking these things. They were only poor by our standards."

The few other customers who aren't taking their McFood and coffee to go sit alone, eyeing this nun in their midst warily. Tyler studies her face. Wrinkled lines that frame her eyes crease tighter as she speaks. The same kind of leathery lines you see on the faces of women who have spent too much time over the years in the sun, tanning. Yet the nun's complexion is a powdery, colorless white as if it has not seen direct sunlight in a long, long time. Like the sheltered face of an aristocratic spinster in eighteenth century France, never venturing outdoors without her parasol, or Michael Jackson lately.

"What were you doing there? I mean, what was your work?"

"I was teaching English to children in a rural village. The Costa Rican government wanted the Peace Corps to help the rising generation master English, to help propel the country forward economically someday."

"Makes sense. English is the language of business just about everywhere," Tyler says, nodding.

"But there was a lesson for us, the volunteers, to learn from the people we were serving. That inner joy does not come from having more money or the things it can buy."

The nun closes her eyes, and a soft smile slowly takes over her face.

"*Pura vida.* They say this all the time in Costa Rica. *Pura vida.* A kind of greeting and a goodbye, like *Aloha* in Hawaii. It literally means 'pure life,' of course. The essence of their happiness, I believe. But they also use it to mean 'Okay, why not?' or 'Don't worry about such things.'"

She reopens her eyes, but the smile remains. "And then I realized it was what we Beats and flower children had been trying to find with all our talk about *peace* and *love*, you know?"

Tyler stifles an inappropriate laugh from the flash of a mental image of this nun tripping out as the Fifties leak into the Sixties, wearing a "Make Love, Not War" tie-dyed tee shirt, and into the Seventies, making peace signs with both hands at a George McGovern rally, the changing landscape of dissent in America. *What's so funny 'bout peace, love and understanding?*

He looks out the window as the cars in a long line in the new drive-through lane lurch forward, making slow, uneven progress. A driver alone in each of the cars, office humps glancing at their watches impatiently, thinking about that first meeting of the day.

Sister Harriet apparently has switched the subject back to the task at hand, saving his soul.

"… were talking about heaven," she is saying, "about meeting up with your wife there someday, remember? Something about the way you talked. You struck me as a person who does have faith inside you, but you don't really let it out too often. And you don't try to understand it, do you?"

"That's about right, I guess," he says. "It takes all your energy just to live this life. And what might come next is hard to know about because you can't see it." He feels his stomach about to growl. The coffee is so hot, he can only sip it. He should have ordered the Egg McMuffin. This nun wouldn't have minded. Maybe she's hungry, too.

"Yes, of course. Most people are exactly like you in that way. Faith isn't something they think about too much, except at a funeral or maybe a baptism, and even then, it's just a passing thought. We're all so busy." She includes herself in that *we* as if she too avoids these thoughts in her own busy life. "So, anyway, that's what I want to talk with you about for just a few minutes. I hope you don't mind. Some people are nervous about discussing such things."

She pauses just long enough for him to object if he is quick enough, but then continues when he doesn't, asking him again if he prays. He says "sure," but the lack of conviction in his voice is the answer she hears. "I remember now, you and I talking about this back in the hospital. You say the prayers you learned as a child, like the Our Father and Hail Mary, right?"

"Yep, sure, the old stand-bys." The two great prayers ending unflinchingly; one in *evil*, one in *death*. Not at all like those *Now I lay my head to sleep* nursery rhyme prayers. Or some feel-good, touchy-feely *We Are the World* verse.

The nun who was a hippie is not impressed. "Well, that's a start, but I have another question. What's in your heart when you say them?" Tyler doesn't seem to follow this, so she adds. "The words aren't so important. God already knows what you're going to say."

"Yeah, and he's heard these same prayers over and over billions of times. It must get so old to him. Like the stars." *Not another rosary!* the Almighty is thinking. *Those same prayers again! Can't you people come up with something original?*

"I don't think it does, actually. He certainly has infinite patience with us, and I can't imagine our prayers ever annoy him anything like our lack of praying must. Remember how I told you how I had been a spoiled little rich girl and then squandered away my innocence, living only for myself? All those years, as a young woman, I never bothered to reach out to God, to ask *him* what I should be doing with my life. He had so much to tell me, but I just couldn't be bothered. I sure wasn't living a *pura vida*. Still, he patiently waited."

Her eyes unblinkingly lock with Tyler's, as if she is reading his thoughts but they are written in tiny type. "What's important is that *you* clear a space in your mind for the connection you're making with him. Get quiet and *listen*. Trust in that *still, small voice*."

There's a TV inside this McDonald's somewhere; he can hear it. It sounds like the *Today Show*'s Willard Scott. He's got some one-hundred-year-olds to congratulate on surviving another year. Each birthday from now on will be their greatest accomplishment as they go on still living, still breathing, longer than seems natural, using up oxygen and the Social Security trust fund that the rest of the population is counting on. If they can make it into a Bill Knapp's restaurant that they have here in Michigan and back in Ohio but not anywhere else it seems, they'll get the birthday special—one percent off their bill for each year they're celebrating. At one hundred, it's all free. *How about that?* After one hundred, maybe Bill Knapp's *pays* them to come in, with their walkers and oxygen tanks. How old would he want to live if science keeps progressing like it has? What is the limit a body can last if you keep replacing the worn-out parts and maybe get a complete blood transfusion every once in a while—like an oil change to replace the old fluids as Keith Richards supposedly did a few times when he was having trouble shaking his heroin addiction?

"You mean really concentrating on what I'm saying. Or, maybe, just concentrate on *him*." Tyler tries to do his part in this conversation he didn't ask for. "That's the hard thing, I think." Just how do you concentrate on someone you can't see, can't hear, really? Your mind jumps to something in the here and now because it's just so much more *immediate*.

Talking to this nun is jarring, making him think about all this God stuff. Like when the Pope had died back when Tyler was starting high school and his non-Catholic friends wanted to know what would happen next, as if Tyler had any answers. The cardinals in Rome picked a new Pope, who chose *John Paul* to be his papal name. Like half of the Beatles. Shockingly, just a month later, he too died. The cardinals huddled again, and elected another Pope, who took the copy-cat name, *John Paul II*. It had seemed the mark of a small man with little imagination, destined to small things. *Maybe that's what we need right now,* Tyler's mother had said, *a calming*. And yet this Pontiff from Poland, JP2, now appears headed to greatness, a people's Pope, credited along with Reagan for staring down the Soviet empire, bringing down the Iron Curtain.

"Yes, exactly," the nun says, after a pause, letting him refocus. "To *elevate* our prayers. In Psalm one hundred forty, King David aims for just that: *Let my prayer be directed as incense in thy sight*. Prayer so real it can almost be seen or smelled like smoke from burning incense. Maybe only a mystic can attain such a powerful connection, but that's what we aim for. So that we might feast on a banquet of grace."

"Not really ready for a banquet," Tyler says. "Maybe just scraps here and there, for now."

She pauses again, letting all this sink in a bit. He raises the styrofoam cup with two hands and takes a tentative sip.

"So, yes, our prayers should be *elevated* but not aimed at someone remote and distant, like stained glass windows high above us in a cathedral," the nun says looking straight into his eyes. "When Jesus taught us how to pray, he told us to direct our prayers to his father in heaven. And, he taught that the Almighty was *our Father*, too. That really caused quite a *stir*."

With this unintentional reminder, Tyler gives his coffee another swirl with the little red stir stick, like a miniature whisk to better mix the granules of sugar he had dumped into the white cup. After another sip confirms that it has cooled just enough, he gulps the coffee, so the caffeine can enter his blood more quickly, unclogging the sticky pores of his brain.

"… understand how radical that was. God had told Moses his name was *Yahweh*—the eternal *I Am*. Over the centuries, the Hebrews came to believe that his name was so sacred that it could only be spoken by the High Priest, softly, and only once a year, on the *Day of Atonement*."

The coffee has that vaguely artificial taste from drinking it from a styrofoam cup. Not as bad as if he'd left the plastic lid on and drank through the little opening, but still. Why can't they give you a ceramic mug to drink from if you're not taking it to go?

"…when Jesus addressed his Father, he used the Aramaic word *Abba*, which is much more personal than *Father*. Have you heard it said that *Daddy* might be a better translation for Abba, as a young child might address his father?"

Tyler shakes his head. This is a lot to take in so early in the morning. "That sounds pretty *far out*, man."

She looks at him for a moment and smiles.

"Well, yes. Indeed. There's been quite the debate among scholars, and it's pretty well accepted now that *Daddy* isn't quite right," she says. "It doesn't capture the sense of respect, awe and wonder—at least to our ears. Part of it is cultural. In Italy and in Spanish cultures, they call the Pope *Papa*—showing both loving endearment and respectful esteem. *Papa* probably sounds too informal to our ears to call the Pope. Maybe *Dad* would be closer to the mark—as a translation for *Abba*."

Thanks, sister, keep saying that word, will ya? Now he won't be able to get those Eurodisco bubblegum songs out of his head: *Dancing Queen. Waterloo. Take A Chance On Me.*

But she continues on. "Wouldn't it be something to talk to God that way? To call him *Dad*. Want to give it a try?"

It's an invitation he's quite sure he's *not* ready to accept, not here in this McDonald's with this ex-hippie nun. What if she has an acid flashback or something? Sensing his hesitation, she quickly adds: "Just try to pray in a more personal way, Tyler."

Switching the subject to something more tangible, he confesses: "I just don't know if I have it in me to be all the father my son needs from me. Without his mother, you know?"

"Well, God knows if you're trying to do the best you can," she says. It doesn't seem to help. Tyler stares down into his nearly empty coffee cup. "But you don't have to do it alone, even if you are a single parent," she says. "Do you remember the odd question Jesus asked a crowd of people listening to him one time? 'What father among you, if his son asked for a fish, would hand him a snake?' He knew, flawed as each of them was, none would knowingly give their child a live snake. It was a pretty low bar, but it was a test these people could pass. Then he said: 'If you then, imperfect as you are, know how to give your children what is good, how much more will the heavenly Father give the Holy Spirit to those who ask him.' What you need the most, the Father gives, in the way of his own Spirit."

But Tyler has that far-away look he gets when his brain has stopped listening. "I don't know," he says. "I didn't really have that close a relationship with my father."

Awkward silence follows his uninvited disclosure. Then, she says simply: "I'm sorry."

"I mean I never felt like anything I could do was good enough for him. I knew he loved me in his own way, but there wasn't a lot of closeness to it."

He pictures his father's unsmiling face as they run through the drills, baseball grounders, basketball jump shots, multiplication tables. Trying to stamp the unformed sheet metal of Tyler's youth into something productive, something usable. And when the ball eluded his glove or his jumper ricocheted hard off the backboard or he couldn't remember the eights—eight times six, eight times seven; he always was forgetting the eights—his father had some little punishment for him, push-ups usually. As if he could punish away the imperfections inside his son. He was preparing Tyler for the bumps and bruises of life, he would tell the boy. Better get used to it. Not going to get any easier.

"Maybe all the more so that you need a father's loving embrace," she says, as if guessing correctly that Tyler's father was not a hugger. "Anyway, I'm sorry to have to leave just as you've brought up something that's probably important to talk about. Let me give you something to read later. Here…"

She slides him a sealed white envelope. "Put it aside where you won't lose it. Someday, after you feel that your prayers have begun to, well … *connect,* you'll know it's time to read this little article I've copied for you. Maybe it will help you make your connection all the more *personal.*"

She gets up to leave the primary color world of McDonald's and reenter the real world where other shades exist. She knows that what she has told Tyler he cannot understand, not yet, maybe never. Just because Jesus may have called God *Dad* or *Daddy,* how can *he* dare to? Jesus was himself God, too, after all, which certainly would give him special privileges with the Almighty, or at least complicate the relationship, him being both Son of God and God himself. Tyler has no pretensions of being a son of a Daddy God. Can't he just stay with *Father* and leave it at that? A final gulp of coffee finishes the cup. But he's hungry still. Maybe he'll grab that Egg McMuffin to go.

26

The little bleachers are nearly full at Divine Mercy's next home game. Tyler and Robbie find a place to sit, but the boy can't see. So, he sits on his father's lap and that helps. Nicki had called Tyler Monday night after he got home from Ohio and told him how the first two games had gone. The plays her coach keeps calling—designed to get the off-guard, her position, open off screens—are setting her up to *score some serious points. Really.* She'd been pleased when Tyler asked about the next home game and said he and Robbie would be there.

Again, the game starts with a wide-open Nicki rising up a split-second after receiving a perfect pass from her whippet of a point guard, Melissa, and another high-arching shot swishing the net. Again, she feels it. Everything seems to move in predestined precision before Nicki's eyes, like a slow-motion replay on television. Like it has already happened for her but not for anybody else. She just seems to know where on the floor to move without the ball to elude the girl covering her. Then she receives the pass, and with the ball in her cocked, cupped right hand, the spot on the opposite inside rim draws her steely eyed focus like an electromagnet, and the goal seems wide enough to swallow a beachball with room to spare. She senses where the ball is going even when it's in the hands of the opposing players. Twice she anticipates a pass coming across court and lunges forward to intercept it, then begins streaking down toward her basket with the nine other players still moving toward the other end.

Nicki is double-teamed the rest of the first half, so she and her teammates execute the plan their coach had them practice the past week. The others become momentary statues at fixed points in the half-court and Nicki snakes tightly through them without the ball as fast as she can, picking off the pursuing defenders. The double- and triple-picks free her, just as the coach had foreseen, and again Melissa is there with the pass, right on Nicki's hands as soon as she's open. At times, it's beautiful. In moments that hang in the spectators' memories like brightly colored wallpaper, they have conquered it, girls no more but *athletes*. Unrestrained by girlishness and running free as mustangs in the open, with the ball as the thing that connects them and holds them apart from the world. Noiseless energy and rhythm run through them like static electricity, sparking from their fingertips. Then in a timeout, one by one they glance into the crowd, at boyfriends and others who judge them each day, each hour. And they're just giggling girls again, mortals alive for just a short time.

In the second half, the other team tries an entirely new strategy: a full-court press with a double-team of the point guard, Melissa. The other three defending players cut off her passing lanes. This results in two quick turnovers and a Fillies timeout. Coach Myers tells the speedy guard to use her quickness to bring the ball up the court herself and she does, easily, time after time. *This wouldn't work with the varsity boys*, Tyler thinks from the stands; *the two defenders would set a tighter trap around the ball handler to force a pass.* But this girl is so much quicker than her slightly tentative defenders, she spurts between them cleanly or draws a foul. They can't close her out.

After Melissa makes three break-away layups and feeds Nicki for three other easy baskets, the opposing coach abandons the press. Nicki is again double-teamed. She stays mostly on the perimeter, keeping her two defenders far outside the paint. The remaining three defenders can do little to stop the four Mercy players they must guard and jostle for rebounds. When Nicki is not closely covered by both defenders, she lofts three-point shots, making two of three. She finishes with 29 points and Mercy cruises to another easy win.

She breathes it all in through her nose, the utter smell of victory. That slow-motion aspect to the game when it starts clicking for her. The kids and the parents in the stands getting loud when her rainbows find the mark, when she makes it rain. That ashen look of panic that came over the girl defending her tonight, who kept trying to keep up but couldn't because the game hadn't slowed down for her. Nicki was raining down points and there was nothing the girl could do to make it stop. The other coach calling timeouts to try to stop the runs Divine Mercy was on, anything to break the momentum, to stop Nicki from raining on them. She breathes it in and holds it deep inside her lungs. That satisfying feeling of *winning*. Then she's swept into the locker room and it's bedlam in there, the girls all shouting and laughing and living the moment. The redhead center Shannon is laughing so hard, she's crying. Girls who haven't seen much playing time hang a little self-consciously on the fringes of the locker room madness, not really sure if they've been invited to the celebration but close enough they might appear to be part of it, not wanting to look excluded. Just hoping to blend in.

Nicki sees it. "Hey, Eberhard," she calls out loudly to Tracy Eberhard, a sophomore and the shortest girl on the team, Melissa's backup at point guard and nearly as quick. But, oh, so shy. "You see how Melissa cut through those loose little double teams they were throwing at her? She was too fast for them. Beautiful, wasn't it?"

"Oh, yeah, totally," the younger girl responds with grateful enthusiasm. Then turning to the captain, Melissa, she says: "Like you stayed so cool under pressure. Just blew right between them until they just had to give up the double team."

"You got real wheels, too," Melissa, a senior, says to her understudy. "You're gonna be the one running the show next year. Mostly what you got to do is get the ball to Nicki when she gets open. Let her light it up."

Nicki acts like she doesn't hear this. She's already joking with some of the other non-starters, getting them involved in the happy confusion, the afterglow. One team. Together, unbeatable. Like a single organism if you could have looked down on the players from the fluorescent light fixtures in the locker room's ceiling. Legs and arms flailing, lots of hair. The indelible shape of victory.

27

After picking Robbie up from daycare earlier than usual, Tyler heads home. Lyvia's coming over for an outing with the two of them, father and son. As he approaches his house, he sees her green Honda Accord in his driveway. She has beaten them here.

"You been waiting here long?" Tyler asks as he jumps out of his car and pulls her into his arms and against his chest.

"Nope. Just got here. How's little Robbie doing?"

They walk around the back of the Cavalier to the rear passenger-side door. Robbie is all smiles as first Tyler, then Lyvia, greet him with exaggerated happy faces. After a quick diaper check and a restocking of his diaper bag with a fresh bottle of juice, some crackers and seedless grapes, the three of them pile into the Cavalier and head west through Livonia and then Northville and finally to fields cultivated by farmers just biding their time until the subdivision developers come calling with the big bucks.

The country road takes them to a combination apple orchard and pumpkin patch, the perfect late October outing. Tyler brings the car to a stop near the front of a huge field specially cleared for parking, outlined with bright orange reflective tape and tassels, like at a used-car lot, gently rocking in the afternoon breeze.

"This place must get packed on the weekend," Tyler observes. "It's great to come out here in the middle of the week."

Soon they are in the middle of a field of pumpkin vines. The soil is churned up where others have trudged, but it's dry and chalky after a bit of a dry spell. The green and yellow vines poking out of the soil are only sporadically clothed with crinkly, dried-up leaves. The pumpkins in this front part of the field have been picked over pretty well and the ones still remaining on the vines have a variety of imperfections and injuries, some beginning to rot, gently oozing pumpkin juice from an open sore. They head deeper into the patch and are rewarded with unblemished pumpkins with surprising variety—round and oblong, medium-sized and just plain huge, bright orange with some swatches of green and yellow. The sun is sinking lower in the sky but still provides a pleasant warmth, the deep blue sky a perfect backdrop for the pictures Tyler takes of his son and girlfriend. Lyvia is down on her knees, sitting on the back of her ankles, to make herself Robbie's size, sharing his vantage point and becoming a child again for a little while.

"Soon it will be Halloween night. You'll get all dressed up in a costume. Your daddy tells me you're going to dress up like a Ninja Turtle. Is that right?" she asks him earnestly.

"Okay. Ninja Tur-tle. Night," the boy responds happily. "Candy."

"That's right, Robbie. You go around from house to house and people give you candy."

"Quite a racket," Tyler says. "All these houses close together in subdivisions. These kids take in a haul."

"But first we have to pick out good pumpkins to take home and cut into jack-o-lanterns," Lyvia says. They talk about their plans for cutting out faces, round eyes and triangle noses, toothy smiles or menacing frowns.

Robbie listens to all this, trying to make sense of it. He drums on the side of a big, oval-shaped pumpkin with open palms, enjoying the chance to interact with nature in this new place. *The lady with Daddy seems nice. He likes her. They smile a lot.*

"Then, right after Halloween will be your birthday. How old will you be?"

"Birfday? Two," Robbie says holding a hand up with two fingers extended. But he looks puzzled.

"That's right, Robbie. You'll be two years old."

Tyler turns back to Lyvia. "He knows his birthday is coming, but we've been concentrating on Halloween for now. All this is confusing enough for him. He can only really look forward to one event at a time. He can't look past that to another thing in the future."

"So, I guess he's kind of the opposite of you in that way," she says, smiling.

"What do you mean?"

"He can't look past one thing to the next. You can't stay focused on one thing at a time."

He laughs, intrigued that she has noticed this about him. He has tried to be on his best behavior as one does in a new relationship, not letting on when he had stopped listening to whatever she was still saying when his mind began to wander. He hadn't been caught yet, he didn't think. Perhaps she's more perceptive, intuitive, than he has realized. She's kept it hidden from him while all along observing him with calculating detail. There's a depth to her he finds vaguely unsettling, a hidden chilly sharpness beneath that glowing warmth wrapped in satiny soft skin. Not her sharp intellect; he gratefully accepts that she is smarter than him in many things. He enjoys seeing through the windows of perception she opens for him with her studious insights, much as Robbie continually opens his windows to simple wonders all around that he might not otherwise notice. Is there something else inside her with sharp edges, like broken glass, or a hidden wound, still oozing unseen pumpkin juice?

* * *

Soon after they return from their pumpkin hunting, Lyvia drives off in her Honda. She is behind where she should be, she says, in her reading and her thesis writing.

Tyler lets her go. He was going to fix a dish with chicken, rice and green peppers, but puts that on hold since it's just Robbie and him. Grilled cheese and tomato soup instead. It's important to introduce his son to vegetables, even in soupy form. His mother-in-law is a relentless harpy never happier than when she exposes in him a raw nerve, but she was right about the food they eat, Robbie and him. He needs to buy more fresh fruits and vegetables, and no longer has the excuse of being too busy since he's been out of work.

There's a message on the answering machine: a woman from Human Resources at Lockery down in Toledo, wanting to set up a phone interview. This is it, he thinks. The job search will mercifully soon be over. His mother will be happy that he's at least in Ohio, if still a couple of hours away. And he won't have to move too far from Lyvia, who has begun to dominate his thoughts day and night.

After dinner, Tyler carries the two pumpkins they lugged home into the living room to be admired for a few more days indoors before they are carved into jack-o-lanterns and placed on the front porch. Cutting into them too early would bring on foul-smelling mold before they even get to Halloween. They had each picked out a largish pumpkin, forgetting that they had trekked far from the entrance of the patch where they had to return to pay for their harvest. Tyler carried a pumpkin in each arm, and Lyvia held hers, so Robbie had to walk the whole way, a prodigious journey for a little one. Eventually, they made it out of there, but now Tyler's back hurts. He sits deep in his recliner as the Reds and A's go at it again. Game 2. Robbie rubs his eyes, worn out from the day of adventure. When he's down for the night, Tyler returns to the recliner. The game is close and keeps his attention, even though the action is spread over three long hours. Breaks between innings are longer during the World Series, to cram in more high-dollar commercials, and the pitching changes and even the walks to the mound to think about a pitching change seem to last longer, so much riding on every decision. October baseball is for the ages. It takes ten innings tonight, but underdog Cincinnati again prevails, 5-4.

Tyler gets up from the recliner, and the room falls away in a wild tailspin. He reaches for the arm of the chair but can't reach it; he's up too high. He tries to take a wide stance with his feet to keep his balance, but it's as if his legs have gone asleep—without the tingle but numb and lifeless. He reaches out to take the fall with his arms, but his side and head have already reached the bottom of their unexpected journey. Fortunately, the carpet provides a soft landing. He lies there confused if unhurt, watching threads of carpet alongside his right eye spin and twist in maddening defiance of what he knows to be real. He shuts his eyes then and collects himself, taking a deep breath. When he opens his eyes, there's no spinning feeling and he can get up on his feet as if nothing has happened.

28

The next night—Friday night and the start of the weekend for those with jobs—Tyler and Lyvia sit at a table with Webb Rucker and Aaron Foster and their dates, finishing up dinner in a Mexican restaurant in Ann Arbor before they head over to the Tangerine Ballroom for drinks and dancing. This was Rucker's idea, the triple date. He has been seeing a girl, Kimberly, for a few weeks and when he heard that Tyler had a girlfriend, he moved quickly with the idea of getting the couples together. Both Tyler and Rucker figured Neticut could come up with a flashy date on short notice to join them, and he has not disappointed. Kelly is a twenty-four-year-old Heather Locklear look-alike, a body wave perm of long whitish-blonde hair, feathered in the front, cascading over bare shoulders and framing high cheekbones and large white teeth when she smiles, forming a mostly pleasing face, although tramped up with a bit too much makeup and lip gloss. A form-fitting white top stretches over her chest and under her arms, plunging behind to leave well-tanned shoulders and much of her back uncovered. Leopard-patterned leggings of some elastic material look painted on, hugging her thin waist and ending mid-calf. Black high-heeled pumps make her slim legs look even longer than they are. She hangs on Neticut and laughs at everything he says, flipping her hair back in place after each hearty laugh. She's apparently in sales at a Cadillac dealership, but she could be a stripper in one of those new, upscale *gentlemen's clubs,* if you can judge by the billboards, Tyler thinks.

Rucker's date is, by comparison, considerably toned down: shoulder-length brown hair with the hint of some curl, brown eyes behind owlish glasses on a mostly forgettable face, white blouse fully buttoned over a smallish bust. Tight-fitting jeans are her only hint of overt sexiness. Kimberly is an analyst at one of the auto suppliers, but could be an accountant or librarian. She doesn't say much and looks down at her feet a lot.

Lyvia is dressed not all that different from Kimberly—slim-cut designer jeans, white blouse—but she makes an entirely hotter impression. Her shape is more comely, for sure, but it's her Helen of Troy face that makes her stand out. Refined high cheekbones like Kelly, but a small, cute nose, too, where Kelly's if you look closely is a bit pointed, and a daintier chin that works with the little nose to provide a softness to her face that really sets off those high, rosy cheeks, not to mention her gray-blue eyes spaced just far enough apart to hint at the depth of her thoughts. Kelly's eyes are a bit beady and too close together; she over-compensates with wide swatches of purplish eye shadow. Lyvia gamely contributes to the conversation, holding back on her braininess. She and Kelly sit flanking Rucker, across from their dates, giving Tyler and Foster an unobstructed view of a television with the World Series. Cincy scores seven in the third, well on their way to a shocking 3-0 lead in the series.

The waitress brings the group another round of beers after they all pass on dessert, and a coffee for Tyler who has offered to be the designated driver tonight. His accident and the death of that McNeary girl has left him resolute in not drinking and driving, and neither his friends nor the women here tonight give him any grief about it.

With another Michelob in front of him, Rucker continues the beer-car brand analogy he had started when Kimberly first ordered a Budweiser, which he had called the "Chevy of beers—solid, all-American, dependable." The Mick he's drinking is, of course, the Cadillac of domestic beers. Neticut's Heineken is the "BMW or Mercedes, a high-quality German import."

"…Dutch, Heineken is," Neticut corrects. "But a Beamer is about right."

"So, what's my beer, Webb?" Kelly says, leaning toward him as if to provide a clear look at her cleavage. She's drinking a Smithwick's, an Irish brew she chose off the menu because she wanted something original and vaguely daring, and because she herself has some Irish blood, on her mother's side, she thinks.

"It must be a DeLorean. That's the only car I ever heard of from Ireland."

John DeLorean had been an eccentric GM executive who left to start his own company, selling a stainless steel-bodied sporty car with distinctive gull-wing doors, that he assembled in Belfast. Unfortunately, the DeLorean launched in 1981 in the midst of a deep global recession. The company went bust the next year. Only a few thousand were ever built.

"Hey, that's the car from *Back to the Future*—Doc Brown's car that Marty drives back in time," Kelly says, flashing lots of teeth. Marty being the character played by Michael J. Fox, who started out on *Family Ties* as Alex, the Reagan-enthusiast teenage son of liberal-leaning parents.

"Yeah, exactly," Rucker says agreeably, enjoying the intoxicating whiff of perfume and beer breath Kelly is giving off. Kimberly eyes Kelly rather sullenly, thinking that her having the Chevy of beers has underscored her inability to compete with these two truly stunning women.

Lyvia chimes in. "If you had that car and could go back in time, where and when would you go?" It's an open question to the table.

"… ten years or so ago and stay right here in America," Neticut says. "Knowing that the Eighties was going to be a fantastic decade for the stock market, and having the names of a few big winners, like Nike and Circuit City, I'd borrow to the hilt and watch my money explode."

"I'd go back to the Fifties and have lunch with Marilyn Monroe," Kelly says, perhaps confusing this with a similar party game. "I've always admired what she did for women."

For once, Rucker has his own opinion to share. "I guess I'd go back to Philadelphia in 1776 and help them get the Constitution right from the beginning. You know, give women the vote and free the slaves and all," he says, apparently positioning himself to his date as enlightened and egalitarian. "That'd save everybody a lot of trouble down the road, don't you think?"

"Well, the Constitution didn't get written until 1787," Lyvia says, gently correcting Tyler's friend. Unable to stay quiet despite her conscious commitment to not outshine the others. But Rucker seems fair game. "You do make a good point that including equal rights for everyone from the start would have been better. What about you, Kimberly?"

"Oh, I don't know. Maybe back to Bethlehem almost two thousand years ago, to be there for the birth of Christ, and see all those angels and shepherds and everything. It would be hard to beat that."

"You know, I was thinking on those same lines," Tyler says, picking up on Livvy's effort to encourage Rucker's mousey date. "Only I'd want to come around a little later, like when Jesus was walking on water and curing the blind and what have you. If you could go back to witness all that, you wouldn't have to take the Bible writers at their word; you'd know it really happened."

"But would you get any credit toward heaven for that?" Kimberly asks back, rising to the occasion. "Believing is no big thing if you see something with your own eyes, right?"

All this Jesus talk makes Rucker and Neticut restless.

"What about you, Lyvia?" Rucker asks. He hadn't known that his date was such a Bible-thumper and looks to draw the attention away from her. He addresses Tyler's date as *Lyvia* because that's how Tyler introduced her to the others and although they have heard him call her *Livvy* tonight, they haven't been given the go-ahead for that level of familiarity. Kimberly and even flashy Kelly are a bit intimidated by Lyvia, who you can tell has a brain, even if she is holding back. Rucker is, of course, intimidated by any good-looking woman, brains or not. Foster is busy silently comparing Lyvia with Kelly. Tyler's date would be smoking hot, he thinks, if she'd just show a little more skin.

"Oh, I guess to travel all over Europe in the late Renaissance, say the early seventeenth century, to be able to get to know Cervantes and Shakespeare, and master artists like Caravaggio and Rubens, even Rembrandt if I stuck around a few more years there," she says wistfully, blowing her cover.

Rucker and Neticut look at Lyvia as if she's some contestant from *Jeopardy* who gets all the answers right. They could know this stuff, too, if it was important to them, they think. Their dates don't know how to take Lyvia. They've always assumed men want them to act dumb and it's been easy enough for them to play that game.

Tyler, who would have bet big money on her naming T.S. Eliot, moves in to help Lyvia by changing the subject. "So, what do you think of this Saddam Hussein, threatening the *mother of all battles* now that Bush is getting all tough with him?"

With *read my lips* clarity, Bush has given the Iraqi dictator a line in the sand not to cross, a No-Fly Zone, on top of the order to get out of Kuwait. You have to spell it out to these despots, or they'll weasel out of what you thought they'd agreed to and still blame it on you. Of course, Bush is spoiling for a fight. He knows there's no way the oily dictator will lose face with his people by backing down to the Great Satan.

"He's got all those tanks, but he's never faced the U.S.A.," Rucker says, relieved that the talk has moved onto a ground he finds steadier. "Our pilots with all their technology will buzz around the sky, pin-pointing his air bases and piles of weapons. How's he gonna stop that?"

"… all those tanks in big packs in the Kuwaiti desert are sitting ducks," Neticut adds. "Our planes will just tear 'em up."

"But what about his *elite Republican Guard* that we keep hearing about?" Kimberly pipes in, showing she can keep up with the boys. "Highly trained troops that will protect their dictator to the death supposedly?" Maybe she's got more on the ball than Tyler first thought.

"They might be tough, but as long as we keep the fight in the sky, they won't be able to do much," Rucker says. "Their air force is a joke. There's no reason for us to go in with ground troops, we can incinerate the whole place, if we have to, from the air."

The women excuse themselves to all go off to the restroom like they do, women. All this war talk has made them want to freshen up.

"That Lyvia you've got there is quite the babe," Foster says in a low voice to Tyler when they've left. "Could be a model if she was a little taller."

He tilts his glass to draw in the remaining slug of beer, then sets it down on the table with a satisfying thud.

A beer glass has to have a solid feel, like a tall mug without the handle, Tyler is thinking. Strange that their three dates all ordered beers, not a wine cooler or daiquiri among them. Women today are constantly vigilant to demonstrate their ability to negotiate the boy's club, to show they have the toughness and will power to be taken seriously with men on whatever playing field they have to compete, certainly in an office environment but it carries over into the social world, too. Yet they also flirt and dangle their sexuality out there as willing objects of desire and lust—they want to win on this playing field, too, where they compete with each other. Men may seem to have the upper hand, but women know better. Aristophanes was dead right; men can be made to do anything, even give up their war-mongering, when women realize the power in their dark, mysterious *sugar walls*.

"Thanks. Your Kelly is definitely hot. How long you been dating her?" Tyler asks, semi-interestedly.

"…not very. Let me put it this way: not tired of her yet. That's a body made for loving."

Tyler becomes aware that they've left Rucker out of all this date appreciation, but what can you say about Kimberly, except maybe she's not as mousey as she first lets on? "Thanks for getting us out together, Webb," he says.

Rucker still swallowing the last bit of his beer, nods.

Foster gives it a go: "All good with you and Kimberly? I bet she can get wild when you get her glasses off."

"I like her. And she's had no complaints, so I guess we're good in the bedroom department. In fact …" he begins, but trails off as he sees the women walking back to the table. Works out well for Rucker, actually—he leaves an impression of some mysterious sexual achievement, yet doesn't have to actually betray the confidence of his lover. Ever the gentleman, he is. And it gives him a story, something to build upon the next time he's out with these two other gentlemen talking about their women.

* * *

The club is loud and it's hard to talk, so they quickly finish off the mixed drinks they ordered, except Tyler, and dance. Quite a range of music: current pop songs like Paula Abdul's "The Way That You Love Me," Paul Young's "That Girl" and Billy Joel's "We Didn't Start the Fire;" and some older ones, including a couple more from Billy Joel, the DJ must be into him: "Only the Good Die Young" and "My Life." Plus, some Motown standards, early danceable Beatles ("Twist and Shout" and "I Saw Her Standing There") and Stones ("Let's Spend the Night Together"). Dancing with Lyvia, Tyler feels uncoordinated, disconnected from her gracefulness. Perhaps because he hasn't had anything to drink. When was the last time he tried to dance without drinking? Probably high school, maybe sophomore year. Moving is difficult on the crowded dance floor. Tyler always feels edgy in crowds, boxed in. Still, it's not as bad as the last time he was in this town, Ann Arbor, at the football game in the Big House last year. Michigan versus the Ohio State University, the biggest rivalry game in the biggest football stadium in the country. More than 105,000 fans packed in bleacher-style seating, each allocated exactly 18 inches no matter how wide their butt and stomach and shoulders. Tyler was hemmed in on either side, the crushing weight of the crowd nearly suffocating him, as if the sea of maize and blue had risen up to swallow him in his scarlet and gray, to obliterate him, make him disappear.

Kelly with her leopard-skin leggings basks in the lusting looks she receives from all directions. But she is not the only one drawing stares. Eyes from all over the club, male and female, are drawn to Lyvia. Tyler can see that she is emboldened by this attention. She dances sexier, swiveling her hips round, then sharply cutting, still in rhythm with the music. She looks at him, smiles, licks her upper lip slowly, laughs and looks past him at all the other eyes and bodies. The flashing lights. The darkness. She seems less real to him here, like a centerfold poster airbrushed to some artificial perfection or an MTV clip of some hottie, a pretend and nameless girl in a fast-paced video with a thin storyline. He doesn't know her, but he's mesmerized by her gyrating body. He pulls her close. She giggles. His right hand embraces the left side of her butt, nice and firm. She lets him hold it there.

"Let's spend the night together," he says in her ears, to the music.

"Yes, let's," she says, looking deeply into his eyes. But she's still not real to him, just a hot body that has his full attention and won't let go.

Then the music changes to a pounding bass beat, the beginning of a rap set, which mostly clears the dance floor, making room for others who must have been waiting in the shadows with their drinks. A younger crowd. Tyler can't understand how affluent, suburban college kids, white or black, are attracted to angry *gangsta rap* with its monotonous shouted-out lyrics about *cop-killin'* and *cherry-poppin'*—not exactly inspiring stuff. And how do you dance to it? The others in the group feel the same way. They make their way out the door.

As designated driver, Tyler pilots the red Lumina minivan Foster has borrowed from work, following the interstate back to Livonia's surface streets. He goes through the intersection of Seven Mile and Farmington, past the little white cross above a pile of flowers and a teddy bear where Linda McNeary left this world; nobody in the car but Tyler notices. Foster continues to tell a joke with a long build up.

Then they are at Rucker's house, where they all met some hours ago. Rucker offers a nightcap, but Tyler and Lyvia pass. He gives the keys to Neticut, who seems sober enough to drive the mile-and-a-half to his house with Kelly. In his Cavalier with Lyvia, Tyler pulls out into the inky black night away from the others, alone with her at last. Or at least once he pays Nicki for the babysitting and watches her drive off in her white Mustang.

He clicks off the front porch light and turns right into Lyvia who had moved in closer to him than he expected and who now wraps her arms around him and gives him a tantalizing kiss.

They make their way to the bedroom. Holding her against him, he frees one hand to reach out and pull back the comforter on his king-size bed and they fall together upon the clean cotton sheets. Then they become as one, disappearing into the other self. Everything's in technicolor like on that dance floor, and he forgets how thirsty he is and hungry, his focus only on her and how good she's making him feel. They reach their destination together and fall into their pillows exhausted, clinging to each other, soon deeply lost in sleep.

But suddenly the other she is high above him, pressed against that ugly tree in the front yard, Christie, arms outstretched against the stumps at either side, floating like a ghost but in pain, and he sees that she's in labor. Her belly sticks out and hangs down covered by a gauzy white fabric like an angel floating there against the tree, and she's breathing hard, like he coached her, *hee hee hee who*. Her eyes are closed and her hair all mussed up, like in the hospital when she had Robbie and he realized his love for her was deeper than anything he'd known before, and it scared him because it made him want to be able to do this for her, to take away the pain, to give to her like she was doing for him but knowing he could not; nothing would ever be like this. She's standing up against the tree and he understands that everything she's done has been a loving sacrifice for him and then for Robbie, too. And when he stirs and realizes it was a dream, one of those intense post-coital dreams that leave you awake and confused while your lover sleeps on, he feels the loss. Of Christie and everything they had. Of the possibilities of this new life with Livvy, now curled sleeping with her back against his front, the inside spoon she has become. Their togetherness fulfilled in sweet pools of ecstasy promising to bring them closer. Yet now he can't help worry that their oneness may be cresting like the high tide the moon brings but then lets recede, leaving a lot of ugliness on the beach. Derailed from the trajectory of his life by so much loss. So much death and darkness to overcome.

He gets up to pee and to twist a Q-tip end in each ear, then climbs back into bed with sleeping Lyvia, her white body dissolving into the white sheets, all grainy softness in the low light of his bedroom, illuminated only by the few beams of moonlight that evade the window shade. The dream of Christie on the tree he still hasn't cut down weighs on him like an iron helmet that a knight in a museum wears. He needs to escape it, or he won't fall back asleep, worrying that the beautiful woman in his bed is not his soul mate. Only one per lifetime, isn't that all you get?

He imagines again that he has the one hundred and five mile-an-hour fastball; he stands on the mound ready to dispatch arrogant Rickey Henderson and the mighty Oakland A's.

29

Tyler opens his eyes to morning and an empty bed. Lyvia emerges from the bathroom wearing one of his scarlet and gray OSU sweatshirts, loose and baggy on her and overlapping the top of her own tight jeans, a towel wrapped around her wet hair. She sees him on the bed rubbing his eyes.

"Don't believe in sleeping in, do you?" he says through a yawn.

"Lots to do today," she says. "On my thesis work. Mind if I borrow this shirt?"

"Not at all. Just don't go back to Ann Arbor wearing that. Hey, I'll get up and we can have breakfast."

"No, you don't need to. I'm just going to head home and make sure I get some real work done before we meet up this evening."

Lyvia had driven herself over to Tyler's house before they met up with his friends and their dates. Her green Honda sits in his driveway ready for her. That she drives a Japanese car is a sore point with him, though he hasn't mentioned it yet.

"You sure you got to rush off?"

"Yep. Lots to do. Are you still up for making Robbie and me dinner tonight, then going to a movie?" No reason the plan should have changed, he thinks. She's acting jumpy around him; it's not like her. He just nods and smiles.

"Ok, I'm counting on it. But..." she hesitates. "I'll drive over here again, and drive myself home tonight after the movie."

All this logistical information seems odd to him, still waking up. And a bit awkward. "You can spend the night again..." he offers.

"No, I can't, Ty. I really need to get work done on my thesis. Sunday, too. And, anyway..." Here it is; he feels the real reason leaking out like sticky sap from a maple tree that becomes syrup but first it's just a reluctant drip. "I don't think we should just start sleeping together from now on. Listen, it was wonderful last night. But we're not ready for this to become the regular thing. You're not ready. I'm not ready."

What can he say? Truth is, she's right. He *isn't* ready for her to be his regular sleepover buddy. But as soon as he feels it being taken away, this promise of regular nightly companionship, he feels short-changed. It's too late to close the box, to put the genie back in the bottle now that he has swum luxuriously inside her and remembers it.

"But it's so nice having you, with me in bed," he says, not really the thing she wanted to hear. So, he adds quickly, "You're a gorgeous girl, Livvy. Your body..."

He never knows how to talk to a woman about her body. Even Christie, he rarely ever complimented her that way. Lyvia is so like Christie in her wholesome beauty. He wants to tell her that he sees that this gift she has is so natural, so innate to her. Yet that would seem to take away her part in it; it's certainly to her credit that she has kept her body toned, right?

"Well, thanks for that. But I don't want it to be just physical. Or even mostly physical. I want something more with you than that."

She walks over close to him, sitting on the bed, his feet on the floor, leans over and hugs him, then kisses him on a cheek.

"You make me happy to be with you, Ty. We'll spend the night together again when the time is right. And I'm sure you'll be much more persuasive when you don't have such a bad case of morning breath."

She laughs and with that she's on her way. Before he has time to fully consider this new development in their relationship, he hears Robbie stirring. Time to get moving with their morning.

* * *

The day slips by. Breakfast, clean-up, making a grocery list, grocery shopping. Lunch, clean up, watch some college football, Baylor against Texas on one channel, Wisconsin at Michigan State on another. Before you know it, Lyvia's pulling into his driveway, like she never left except they each have had a chance for a little space. Just enough that they're glad to see each other again, and Tyler's already wondering if she'll give in and spend the night.

The three of them go for a walk together around the subdivision, Tyler pushing Robbie in the stroller because if the boy walks, it takes forever. Then Lyvia plays with the boy in the living room, Duploes and stuffed animals, while Tyler fixes dinner—meatloaf, mashed potatoes from flakes and frozen peas. Nothing fancy, but it's within Tyler's wheelhouse as a cook and it's food that Robbie will eat. Having the boy gives him an excuse to keep it simple. Livvy doesn't complain, though she does find the meatloaf rather bland. If they're going to be a couple, she's going to have to teach him to work in some spices into his cooking. There are other things as well she will need to change about him—the annoying way he pretends to listen while his mind blissfully runs away, his inability to focus, the lack of a defining style in the clothes he wears, and so forth. There's a lot to like about the guy; he's worth trying to fix, she thinks.

Nicki arrives to take over with Robbie so Tyler and Lyvia can go to their movie. They have lots of choices but find reasons to reject them, one by one: *Pretty Woman* (Tyler wasn't up for another chick flick), the *Exorcist III* (too scary, they both agreed), *Death Warrant* and *Marked for Death* (action films for guys, Lyvia said), *Presumed Innocent* (she's already seen it) and several others. They settle on *Pacific Heights*, with Melanie Griffith, Matt Modine and Michael Keaton, so it should have been good but turns out to be a dopey sort of thriller about a yuppie couple who try to evict an unbelievably annoying tenant, who goes psycho on them. Tyler finds the movie stupid to the point of being funny and almost likes it. Lyvia is just disappointed they've wasted their time and Tyler's money when there were better choices. Even that mob film *Goodfellas* is supposed to be worthwhile.

It's after eleven-thirty when they get back to Tyler's house. Lyvia begs off coming in. She's still got to drive back to Hazel Park and she's tired. The movie disappointment clearly has taken a toll. Tyler doesn't fight it. He kisses her beside the Accord where Nora Johnston can see them if she's looking through her curtains.

As Lyvia settles into the driver's seat of her Japanese car, her window slides down. She looks at Tyler, her mouth turned a bit sideways, like she's sizing him up and he's not faring too well. Then she blurts out what must have been building inside her.

"All this that you've been through has been hard on you, even if you won't admit it. But you have to *wake up*, Ty. Sometimes I think part of you is still in that hospital room, still in a coma, insulated from the ups and downs of life. I don't know how you were before I met you, how you were with Christie, but I think you probably had more enthusiasm, that you felt things more deeply."

He doesn't know how to respond at first. When it's clear that she will wait him out, he mutters, "I feel the downs, believe me. I just don't let on."

"Go ahead and show it, when you're ready. It's natural, I guess, for you to hold back after such a loss. But we can't get serious until you let go." She says this not meaning exactly *let go of Christie*, but that's the way it comes out. She adds too late: "Of what you're feeling, what you're holding back."

"Okay," he says simply.

She begins to back out of the driveway, and he lets her go. For now. *That little Honda is quiet*, he thinks. You hardly hear the engine; you have to give the Japanese credit for that. What had he said or done tonight that made her see him as remote and unfeeling?

He walks into the house, closes the front door behind him, hangs up his keys on the hook on the wall and lumbers toward the kitchen. *What a weird evening.* The movie start time was too late; they were both spent by the time the five or six previews—loud and over-acted, selling too hard—were finished. Then it was awful, the movie they'd chosen together. Lyvia felt cheated somehow. He had just rolled with it. Then she gives him that speech out by her car, that she doesn't want him to just roll with the ups and downs. He thought he'd been doing pretty good with all this loss, not just Christie but everything. Maybe they do need a break. Not that many hours ago, he and Lyvia were making love, their bodies fitting together so well. Now she's pushing away. Who can figure? *Maybe she's the one who has issues*, he thinks.

As he walks into the kitchen, he sees Nicki sitting there, elbows on the kitchen table, head in her hands. She looks up for a moment, eyes red and wet.

"What's wrong?" Tyler asks cautiously.

Her face disappears back into her hands. She tries to compose herself, to shake it off. But when she looks up, hers is the face of a wet kitten, miserable and self-absorbed.

He sits down next to her and waits. Eventually she tells him. For several days, she's been worried. Her period is late. Tonight, away from her house and her parents, she had used a test kit she'd bought at a Perry Drug Store. *Positive.* She knew it would be, just knew. How would she tell her boyfriend? And her parents?

"Slow down, Nicki. Don't you think you should try the test again, maybe tomorrow, see if you get another positive?"

How does a pregnancy test kit work, he wonders. A bit of blood or does she pee in a little cup? He can't remember if Christie had ever explained it. A piece of litmus paper like in high school chemistry class dipped into her bodily fluid, able to react somehow to a chemical change inside her. This girl should be shooting hoops and giggling with her friends on the phone, not making her blood or pee rat out the secret of how her own body is changing, her own chemistry altered by this new life inside her oblivious to the chaos it is about to unleash.

"Yeah, I guess," she says. She will do another test. But she knows; she just *knows*.

"I didn't even know you had a boyfriend. How long have you been going with him?" Tyler asks.

"Two years almost. Well, a year and a half. It'll be two years next spring. I don't know."

"What's his name?"

"Chris."

"How long have you been, you know, having sex?"

"It was only a few times, and we tried to be careful. But a couple of times things just happened before we were ready."

"Does he know yet?"

She shakes her head.

"How's he going to take it? I mean, what will he say?" he asks, not really wanting to be this involved but there's no choice now; he's in. He owes it to her anyway. She was there for him and Robbie when he was lying unconscious in the hospital, helpless.

"I don't know. We're just two kids. C'mon. He isn't ready to be a father."

Tyler pictures a skinny, pimple-faced Chris, holding a bag of buttery popcorn as he waits for Nicki to come out of the movie theater bathroom. She's in there doing her chemistry experiment. Boy, is he going to be surprised. "What about you?"

"I'm not ready to be a mother. No. I'm not. I'm not."

"Yeah, it's tough. You have your whole life in front of you. Hell, you have almost two years of high school still ahead of you. You shouldn't be having a baby right now. It's really a tough break."

"So, what do I do?"

"Maybe you decide that you have the rest of your life to have kids. You'll have a baby again when it's time, your life is more settled, you have a husband. Having a husband first would be good, Nicki," he says, trying to get her to smile.

She does smile, just the slightest bit, then rubs her red eyes. She's crying again. "I really screwed up," she says.

Mistakes, we all make them. Some of them lead to nothing and we don't even have to look back, to think twice about them. Others have consequences—messy, inconvenient, embarrassing, terrible consequences.

"Lots of people who can't have kids would love to adopt your baby, Nicki."

She looks up at him, confused by what he has said. Then it sinks in, and she turns away, understanding he's not on her side. "Maybe I don't have it at all," she whispers.

Tyler doesn't answer at first. Not until the words are right. *What are you talking about?* is all he can think to say, but as he places his hand on the back of her head and starts to say it, he stops himself. Instead, he gently pats her wild, thick hair and says nothing. Not saying anything that would shut her down. He can't imagine being in her shoes right now, a sixteen-year-old in a Catholic girls' school. Not his place to judge.

"Maybe I should do what just about all the other girls would do if this happened to them. You know they would without even thinking about it. *Just end it.* Then I don't have to tell my parents, don't even have to tell Chris, mess up his life. Or go to school with a big pregnant belly. Then it's just done and over."

But would it be over? Or become an emptiness that won't go away? A darkness inside her womb, never meant to be a killing field.

"You aren't like that," he says, not really what he wanted to say. *Don't pile on with guilt.*

"You don't know who I am. I mean, *I* don't know who I am," she mutters.

"It's too much all at once. Take it slower. Do the test again. Then go see your doctor." This all seems like good advice, right?

"What about basketball? I mean, we're 6-0. It's been a dream season, so far." Nicki says hoarsely. "But this is a *nightmare*. I don't want to quit the team."

"I don't know. I think you can probably still play for a while, maybe even the rest of the season. What is it, your basketball season, two more months? Exercise is good when you're pregnant, I think."

Isn't that what they told Christie? Not that she was playing basketball, but running and playing some tennis. She was encouraged to continue working out. Dr. Klira told her that. And wasn't there an Olympian woman who was pregnant, years ago, won a gold medal in figure skating maybe? All that spinning and jumping and landing, it would have to be harder on a developing baby than playing girls high school basketball.

"Yeah, right. Divine Mercy is going to let a pregnant girl out there on the court in front of all those people. The parents in the stands would go: *Look at the little slut who's knocked up. Serves her right*. No way. They wouldn't let me embarrass the school like that. School tradition and standards and all. They'd tell me it was for my own good that they hide me away."

She's probably right, Tyler thinks. But they're getting ahead of themselves. "Ask your doctor, Nicki."

"I don't have a doctor. My *family* has a doctor. Even if I went to him and told him not to say anything to my parents, would he?

And I don't even have a health insurance card. My mom always takes care of that."

"If you want, I could make an appointment for you with my doctor. Christie used to see him for all that female stuff. We could just pay him cash. It can't be too much for one visit. You can just pay me back a little at a time as you baby sit."

"Yeah, okay. Sure. Whatever. What can *he* do about it?"

"He can make sure you know enough to make a good decision." *She's pregnant;* Tyler can't believe it. She seemed so innocent, just a happy little jockette. But it's not hard to see that boys her age would be drawn to her.

"I can't wait too long. I just want to be out of this mess. And if that does mean ending it, I want to do it while it's just a little piece of tissue, like some fish bait or something, that can't feel anything. I was thinking of going to a women's clinic, where I'd be more, you know, anonymous and they wouldn't ask a lot of questions." Why can't he be on *her side* and just support her in this? Then nobody else has to know. Maybe she shouldn't have told Tyler; he still thinks of her as just a kid. That's why he's so shocked by all this.

"Let's get you to a real doctor. Really. I'll go with you if you want."

"But if I decide to get it taken care of, you won't get in the way, right? Won't tell my parents?"

He assures her that he won't tell anyone. "But I hope it doesn't come to that."

"You hope. What about me?" she says angrily. "Do you know what all this is going to do to me? You wouldn't lecture me about having the baby and giving it up for adoption if you thought for a minute about me, still in high school, remember?"

He just shakes his head. Nothing more he can say. Sex elevates women higher than they can imagine, but also makes them volatile, unpredictable. He finally goes to bed with his gorgeous girlfriend, and she immediately gets all icy on him. And this sixteen-year-old here unleashing the genie of sex before she was ready and it's changing her chemistry, upsetting her apple cart, intent on bringing forward a new life.

"I better get going," she sputters. "Don't say anything to anybody yet, you can't! *Please*. But thanks, Tyler, for talking it through with me."

She blows her nose in a tissue from the box he handed her. Then she rises up on tippy-toe white sneakers and hugs him around his neck, her little body pressing against his.

"It's going to be okay, kid," he says, but it's not him with a baby already growing inside his belly, with other girls at school to face who can be so mean. And having to tell her mother and father. That would be tough.

30

Sunday afternoon and Game 4 of the World Series sitting inside his VCR, taped last night while Tyler and Lyvia were at the stupid movie. He tries to avoid hearing how the game went, hurrying out of church without much chit chat, so he can watch it with some suspense. But his heart's not in it, not with the NFL games coming on. He flips open the *Free Press* to the sports section. Cincy beat the A's again to sweep the series. The end of another baseball year, yet another death but a tiny one, hardly grieved. Might as well watch some football.

First, he has a job to do, now that Robbie has gone down for his nap. Out front, Tyler stuffs little yellow rubber earplugs deep into the spiraling tunnel of each of his ears. He pulls the cord on the chainsaw borrowed from Webb Rucker's brother. It starts right up, making quite a racket but hopefully not waking the boy inside. He cuts the trunk at an angle, starting about a foot off the ground. Then he'll cut the stump off as close to the ground as he can, so he won't leave a bump he'll have to mow around. Wood chips fly, making it hard to see.

The noise and the blurring sawdust somehow clears his mind. Her *sacrifice*, he can see now, had been given without reservation, without conditions. He and Robbie always had come first unquestionably. Offering her very self to him and to Robbie without reservation. The only requirement for him was to accept and receive that gift, honoring her by taking it in. But he was left without answers. Didn't even know the right questions because of a blindness to what cannot be seen or touched or measured. Trying to find faith through knowledge instead of the other way around. Understanding remains elusive.

The dead tree comes down without a fight. The eye sore removed. His promise kept. His neighborhood honor restored.

He never could live up to the potential she saw in him, of course, that better self. He was always letting her down even if she never told him so. Only rarely in moments of weakness did she complain or grow angry. Maybe if they had had more time together, they would have fought more, who can say now? She never made him feel like a loser, letting most of his little failures and indiscretions slide. Nobility is forgiving others for the slights, real or imagined, that we allow to wound us. But we do seek justice, if only to contain the evil residing in these others. For our own transgressions, we often take a different tack. First, minimizing their significance. *Not really a big deal. No one was hurt. A victimless crime.* Then attempting to explain away our role, our guilt. *Not really our fault.* When our excuses are exhausted, we plead for *mercy*. Blind justice would crush us, can't have that. Mercy is a gift we ask for, to be granted, not earned.

He cuts the fallen tree into manageable pieces he can give away if he can think of anyone who has a real fireplace. Everyone these days has an instant-on gas fireplace; so much easier than burning logs. Below the ground, the tree's massive root system remains unseen, still holding the Earth together.

She never burdened him with doubt. She assumed he would be faithful, truthful and loving. Inviolable *trust* in him. When we expect the best in those we love, we may succeed in bringing it out of them. Trust in a being we cannot see is harder. Letting go of it all—the worry, the anxiety—that can envelope our bodies, cloud over our senses. We want to control everything though so many concerns lie far beyond our grasp. Better left to the Master of the Universe, but we still won't let go until there is no choice. Like a golfer finding his ball in the rough with only a blind shot from there. He figures the distance and feels the wind and knows the green is out there, somewhere around a corner of taunting trees and hidden hazards. Then he must get into his stance without seeing the target, envisioning the shot that cannot be seen. He brings the club back smoothly and confidently, turning then and driving his fists down to begin the swing, whipping the club face around a steep and glorious arc. Down onto the tiny single dimple on the ball he's staring at, striking that very spot with quiet fury. Sending the ball flying on a journey of faith, out of sight on the far side of the trees. Believing in the shot as he conceived it must be.

31

Tyler is about to leave the house Monday morning, later than he'd planned, to drop Robbie off at daycare and spend another hour or so with Cuhlman. Hoping that the old man won't turn moody again, making him feel like he's a bigot.

Tyler had begun to seriously think about Cuhlman's memoirs as a book-in-the-making. If he can't find a job, he'd make it as an author. Why not? He had found a real hero with so many stories to tell. Playing in the negro leagues with Josh Gibson and Satchel Paige, then killing Nazis in a machine gun nest on D-Day, who else could say they'd done all that? It was an idea with real potential. He had thought about calling it *Memoirs of a Great American*. Or even *The Greatest American*. But not after the old man suddenly went off, as if Tyler was against him somehow, on account of the whiteness of his skin. Imagine that! Better to forget about it as a book. Just finish out the simple project, a nice keepsake for Cuhlman's kids and grandkids.

With his son in his arms, the diaper bag strapped over one shoulder and a little gym bag with a notepad and the tape recorder over his other shoulder, the phone in his kitchen rings. He picks it up with his left hand and holds it to his face without dropping anything. It's a nurse from his doctor's office; the results are in from his MRI. He needs to come in to see Dr. Klira to discuss whatever those results might be. Can he come in tomorrow afternoon? Tyler scans his brain for conflicts.

"Can we make it for around three-thirty or four?" Tyler asks.

This could work out perfectly. He'll pick up Nicki after school and bring her with him to the appointment. Maybe she'll have to skip out on basketball practice for once. He'll ask Klira if he can squeeze Nicki into his schedule while she's there. He'll pay for it as a separate visit, of course.

Nicki fights him at first, loudly, on the phone when he calls her. Her parents must not be around. But she relents when he's firm with her, telling her she needs the best information she can get as she makes a big decision. She says she'll walk a couple of blocks from the school and he can pick her up at a Mobil gas station. They have a little quickie mart where she can wait so no one sees her going off with him. She's making it all so clandestine, cloak and dagger, clearly worried that one of the big mouths at school will guess her secret, the mystery brewing unseen inside her still-flat belly.

32

They drive silently to the doctor's office the next day, Nicki and him. The seriousness of their mission weighs oppressively on them, so he flips on the radio and hits the button to bring up the Top 40 station he still has on one of the presets. The B-52s' campy "Love Shack." *The whole shack shimmies, yeah, the whole shack shimmies…*

Tyler reminds himself to tell the doctor about the spinning head he's been feeling. It might be important, something inside his brain that could relate to whatever that MRI has turned up, his neurons possibly scrambled, not that he really wants to know.

He signs in at the desk and sits down in the waiting area with Nicki. She tries to act bored, but he can see the terror underneath her skin. He flips through a *Sports Illustrated*, the College Football Preview issue from a couple of months ago. Eventually, a nurse calls Tyler's name. He motions Nicki to follow him. They're led into one of the rooms, where the nurse takes Tyler's blood pressure and temperature, like always, then tells him to wait for the doctor. She doesn't ask about Nicki, who sits quietly on a chair by the window.

A few minutes later, Dr. Mohammed Klira throws open the door and hurriedly enters the room, his head down scanning notes on a clipboard he had undoubtedly just been handed as he bolts from one patient to the next. He extends his right palm to shake Tyler's hand, just as he notices the teenage girl sitting by the window.

"Dr. Klira, this is Nicki Saliba, my babysitter," Tyler says, leaving out for now any explanation for why he has brought her here.

"Please to meet you, Nicki. But Tyler, you're too old to need a babysitter," the doctor quips, smiling.

"Yeah, right. Well, I'll explain in a minute. But first, what about the MRI? And, before I forget, I should tell you that a couple of times in the last few weeks I've had some strange dizzy spells."

The doctor tells Tyler that the MRI of his brain shows a very small dark patch, a shadow of sorts. It may be significant; it may be nothing. He wants to hear more about the dizzy spells.

"The room just starts spinning. It's only happened twice or maybe three times, all in the last few weeks. I hadn't been drinking or anything. The spinning only lasts a few seconds, but I don't want it to happen when I'm driving."

Has he had any severe pain associated with the dizzy spells, in his ears or head?

No, Tyler says.

The doctor makes some notes with his pen. He takes a black instrument out of one of the pockets in his white smock. It's like a flashlight but with a magnifying glass attached that he uses to peer into Tyler's eyes, first one, then the other. Then he pulls out a little adapter piece and uses the light scope to look deep into each of Tyler's ears. *What do all these windows into his head reveal?*

The doctor makes a few more notes on the clipboard before saying, "Looking at your eardrums is important. A perforated eardrum is not an uncommon cause of the *vertigo* you have experienced. Balance and equilibrium are controlled in your middle ear."

It occurs to Tyler that he may have been the culprit, with his deeply inserted Q-tips hunting inside his ears for a little wax. His quiet little addiction to the swirling, the tickling; could it have been his undoing?

"But a ruptured eardrum is almost always accompanied with severe pain, which you haven't had. And your eardrums look fine from what I can see."

Sweet relief cascades down Tyler's back when his doctor seems to move away from the inner workings of his ears.

"I'm more concerned about the small dark spot on your MRI. We'll have to keep an eye on this. This shadow is so small I might have missed it all together. Hopefully, it is merely the last remains of your brain getting over the trauma that left you unconscious for a couple of days. A ruptured blood vessel produces a pool of blood, we call it a *hematoma*, that clots and eventually heals up. What we don't want, of course, is an active hematoma that continues to put pressure on your brain. You only have some much room inside your skull that your brain has to fit into. It is a tight squeeze. That is why there are so many folds in the brain tissue."

"Would that hematoma explain the dizzy spells?" Tyler asks.

"Possibly. But vertigo can also be caused by severe stress and anxiety. A lot of stress in your life since you lost Christina. We discussed this a bit when you were last in to see me. And your job, too, you said?"

"Yeah, I was let go right before the accident. So, yeah, a lot of loss. I try to roll with it, but it *has* been a lot to deal with, sure."

The doctor asks Tyler if he wants him to prescribe a medication to help relieve the stress and prevent anxiety. But Tyler is reluctant to start taking something to further *numb* his system. Lyvia's already accusing him of insulating himself from the highs and lows in his life.

"No, I don't want to be medicated. I can get through it on my own."

"Okay, we'll have you redo the MRI in two months," the doctor says. The thought of repeating the awful test terrifies Tyler, but the doctor is already writing out the script and doesn't see the pained look on his patient's face. "In the meantime, you keep track of any more dizzy spells and if they are severe, or if they occur more than once in a two- or three-week period, I want you to come see me right away."

"Do I really have to go back in that awful torpedo tube again?" Tyler moans.

"We can't take a chance with your brain, Tyler. You know better than anyone," the doctor says, his second reference to Christie, this one an unintentionally cruel reminder of the tiny explosion inside her brain. The doctor moves toward the door.

"One more thing, Doctor Klira," Tyler says, knowing his time is short. Better get right to it. "It's why Nicki is here. She thinks she's pregnant. She's scared and confused and hasn't told her parents yet. I wondered if you could see her and at least figure out if she really is pregnant."

"This is highly unusual, Tyler. Nicki, you should go to your own doctor who knows you."

"That's the thing, Doc," Tyler says, still speaking for the girl. "She'd normally see her doctor with her mother. But she's not ready to tell her parents yet. I can step out of the room while you talk with her." The doctor frowns. Probably doesn't want to take on this new complication to his busy schedule.

"Why don't we both step out of this room for a minute, Tyler, and talk about this. Nicki, please wait here." She nods her worried head and stays seated while the two men scoot out the door. The doctor leads them into another small room and shuts the door behind them.

"How old is that girl?" the doctor asks with a tone Tyler has never heard him use before. Like a parent would use to scold a young child.

"Not quite seventeen."

"That's not good, Tyler. She's underage. We're talking about statutory rape here. That's a felony. It can't be ignored."

"But her boyfriend is the same age. At least I think he is. I guess I never asked her."

"Is that really the story? Or is it you who is worried about being the father of this girl's baby?" The full weight of the doctor's accusation falls on him like a giant hail stone, hard and heavy and icy cold.

"Me? No, no. That's *not* what's going on. I'm just trying to help out my babysitter. She burst out in tears the other night when I came home and told me she'd missed her period, and that she'd done a home pregnancy test." He blurts this out to clear up the confusion, but isn't sure it's helping. "I didn't even know she had a boyfriend, but she says she's been going with this kid for a year and a half and they've been sexually active for at least a little while, she said."

The doctor looks Tyler over, unsure what to do. "She has to go to her own doctor."

"She won't go. She's scared and desperate and can't imagine telling her parents. Going to her family doctor won't work. But I'm afraid if she goes to one of those women's health clinics, they'll just talk her into having a quick abortion before she can make a good decision. Or at least a decision she can live with the rest of her life."

"I will talk with her, but in generalities only. I cannot take her on as a patient unless one of her parents comes in here with her."

The two men reenter the room where Nicki still sits, waiting. The doctor explains he will speak with her briefly, but would need her parents' approval to take her on as a patient. He lets her decide if she wants Tyler to stay in the room while they talk briefly. She says she does.

"I am sure you are scared and wish this had never happened. Tell me, how long has it been since your last period?"

"Six and a half weeks. September seventh. I'm always pretty regular, every twenty-seven or twenty-eight days."

"And did you have unprotected intercourse in mid- to late-September?" the doctor asks, sounding a bit like a trial lawyer.

"Yeah.... My boyfriend and I have tried to be careful. We've only had sex a few times and he's usually worn a condom. It's just a couple times we ... and he didn't. I mean..." she sputters, but her meaning is clear enough. She's trying to be brave, to be adult, but she just wants to leave. *Why did Tyler make her come here?* He made it sound like his doctor would be sympathetic and helpful, but she's not seeing it.

"And a home pregnancy test resulted in a clear positive?"

"Yes. Twice, just to be sure." She's no longer able to appear grown up. Cowering in the chair, she's just a little girl without her mother, looking with downcast eyes like she's about to suck her thumb.

"Your doctor can perform a test of your urine using a very similar methodology. But the test you used is generally quite accurate. False positives are rare. He can also test your blood for elevated hormone levels, to further confirm the pregnancy and to give you a better indication that your body is reacting as it should to this new development."

Nicki looks like she's going to throw up. Tyler has never seen her so pale.

"How big is it right now?" Tyler asks.

"Tiny," the doctor replies, still talking to Nicki. "At four and a half weeks after conception, the fetus is about the size of a sesame seed."

Like on the bun of a Big Mac. How could this miniscule thing have so much power over her? It just isn't right. But maybe being so small is a good thing. Who would miss one tiny seed if she would get rid of it?

"But you may be closer to six weeks pregnant; we do not know yet. At six weeks, the circulatory system of the fetus has already developed, including a tiny heart, although it still looks like a miniature translucent tadpole. At nine weeks, he has grown much bigger in relative terms, though still smaller than a grape. By this point, he is visibly a tiny human, with toes and fingers and a face with a nose and little ear lobes."

"So, there's not much time," Nicki blurts out.

The two men look back at her silently.

She continues: "I mean, if it's just a miniature tadpole not much bigger than a seed, it's really not much different from a sperm or egg that never got used in the first place, right? But once it's a little person, I wouldn't want to, you know, end it like that."

"You are correct in drawing a distinction in visual appearance. Before nine weeks it does not look very human at all. It could be a baby frog. But, then again, it's not a frog or anything other than a developing human. All the genetic material that this human being will ever need to fully develop is already contained in the cells of the most primitive, tiny fetus. *Ending it* at a very early stage, as you say, might not be seen as taking the life of a baby, but it certainly is taking the life of a human."

It's all too much to bear. As Nicki absorbs these last words from Tyler's doctor, her eyes dart around the little office room, searching. She jumps up suddenly, lunging for the wastebasket on the floor in a corner and tries to heave, but nothing comes up.

Dr. Klira moves toward the door. "I'm sorry to upset you, but you should know these things."

"Just one more thing, doctor," Tyler says. "If she does decide to have the baby, can she continue to work out and run hard? Nicki plays high school basketball."

And just then she does throw up, in two short spasms.

The doctor waits to see that the girl is done vomiting and doesn't need his attention. "She should certainly listen to the doctor who will be following her. And, of course, her basketball coach has to be made aware of her condition. I would not want to say anything about her individual situation myself. But, in general, a young woman in good physical shape can continue to maintain fairly strenuous exercise well into the sixth month of pregnancy or even beyond, though she should be careful not to get overheated. Of course, playing basketball is more than exercise. There can be rough contact, and she could fall down hard. For the first trimester and into the fourth month or so, the baby is very well protected. But after that it might not be safe for a young woman to play a rough sport. Again, I am not speaking about Nicki and her unique situation. There can be complications."

He turns again to face the girl, still hovering over the wastebasket.

"Nicki, I know this is upsetting. You can get cleaned up in this adjoining little bathroom and rinse your mouth out. There are paper cups in there. Then go home and talk with your parents. Have your mother take you to your regular doctor. He will know best."

"She," the girl says, turning her head to respond. The color is coming back to her face, though she has flecks of vomit in her hair. "Our doctor is a she."

* * *

A sesame seed! *Oh, my God!* This thing inside her is so small, a nothing, certainly not recognizable as a baby, but splitting and growing every minute. She has to stop it before it ruins everything, she thinks, her mind racing. Already she is a wreck, not able to concentrate on anything at school or at practice. She's got to get her head back in the game. A couple of her friends have noticed the nervousness, the jitters she feels all the time. Asking what's wrong and of course she says "nothing" and that ends it, for now. She wishes she could end this thing altogether.

But, *Oh my God*, throwing up in that doctor's office! So embarrassing! How could Tyler do such a thing to her? And then this doctor, so above it all, wouldn't even run a test on her, make sure she's not freaking out over nothing. But she's already run a second home test with the same result. Preggers. It was so easy to joke around with the other kids about somebody else. Like that girl Bobbie on the soap *Home and Away* a lot of her friends watch, taping the show on the VCR 'cause it's on during school. A big build up before Bobbie finally tells her mother, and they still haven't told her father because he won't handle it well. *Who would handle it well?* Nicki's still sixteen, same as that Bobbie girl, and even if she's felt grown-up for quite a while and can hardly even remember thinking like a kid, she knows she's not ready to have a baby in her life. Just a junior. She's going to have this belly hanging out and how's that going to fly at Divine Mercy, walking the halls and just feeling all the stares, the snickers. Preggers. *Don't be like her. That's what happens to a slut. A little Arab slut.*

    She doesn't feel like a slut. She just let Chris take things too far. He just expected that they would make out any chance they were alone. Then they'd gone all the way and the world didn't fall apart, you know? He had used a condom, except once, and that one other time it broke anyway and his funky smell all over her. Billions of Chris' microscopic sperms swimming up inside her, racing to find an egg and guess what? They found it. On the film the girls had watched in Health class, these sperms, like tadpoles but with whip-like tails, surround the much bigger but still microscopic egg and attack it, like they're raping it almost, until one does break through the cell wall which then instantly becomes like concrete to keep the other sperm attackers from breaking in, too. That very second everything changes: the microorganisms of sperm and egg becoming one thing, their DNA combining to form a single tiny being. Is that when God rushes in with a soul and a future reservation to heaven if this human-to-be will just accept it and maybe act just a little grateful once in a while? Or does he wait to bring his great gift until this tiny patch of cells develops into something more recognizable as a baby, created in his image after all, not created to be a frog like a tadpole is. At least until it's the size of a grape but with fingers and ear lobes, like that smug doctor had said, at what? *Nine weeks*, she thinks.

And Chris has been a bit of a jerk-off lately. She wondered if he was about to break it off, and she sometimes had hoped he would. Everything was getting kind of tiresome, you know? Of course, she was still hoping that somehow this fertilized egg would come loose off the wall of her womb and pass out of her like the bloody stains of her period, maybe when she sat on the toilet and peed, it would just come out and she'd not even notice this sesame seed floating on the toilet water below her and then flushed away like all the other waste that comes out of us that we never give a second thought. A lot of girls, women even, lose a baby early on in the pregnancy. That would be the best. But maybe she has to help nature along. That's what the other girls would do. Go to one of those clinics. Try not to be seen if there are any people protesting there, saying rosaries for the unborn martyrs and all. If she does it before God moves in and makes those cells his own, it won't be so bad. And nobody would have to know.

She just wants her little life back. Shooting hoops. That's when she feels most alive and in control. Getting in one of those rhythms where she can't miss. Raining down from all sides of the court, her shots flicking the net clean, no iron. Coach Myers saw her like that a couple of times in practice before they'd played their first game this year. *In the zone*, shot after shot. She began to see what Nicki could do for her, for the team, and then she changed the offense to run more plays to cut Nicki loose. *That would be so cool*, she had said to her coach when they had met alone in the trainer's room. There would be pressure on her, the coach had said. But Nicki hadn't flinched. She got a taste of what it could be like in that first home game. To be the star, the scorer, carrying the team. And, yeah, she is determined to play aggressive defense, too. Like that one nurse at Tyler's hospital, had said, *defense never gets cold*. So far, the team is undefeated and Nicki is playing like an

All-Star. But all this is going to come crashing down if this sesame seed has its way. *It isn't fair, you know? Just isn't fair.*

And Tyler, after that awful doctor's office visit, dropping her off a block from her house so she could act like she was just getting home from being dropped off from practice. Telling her that she should pray about it. What was that all about; now is he going to get all preachy on her? 'Cause if she prays, where's that going to lead? She can't see God making her feel that, you know, *Sure, it's okay.* Just flush this little speck of a baby out of you like a bad germ. *My creation*, he would say, *but it's fine. Do what you must.* Sure, right? It's not soon enough if he's already moved in with one of his souls, put it inside her little fetus. How does she pray about *that* and still get the answer she wants, to make it all just go away?

33

Tyler's on the phone with the hiring manager at Lockery, the phone interview already nearing an hour. It's so hard to know how it's going when you can't see the other person. Some of Tyler's answers are too long, and rambling; even he gets bored listening to himself. But he must be scoring points. The voice on the other end of the telephone keeps asking questions. Tyler has figured that this company, so tiny compared with GM, will be in awe of his experience with the automotive colossus and quick to make an offer.

The call ends without Tyler having a clear idea of the next steps. He feels run down, worn out by the mental exercise as if he'd been there in the Lockery building for the interview but had to keep his eyes shut. He feels the room begin to spin, yes, definitely. That's one time. He needs to write this down and remember it for his doctor. He wants to call Lyvia to tell her about the interview, but he's talked out. He reaches instead for the television remote.

***

Nicki's game uniform shorts seem tighter around her waist than the last time she put them on, less than a week ago. It's her *imagination*, she tells herself. The little invader inside her is still smaller than a pinhead. She has trouble concentrating during the pregame drills and still seems out of sync as the game gets underway. Tyler and Robbie again watch from the pull-out bleachers in the Divine Mercy High gym. The other team, Bloomfield Hills Marian, gets off to a fast start with two fast-break layups off turnovers. Coach Myers calls an unusually early timeout to settle the team down. They return to the floor with new focus, thinking only about executing the set play they discussed during the timeout. Melissa dribbles quickly up the court, losing her defender at the midcourt stripe. As she nears the foul line, the Marian interior defenders rush up to block her path, leaving Shannon uncovered just to the left of the basket. Melissa's bounce pass splits two defenders and arrives at waist level for the red-headed center, who makes the easy basket. They run a similar play the next time down, except Nicki slips unnoticed behind the three-point line on the far-left baseline. This time, when Shannon gets the bounce pass from Melissa, the Marian defenders are ready for her. But instead of forcing the shot, she flings it out to Nicki, who catches the ball and brings it up behind her right ear as she bends her knees, ready to spring. Then she's rising up on the toes of her sneakers and sending the ball on that rainbow of hers with perfect backspin. Her follow-through brings her right hand out in front of her eyes with their unsettling, steely gaze, palm down, fingers extended. She can still feel the imprint of the pebbled surface of the ball spinning off her fingertips as it comes down off the rainbow and snaps the net.

It takes four more makes out of five shots from Nicki before Marian figures out that she's the one they have to closely defend. Shannon and the others don't draw as much attention, and each of them contributes at least a couple of baskets. The Fillies hold a comfortable lead in the second half, when Nicki goes off on another tear, sinking three mid-range jumpers and two more threes, both from the right baseline corner.

Tyler looks at Nicki, so alive in the flow of the game, forgetting for a time the tiny thing in the tunnel of her teenage uterus. She moves with graceful confidence as if she knows the lucky places on the floor to set up and shoot. But it's not luck, as she demonstrates with deadly repetition, her smooth follow-through leaving the slender fingers on her right hand pointing at the little spot on the orange rim out up ahead of her. How can she forget for even a minute or two that she's carrying another life inside her, he wonders. Creating havoc with her future. That miniature *tadpole* inside her, like a shrunken version of that little girl Jessica when she was trapped in a dark well in Texas and the whole country was watching on CNN, Tyler remembers, fifty-something hours it was until the firemen rescued her finally and brought her out whole, back into the world alive. But for this other life hanging onto Nicki's uterine wall, who will be watching if it's snuffed out or if it's allowed to live?

* * *

Tyler sticks around after the game to let Robbie finish the popcorn he had bought the boy when he got fussy, sometime in the second half. As they finally make their way out to the parking lot, Tyler sees Nicki leaving the side door of the locker room, carrying her gym bag over her shoulder. He scoops up his son and hurries over to her before she gets out to the cars, where her parents undoubtedly are waiting for her.

"You were unreal out there, Nicki," he calls out to her. "On fire."

"Yeah, it has been pretty unreal," she says. The music in her head, providing the rhythm. Everyone else and even the ball seemingly moving in slow motion. Unreal.

"You keep shooting like that and you're going to get a scholarship to some college that'll be glad to have you."

"Yeah, I don't know. A lot's up in the air right now, if you know what I mean."

Tyler knows. He just nods and gives her the chance to finish the thought. Instead, she shifts to a new subject.

"Hey, I've been meaning to tell you something, if you want to hear about it. Maybe not. My friends heard a little more about that Linda girl who was driving the car that hit you that night."

"Go ahead and tell me," Tyler says, before really considering it.

"Well, she was a good student. I mean, really good, practically all A's. Taking a bunch of AP classes as a junior."

Great, Tyler thinks. Their crash has cost the country, the world even, somebody who could have been a productive person, maybe made a difference with her life. We'll never know.

"She'd been pretty quiet, not very social, you know? But kids are saying she'd come out of her shell a bit this summer. Going to parties, going out with boys."

Living a little more dangerously, he supposes.

"And something else," Nicki continues. "You know I guess it just sticks out because people, I would think, are gonna only say good things about somebody after they're, you know, gone. But the kids over at her school are talking about her, saying she had picked up a bit of a mean streak. Not just behind a kid's back like girls do, but she'd get nasty right in their face, they say."

What does it matter, Tyler is thinking, this petty meanness? So, the girl had grown a backbone. Now she'll never get to use it, to flex some muscle on anybody.

"Yeah, okay. Even if she had become a jerk at times, it doesn't change anything," he says sullenly. He feels sorry for her, this girl, he does. But he's also feeling sorry for himself that he had to get mixed up in this teen tragedy. The mark of this death is on him, like a stink that won't wash off, like those other deaths that surround him, pulling him down from the path he should have been on. We know that life isn't fair, but still we expect it to be, and are then sorely surprised when unfairness leaps up in our way and forces us off the road we want to be on, just minding our own business.

"Nobody seems to know when she started drinking..." Nicki says, but trails off when she sees from the far-off look in his eyes that he's no longer listening.

* * *

Tyler presses the PLAY button on his answering machine. It's the HR manager at Lockery, hemming and hawing. *It was so good to speak with you last week. Your experience is indeed impressive.... But we've decided to go in a different direction and wish you the best in your job search.*

Great, he muses, no job offer, and not even any feedback to help improve for the next interview. *Oh, well.* Another opportunity is bound to come up soon, maybe a much better one. He's counting on it. He's spent the severance now and the health insurance has run out.

He does call Lyvia this time. She hears his bad news and offers the same kind of encouragement he was already telling himself. He pretends to be heartened, but feels himself growing numb. Being without a job, he thinks, is to watch your identity vanish, like losing your driver's license and not being able to get a new one. Your job is who you are.

34

Riding on his bike with Robbie behind him, in the slightly larger toddler seat he found at a yard sale. Unseasonably warm for late October. He points out the houses that have gone in big with Halloween decorations. Giant cobwebs and furry spiders, rows of tombstones and witches on broomsticks.

When did people start decorating for Halloween like it was Christmas? Just one non-stop commercial holiday once the leaves start to fall. The stores can't wait to start playing the Christmas carols over the intercom to get their customers into the buying spirit of the season. Robbie is happily humming some tune in his mind, soaking in the gentle warm autumnal sunshine and the cross breeze throwing up crinkly dry leaves into crazy swirls as they go by. He doesn't understand much about Halloween, of course, just pumpkins and cartoonish witches. And *goats,* as he calls those white apparitions made silly instead of spooky by Madison Avenue, modernized Caspers. What thoughts of the afterlife can there be in the head of a toddler? Perhaps it is true that *the scent of heaven can be smelled from a distance of seventy years.* But if the very young really can sense the eternal, they don't let on. It seems all about cartoons and cereal to them. God seemingly as remote from their consciousness as asparagus unless you push it on them. But maybe they just don't know how to tell us what they feel towering above them, all the adults around them looming like giants. Is there anybody even higher up there to them?

For something different and in keeping with the season, he heads farther west than he usually rides, through the neighborhoods between Seven Mile and Eight Mile to Glen Eden Cemetery, a sprawling maze of roads and paths through the fields of the dead. The real tombstones aren't as cheerful as the decorations because you know there's a body down below each one. But it's all the same to Robbie, who continues his mindlessly merry humming.

The roads are empty today of hearses and mourners, father and son on the bike ride alone except for the occasional squirrel scurrying around the leaves and twigs between the headstones, nature going on oblivious to our casualties. Why should these creatures mourn the dead among the great spoilers of the Earth? At least that's how we've come to look at ourselves.

We give ourselves a lot of crap, Tyler thinks, the modern peoples of Western civilization at least, for being wasteful and unthinking stewards of our planet, destroying all that is natural and untainted. But nature, too, can be so inefficient. He helped his father some years ago back in Akron clear out a huge old hornet's nest from the shed behind their garage. A giant ball of papery catacombs, an insect Taj Mahal, evidently built the year before and then abandoned. Why work so hard to build such an edifice for just one season? Why not come back and make it home again for another year? Or corn, towering majestically six feet tall, all that stalk and tassel, but just one ear for each plant. Couldn't that tree-like stalk hold another ear or two?

The cemetery road leads around back to the entrance. Tyler stops the bike for a moment to adjust his helmet, which doesn't seem to fit his head very well.

"Daddy?" Robbie says, into the stillness around him now that the scenery has stopped moving and the wind has died down. "Daddy, I hungry."

"I hungry, too, Robbie. We'll head home and get some lunch. Peanut butter and jelly. Maybe some soup, too."

This information seems to satisfy the little one, who returns to his humming. His father pushes against the pedals and the scenery again moves behind them, the wind blowing again onto the boy's happy face.

After lunch, Tyler puts Robbie down for a nap. With a full stomach and after all that fresh air, he doesn't fight it and is soon sound asleep, snoring gently in that toddler way. Tyler scoots down to his basement workshop to begin painting the bookshelves he has made for Robbie's birthday. He'll get him a couple of new toys, too, of course, but he's really looking forward to giving his son something he's built with his own hands. The pieces have come together perfectly, smooth surfaces the product of hours of careful sanding, here and there for the past few months. Now he applies the paint, red—Robbie's favorite color—in steady brushstrokes. Just as he finishes the first coat, the doorbell rings. Lyvia coming over for dinner that they're going to make together. They've seen each other less frequently the last ten days, and there haven't been any more sleepovers. They've both been acting as if everything's normal between them, and he's content to go with that, for now.

Tyler opens the door and lets her in, though he lingers on the porch for a moment before following her inside. "Devil's Night, tonight. Just keeping an eye out for any mischief makers."

"A little early for that, don't you think?"

It's not even five o'clock with just the hint of dusk coming on, though Tyler has had his lights on for an hour. Lyvia follows Tyler into Robbie's room. The kid had been sleeping all afternoon, and is now holding on to the bars of his crib, jumping up and down excitedly, ready to rejoin the waking world. Or rather, to have the world rejoin him. Sleep stops the clock and everything else to a toddler; the world in front of their eyes ceases to exist when their lids close down.

"Lid-dy!" he says happily, the first time she's heard him try to say her name. She lifts him up out of the crib and squeezes him against her upper body.

"Yes, that's right, Robbie. I'm glad to see you, too."

Tyler smiles proudly. Nice to have the boy working on his woman, making her feel part of the family.

Lyvia takes charge in the kitchen, fixing a chicken stir fry using a wok she uncovered in one of Tyler's cabinets on an earlier visit. She takes an occasional sip from the bottle of Miller Lite Tyler has opened for her. He's nearly finished with his. Robbie sits in the recliner, mesmerized by some show on a new network for kids, Nickelodeon, that Tyler gets now with his basic cable. Something he might have to cut back on if he doesn't get a job soon. Until then, the boy can gorge on cartoon animals and sitcoms set in fanciful junior highs. The chicken crackles in hot oil in the deeply concave pan releasing an alluring fragrance that makes Tyler all the hungrier. As she pours in the ingredients she brought from her apartment—fresh pea pods, chopped celery, mushrooms and onion, along with some spices he doesn't recognize—she asks again about their plans for Robbie's birthday, the day after Halloween. Lyvia has an early morning class on Thursday, but then is free to spend the day with them. It looks like the weather will cooperate—chilly but sunny—for an afternoon at the Detroit Zoo. There's a new polar bear exhibit Tyler read about in the newspaper that features a big artificial pond of clear water with a glass wall so you can watch from underneath as the bears swim by. Talk of Robbie's birthday seems to trigger a related thought in her mind.

"So, when is *your* birthday?" she asks Tyler.

"Earlier this month," he says flatly. "October 6."

She looks at him with dismay. "What, we missed it? How could you not tell me? Didn't you think I'd like to help you celebrate?"

He has no answer. Just the sheepish look of someone only now realizing the error of his ways.

"Somebody else you wanted to be with instead?"

No, no, he says. He just didn't want to put any pressure on her to get him a gift; they'd only been going out a little while.

"More than a month. Enough to know we cared about each other, at least I thought so," she says, confronting the unwelcome notion that perhaps he is less than she has made him out to be.

Later, he asks her when her own birthday falls, not wanting to compound the problem by missing hers.

"February 5th," she says matter-of-factly.

That's just great, he thinks. Christmas, her birthday and Valentine's Day in quick succession. Each holiday will ratchet up expectations for the next one. Three opportunities to underperform if he doesn't get the gift right. This is just the kind of pressure he was trying to save her from, and look where that got him.

Robbie doesn't fight it when Tyler puts him to bed early. He has two big days coming up and is going to need to have banked some sleep. Then Tyler and Lyvia retire to the family room. She's still giving off a chilly vibe, the perceived slight of the missed birthday an open wound for her. He would have forgotten it by now if not for her sullenness. No point in reopening the hurt by trying to further explain. Maybe the good Thursday night TV will help. *America's Best Night of Television on Television,* NBC calls their Thursday programs. Not exactly a snappy slogan; it doesn't do the shows justice.

First up is *Cheers.* Cliffy sits on his usual barstool telling his friends of plans he has to freeze his head after death, but they make fun of him for it. Then Frazier pulls a prank on the other patrons by bringing a metal box to the bar supposedly containing a frozen head. There's a little cassette recorder in there instead. Next up is *The Cosby Show,* which used to be great but has about run its course, now with Elvin and Sondra thick in the plot, it almost makes you wish for more Theo. On this episode, Clair has begun menopause, surely the show's death knell. Sitting on the couch, Lyvia has her arms crossed and a slight frown on her face.

Tyler decides to change things up, go a different route. "Tell me something more about you, Livvy. Maybe about your childhood, growing up and all that."

He lowers the TV's volume with the remote clicker. And in opening this new vein of conversation, he is accidentally brilliant. She has secretly been waiting for him to care enough to ask about her past.

"Oh, there's nothing too interesting, really," she lies. Everyone's story is uniquely interesting because it is his own. Or her own. "I grew up in St. Charles, a suburb of St. Louis on the Missouri River," skipping over her Eureka birth this time. "We had a little three-bedroom ranch, a lot like your house here. I'm an only child, so there was plenty of room. They still live there, my parents, in St. Charles. My Dad's a postman. Mom's a *librarian*, if you can believe it. They both love to read and passed that on to me, as you know. There always were books lying about our house, each with a bookmark of some sort showing where it'd been left off. On the end tables in the living room, and across the shelf under the coffee table. In wicker baskets in each of the bathrooms. On either side of my parents' bed. And in my bedroom, too, of course. Everybody was always reading several books at once. That way you have something already started no matter what mood you're in." Remembering her mother and father as great readers reminds her to backfill her story to the beginning. "You might have wondered where my name comes from?" She trails this off as a question.

"It *is* pretty unusual. It seems musical to me." He clicks the TV off altogether.

"It's a shortened version of *Olyvia*, my legal name, from Shakespeare's *Twelfth Night*, but spelled with a 'y', my mother's insistence on originality. My parents loved the classics. But from my earliest memories, they called me *Lyvia*, wanting me to have a unique name, no one else's."

Then she tells him about her quiet town, St. Charles, and the Catholic high school she attended. Her first boyfriend and kissing in his car. Nothing more, she adds oddly. Not Tyler's business; he wouldn't ask about such long ago details.

"What brought you up here to the U of D?" Tyler finds himself listening for once, really listening, focused on the bullseye within her words, her story.

After high school, she says, she went off to the University of Kansas in Lawrence.

"That was a big step for me. A three-hour drive from home. A *big* university. And there, the world opened up for me."

She studied Western literature, of course. After graduation, she took three months off to travel. New York and Boston. Then all over Europe.

"I had saved some money from working part-time jobs at college and over the summers. My parents were good enough to foot the bills for my college, so I could put away some savings. After Paris and London, Rome and Vienna, everything back home seemed so small and *insular*. So, when I was looking for a grad school, I knew I wanted to go farther away, to a big city. And the discipline of a Jesuit university appealed to me, although U of D is actually quite *liberal* in its approach to learning and academics."

"Wait. You went off to Europe for three months of travel, by yourself?"

"No, not by myself. With a companion. We were in love, or so I thought. We were going to get married, at least that's what I told myself. The romance of it all, these European cities, blinded me to what a self-centered jerk he was."

Tyler's beer bottle has gone dry. And he has to pee. But it would be rude to break the momentum of Lyvia's story. This is not the time to be rude, just as she is remembering this former lover to have been a *self-centered jerk*. "In what ways?" he prods.

"In a thousand different ways, Alex would put himself first." Now he has a name, Alex, making this specter a little more real, and so a bit threatening. "Especially when he wanted to smoke. The need for a cigarette or a drink often seemed his most pressing thought."

"Your boyfriend *smoked*?" Tyler is stunned. He can't imagine getting close and intimate with a smoker—the stale breath, the smelly clothes, yellowy teeth and fingers, all shades of the same slow death. Why would she want to be part of that?

"I smoked, too. A bit," Lyvia confesses. "Something I picked up in college. Stupid, I know."

Tyler is genuinely appalled and doesn't try to disguise his revulsion. He just can't imagine this fresh, vibrantly wholesome girl bringing a dirty cigarette up to those moist, tender lips and inhaling that stench, fouling the insides of her pure, alabaster body.

"I quit before I came home from Europe. Haven't had a smoke since."

Tyler pictures a gray cloud of disease and decay still clinging to the linings of her lungs, blocking each glob of hemoglobin flowing through her pulmonary arteries from completing its essential capillarian transaction, swapping carbon dioxide for fresh oxygen. The pulmonary veins, expecting to take a load of oxygen-rich blood to return to the heart so it can be pumped throughout her delicate body, instead receive blackened parcels of blood, heavy with carbon and lifeless. That's what he imagines, while Lyvia is remembering only the pleasant mellowness of an occasional cigarette, discarded after a few light puffs.

"We did drink quite a bit, those months in Europe. It became a problem. Alcohol is a funny thing. It can make a shy person bold. That's what it did for me. I guess it still does. But I think it more typically exaggerates a personality—the brave grow brazen, and the obnoxious become unbearable. That was Alex. Worse, he would turn his anger on me."

"Did he hit you ever?"

"Yeah, he did. More than once. I was so stupid to take it."

She describes the abuse she endured. An angry shove, a rap on the side of her head from the butt of his open palm, hard enough to knock her off her feet, once tumbling down a stairwell and lucky to have not been more seriously hurt.

"Of course, he apologized right away each time and said he would never do it again. I wanted so much to believe him. To focus on the romance of being in these fabulous European cities with my lover, rather than admit I was stuck with a mean, conceited and frightened bully. I was so far from home. And I guess I still didn't believe in myself enough to run away from him."

"How did it end?"

"He stole from me. That's what finally woke me up. Stole some money, like forty dollars. Just stupid. That's what did it for me, not the hitting or the lies. He had stolen so much from me, my innocence, my trust and even my hopefulness. But then I realized he couldn't take my spirit from me. It was mine to keep or lose, though I'd certainly lost it at that point." The bruises remain inside even after the body heals over. "In the two-and-a half years since then, I've found it again."

Tyler moves closer to her on the couch and puts his arm around her shoulders. He will never do these things, he tells her wordlessly. That's not his way. A jerk in other ways, perhaps, but not as blatant as one who'd hit a woman, lie and steal. In smug self-satisfaction at being better than this misogynist in her past, this *Alex*, he is blinded to his own material deficiencies. He will be the center of righteousness she needs and deserves, if they each find the other worthy of a *long-term relationship*. He is a survivor, a winner. Can't she see that?

35

Late November

Nicki cocks the ball back behind her right ear and smoothly sets it on course toward the hoop, but it rims out. Another miss. Oh-for-six tonight and Mercy trails by ten, the biggest deficit they've faced all year, their undefeated record in jeopardy. She runs back down the court dogging the opposing two-guard, playing relentless defense. *If I can't score, at least I can keep my man from scoring.* Nearly halftime and she has just three points on three-of-four shooting from the foul line. Before the game she had vomited; told her teammates she might have a touch of the flu. Coach Myers has been giving Nicki frequent breaks to come over to the bench, drink some water and rest. She plays three- or four-minute stretches, then sits for two. Divine Mercy already has clinched a division championship. Now they're trying to preserve an undefeated record; that would be a first in the school's history. Only one more regular season game left after tonight.

The coach has known for three days about Nicki. She's spoken twice to Nicki's doctor, who assured Myers that even vigorous exercise would not be harmful to Nicki or her tiny baby. *As long as she doesn't get severely overheated.* And neither should the jumping and bumping and even falling to the wood floor affect her developing baby. Floating inside a bag of fluid, the *amniotic sac*, a thin but tough set of membranes inside Nicki's womb, at nine-and-a-half weeks now the fetus baby weighs about a tenth of an ounce and is just a bit larger than a grape. In a private meeting with the coach and school principal, Nicki and her parents had signed an indemnification agreement holding Divine Mercy High School—and any and all of their basketball opponents—not legally responsible should anything happen to her or the baby. All agreed to keep the girl's secret until the end of the regular season next week. Then, all have agreed to meet again and decide what further course to take. The little life inside her will nearly double in size and weight with each passing week. Nicki isn't showing and won't for perhaps another month. But well before then, she will need to tell her teammates. And the school will need to inform the Catholic High School League.

The principal had wanted to end Nicki's season immediately, of course. Nicki begged her to let her play *just a little while longer.* All of them—principal, coach, the star player and her parents—worry about how the rest of the school and the other parents will react. Nicki's own parents had been upset, of course, and still seem numb with shock and disbelief. But each of the adults in the principal's office that day are clearly impressed and proud of Nicki for taking responsibility for the living being inside her. Tearfully, she apologized to all of them. What she and Chris had done was wrong; she knows that now. Tiny tears welling in her eyes when she had told her parents a week earlier, but not the torrents she had feared. *It was wrong.*

She had decided, after hiding her secret from everyone around her, that she could not make it right with another wrong, a bigger one. She didn't mention to her parents that she had considered doing away with it. She told them only the plan she has come to now, to carry the baby to term, then put it up for adoption, so some couple somewhere unable to have a child of their own can receive a priceless gift. *So that something good may come out of it, after all.*

It will be hard, so hard, she knows. Going to school like that, belly swelling month after month all winter and spring. *Oh my God!* They'll laugh and snicker behind her back and make her feel as small as that seed once was, now overtaking her life, oblivious to the havoc and tears and humiliation. *Oh … my … God!* How will she do it, bear with it all?

She had been trying to put it out of her mind, as if she could will herself not pregnant simply by refusing to acknowledge it. This new life seeking safe harbor inside her. Her *uterus*, that funny word, sounding like something a cow has or, as you get used to hearing it, something women have, not girls, not her, not yet. Like her small intestine or gall bladder, not something she really thought much about. But here was this growing mass of life, affixed to her uterine wall, an unseen and unwanted squatter. If as a sesame seed it had lost its grip on that wall and slipped away forever, she would not have grieved it, but now that it is coming up on ten weeks and this tiny mass of life has its own heartbeat and even primitive brainwaves, she is told, she can no longer ignore it. Not just a part of her, but its own *self*, a translucent tadpole just an inch long yet with so much *potential*. She had begun to think and wonder about the life she might grow into—Nicki fancifully thinking of the fetus as a girl-to-be—playing in a sandbox, chasing after a soccer ball, going off to college, maybe doing some good in this world as a teacher, a nurse, a biologist maybe, or a business executive. And as a mother herself, someday, bringing her own children into the world. All that potential inside those dividing cells as surely as Nicki's DNA resides there. And Chris's, too; can't forget him. They haven't been together in like forever it seems, just went their own way, he not protesting when she broke up with him more than three weeks ago it must have been. She will have to tell him, of course, now that she has decided to have the baby. Not that she wants anything more to do with him, but he should know.

The decision she made really was hers alone. She had been confronted in her restless mind with what this little girl inside her might do someday. She could not snuff that out, deprive the world of whatever good her girl might be destined to do in her life. Yet, it still felt remote and theoretical, all this fuzzy future potential, not certain at all. And then, though she did not want to, Nicki thought of the girl quite separate from her potential. Not all the good she might do with her life but just her *being*, her little life itself. Even if she grew up to be average, or less than average, was she any less deserving of this chance to live? Who had given her, a suddenly pregnant seventeen-year-old, the power to end this tiny self, or to let it live and grow and inherit her rightful place alongside everyone else? Not old enough to vote or buy a beer or cigarettes but able to decide on her own to put an end not just to all that potential, but to this very life itself? She knew then that she couldn't kill off this little life cozying up inside her, asking only for a few months of sanctuary after all. Just wanting her mother to be a mother. To just let it be.

The crowd here today doesn't understand why Nicki keeps getting pulled from the game. Her shots haven't been falling, but the coach has to stick with her, right? She's been the unquestioned star of the team all year. Some of the fathers yell from the stands, *What are you doing, coach?* and *C'mon, put Nicki back in!* She blushes at the attention but tries to ignore it. Nicki reenters the game just before halftime and makes her first basket from the floor, a little eight-footer to the right of the key that she kisses off the glass. But her team is still down by eight as they run into the locker room for the half. During the break, the coach implores the team to reach deep for some extra effort to help pick Nicki up. *Not feeling well*, the girl says. *What's wrong?* they ask her.

"Nothing," she says. "It's nothing."

Melissa directs an up-tempo attack and a trapping defense in the second half, and Mercy begins to come back. Nicki continues to play only in spurts, and continues to miss most of the few shots she attempts. But she comes through on defense, with a flash of her right hand stealing the ball as it is dribbled just a bit carelessly by the other team's shooting guard, and then intercepting two passes that she anticipates perfectly; all three turnovers lead to easy layups by her teammates. The Fillies take the lead for the first time with three minutes to play while Nicki rests on the bench. For the next minute and a half of clock time, neither team can score, shots on both ends of the court rimming out. You can tell that players on both teams feel the tightness of the moment and become a little smaller in their minds, timid. When Nicki returns to the game, the noise from the stands grows louder, but Divine Mercy gives up a quick basket on a defensive breakdown to fall behind by one point. Then Melissa and Nicki execute a set play, a pick-and-roll that springs Nicki on the right side of the lane a step ahead of her defender just as the ball arrives on her hands from Melissa. But as she goes in for the layup, the two tallest opposing players slide over across the paint to block her path to the basket. Nicki reaches out with her right hand around one of the defenders and bounces a pass to a suddenly wide-open teammate—the tall redhead, Shannon—on the other side of the lane. Her hurried shot rattles around the rim but drops, putting the Fillies ahead again by a point. A few seconds later, Melissa steals the ball from the opposing point guard just past midcourt and streaks ahead for what looks to be an easy layup and a three-point lead. But instead of going in for the score, she dribbles to the far sideline, then back toward midcourt before reversing herself again, now zig-zagging around opposing players trying desperately to foul her. The horn sounds before they can catch her, preserving Mercy's perfect season.

Inside the locker room, the girls stomp their feet and dance about, delirious with their latest win. Nicki sits in front of her locker and smiles. Her nine points are a season low, but they remain undefeated.

"Wow, I was really worried near the end," one of the starters admits, "especially when you weren't in there, Nicki. You feelin' okay?"

And then it just seems like the right moment to let it all out.

"I'm not really sick or anything," Nicki says. "Just pregnant."

All eyes now on her in the sudden silence. She stands and lifts up the bottom front of her jersey to show them her flat, taut stomach.

"Ten weeks now," she says. "Thirty still to go. It's going to be a long winter and spring for me at school…"

Tears stream down her cheeks. Her teammates huddle tight around her as if in a group hug. Their coach hangs back, letting them work it out, for now. *Can you keep playing? Do your parents know? What does Chris think? Will you keep it?* She wipes her face with a towel and answers their questions, beginning the next phase, the public spectacle.

36

Early December

Robbie sits on Lyvia's lap next to Tyler in the pull-out bleachers in the Divine Mercy gymnasium that doubles as the school cafeteria. After a couple of hours sledding, the three of them, they changed into dry clothes and headed out to watch Nicki's basketball game. A cheap date. Both teams are warming up, running layup drills as the clock at the scorer's table winds down to the tip-off. Everyone knows about Nicki. At least everyone in the stands on the side of the gym behind the Divine Mercy bench.

Many of the parents are outraged that the girl continues to play on the team. *She's going to lose that baby. Then you just know there's going to be a lawsuit!* Some are outraged for a different reason, not quite calling Nicki a tramp or worse, but thinking it: *It's a scandal that she's wearing a Mercy uniform. Just embarrassing! She should stay home—bad enough she's still in school.* Parents have gone to see the principal, demanding action. Principal and coach both may lose their jobs over this.

A small contingent of parents and a good number of Nicki's Divine Mercy classmates see it differently: she's a hero for choosing to let her baby grow to full term inside her, whether she ends up keeping it or putting it up for adoption. Her teammates, save one, have rallied behind her. Since very early in the season, when Nicki started raining down points on every team they came up against, this has been *her* team. They've been in awe of her, along for the ride as she lit the nets on fire game after game. And never got all full of herself, never lorded it over them. They have loved her for it. This new development has only drawn them tighter around her. Except for Melissa. The one teammate who has clicked so well with Nicki, the speed-demon with the perfect passes always arriving just as Nicki finds an opening in the defense. Off the court, Melissa is keeping her distance.

Nicki had called Tyler after the last game to let him know the cat was out of the bag. So, he had finally told Lyvia, after keeping Nicki's secret for so long. He explained how Nicki had told him the night they'd seen that awful movie, then how she'd thrown up in his doctor's office, how she made him promise not to say a word to anyone. And how *she* had kept it all secret while she weighed it all over in her mind.

"Ty, what finally made her decide to have the baby?" Lyvia had asked as they were driving to the basketball game.

"You should talk to her, ask her about that," he said. "But here's what I think. It's the decision she always wanted to make. She was just overwhelmed. She had to get over her first impulse. You know, to just wish it all would go away."

"It's a lot for her to take on. A lot for anyone to take on."

"Yeah. Like any seventeen-year-old girl, I guess, she just wants to fit in."

Lyvia gives him that raised eyebrow look. "When did she turn seventeen?"

"Toward the end of October, it turns out. She hadn't told me it was coming up, her birthday. A lot of that going around, I guess."

A week after they had gone together to see his doctor. He certainly would have acknowledged her birthday in some way, a card if nothing else. Nicki was dealing head-on with the realization she was pregnant and could have used whatever cheering up he could have offered. It wasn't until two weeks later when he had referred to her as a sixteen-year-old and she had corrected him with her new, almost-adult age that he had learned he'd missed her birthday.

"Like I was about to say," he begins again with an exaggerated grin and a shoulder shrug as a way of a peace offering, "there's no way to fit in at her school with a big, pregnant belly. And she wanted so bad to keep playing basketball. For a while, she just kept playing without letting on to anyone." The hardwood court being the only place where the girl is confident enough to want the spotlight, Tyler says; she must have found her courage there. "But now that everyone knows…" he trails off. "It's got to be really tough on her."

Once again, the team gets off to a slow start. Nicki puts up an air ball from just inside the three-point line and, a minute later, her twelve-foot jumper clangs off the back of the rim. Then she comes out for an early rest. The point guard on the opposing team, St. Francis Cabrini from Lincoln Park, swishes her first two shots. Evidently, she's their star player. Then she steals the ball from Melissa and runs ahead for an uncontested layup. On Mercy's next possession, Melissa works the ball into Shannon down low, who misses the short shot. She does get her own rebound, but then misses the easy put-back. Divine Mercy is down 8-0 when Nicki comes back in. She comes off a pick and is open for just a second, but Melissa doesn't see her. Instead, the speedy guard splits two defenders with a slash to the basket and lays it in. Nicki high-fives her teammate as they run back up the court on defense, and that seems to help mend some of the invisible rift between them. Melissa finds Nicki with crisp, on-the-money passes the next two possessions, and she buries them both.

The next time Nicki touches the ball, she hears from the visitors' stands clear as day: "...that's the one that's knocked up. The *A-rab* girl." She bounces a pass to Shannon, underneath the hoop, who puts it in off the glass. *Don't listen to them*, she tells herself.

But the voices grow louder. Some of the Cabrini boys in the bleachers taunt her openly whenever she touches the ball. *Baby, love! Oh, baby love!* somebody sings in mocking falsetto. Nicki misses the shot, but Shannon rebounds and passes back to Nicki, who misses again.

Several loud voices in the stands join together: *You're having my baby. What a lovely way of sayin' how much you love me.* Some of the Cabrini cheerleaders glare at their obnoxious classmates with disapproving frowns, but some of the others giggle, which serves to embolden the boys. They whisper something among themselves and chortle loudly. On the next possession, Nicki catches a pass on the side of the court near the visitor's bleachers and begins to dribble as a male voice sings loudly, *Telling other things but your girlfriend lied. Can't catch me...* and it seems half of the Cabrini students join in to finish the lyric: *'cause the rabbit done died!*

Nicki passes the ball back to Melissa and glances over at the scorer's table. Her replacement has checked in and waits on one knee to sub in for her at the next whistle. *Just keep your head in the game a little while longer.* The ball sails out of bounds when Melissa fires a pass ahead of a teammate who had stopped and began cutting the other direction.

The sound of the referee's whistle signals the reprieve Nicki needs. She runs over to the bench without meeting any of the eyes tracking her every movement, pulls a towel over her head and sobs. She allows herself to cry, flushing out the meanness that has penetrated her very being, for a solid minute like a long exhale.

Then, she wipes her eyes and tosses the towel behind her, willing her mind back into the game, watching the opposing team for any weakness she can exploit.

"Nick, check back in," her coach tells her. "Just keep taking your shots. They'll start to fall."

Then she's on the floor again, into the flow and the music in her head comes on, blotting out all the noise in the gym. She floats to where she's supposed to be, everything in slow motion. Melissa sprints right up the middle of Cabrini's defense. Three players in the interior converge in the paint to stop her, but she's already dishing off a smooth pass that smacks against Nicki's awaiting palms; caught, cocked and released in beautiful rhythm on the trajectory to its rightful home, snapping the net with that satisfying note. Nicki turns to catch Melissa's eyes. Smiles exchanged and they're back on that same singular page, unstoppable again, at least for a few minutes. Nicki buries another jumper but as she runs back up the floor to be ready on defense, she sees her replacement already checking in.

"Coach," she says just loud enough to be heard as she runs by her. "Just a couple more minutes."

Myers brings the sub back to the bench. Nicki makes the most of her court time, scorching the net on each of the next three possessions before she finally does come out, the score tied. As she runs to the bench, most of the crowd on Mercy's side, students and parents alike, rise to their feet, clapping and calling her name.

Something apparently is said at the halftime intermission to the boys in the Cabrini stands; there is no audible taunting of Nicki in the second half. Mercy takes firm control of the game and wins by ten, with Nicki leading all scorers with 23 points despite her reduced playing time. For the first time in school history, the Divine Mercy varsity basketball team completes an undefeated regular season. In less than a week, they begin play in the Michigan Catholic High School League quarterfinals. The CHSL champion will move on to District competition in early January, facing the best teams from private and public schools alike, hoping to advance to the State championship tourney. But the Mercy girls' dreams are tempered by the realization that Nicki's season surely is nearing its end. Soon she will be showing. Even before her doctor and her parents decide enough is enough, Divine Mercy's administration will surely yield to the pressure and order her off the team.

***

After the game, a hulking *Free Press* reporter catches Nicki before she makes it off the court. At least six-four with rangy arms and legs and a bit of a gut, he dwarfs her standing there on the hardwood floor, even as he slouches to come down closer to her level. His breath and clothes smell of cigarettes. With loose-fitting jeans, weathered canvas sneakers and an old puffy parka with a dirty fake-fur collar, he could be a vagrant wandered in off the street. But he's got a reporter's pad in his left hand and holds a cheap pen in the other, so he must be legit.

He compliments Nicki on her shooting, then asks her about the taunting.

She just looks at him a second, thinking: *Oh, God, here we go.* "You just got to tune that stuff out," she says. "Play through it, you know?"

"Is it true you're pregnant, then? How long will you be able to keep playing?"

She glares at him wordlessly, then runs ahead into the locker room. *Unbelievable! Now it's all going to be in the paper for everybody to see....*

***

Lyvia returns with Tyler and Robbie to their Livonia house. After dinner, they watch television in the family room. The war coverage no longer runs day and night, but the news anchors interrupt pretty often anytime they have some breaking news. One of the Hollywood award shows is on, the *Golden Globes*, and Livvy wants to see it. *Dances with Wolves* is the big winner, about a Civil War vet who becomes an Indian. It sounds more intriguing to her than it does to Tyler, but he likes Kevin Costner from his baseball movies, *Bull Durham* and *Field of Dreams*. Maybe they should go see it.

Then there is an update on the war. It's not really breaking news exactly but a bit of a summary of what's happened today. They must figure America needs its fix of war news. Air strikes continue unabated with very few coalition causalities, softening the Iraqi defenses for the inevitable ground assault. As many as five hundred thousand troops are being readied for the invasion.... Two Iraqi Scud missiles have struck Israel. There's video of journalists and citizens huddled in bomb shelters, wearing gas masks, but apparently no chemical agents have been released in the explosions. The Department of Defense announces more Patriot anti-missile systems are heading to Israel.... *In other news, Eastern Air Lines has gone out of business after 62 years.* That last item leaves a pall over Lyvia and Tyler sitting close to each other on the couch, another brutal reminder of the ever-sickening economy and his continued joblessness.

* * *

Is Tyler really any different from the other guys she has dated since she fled from Alex, she wonders. Can he be trusted to be who she wants him to be? It's a mind trap, a whirlpool, that begins in doubt, leading to distancing, and finally to the end: another short, severed relationship. Still, she lets her mind go there because his own mind is anything but an open book. Will he ever let her into his interior world, dropping his defenses because he fully *trusts her?* She needs help from above to let it all just be until she can know, they can know, if they are meant for each other for keeps.

37

The next morning, Tyler and Robbie head out in the Cavalier to Harper Woods, to meet up with Lyvia for mass at her church, St. Peter the Apostle on Anita Street near the Eastland Mall. A newcomer to the state might want to pronounce the massive shopping center *EAST-lund*, but in Michigan they say *east-LAND*, like it's a whole country. Lyvia drove home last night shortly after Robbie finally went to bed. Not even making excuses about things she has to do. She just wants them to take it slower with them *getting physical*, as she calls it. He doesn't try to argue with her, tries to see it her way.

They sit in a pew toward the back in case Robbie gets fussy, though for now he seems content to quietly flip through a picture book with Joseph, Moses, Sampson, David, Daniel and a few other Old Testament superheroes. Tyler looks up at the stonework high above them. It's an impressive place and he can imagine God up there, more so than in the wooden rafters of the newer churches near him, built after Vatican II without kneelers or stain-glass windows even. God surely is in those churches, too, but it's harder to feel him there, you have to catch him in the music. Unless it's one of those folk masses rocking out with guitars and drums and tambourines that seem to be more about us than him. When the choir's good with an organist who knows what she's doing, it helps keep Tyler firmly planted in the service, instead of wandering off into his daydreams. When he catches himself drifting, he'll say a silent prayer in his head, but it seems like a one-way conversation, never hearing anything back. Those fearless men in Robbie's picture book got messages back loud and clear. Like Moses' burning bush with the booming voice inside. Even Joseph, who had to interpret the visions he received in his dreams, didn't have too much trouble making sense of them and he turned out to be right on the money, every time. Why can't he just turn on the TV or the radio and have God come on and just *speak* to him? That would be the way to do it in the modern world, Tyler supposes.

After church and brunch at Bob Evans, Lyvia really does have some schoolwork to do. Tyler and Robbie head back to Livonia. The boy falls asleep, of course, and stays zonked while his father carries him out of the car and into his little bed. Tyler settles down in front of the tube for a little football. The sad-sack Lions keep it close with the mighty Chicago Bears, but Tyler senses a disappointing finish. He pops a tape in the VCR and hits *RECORD*. This frees him to work in the basement on his latest project, a bookshelf for Livvy for her birthday coming up in a couple of months. It will be bigger and more ornate than the one he made for Robbie, made of oak that he can stain rather than the painted pine now sitting in his boy's room. Later he returns to the game, fast-forwarding through most of the second half until he sees that the Lions hold a narrow lead late in the fourth quarter. He hits *PLAY* and watches it from there: the Bears kicking a tying field goal as time expires, then hitting on a fifty-yard pass in sudden death overtime to win it. Typical Lions.

He grabs the sports section from the thick Sunday *Free Press* sitting on his coffee table and turns the pages in the Sports section until he gets to the area high school games. There's a decent-sized story about Divine Mercy's win headlined:

FILLIES COMPLETE UNDEFEATED SEASON

And a really nice photo—*how about that!*—of Nicki shooting a jumper with that perfect form of hers. He glances down and scans the type under the headline. He stops and rereads it slowly:

> As she has nearly every game, junior Nicolette Saliba led Divine Mercy in scoring, with 23 points. The game was marred in the first half by spectators in the Cabrini bleachers loudly taunting Saliba. "You just have to tune that stuff out and play through it," she said.
>
> Saliba would not confirm widespread speculation that she is pregnant. Fillies Coach Virginia Meyers also declined to comment on her star player's condition.

38

The girls run suicides, gasping for breath, sprinting from midcourt to the baseline, squatting down to touch the wood floor, then racing back the opposite direction. They must maintain their conditioning, an edge they cannot afford to give up. While they run, their coach racks her brain for schemes to manufacture offense for a playoff run without their top scorer. Nicki sits on a bleacher bench in street clothes, while her teammates run the torturous drills. A blood spot on her underwear Sunday—three days ago—led to a hurried doctor's visit Monday, her mother at her side. The ultrasound had showed everything normal for a healthy pregnancy at twelve weeks. Nicki could clearly see her baby's beating heart, and make out the fuzzy image on the black-and-white monitor of the baby's head and belly and legs curled up, laying on its back—appearing to be sleeping comfortably as if on some kind of hammock inside her on a warm and sunny day. The images make it all the more real to her. The bleeding has not reoccurred and there seems to be no cause for worry for the health of the baby. But her doctor has pulled the plug on her basketball season. Even greatly reduced minutes might put the baby at risk. Neither Nicki nor her coach makes any attempt to argue.

The tension with Melissa has returned. She has all but stopped speaking with Nicki. The quicksilver point guard can't put her feelings into words, can't describe the abandonment she's feeling, the betrayal. Their magical undefeated season will surely come to a crashing end with their star player unavailable because she got herself pregnant. *How could she do such a thing?* Nicki will come back for her senior year after she has the baby and then gives it up. She'll probably score even more points next year and the team will make a deep playoff run. But Melissa's a senior *now*. There's no next year for her. She's not going to play in college—she's short and can't jump and for reasons she can't understand, she can't shoot very well, no matter how hard she practices. This is her chance, right now, and Nicki's gone and ruined it.

39

When the team practice has ended, Nicki works with Melissa and some of the others who can stay late. She reminds them of the shooting technique she had shown them early in the season, after that second game when she'd first lit up the nets and they all came to her and wanted to know how she had done it. She had told them about aiming at a small piece of inside iron on the far side of the rim and to shoot with good form, with springiness in the legs and a good follow-through with the shooting hand. Flicking the wrist to put backspin on the ball so it will fly straight and true as it climbs a high, floating arc on the way to the hole above the net. Most of them aren't able to focus on a single spot of the far-away rim in frenetic practice drills, let alone in a real game. Her lessons do seem to help Melissa, who so wants to be able to step up and carry the team. But she gets frustrated easily, sulking when she misses a couple of shots in succession. There's not much time to learn the new art. The heaviness of doubt cannot easily be overcome. A shooter must first believe in the shot. And the girl who most believes can no longer play.

40

Tyler is watching NBC's Thursday night lineup alone; Lyvia's busy with school and Robbie has conked out early. On *Cheers*, Cliffy complains about some hippie radicals protesting this, that and the other thing, all in the name of world peace. "These peaceniks *ah* gonna get us all killed," the paranoid mailman insists in his *hahsh* Boston accent. "The *Rooskies* see us as *sahft* and the next thing, it's *nucleah ahmageddon*. I say there's only one way to deal with these hippie freaks. We *aht* to bring in the *national god*, I say."

Tyler opens a Miller Lite and sits back down on the recliner. It's not typical for him to drink even a single beer when he's alone, but he has a thirst for something other than soda pop or Kool-Aid. Maybe his taste buds are finally growing out of adolescence. Livvy has gently been on his case to expand his culinary repertoire to include some spices here and there, and he has to admit she might be on the right track. It would be a change from how he was raised; his mother never ventured much beyond salt and pepper in her cooking. Perhaps it's time to declare his independence, be his own man and all. He better do it while he can; if he doesn't get a job soon, he might be making that humiliating move back in with his mom. Like Cliffy, the postman.

Nah, he thinks, it won't come to that. He's had two phone interviews in the last week for decent jobs, with Proctor and Gamble in Cincinnati and with a drug company, can't remember its name, in Chicago. Getting close to the holidays and the year-end. Corporate managers watching their budgets are careful to spend all they have left by the end of the year—and fill any open headcount—for fear that they'll lose it forever when budgets and headcounts get established for the new year. It works against trying to be efficient, but it's how the game is played. He thinks back to old Cuhlman in the hospital talking about competing with the Japanese and their ability to *sacrifice.* Wonder if that carries over to how they watch their budgets?

41

Despite its undefeated record, Divine Mercy enters the post-season a badly flawed team lacking a legitimate scoring threat. Nicki and her graceful rainbows had forced opposing defenses to concentrate on her, opening up other options for Mercy. But without a strong outside shooter, there is no one to make the other team pay for keeping its defenders down low and in the paint. The Fillies' first opponent, Orchard Lake St. Mary's, deploys a tight 2-3 zone to prevent Mercy from working the ball inside for close shots. Just daring the Fillies to shoot from outside. But Melissa and the others can't make enough of their shots; the rain never comes. Divine Mercy loses badly. The dream season is over.

42

Girls in their plaid uniform skirts and white blouses peer into pale blue lockers up and down the long hall, vigorously chewing gum they'll have to spit out at the next bell. Others congregate in chatty bunches. Nicki finds the books she needs for her next two classes and with a foot in its white Puma sneaker, slams the locker door shut. New sneakers her mother bought her at the mall last week, her swelling feet no longer fitting in her old pair. She ambles purposefully down the hall, a bit of a hike to reach her next class, Chemistry. She comes upon Melissa and two others giggling as they watch her approach. The girl who was the team captain now covers her mouth, muffling her words before they reach Nicki. Something about Arabs? Or about being pregnant? Or maybe two slurs together. *Whatever.*

The comment has its desired effect, and the other girls nearly collapse in laughter, still watching Nicki walk toward them.

"Hey, Melissa," she says, "can I tell you something?"

The dark-haired senior, shortest of the three, shrugs her shoulders dismissively but walks over to meet up with her former court companion.

"C'mon walk with me a minute. Your next class is in the science wing, right?"

Melissa nods and follows along, wondering what she's in for. Still giggling, the two other girls watch them leave.

"I know you're like disappointed how the season ended," the taller girl says in gross understatement to her sullen teammate. "But you got to move on. I've been thinking. You got a real good chance to play at college. Seriously."

She looks over at her doubtful classmate.

"I mean, your quickness—you can't coach that. Your ball-handling and passing are excellent. You could be so valuable, *really*. And your defense, too. You should keep practicing. All the way through to the end of summer. I bet there are lots of small colleges that would be happy to have a walk-on with your talent. Make the team and you get a scholarship."

Melissa looks up at her friend as they near the science wing. She had expected a tongue-lashing from Nicki; it's what she deserved for the hateful things she's been saying. This unexpected olive branch is harder to take. She says nothing.

"We just gotta work on your *shooting*. I can keep helping you with all that. It'll come if you just keep working on it. And it would be a favor to me as well—you know I'm going to get stir-crazy carrying this baby around inside me all winter and spring. Will you? With me?"

Science without religion is lame; religion without science is blind.

ALBERT EINSTEIN

He will come to save you ... Then will the eyes of the blind be opened... Then will the lame leap like a stag.

ISAIAH 35:4-6

IV. MOONSHOT

43

January 1991

In the Livonia library again, his Tuesday routine. Scouring the same newspapers, hoping for an uptick in employment opportunities with the new year. But the morass of recession has thickened. The economists don't even debate it anymore. A couple of out-of-town leads, but not really good fits for him, each a stretch, and in this economy a stretch candidate has no chance. None of the leads he'd been following before Christmas led to any in-person interviews. Another month of this and he'll have to sell his house, if he can, and move back with his mother in Akron. He should have the house up for sale already, who knows how long it will take to find a buyer. But he has put off such an admission of career failure, that *For Sale* sign a beacon of hopelessness, giving all those neighbors he never talks to something else to whisper about.

Funny, he never figured that getting another job would be difficult. It was the prospect of finding a worthy replacement lover that seemed so daunting back in the summer. It was all so easy somehow the way he found Livvy and she had responded to him, and all so impossible to find work in his field. Now if he has to move away, retreating in humiliation back to his mother's home in dreary Akron, he will surely lose her as well.

Daytime darkness dampens his spirits all the more. Winter in Michigan brings day after day of impenetrable cloud cover. Gloominess covers his head and seeps into the pores of exposed skin on his face and neck, into his bloodstream, choking him from the inside. He finds his vision is cropped; he perceives only what is directly in front of him. It's as if his brain is conserving energy in crisis mode, blocking out what he'd ordinarily see on the peripheries because it takes just too much effort to take it all in. He notices that he walks more slowly than normal, and his posture is stooped. He better shake it off soon. He's in no shape to interview if he would even get the chance. He will need to put on the demeanor of a winner as surely as he'll need to don a freshly pressed suit, crisp white shirt, a smart tie and polished black shoes. But the psychic garb won't be as easy to dress himself in; he has to shed the bad vibes first. That will require him to summon energy and will power he just doesn't have right now, to rise above the gloom and self-doubt.

Doesn't help that he's not been sleeping well. Night after night he wakes up around three o'clock. Robbie's sleeping through the night again, thank God, but now it's his turn to wake up suddenly, inconsolably. Everything seems bleaker at three a.m. He's never sure if the darkness in his very soul at that hour is just transitory pessimism to be shaken off or if he really does see so much clearer in the stillness finally inside his head in his blackened bedroom several hours before the dawn of a new day, that his prospects are sinking quickly, and it is only in the dark of night that he confronts his painful reality. That it is, in fact, high time to panic. Night after night, he hides from these thoughts by disappearing to his mental hiding place on a pitcher's mound with his mighty fastball dispensing one batter after another until sleep mercifully returns. Maybe later in the week he'll feel stronger. Ready to compete again if he can just get the chance.

The front pages of the newspapers are all about Iraq. Three days ago, the United Nations authorized member nations to expel Iraqi forces from Kuwait if they don't leave on their own by today. To no one's surprise, Saddam is not backing down. The Senate and House have voted to authorize President Bush to use military force against Iraq as part of a coalition he has put together over the past few months, though Democrats in both houses of Congress mostly voted against it. This week will likely not end without the beginning of war. Other than that hiccup in Grenada, Tyler has not seen his country at war since the ignoble conclusion of the deeply divisive Vietnam War in 1975, when he was just eleven years old.

Most of the newspapers' front pages also mention the Soviet Union's aggression in Lithuania. Mikhail Gorbachev, he of the Nobel Peace Prize and the worm-like birthmark, has sent Soviet tanks and troops into Lithuania to crush an independence movement, making unsupported accusations that Lithuanian nationalists are preparing to "unleash direct military actions and pogroms" against Russians living in the tiny puppet nation. Is it too late to get that Nobel Prize back?

In the *Free Press*' business section, Tyler sees this story from the AP wire:

Bridgestone Leaving Akron

Bridgestone-Firestone Inc., the heavily indebted tire company, said it would move its headquarters to Nashville from Akron, Ohio, by the end of the year.

The move will consolidate the company's American operations, but it deals an unexpected blow to Akron, also headquarters to the Goodyear Tire and Rubber Company and long regarded as the tire capital of the world.

Ever since the Japanese bought out Firestone, there have been rumors that they'd be moving. Now it's happening. Out of unionized Ohio and on to Tennessee. Tyler wonders how well all those Japanese managers' families will fit in down in the land of Dolly Parton and Hee Haw. But it is that old radio jingle you used to hear all the time that plays in his head:

> *Wherever wheels are rolling,*
> *No matter what the load,*
> *The name that's known is Firestone*
> *Where the rubber meets the road*

His eyes move to a feature story, still in the *Freep's* business section. An interview with a young, high-flier in the health care industry, speaking immodestly about her latest promotion. It's not merely her good fortune, she is saying between the lines; she *deserves* her success. Then she pretty much comes right out and says it, though keeping it clothed in an abstraction: "The best people will always have the good jobs." He knows better. The winds of fortune blow unevenly on the sails of those at sea in their professional lives, launching and maintaining careers. It's as much who you know as how well you perform. Being in the right place at the right time. Or not. And though corporations have always been bastions of the white male, the tables lately are turning. Making up for past injustices and to speed up the pace of change in the makeup of their ranks of managers, companies now look favorably on diversity candidates and women. Fair is fair, but it's not a great time to be a white guy looking to get back into the mix.

* * *

After dinner, Tyler puts a little coat and stocking hat on his boy and takes him out on the front porch. They look up at a dazzlingly bright full moon until the boy complains of the cold. "Remember what it looks like, son. We'll come out again after a bit and see if it's changed."

Back inside, Robbie plays with some toys while his father cleans up from supper. They watch a little TV. Then Tyler bundles up his son again and they go back out on the porch. There's a significant bite missing from the moon, perhaps a third of it obscured by the Earth's dark shadow. As they look up at the lunar eclipse, their usual roles are reversed: Tyler is awestruck, while his toddler son grows bored with the seemingly mundane. He's seen less-than-full phases of the moon plenty of times; what's the big deal? They come out on the porch one more time before bedtime, the moon now reduced to a sliver. The rest is black, but you can still make it out, unlike with a regular crescent moon, and with the hint of a blood-red glow around the perimeter. Still, Robbie doesn't notice anything special about this moon. He looks instead at the feeble figure of a snowman on their front lawn, the inexpert craftsmanship of father and son in a bit of a hurry to beat the numbing cold invading their fingers as their gloves grew wet.

* * *

With Robbie down for the night, Tyler calls Lyvia. He hasn't seen her since before Christmas. She drove back to St. Charles for a holiday visit with her parents during her break between semesters. He in turn managed to get away with Robbie to Akron for three days, though his mother had all but begged him to stay longer. His gift to Lyvia before she left had gone over well, a leatherette-bound collection of Shakespeare's plays that Tyler had found on a clearance table at Barnes & Noble a few days before they exchanged presents. Just the right combination of elegance and simplicity, matched well to her love of classic literature, and it had only set him back $14.95. He had written a nice note to her on the inside front cover and signed it, *Love, Ty*. And he is happy with her simple gifts to him—a pair of leather gloves and the board game *Trivial Pursuit*.

He mentions the news from back home about Firestone, another nail in the economic coffin enveloping Akron where his mother hopes he will return, though he doesn't mention that last part to Livvy. She asks also if he's heard anything from his expecting babysitter. Lyvia met Nicki in November and the two immediately connected. No, he says, adding that he hasn't had need for a sitter since she's been gone visiting her parents.

"That's a good thing," she says, her bright smile coming to him right through the phone line.

Before Livvy had left for Missouri, she had spoken with Nicki one evening at Tyler's house. It all flowed easily that night, building on that connection they'd made from their first brief interactions. Nicki liked the way Lyvia spoke to her as an adult. Lyvia, in turn, saw a bit of herself in the spirited teenager. Several days after Nicki's last basketball game, Lyvia had expressed her admiration at how the girl was handling herself—leaving the pregnancy part unspoken but fully understood. Closer to Christmas, before she and Tyler went out for the evening, Lyvia delved deeper. Nicki had been busying herself with Robbie and his Duploes while waiting for Tyler and Livvy to leave on their date. To some Italian restaurant in Westland. They hadn't seemed to be in any hurry to get going. Then Livvy sat down on the couch next to the patch of carpet where Nicki sat back on her heels playing with the boy. Tyler pretended to busy himself in the kitchen.

"I just want to tell you again, Nicki, how impressed I am with your decision to go ahead and have your baby," Lyvia said. "It had to be a terribly hard decision. And a brave one, really."

"I don't know," the girl said, sensing a deeper conversation was coming. The girlish shyness she feels around most adults evaporates when she talks with Livvy. Might as well *put the moose head on the table*, as one of her teachers often says. "To be honest, I had just about made up my mind to sneak off to a clinic and just *end it*."

"I'm sure that would have been a whole lot easier. And would've meant you could still play basketball. What made you decide not to?"

"Actually, it was Tyler. When I first told him, back in October I guess, he seemed to just assume that I'd have the baby. Like, it never occurred to him that I wouldn't. That kind of hit me in the face. And then later, after he took me to his doctor—which was *so* embarrassing—he told me to *pray* about it. That wasn't like something he would normally say to me, you know?"

Tyler then had plopped down in the recliner chair and didn't even pretend that he hadn't overheard their whole conversation.

"At first, I was pretty mad at you," Nicki said, looking at him. "I didn't want to talk to God about being *pregnant*. I mean, it was pretty clear God wouldn't tell me what I wanted to hear. You know, to go ahead and have an abortion. So, I just avoided the subject with him."

"But you didn't have the *abortion*," Livvy said, repeating that charged word now that Nicki has used it. "That was so brave of you."

"I don't know if it was being *brave* as much as just being *frozen*. Not knowing what to do so I did nothing for a while. Basketball season had started. I was playing well, better than I could have dreamed, really. And we were like winning all our games."

Tyler smiled, thinking he knew what was coming. *She had found her courage on the court and it carried over to what she should do about the pregnancy.* But that's not what she had gone on to say.

"I didn't want to mess that up, the basketball. I guess I just tried to forget about the baby and all. Put it out of my head. To just *play*, you know? But then one night in bed I kind of *accidently* prayed about it. This sounds dumb, I know."

Lyvia shakes her head and smiles, encouraging the teen to continue.

"When I said my usual prayers that night, it just kind of came up. Then I started crying. I found myself saying almost out loud that I was sorry about everything, you know? And it was like I heard this tiny voice in my mind saying, '*It's going to be all right.*' Then I knew what I had to do. And that I could do it."

Tyler had taken this all in, like being in the front row at a magic show, only this was real. Just as he was feeling smugly righteous in having Nicki give him credit for turning her to prayer in her time of crisis, the teenager had described something he has never had with his elusive God: a real conversation. Something to keep aiming for, like that mysterious other side of the rim.

"Hey, I know it's not exactly the same thing as playing on the team," he said. "But don't forget, we still got to have that rematch of HORSE. Maybe I won't go down as easy next time. Might even beat you."

A smug look came over her face, and then she laughed, loudly, from somewhere deep inside her.

"No chance!" she taunted. "No way."

* * *

Talking to Lyvia on the phone had been a pleasant way to close out his day, but now he feels the restlessness returning. As he lies in bed after his latest little one-way talk with God, Tyler feels the cloudy fear coming on. The languid uneasiness that envelopes him at night lately. He can't fall asleep when the worrying sets in. As usual of late, it stems from his being out of work. It's not just his depleted savings. Or the balances on his two credit cards that have grown the last couple of months when he made only the minimum required payment, submitting to the usurious interest rate they charge those too stupid or indigent to pay the balance in full each month. The longer he stays out of work, the bigger the stigma and the harder it will be to land a job, he knows. Companies aren't in the business of putting the unemployed back to work. They want winners. And winners aren't out of work, they think. *The best people will always have the good jobs.* There's the fear and the reality that being out of the corporate world too long makes you stale, unable to compete. In the bright light of daytime, he knows that, even a little bit stale, he is much more forward-looking and capable than nine-tenths of the stiffs currently holding down corporate human resources jobs, and this knowledge gives him the confidence he needs to interview well when given the opportunity. But at night, it's only bleakness he feels. If he gives in to it, he will be racked by fear and stress, breaking out in sweat. For hours, sleep will elude him, and without sleep, he will be useless the next day. When he feels that bleakness heading his way, he knows how to shut it off. He again conjures the self-image of the big-league pitcher with the one hundred five mph fastball, standing on the mound at Tiger Stadium, staring down the next hapless batter.

44

Tyler and Lyvia collaborate in her kitchen on a recipe she found in one of her cookbooks—a spicy chicken coconut curry. She had to convince him to try a dish that's out of his comfort zone. Ginger, red peppers, cilantro and curry powder aren't ingredients he would have chosen to include, but he agrees to give it a try. And though he drinks a lot of ice water with dinner, he's pleasantly surprised at how well it turns out.

Afterward, they retire for a glass of wine in her apartment's tiny living room. The TV stays silent, further evidence that she wants to talk. He first picked up this notion when she had suggested he come to Hazel Park to her place, requiring him to get Nicki to babysit and for him to return home to relieve her. Thus, she has made it clear that once again there will be no sleeping over. Come to think of it, their phone calls to each other since she left for Missouri before Christmas have been a little strained. He had written it off to whatever weirdness she was encountering with her parents in her old home, but perhaps it's *him* who is weirding her out.

She doesn't let him wonder much longer. "Tyler, I want to know what you think of us, where we stand." It's certainly a subject he's thought about, particularly as he's missed being with her these past three weeks. Still, the bluntness of her question catches him cold.

"Well, I've told you that I love you." In his mind, this is true. He *has* ended phone conversations with a hurried *love you,* but he hasn't yet strung all three words together in a face-to-face proclamation, and neither has she. "That pretty well says it, don't you think?"

She gets that quizzical mouth-turned-sideways look of hers, and he knows he's on thin ice. Her wintered white skin looks particularly pallid in the low light of the single lamp in her living room.

"How do you know you love me?" she asks.

He stammers something about how she makes him feel, how she's always on his mind these days. How he misses her body when she hasn't been around. And, *bingo,* that last line elicits a response from her.

"That's the problem. I know we have great chemistry between us. Of course, I feel that way, too. But would you still be interested in me if you knew there was no chance we were going to have sex again?"

And clearly that gets his attention. "What do you mean?'

She knows it's wrong, she tells him. They're not married; they have to wait. "But I know you've *been* married. You've gotten used to sleeping in the same bed with your wife. And I'm sure it's not easy for you to go back to a relationship that's not *physical.*"

"Is that what we're doing?"

Yes, she says, if he wants their relationship to continue. This agreement—she doesn't call it an *ultimatum*—will either bring them much closer together or will quickly break them up, she knows. She would miss him terribly if he chooses to end it. But she would understand, *really.*

He's smart enough to know in an instant what he has to tell her. That, of course, he wants them to stay together. That's what is most important. He will accept the deal she has set out, and more than that, he will try to understand and embrace it.

It's a calculated response—if he even hesitates to accept, there's almost certainly no going back to her. If he does accept the no-sex rule, well, maybe she'll give in once in a while, who knows? He does know that he cannot, will not, let her go. In that instant, he does know that he loves her, and he tells her just that, more clearly and more slowly than he has before. She smiles and melts her body into his and they kiss. And already he's thinking maybe she'll give in, but of course she doesn't. Soon he's back on Eight Mile Road heading west to Livonia, wondering what exactly he's agreed to. It is the same deal Christie and he had before they married. But his body *has* gotten used to the rhythm of regular sex and the comfort of sleeping in the same warm bed with the one you love, even Livvy said she understands that. How can he be expected to give all that up now?

* * *

Nicki hears him coming in and pulls on her furry winter coat to leave. Robbie's asleep, of course.

"What do think of Lyvia?" he asks her.

"Livvy? She's great. I really like her. She's smart and funny. And really beautiful, too, but she's not on any high horse, you know? Why, is there something going on between you?"

"No, I guess not. I think we're going to be good."

"Cuz you'd be stupid to let her go, if I can tell you that."

He smiles and assures her that she can indeed tell him that. Then he lets the wise little teenager go, not even asking her how she's doing with that baby growing inside her. She must get sick of everyone always asking.

45

Tyler wakes to the sound of Robbie crying. It's still dark, but must be almost morning. The house is freezing. He turns on the hallway light and staggers over to the thermostat, bleary eyes slowly adjusting to the assault of incandescent brightness. The thermostat's set to kick on the heat at sixty-four degrees, the nighttime setting in this winter of jobless austerity. But the thermostat says the actual room temperature is only fifty-two degrees. Tyler goes into the bathroom and puts his hand down across the metal air duct on the floor against the wall. Nothing. Something's wrong with the furnace.

After changing his son's diaper, Tyler pulls a sweatshirt over Robbie's one-piece pajamas. He carries the boy across his shoulder and heads down to the basement to take a look. The pilot's on, but the burners won't kick on. There's nothing obvious for him to do to make it work. He'll have to call a repairman as soon as it's really morning.

"Cold, Daddy," Robbie tells him.

"Yeah, me, too." They go back upstairs and add to the clothes they are wearing. A jacket and wool hat for the boy; a sweatshirt for Tyler over the tee shirt and cotton pajama bottoms he wore to bed. And a pair of white athletic socks to cover his freezing feet. Something Robbie doesn't have to worry about in his one-piece sleeper with its little footies. Tyler holds his boy against his chest as he gets back into bed and pulls the sheet and comforter over both of them. The boy is restless at first, so Tyler tells him a story, reciting as best he can the story of Thomas the Train that he's read to Robbie countless times at bedtime. Both doze off about the same time, keeping each other warm and comforted.

Then it is morning. After cereal and toast, Robbie climbs into the recliner to watch cartoons clutching a blanket, while Tyler finds the number for the repair service. They'll be able to send a man out this afternoon between noon and four. In the meantime, the house will only get colder. There's a fresh layer of snow outside and the temperature isn't supposed to get over twenty degrees. A howling wind whistles through invisible leaks around windows that probably should have been caulked in the fall.

Worries seep into Tyler's being through equally invisible cracks in his consciousness. How much is this furnace repair going to cost him and where's the money going to come from? Still a little more left on his Discover card before it's maxed, but he already feels buried in debt that must be paid back at ridiculous interest rates. The house is twenty-two years old. What else is about to fail? The water heater? The air conditioning unit, or the refrigerator, maybe? He doesn't have any idea how to fix any of these heating and cooling machines and will be at the mercy of the repairman, taking his word on the extent of the damage and the cost to fix or replace them. Worries that would bounce off his thick skin if he was still working and maintaining a positive bank account balance. As a jobless pauper, he has no defense against potentially ruinous expenses. What other calamities hide in the woodwork waiting like hissing snakes to spring upon him?

Snakes, indeed. He's behind in his payments for the COBRA health insurance plan he's been on since his GM coverage expired. And he's got that appointment for next week for another MRI, another big deductible to pay. Even more worrisome is the test itself. Being strapped down like a death-row prisoner on the motorized gurney and sucked into the dark nothingness inside the fearsome metallic torpedo tube with its cacophonous grinding and clanging noises assaulting him to the core, the *very fiber* of his being. Taking a movie picture of the brain folded inside his skull to determine if the hematoma is still slowly seeping blood, setting in motion a time bomb like the one that was inside Christie's head. If that's a snake ready to uncoil and explode inside his skull, who can stop it? And then Robbie will be an orphan, raised by his over-caffeinated, cynically calculating grandmother and his spineless grandfather in some steamy retirement community in Florida without any other kids his age. How soon before he forgets his mother completely, then forgets his father, too? Why have they left him, he'll wonder, and then sent him to this humid swampland of tired retirees constantly complaining about ailments he does not want to understand? Without a job, Tyler has no defense against all these slithering worries. *Who* is he anyway, without a job? Without a wife and perhaps without his health? A failure, a lost cause. Strapped on a gurney and pulled into the void, never to escape the noisy hell. How can he withstand all that *noise*?

These fears and worries paralyze him in deep despair when he lays in bed in the darkness, shaking. Here in the morning daylight of his kitchen, the hissing fears should recede into the shadows, but now they're worse than ever. And he has an interview tomorrow at a big automotive supplier, Lear. He has to get a hold of himself, can't sink any deeper into the abyss of snakes.

* * *

The repairman arrives while Robbie's napping. The doorbell wakes the boy up. Strike one against the repairman. The three of them go down to the basement, Robbie clinging to his father's neck and shoulder. The furnace is in bad shape, the repairman says dourly. Something in the burner is fried, the sensor at least. The manifold really needs to be replaced, too, but then you might as well get a whole new furnace. We're talking $2,500 or so, fully installed, he says. Tyler's stomach goes sour; he's going to need to chew some Tums when he gets back upstairs.

"How about if we just keep it to what's needed to get it working today?"

The repairman pokes around a little more, than starts scratching out something on a pad of paper on a clipboard. "I can get you up and running for $485," he says. "But I might be back out here before the winter's over. This beauty's on its last legs."

An hour and a half later, the furnace makes a big *wooosh* as the burners ignite and begin to heat the air that will be driven throughout the frigid house.

"See how most of those flames are more yellow than blue?" the repairman asks, pointing with his pen into the furnace before he replaces the metal cover. "Not very hot. Inefficient. I'm telling ya, your manifold's bad. The orifices are all mostly clogged. I tried to clean it up best I could, but they make 'em so they can't really be cleaned. You gotta replace the whole thing, you know?"

Tyler just wants this guy out of his house before he finds something else. The gas bill is bad enough in the winter; he hadn't figured on repair costs, too. As he's writing out the check, Tyler finds himself morbidly asking about the life expectancy of the water heater and air conditioning unit. Sure enough, they're all made to last *fifteen to eighteen years, tops*, the repairman says. Tyler's on borrowed time already.

* * *

That evening, January 16th, the television is all Iraq, all the time. Tyler's watching NBC's *Special Report: America at War* while Robbie plays with his dad's old Matchbox and Hot Wheels cars they brought back from Ohio. Warmth is slowly creeping back into the house, though father and son each still wear a sweatshirt over their regular indoor clothes. Type crawls right-to-left on the bottom of the screen:

WHITE HOUSE: LIBERATION OF KUWAIT HAS BEGUN!

Tom Brokaw tells viewers who may have just tuned in that two hours earlier, about seven o'clock Eastern time, which would be four tomorrow morning in Baghdad, "allied air forces" began a massive air attack on military targets in Iraq and Kuwait. The attacks have continued relentlessly, carried out by F-15 Eagle and F-111 Stealth fighter-bomber jets taking off from six aircraft carriers in the Gulf region as well as from two air bases in Saudi Arabia, and scores of Tomahawk cruise missiles launched from untold numbers of ships in those carrier fleets. British, French and Saudi jets are also participating, we are told, flying hundreds of *sorties*, a strange, new word for Tyler that apparently means "flight missions."

Ground forces have not yet been engaged, Brokaw says. A map of Iraq comes up on the screen and the voice of an NBC News reporter can barely be heard over the sounds of air-raid sirens and sporadic explosions. Brokaw makes war-time small talk while awaiting President Bush's any-minute-now speech from the White House briefing room. Speculating out loud why Bush hasn't chosen a more formal setting for such a momentous occasion, the anchorman offers an explanation:

He likes informal settings. He does not like competing with the images of Ronald Reagan, who was without peer when it came to making those addresses to the nation in the majesty of the Oval Office. This president has always been more comfortable in an active setting.

Then suddenly, from the White House, President George Bush appears and begins to speak:

As I report to you, air attacks are underway against military targets in Iraq. We are determined to knock out Saddam Hussein's nuclear bomb potential. We will also destroy his chemical weapons facilities. Much of Saddam's artillery and tanks will be destroyed.

Robbie begins to fuss. It's well past his bedtime. But Tyler cannot take his eyes off the screen. He's never witnessed the onset of a war, and this one is coming live on TV. This is history. And, in fact, the President makes that very point just now:

This is an historic moment. We have in this past year made great progress in ending the long era of conflict and cold war. We have before us the opportunity to forge for ourselves and for future generations a new world order—a world where the rule of law, not the law of the jungle, governs the conduct of nations.

There it is again, that *new world order* Bush is so anxious to usher in, and tonight is when it all begins. The President quotes from several soldiers on the ground, preparing to fight, including a master sergeant in the 82nd Airborne:

We're here for more than just the price of a gallon of gas. What we're doing is going to chart the future of the world for the next 100 years. It's better to deal with this guy now than five years from now.

Tyler picks up a limp Robbie, changes him into a one-piece sleeper and lays him down to bed. Tomorrow he's got that interview. With all the fuss over the furnace, he hasn't taken time to review his notes, answers he has prepared for all sorts of potential questions. The main thing is to push away the stress that has invaded his psyche today, the hissing snakes all around him. No more thinking about his depleted finances, the deteriorating condition of his house, his upcoming date with the dreadful torpedo tube. He can't face any of that right now; it's all so overwhelming.

He's got to get himself together. Then he can put on the self-confident demeanor of a winner, wear it like a mask to the interview. Tyler's been so jumpy lately. Lyvia's insistence on avoiding "being physical" isn't helping, he frets. If he could only just relax. Maybe a beer would help. Or a rum and Coke. In his little liquor cabinet, he finds a half-empty bottle of Bacardi that's been in there who knows how long, and pours a bit of it into a glass. He adds some Coke from a can in the fridge and two ice cubes from the little plastic tray in his freezer.

In this *job search* game, he only needs to prevail once—just one job is all he needs to win. To enter the *promised land* of full employment. Of having his career back on track. Of *being* someone again. It hasn't been easy; God knows how much longer he'll have to wander in the desert of the unemployed. Forty years it was that Moses led that complaining band of Israelites through the desert. And then, after all that, God didn't let him into the Promised Land, punishing Moses because he impatiently hit a rock twice with his staff before the water flowed out as God had said it would. Even though God had never actually said, "Only hit that rock once, okay, Moses?" Seems like an awfully stiff punishment for a marginal offense, Tyler thinks.

He lumbers back to the living room and clicks the TV channel-clicker to CBS. All this war coverage and commentary is adding to his jumpiness, but it's addictive and he can't turn away from it. Dan Rather is asking a retired general who seems to be in the know, "The plan, in so far as you knew it, and we have to be careful here, the plan was to minimize civilian causalities. So, you aren't talking about bombing to terrorize a civilian population?"

The general reassures the nation, the world even, that America would never pursue war in that fashion. "On the other hand," he says, "there is great terror that comes with war."

CNN has its own retired general from a studio in Washington with the backdrop of a large video map of the Middle East showing the rough location of coalition fleets in the Persian Gulf and the Red Sea, and troops in Saudi Arabia denoted by three blue-colored silhouette figures of army men holding automatic rifles facing off against three identical silhouette figures but in red, showing the menacing Iraqi troops, in tiny Kuwait.

Did he lock the front door? Of course; he does so every night without fail. Still, he doubts. He ambles into the living room, to the front door. Locked. He pulls back the curtain a bit and gazes out the picture window at motionless quiet, like a great black-and-white print. His snow-covered lawn is a blanket of white, moonlit, framed by the black asphalt of the salted subdivision street. Underneath the snow, his front lawn waits for a spring awakening, renewing its redolent wet plushness, Tyler's reward for all his watering, fertilizing and weed control. Barren for now in hibernation, but scheming all the same to break out in splendor when given the opening, as are the hard, stubby embryos of buds on the maple and oak trees.

Weeks of bitter cold still to bear, but the thaw is coming for those who wait it out. Can Tyler's job-seeking self last that long? Waiting for the break in the tundra his career has become, albeit in a crappy economy, but still. He knows that it's on his shoulders to persevere and eventually to win out. Those with jobs will continue to believe that the deserving will always have the good jobs, and they will hold those out of work in contempt. Just as all those lucky in love believe they deserve their just rewards, and look with suspicion on those who remain single and alone. He feels a lightness in his head as he stands looking out the window. Not dizziness, exactly. Not that spinning vertigo sensation but a feeling of tightness and constriction, being crowded somehow, though he's alone in the room. *Anxiety. Doubt. Fear.* They are his unwanted companions, stealing his oxygen and clouding his vision.

"Father. I need you." Tyler's addled cry for help, though barely a whisper, echoes about the empty room unanswered for now, but perhaps not unheard.

46

Robbie plays in front of the TV in his one-piece jammies, yesterday's unbearable chill already forgotten, while Tyler fixes their breakfast. Scrambled eggs instead of their usual cereal. It will be good to start out with some protein today. Tyler's already on his second mug of coffee, trying to compensate for a short night of sleep. Having succumbed to a bit of a panic attack staring out the window into the nothingness, he had stayed up even later so he wouldn't lie in bed awake.

Now, instead of the usual cartoon Care Bears, Robbie's trying to make sense out of Bryant Gumbel on the *Today Show*, turned up loud so his father can hear in the kitchen. "Good morning and welcome to a special edition of *Today* on a Thursday and one that finds the country at war with Iraq," Gumbel says in a somber tone, unusual for him.

"And probably not having had a lot of sleep last night," says Deborah Norville, as if she is talking directly to Tyler. "I don't know anyone who didn't stay up most of the night."

She has shed her glasses and has her big hair all poofed up. But she's keeping it all business in a white turtleneck sweater halfway up her neck, and further wrapped in a gray suit jacket with those masculine shoulder pads. Now Gumbel's talking again:

...preliminary reports indicate relatively light Iraqi resistance. At this hour Baghdad radio is claiming Iraqi forces have brought down 14 U.S. war planes, but that's a claim the Pentagon has labeled 'ridiculous.'

* * *

Maybe this will be the one. It's about time he catches a break and lands a job. Dressed in a navy blue pin-stripe suit, white shirt and red tie, Tyler pulls into the parking lot of Lear Automotive. Feeling pretty good, all things considered. A global manufacturer of seats, instrument panels and electronics, Lear has huge contracts with each of the Big Three domestic car companies, most of the Europeans and even some of the Asian makers, though the big Japanese companies buy mostly from within their own *keiretsu* networks of in-bred suppliers loyal to the top of the Japanese food chain. Lear moved its headquarters to Southfield years ago, in one of the first waves of so-called *donut growth*—bustling suburban prosperity in ever-expanding rings around increasingly vacant and battered Detroit. Tyler would be hard-pressed to find a large company closer to his home. Southfield is kitty-corner to Livonia, just east of Farmington Hills. A twelve-minute commute would be pretty amazing, considering he lately has expanded his job search to the entire Midwest and Northeast.

Tyler made it past a fifteen-minute phone-screen interview a week ago to advance to today's in-person meeting with a mid-level HR type, the internal recruiter at Lear. Tyler and some unknown number of other candidates being brought in over the next several days will compete to make the next cut and, hopefully, a final round of interviews, unless there's still another round after that. He feels like a late-round NFL draft choice working hard in training camp with several roster cuts to come, hoping to make the team. He heard about this opening from Neticut, who has carefully cultivated a powerful network of well-connected associates who share something in common with him—most are Finance types, alumni of Yale or Harvard or MBAs from the Wharton School and, of course, GM junior executives and former GMers who have gone on to take promising positions at other companies.

"Tell me about yourself," the HR manager says to Tyler as he's still settling into the swivel chair in the little conference room on the ground floor near the building's front entrance. No sense bringing first-level candidates very far into the belly of the corporation.

It seems like an ice-breaker question, an invitation to share something personal. But Tyler knows better. It's a trap, a weed-out question right at the start. He could answer with something like, "I'm a single father of a two-year-old boy. My wife died a year ago." A sympathy ploy that would likely backfire, indicating a possible reluctance to work long hours or to travel for the job, making it easy for the interviewer to disqualify him. Or he could offer some other bit of personal information, trying to be memorable but likely only detracting from his business persona.

Instead, he says, "I studied Human Resources management at the Ohio State University, earning my Bachelor of Science. With a minor in Computer Science. For the past three-and-a-half years, I worked at General Motors' Garden City Stamping Plant in three different personnel roles, including resource evaluation and staffing. I consider myself a strategist and a change agent, someone who can help nurture and develop a winning culture at Lear."

That last bit is somewhat of a gamble; if Lear's HR team is really looking for just another corporate lemming to follow orders and not ruffle any feathers along the way, he's just given the interviewer good reason to rule him out. Tyler's taking a calculated risk that the job specification he received before the phone screen—detailing an opportunity for "a *strategic* manager to help enhance *employee engagement* and an *empowering culture*"—was not complete b.s. The intelligence he received from Neticut seemed to corroborate the sincerity of the job description. But human resources people are notoriously inscrutable and, true to form, the interviewer gives no indication whether Tyler has answered well or stepped into quicksand, only to slowly sink into job-seeker oblivion, even as the interviewer continues on stone-faced.

* * *

Tired and talked out by the interview, Tyler walks to his mailbox and retrieves its contents: a couple of bills, three fliers for companies selling products that don't interest him, and a letter from his mother. He tosses the fliers into the kitchen wastebasket and the bills in a little wicker basket which collects mail that must be dealt with later. Then he opens the letter. His sister is coming home, his mother tells him. She's moving to New York City and will spend a few days at home in Ohio; Celia's not sure exactly when. But, Tyler's mother writes, it would be so nice if he could plan to come down at the same time.

It's not clear in the letter what is bringing Celia to New York—a missionary outreach to the South Bronx? Or maybe she or her husband has taken a high-paying job in Manhattan. It would be good to see her, but much better if he had a job by then. Unemployment is such a downer, a cloud hanging over him. His mother will keep pressing him to move back with her and he can't dismiss that so readily anymore now that his meager savings have evaporated.

He flips on the television set again for some more war news. Another retired general is giving a quick tutorial on the weapons each side has at its disposal. Iraq has begun launching Scud missiles of an old Soviet design toward Israel and Saudi Arabia. But the U.S. has installed Patriot anti-missile installations to shoot the Scuds out of the sky before they can reach their intended targets. The names of these armaments tell you a lot about who has named them; surely the Iraqis have a more impressive name than *Scud* for their primary tactical ballistic weapon. That Patriot system sounds a lot like the so-called *Star Wars* network Reagan wanted to develop that could have shot down Soviet intercontinental ballistic missiles on their way to New York or Washington. Or Detroit, for that matter. But it was too expensive, we were told. Yet, we developed this Patriot setup, and it seems to work fine against the admittedly plodding Scuds. Old man Reagan probably went ahead with the Star Wars program in clandestine fashion, like the whole Iran-Contra thing, and made sure it was secretly deployed even though it had never been authorized by Congress. If it makes us safer against nuclear attack, more power to him, Tyler thinks.

He glances through the *Free Press*, while the TV plays on. The lead story includes quotes from an assortment of world leaders. Saddam Hussein is defiant as ever. "The great showdown has begun! The mother of all battles is under way. We will not fail!" The Reverend Billy Graham has an interesting line: "There come times when we must fight for peace. I pray we will be on God's side."

* * *

"How'd you do in the interview?" Nicki asks Tyler suddenly, before he goes out for the evening. Another Saturday night the girl won't be spending with kids her age. She had said she didn't mind; she would be happy to sit for him. *Nowhere better to go*, was the unspoken rest of the thought. Oblivious to her absence from the expected social circles, the life inside her expands. Still not showing in the clothes she wears, now fully four months since that fateful encounter with her now-ex boyfriend. A minute ago, she had told Tyler, in response to his question about how she has been feeling lately, that her infrequent bouts with morning sickness seem to have passed. She's full of energy these days, she says. *Amazingly normal.* Other than feeling hungry all the time despite all she's eating, and soon needing to move up another size in her clothes, already a five now when she should be a four. Without thinking, she lifts the bottom of her sweatshirt, like she'd done in the locker room with her teammates when she'd told them, and shows him the hard little bump just above her belly button. He wants to press his hand against it, like he had with Christie so many times before Robbie came, but he stops himself. And just then she feels the awkwardness of her bared abs there for Tyler to examine. She pulls the oversized shirt back down to cover even the front of her jeans and abruptly changes the subject to ask about the job interview he must have mentioned when they'd spoke on the phone.

"Pretty well, I think. It's hard to know." He looks for his gloves, not that he needs them to drive, but in this weather, you have to be prepared. Car trouble in January in Michigan can be dangerous for those who leave home without ample protection from the cold. "I feel like I'll get called back for a second interview, but you never know."

"*Trust*," she says simply, looking straight and intently at him, smiling to take away the seriousness of the single word, but it still hangs there.

She looks away. Direct, sustained eye contact is still unusual for her with him except when they're talking about basketball. As they had been a few minutes earlier when he had asked if she'd gone back to the gym to shoot around any since the season had ended, and she smiled and said *yeah*, she'd been helping one of the girls from her team practice her shooting two or three times a week. And sometimes she goes alone, just for fun, keeping the rhythm of her shooting motion intact. Still making it rain, he supposes.

Then he'd asked how she was doing with her pregnancy, and she so quickly had changed the subject to his job search. It makes him wonder which conversation her one-word answer was meant to fit, or maybe all of them somehow.

In midwinter the still-deep hue to Nicki's face and neck stands out compared to the wan faces all around her. Most have lost all the color in their skin. Lyvia is so much whiter than this girl, of course, and Tyler is, too. By the middle of January, the sun has become a rarity in Michigan, hidden day after day behind rolls of gray. The lack of sunlight takes its toll on the skin of seemingly everyone he knows, except Nicki. As Tyler glances in the hallway mirror putting on his winter coat, he sees their two reflections together. His looks pale and lifeless next to the healthy olive glow her calm image gives off, a teenaged aura of quietly conquered fear.

47

Another few hours in the library Monday; he's down to once-a-week to cut back on his burdensome daycare bills. Going through the newspapers, hoping to score another promising job lead but finding none. Then he sits at one of the computers they have there in a separate glassed-in room, typing up the rest of his notes from his sessions with Cuhlman. Part of his natural compulsion to tidy things up. He'll meet up with the old man at the nursing home sometime and give him the pages of memories and the tapes. Not a published book as it might have been, but something personal for Cuhlman's family. The old guy is all right, really, calling himself a *friend* before Tyler had even considered the notion. Yet, he had intimated that Tyler had some share of culpability in the racial inequities everywhere around them. Tyler still bristles at that.

When he returns home, there's a message on his answering machine. It's the internal recruiter at Lear inviting him to come back for a second interview. That was pretty quick. *Maybe this is the one.*

* * *

He's thinking more and more that *she* is the one. So often these days, when his mind wanders from whatever he is supposed to be thinking about, he thinks of her, his Lyvia. It's more than physical, lord knows there hasn't been enough physical action lately; it's more than chemistry. Everything about her makes him smile, probably with a ridiculous goofy grin if he ever would catch himself in the mirror day-dreaming about her. He *loves* her, he knows. But can he trust it, this love? Undeniably on the rebound, still missing his Christie so badly, so *deeply*. Is his love for Lyvia just a replacement love, filling a void for now that so cries out to be filled, only to one day spoil and rot because it never did measure up in his mind to the once-in-a-lifetime love that came before her? He is sure in his heart that he is not dishonoring Christie by embracing a new love, that his time with her is made no less eternal than it ever was. But can he trust it, this second and on-the-rebound love?

And Lyvia's so good with Robbie. *Let's face it,* at this point they're a package deal, him and Robbie. It wouldn't be fair to saddle someone he's merely dating with the "Mom test." And just unnecessary. But if she's quite possibly "the one," it's more than a fair question of what sort of mother she would be. It's essential. Not a hypothetical someday when they have a kid together, but from the get-go, a wife will have to be a great mom to Robbie. And she will be, he knows now. *She's the one.*

* * *

Sitting beside her in the booth at Big Boy, an inexpensive and casual date, but still pleasantly intimate because they're so few people there, Tyler stacks Lyvia's finished plate on his and pushes them both aside. Then he reaches around into the large, inside pocket of his winter coat hanging on a little brass hook between their booth and the next one. He sets an envelope on the tabletop in front of his now-curious date.

"I've been meaning to show you these photos I had developed."

Lyvia moves slowly through the images of Robbie at the playground, the fall colors clearly indicating how long ago Tyler had taken the pictures.

But Lyvia doesn't complain. "How darling he is!" she exclaims. "What precious, beautiful photos. You have such an expert eye."

There are thirty photos for her to examine. The envelope contains the full set of twenty-four images after he replaced the ones his mother had chosen to keep plus a few additional close-ups. He had taken the negatives to a camera shop in Dearborn he likes, leaving specific cropping instructions to make a number of the best ones even more dramatic.

"If you really like one, we want you to have it. I'll get it enlarged and put it in a frame for you. And Robbie and I will autograph the back."

She leans over and kisses his cheek. She continues to examine the photos, looking for the one she will claim. She comes to the earlier pictures of Robbie, when he was fully a year younger than he is now.

"I had the roll in the camera a long time," he explains. "I'd forgotten all about it."

And then she comes to the first portrait of Christie, staring up from the beyond, there on the tabletop at Big Boy. Lyvia gasps.

"She's so lovely. Just gorgeous, truly," she says. "I've seen some of the pictures of the two of you together that you keep around your house. But I had no idea." She looks through the rest of the set, including a couple of extra close-up prints from the camera shop order. "Thank you for showing these to me. They must mean a lot to you."

She asks him to tell her stories about Christie and his life with her. They get coffee, being careful to protect the photos, and linger there for nearly two hours. He tells his lover all about his wife—how they'd met at a crowded dorm room party, how on so many lazy, sunny days they'd sit on the warm grass on the OSU quad in the open space framed with leafy trees and massive brick classrooms. How they had fallen in love, how he had proposed to her in that restaurant and then moved with her to Michigan when he took the job at General Motors. And how they had brought Robbie into the world together. He even rats her out a little, gently and fondly.

"She never was that good at keeping up with housework, really. Everything was always just a bit messy. But it didn't matter. She was a *perfect* mother to Robbie, took so much time with him. Gentle, so loving. I don't know if she taught me how to love my boy the way I do now or if it would have come to me anyway, you know, naturally. But she sure set an example for me to try to follow."

He has to wipe his eyes frequently as he tells her all this. And this new spark in his life laps up every adoring detail from him about Christie without the slightest sign of jealously or impatience. It opens a deeper channel of connectivity between them, and he loves her all the more for it, fighting his natural instinct to change the conversation to something safer.

A silence settles over their booth in the Big Boy. Tyler drinks in the moment, letting it lead him, staying patient for once. Lyvia looks down into her coffee mug, uncharacteristically quiet. He fights a jittery desire to break the silence, until he cannot wait any longer.

"What's the matter?"

She turns her head slowly toward him and nods, lips pursed. "There's something else. That I haven't told you. I guess I didn't want you to hate me for it."

"What? There's nothing that could make me hate you." Clearly the right thing to say no matter where this is headed. But he can't help being unnerved.

"When I told you about Europe, about Alex…there's more," she stammers. Taking another gulp of coffee, she continues without pausing, not letting him interrupt. "I did something terrible and it's time you know about it. I had already made up my mind to leave him, when I discovered I was pregnant. I wasn't sure how far along I was, but then I realized I had missed a whole cycle. Before I came home, I went to a clinic in Vienna, confused and scared. Ty, I allowed myself to be talked into having an abortion. A couple of hours later, it was over. As I walked back to the hotel for my last night in Europe, I should have felt relief, if you believe what the world tells you. I mean, I'd become pregnant accidentally in an abusive relationship. So, I did just what anybody would do, right? I was closing out an unfortunate chapter in my life to start over."

His eyes focus on the tiny lines on her forehead above her eyes. Three shallow valleys running parallel across the pale expanse at the top of Lyvia's delicate face just below her hairline.

"Immediately I was filled with regret. I knew I'd done something horribly wrong. It wasn't just some tissue that I had expelled from my body. What right did I have to end this life inside me? Didn't my own baby have the right to expect my womb to be a safe place? I cried all night."

She stops there, looks into his eyes. He does not fight against the silence, and it is short-lived this time. "When I arrived home, it was pretty obvious to my parents that I was an emotional wreck. I told them just enough about the abuse from Alex for them to know that I just needed them to shelter me for a while, without a lot of questions. To this day, I haven't told them. You're the only one who knows now."

He puts a hand over one of hers. He purses his lips in a tight smile, hoping to show the understanding and compassion he is sure he is feeling.

Tears are now streaming down Lyvia's cheeks. "I started bleeding at the airport in Vienna. Something had gone horribly wrong with what was supposed to be a simple procedure. I bought some maxi-pads and got through the flight and the next couple of days at home before I could be seen by a doctor without my parents' knowing."

He pulls her close and just holds her there. "I'm sorry … I didn't tell you … all this sooner," she says haltingly, between stabbing sobs. "It wasn't fair to you."

He doesn't know what to say, so he says nothing. The silence lingers and demands a response.

"I'm sorry, too," he says finally. "That you went through all that. And that you're still hurting inside. But I don't hate you, Livvy. Not at all."

She says she wants him to think it over for a few days and she will understand if he wants to break it off with her.

He shakes his head immediately. *How can she even think that?* he wonders. "I'm not going anywhere," he says softly.

"You don't understand. Let me finish. That doctor who examined me back home said that my uterus had been badly damaged and even when it healed, would be forever scarred. And that I'd never be able to get pregnant again. I'll never be a mother, Ty. I should have told you sooner. I'm so sorry."

As this all sinks in, he holds her more tightly. "I'm not going anywhere," he repeats.

* * *

"The kids at school giving you a hard time?" he asks the girl before she walks out to the driveway where her Mustang waits. She turns to face him as she pulls on her winter coat, then hooks her thick, untamed hair with her thumbs, pulling it up and out from inside the coat. Shakes her head to let the tresses expand and fall across her shoulders.

"Some of them, yeah. There's one girl who thinks she's so clever, calls me *Spaghetti Sauce*. You know—Prego, the tomato sauce—only she says it like *Preg-oh*. So that gets old. But I'm kind of used to some teasing. I don't let it bother me."

Nicki goes on to explain that in grade school and junior high, some of the kids, mostly other girls as it turned out, would call her names because of her skin tone and Middle Eastern heritage. "'*Little Arab girl*', they'd call me. It used to really get to me, you know? I used to hate that."

"But not anymore?"

"Not so much in high school. They can tell that I've learned how to deal with it. Kids are basically all right, you know. They're just mixed up or angry at themselves, *especially the girls*. You even said that to me, remember? *Girls are the worst*. A lot of girls kind of turn into monsters for a while as they grow up."

Tyler smiles at this. At least he won't have to worry about that from his child, his *son*. Those teenage years will be tough enough to go through as a parent. Luckily, he has plenty of time to get ready. "But how do you deal with the bullies?"

"You just treat them straight-up like anybody else. That's what my father taught me. Don't yell back or try to avoid them. Just, you know, be friendly around them. They see you aren't letting them get under your skin and that, like, they kind of enjoy you being around. Because you made them feel just a little better about themselves."

"Sounds like your dad knows what he's talking about."

"Yeah, I'm sure it was hard for him being, like from an Arab family, Lebanese actually. To move here as a young man and raise a family," she says.

"I didn't even know for a while that you were, you know, part Arab. You seem so *American*."

"Thanks, I guess. My parents were good about helping my brother and me fit in and all, but still be proud of the families we come from. They want us to visit there someday, but practically my whole life they've been having a civil war. Lebanon, not my parents. Supposedly it's over, the fighting, but after like fifteen years, how do you know from a few months of peace if it's for real?"

Tyler asks her if this war in Iraq that is all over the news has made it harder for her with her Arab name and olive skin.

"Yeah, I do feel it more lately, the way people look at me sometimes. It just seems a little more tense, you know? Like nobody knows what's going to happen next. But at school it's not too bad."

"It's going to be harder as you begin to show, don't you think?" Switching the subject, but not a whole lot, really.

"Totally. Real hard to fit in with a big, pregnant belly. My mom wanted to pull me out of school when she found out. She said she could home school me for the rest of the year. She couldn't imagine what it would have been like for a girl *expecting,* as she says, in the little high school where she grew up. But that was in *Wisconsin* and like a million years ago," Nicki says as she rolls her eyes in that girlish way. "I'm going to be okay. And who knows, maybe I can help make it easier for some other girl to choose *not* to get rid of a baby she's not ready for. That would be something good, wouldn't it?"

"Yeah, it would," he says. "That's a real tough call for any girl to make. Or woman, even."

48

The TV reports show thick clouds of black smoke rising up from Kuwait. Facing sure defeat, the Iraqi armed forces have begun blowing up Kuwaiti oil fields. By nightfall, it looks like the whole country is in flames. Iraqi troops also apparently are dumping millions of gallons of crude oil into the Persian Gulf. Petulant Saddam Hussein strikes back at the world that is pushing him out of power by unleashing an epic environmental disaster for no reason other than to somehow avenge his humiliating defeat.

Tyler flips off the set and resumes studying for his upcoming second interview at Lear. He has been through the stories he can share to provide examples in response to a myriad of potential questions. He has boned up on the latest developments in the HR world. He has read through Lear's annual reports for the past three years and all of the press releases it has issued over the same time period. He has thought of smart-sounding questions he will ask each of the Lear people interviewing him when the time is right. He is going to be ready and he is going to be good. He doesn't have much time left; he *has to* get offered this job. Otherwise, he'll have to return to Akron a broken and beaten man, tail between his legs, to live at home with his mother. He hasn't mentioned this possibility to anyone, certainly not to Lyvia, and not even to his mother. No reason to get her hopes up when he still might be able to avert this fiasco.

He finds he can only study up on Lear and his interview answers for about twenty minutes at a time. He's still jumpy from having to repeat the awful MRI scan this morning. Dr. Klira had strongly recommended he go through the same procedure as before, not opt for the less confining alternative MRI test reserved for the truly claustrophobic, so they could make the most accurate comparison to the previous scan. That was the worst part—because his baseline scan had been made in the torpedo tube, all subsequent scans would need to be done this way as well. *Trapped inside a trap*. Knowing exactly what was to come, he dreaded it for days. Strapped down again and pulled head-first back into the terrible pallid womb, bracing himself for the high-pitched screeching. When fully inside the abyss of the cold, unfeeling metallic tube, a devil's symphony of shrieks and screams again pierced his head, pushing him to the edge of panic.

"You don't know how much I hate that," he had told the blonde technician when he had finally emerged feet first from the torturous tube.

She continued to scribble onto her clipboard and didn't reply at first; probably hears it all the time.

"It is a little discordant, isn't it?" she said finally, without ever looking up.

When Tyler gets home from picking up Robbie at day care, he goes straight to his bathroom and pulls a Q-tip from the big blue box in the vanity drawer. The little cotton fibers swirl inside one ear and then the other. The forbidden tickling soothes his head. He is careful as always not to go in too far; the clucks at Johnson & Johnson need not fear him coming after them with a stupid lawsuit.

Back in the kitchen to check the telephone answering machine. Two messages wait for him. The first one is Neticut: "…*Street Journal* this morning has an ad from Lear for the Human Resources job I told you about earlier. Hope you moved already on my tip 'cause they're going to be flooded with résumés now."

The second message, from his mother, is longer. Celia's plans have changed. She's going to be delayed getting things finalized in Singapore. So, her visit in Akron will be shorter. "Not sure why they can't delay when they have to go off to New York," his mother says with irritation. It's clear from her tone that she is feeling hurt by his inconsiderate sister and her husband and their new, uncertain plans. Why does she have to be the one short-changed in all of this? Dorothy Manion just wants to be with the daughter who lives in her memories, the sweet youth she was before getting in with some of that *bad crowd* in high school. She wants her little girl back at home with her, in that bedroom kept as if it had never changed, and sooner than later. *Please.*

49

This is going well, he thinks. His second in-person interview at Lear, this time with the hiring manager. She had let him know from the outset that she was impressed by his answers as they were reported to her from the first interview, from that stone-faced HR functionary Tyler found so difficult to read.

"You see yourself as a strategic *change agent*, and you say you're interested in helping to instill a winning culture at Lear. Tell me more." In this way she opens the door for Tyler to expand on the thought or to stammer and fumble his way through the answer if it is not truly written on his heart.

This is a point-of-view he does believe in, for himself and for the field of human resources, so he finds himself enthusiastic and expansive in his response. Again, it's a bit of a gamble, taking this manager at her word that she indeed is interested in hiring someone to do more than mindlessly follow her orders in enforcing the status quo.

"Human resources professionals can help bring out the best in the people they serve," he says. "We should encourage their creativity and help get ideas to percolate to the organization's leadership. We can help them, the employees, understand and believe in the overall strategy. And help management empower them to use their creativity in making that strategy succeed. That's an exciting vision for our profession. For too long we've been focused on making sure the rules get followed, when we should be helping to inspire the best performance from people at all levels in the company."

This is radical talk coming from a low-level HR person who doesn't even have a job at the moment. But he can see from this manager's smile and the way her eyes gleam as she listens to him, that she is favorably impressed, and it gives him confidence and hope. He makes sure he also stresses that he is a team player and a collaborator; he knows he can't come off as someone who thinks he already has all the answers. Or as a reckless *cowboy*, off doing his own thing. That will never fly in the corporate world. He will be a good listener, and he will follow orders as required, he makes clear without having to say it.

As soon as he gets home, Tyler calls Lyvia and lets her know that he has good feelings about the interview, about this potential boss and about the company. This job could be just what he wants, he says to her excitedly. And it surely is what he needs. He is *just about going broke*, he confides to her. But he says it with an exaggerated voice to avoid alarming her and perhaps to protect his own fragile ego. He can hardly bring himself to believe that he really is nearing the end of his line.

"Oh, *necessity's sharp pinch!*" she exclaims mysteriously.

When he does not respond, she adds: "Shakespeare? C'mon, don't you know that line?" More silence. "*King Lear*, of course!"

He laughs, glad to have her on his side even as she chides him gently. Not the first time she has gone over his head with a literary reference, and it promises to not be the last. She will be patient with him she has decided; he may be worth it.

* * *

Robbie's down for the count rather early, just after eight o'clock. Tyler sets down the book he'd been reading to the boy and moves to the kitchen. He lifts the phone from its cradle and dials the number he pulled from the Livonia phone book weeks ago and now knows by heart. A call he has made many times in his head.

"Hello?"

"Roger? McNeary?" he stammers.

"Yes. Who is this?"

"Tyler Manion. I'm the one who was in the accident… with your daughter. I just…" Tyler's voice falls off, searching for words that might make this easier.

"Oh, yes, I know," McNeary says after a time, no emotion in his voice, "But it should be your lawyer, talking to our lawyer. Really, it's out of place, you calling us at home."

"Lawyer? No, it's not like that. I don't even have a lawyer. I mean, I just…" Tyler reaches back to the script in his head. "I just wanted to express my condolences to you and your wife."

"Oh, well, then, thank you."

"And I wondered if we could talk for just a bit. If you don't mind terribly. Not for any lawyer business, or anything. Just as people, as fathers, you know?"

No response.

Then, Tyler hears a heavy sigh.

"Maybe just a bit. Go ahead."

Tyler had planned to ask if he could come over to visit them in person, Linda's father and mother. Maybe to step briefly into Linda's room, look at some photos. But in the awkwardness hanging heavy over the phone line, he knows this is all there is going to be.

"I can't imagine what you and your wife are going through. There's no way to say it… not…"

"I know a little bit about what you've been through yourself," the voice on the phone says, slowly. But then in spurts: "Our lawyer told us. When you were in the hospital. That your wife had died earlier this year. So, you do know a bit of what we're feeling, I think."

"Yeah. The suddenness of it all," Tyler says, off script, in the moment now. "How you want to undo it, but you can't. How you hear her voice and you think for just a second she's back with you."

"Yes, that's about right. I just want to be in the car with her. Drive her safely home, from that awful party. 'We can talk about it later,' I would say. 'Let's just get you home, Linda.'"

"I waited some time, a few months, to call you. But that's not because I think it might be any easier for you now. To talk. I know it still hurts. Still burns."

McNeary coughs and breathes hard into the phone. "Thank you," he says finally.

"Can you just tell me a little bit about her?" Tyler asks. "I know she was a good student. Where'd she want to go to college?"

"U of M. There was no doubt in her mind about that. She wasn't sure what she wanted to study, maybe engineering, maybe something in science. Smart in everything, she'd have her choice. Always made A's. Up until lately…"

"What changed? If I can ask you."

"I don't know. Started hanging out with the wrong crowd. We knew she'd been lonely, not many friends at school. She so wanted to belong, be part of what was going on. But she'd always been bookish and shy. We just wanted her to be happy, so we didn't fight it, when she started going out. There was drinking going on, we can see now. We should have stopped her… she was a lost sheep around those other kids. Didn't know any better. She wasn't prepared for all that."

"That just sounds like growing pains. You can't blame yourself…" Tyler stops himself. He never liked it when others tried to tell him what to feel or not feel, after Christie died. It always hit him the wrong way.

"She was out of control," McNeary says, through a haze Tyler can feel all too well. "We were just starting to see it. Out of control."

"It's just…" Tyler tries to say, but McNeary cuts him off, thanking him for calling. The line goes cold, like the two young women who have left them, far too soon.

50

None of the old magazines in the waiting room at the office of Dr. Mohammed Klira interest him much, so Tyler stares ahead at the blankness of a white wall until a nurse ushers him back to one of the treatment rooms. Soon Klira himself steps into the room and warmly greets his patient, extending a brown hand for Tyler to shake. "Good news," he says. "The hematoma is no longer apparent on your latest scans. I would like to say you are completely over your accident from this summer. But tell me, have you had any more vertigo?"

"Not for at least a month, I don't think. Maybe I'm over that, too. Not that the stress has gone away." Then he thinks to add a little more explanation. "Still haven't found a job yet."

The doctor has Tyler update him on his job search, concluding on the hopeful note that he has interviewed well at nearby Lear for a good job. Then Klira asks his patient about his son—is he sleeping through the night again?

Yes, the boy is doing fine, Tyler says. He seems to have gotten past that *regression* of a few months ago and seems as happy and well-adjusted as ever. Tyler tries to do his part to keep the conversation on track—but then can't help taking it off on his own tangent. "So, I think we're both handling the *stress* pretty well. Of course, it's hard to relax when all you see on TV lately is about the war. Not that it affects me directly, it's just, you can't escape it. Have you seen all those burning oil fields they keep showing? Thick, black smoke everywhere."

"It is on everyone's mind, I am sure," the doctor says. "The war over there. But at least you do not have to worry about a deranged idiot mistaking you and your family for some kind of enemy."

Klira goes on to explain that one of his partners, Dr. Ashraf, two nights ago had his living room window shattered by a thrown brick. Taped to it was a piece of notebook paper crudely lettered with black marker: *ARABS GO HOME!* Now his wife and four children are terrified to be in their own house at night.

"You could not find a gentler, more kind human being on this Earth," Klira says of his colleague. "It is a violence to terrorize this man's family, it is."

Tyler realizes then that he doesn't know a thing about this man who is his doctor—if he's married and has kids, what he enjoys doing in his free time, where he grew up and went to college. What his house is like, his yard. This doctor has made it his business to get to know Tyler and his toddler son who isn't even his patient—and knew Christie all the more so. This doctor who she had so wanted to deliver her baby into the world, the most intimate act imaginable. But Tyler has not reciprocated in asking even the most superficial *"How are you and your family, doctor?"*

Then Klira apologizes to Tyler for getting off the subject of his patient's visit.

"I should be the one telling you I'm sorry," Tyler responds, disheartened that some moron here in America today would act with such misdirected malice. *Even now this stuff still goes on*, he thinks. A new life for bigotry, fueled by the excitement of war, the clamoring for a righteous ass-kicking. *We have enough enemies without turning on our own*. "That you or he would have to worry about such a thing in this country, it's terrible. To a doctor of all people."

"Anyway, there is also the weather, contributing to our stress," Klira says, glancing at his watch. "The long, gray winters here can be tough on all of us. It can be depressing. When we do get the occasional sunny day, try to get outside, even if you have to wrap up. Another month or so and we should be through the worst of it."

* * *

Robbie sits quietly on the couch next to his dad as they look through a picture book. Tyler emphatically names various objects on the colorful pages—the fire truck! the puppy dog!—and his son points to them with a chubby index finger. But Tyler's mind is running far from firemen and their black-spotted Dalmatians. Tomorrow marks a full week since his interview at Lear that he had felt so good about, and he hasn't heard a word from them. Of course, they're busy. He shouldn't worry. He felt so good as he left the office there. But he knows that these companies look at so many applicants before choosing one to hire. They may really like him, but he could still finish second to some other accomplished candidate. There's no prize for second place, just another name for *loser*.

After the clean bill of health from Dr. Klira, he should be feeling good about everything. But that talk of an anonymously thrown brick shattering the sanctuary of an innocent homeowner here in the peaceful suburbs—*a doctor!*—has left him a little unsettled. If he would just hear from Lear, it would chase away every other worrying cloud from his mind.

The evening news begins with a report of eleven U.S. Marines killed in an armored personnel carrier near the Iraqi town of Al Khafji. Not by Iraqi troops but by the *friendly fire* of an anti-tank missile launched from an U.S. Air Force fighter-bomber. Mistakes happen. Collateral damage in an otherwise flawless campaign. But don't tell that to the mothers of those eleven young men.

"You've never said much about the war," Tyler says to Lyvia. "What do you make of it all?"

She shakes her head and looks down at the carpet. "It's tragic," she says simply, but then immediately amends her comment: "No, far worse than tragic. Deliberate."

He waits for her to say more. These college students are always against war. But isn't there an undeniable *justice* to it sometimes? Not that anybody wants to see American boys coming home missing limbs, or dead.

Finally, she does elaborate, but her concern seems more for the Iraqi people than the coalition troops. "The man's a menace and a monster, that Saddam Hussein. And he needs to be stopped. But isn't there a better way than all these Iraqi soldiers having to die for him? And the civilian casualties, too, must be horrendous. I'm sure nearly all of them wish he would just get deposed so they could all go peacefully back to their lives."

"What about our own soldiers getting killed over there?"

"Yes, of course. I just meant that it's pretty one-sided with the Iraqis taking the brunt of it. But any loss of life is heart-breaking. These eleven American soldiers killed just today from our own mistaken missile? Senseless. But what should we expect? War is just *killing*. You can't make sense out of it, I don't think." And just when he thinks she's gone completely soft, doesn't understand the necessity of fighting, the *justification* when there's a tyrant over there terrorizing his part of the world and must be stopped, she adds: "Seems like we could just knock him off quietly, that Saddam, don't you think? Instead of killing all those Iraqi people, couldn't we just send a cruise missile into his palace and be done with it?"

Tyler points out that the dictator has countless royal hangouts and hideouts, and supposedly a whole bunch of look-alike doubles dressed up to fool would-be assassins.

"Yeah, but c'mon," she counters, "don't we have spies and such to know where he really is? If we don't, we should, I think. Seems to me a few really good spies could save us—and the world—a whole lot of trouble." To this Tyler can only agree.

51

He's home to catch the call when it finally comes. The hiring manager from Lear, pleased to ask Tyler to come back in to see her; she has an offer to present him. He squashes his impulse to shout out *Yes!* but he does thank her profusely. Making it clear with his enthusiasm that he wants the job badly, which may hurt his ability to negotiate the most favorable salary. But maybe it also further endears him to the manager who will be his boss, getting him off on the right foot before he even starts.

He telephones Livvy, but only gets her recorded voice. "Call me," he says excitedly, "Got some good news from old King Lear."

She will be thrilled. Landing a good job, one in which he may very well be able to apply himself in ways he never could at GM, will free his mind and spirit. He will be loosed from the discouraging reins which bind the unemployed in ways that those with jobs, however uninspiring, can never really appreciate. And, of course, she'll be pleased and relieved that he doesn't have to move.

Next, he dials the familiar phone number in Akron, memorized as his own when he was a child. His mother will have an entirely different reaction. Pleased her son has landed a good job, but disappointed that his unemployment hadn't resulted in him moving back home. Before he can tell her his news, she blurts out her further irritation with his wayward sister. Her departure again has been delayed. Now she and her husband will have to fly directly to New York City, won't be coming home at all. Just when she was so looking forward to having both Celia and Tyler for a nice long visit. He can hear the anxiety in her voice, the unexpected and disappointing news jagging into Dorothy's head.

"That's really too bad, Mom. But let me give you some better news. I'm being offered a really good job with one of the biggest automotive supplier companies, a job that will really interest me." He finds himself repeating the *really* without meaning to, just trying to settle her down.

"That's good," she says flatly, then forces herself to add, "Where is it?"

"That's one of the best parts," he says. "It's close by my house, in Southfield, just a few miles from here. Robbie and I will still be just as close to you. We're not moving away." That's one way to spin this news to his mother, who already thinks there's an unbearable distance between them.

"Well, that *is* good news," she says flatly. "I'm happy for you. And I look forward to having you and Robbie come visit for as long as you can until you have to start this new job."

Tyler hadn't really thought this through—how soon will they want him to start? He needs to meet with his new manager and hear the offer. Even if he accepts it right on the spot, which he is inclined to do, there may be some other steps. He'll need to take a drug test for one thing. The phone silence builds while he tries to sort out this immediate future, and he can hear his mother's quickened breathing through the phone.

"I still have to meet with my new boss and actually accept the job," he says finally. "But, sure, Mom. We'll come down for a visit, Robbie and me. As soon as I can, I'll let you know when to expect us." Then, on impulse, he adds: "Hey, maybe Lyvia can come. She's the girl I've been telling you about."

He and Robbie had come to Akron for Christmas. There were more photos to share and some small presents. Dorothy hadn't asked much about Lyvia, still thinking Tyler shouldn't be distracted with dating anyone so soon, should just concentrate on Robbie for a while. And still quietly harboring hope that the two of them would move back in with her.

"I'd like you to meet Livvy. She's really becoming pretty special to me," he says. *Really*. But then by the silence in his ear he can tell that the uncertainty of her possibly meeting this new woman is noticeably amping up his mother's angst. "Anyway, she might not be able to break away from her Master's work. It was just a thought."

He still finds himself irritated now and again by his mother's paranoid depression. Felt an internal anger swelling a couple of times over that Christmas visit, but he'd been able to squelch it. He's seeing now that he has failed for so long to protect her. And that he owes her that. She who has always been so loyal to him, largely making up for the emotional distance his father kept from him. He knows that she has been battling these demons, this *cloud,* since he was old enough to notice, and he seldom has cut her any slack for it. So maybe he does owe her. But couldn't she just buck up a bit more? Would it kill her to welcome Livvy into her sad, little house next time he drives down?

52

They sit in the mezzanine, far from the stage, but at least in a center section of the magnificent Fox Theater. Celebrating Lyvia's twenty-fifth birthday, a milestone largely ignored in this country as it falls between the dawn of legal drinking at twenty-one and that first birthday to be feared—thirty, the sunset of youth. She is wearing the red outfit, including that festive hat, recalling their first meeting at a much humbler venue with its third-rate *farce*, as she had called it. Tonight, it's a traveling troupe bringing the Broadway hit *Sweeney Todd* for a week of shows in Detroit. A lively musical even though it's about a murderous barber, set in the bleakness of nineteenth century London. The title character slits the throats of his customers; his lover disposes the bodies by making them into meat pies she sells to unsuspecting customers. Despite the gruesome plot, it's charming and top-drawer, with soaring music and clever writing. And that vengeful barber is somehow a mostly sympathetic character.

Tyler sprang for the rather pricey tickets hours after accepting the job at Lear. Having escaped financial ruin, he wanted to treat Lyvia to a classy night out. He won't start working for another week—just time enough for a three-day visit with his fear-addled mother in Akron—and won't see his first paycheck for nearly a month, but his credit cards aren't completely maxed and he knows now that he'll soon be able to pay them down. He insisted that Lyvia wear the red dress and hat, and she bought him a matching red tie to wear with a white button-down shirt and navy blue blazer. Although the show is quite good and holds his attention, he can't keep his eyes off Livvy, that stunningly captivating face under the red hat fixated on the stage, eyes and mouth expressively in sync with each dramatic turn of the story, every clever lyric. He still can't quite believe that this alluring, brainy woman is paired with him, despite all his shortcomings. Dinner at the swank Rattlesnake Club earlier tonight, followed by this Broadway production at the Fox; she has to be impressed by all that. He needs her to know how important she is to him now. He needs himself to know it, too. Now that a critical bearing point of his identity has been restored, his unemployment mercifully ended, he feels on a better heading to navigate whatever rough waters still may lie ahead for them. And to take her on as a passenger or co-captain perhaps.

"Let's stretch our legs," she says at the intermission. "Come along, now. I don't dare leave you here for fear you might molest some innocent damsel in the next row."

They share a sparkling water in the lobby, soaking in the splendor of their victory for now over all that could have torn them apart.

53

March

    Early morning Saturday sunshine pours through the picture window onto the carpet in the family room, beckoning Tyler to come over and bathe in its rays like a lazy house cat. Used to getting up early now that he is working, sleeping in on a Saturday would be a waste of one of *his* days. He walks from across the room and crouches down, then kneels, sitting back on his heels like that Indian girl on a box of butter, Land O'Lakes. Something in one of his thighs creaks audibly but it doesn't really hurt. Just not used to stretching this way. He feels the sun's warmth on his cheeks and forehead and even through his thick, brown hair that needs to be cut one of these days, so that he feels like that Indian, one with nature even through the plate glass window. In the glare of morning sun, he sees his own image in reflection upright and strong, motionless, and beside him is his Christie with that thick shoulder-length reddish hair and those brilliant blue eyes against the whiteness of her face, her image not as tall as his even though he's not standing; perhaps she's kneeling, too. Her warmth and the softness so close he can breathe her in, her fresh scent and endless effervescence, that happy charge of energy inside her releasing just when he thought she had to be coming up for air. The shared secret of that crazed smile; he remembers suddenly what had made her laugh just as he took that photo more than a year ago now—he'd said that he saw so much of her dad in her, the way she could *embrace life's wonders without ever taking a grip of its jagged edges.* She'd thought that a funny thing for him to say, and left the question unasked of what he might see in her of her mother. Their shoulders in the window glass here almost touching, not unlike the stoic farmer and wife in that painting you see all the time in magazines, *American Gothic,* but there's no pitchfork between them and the only church is that rising sun, and their faces are not blank and haunting but smiling and radiant. Christie hovers then, an angel in a liquid robe blurring; she smiles with a serene placidity though she must be aware that she has gone away from his world; she can see him still. He listens but there is no soundtrack, no voice that would make her being here with him in this brief moment complete.

Her image recedes and it's Lyvia there beside him in the glass as if she'd always been there, a different sort of smile on *her* face, that way her lips turn up knowingly, not smug so much as content for the time being, but always thinking ahead. There's no surprise for him that the woman in the window has changed; he just absorbs it like one of Robbie's Huggies would. Then perhaps greedy in wanting to see her a little clearer, Lyvia, as enthralling as that first time he saw her, disguised as an untouchable stranger in a red hat, he squints into the picture window and understands there can be no reflection with the brightness on the other side; it's all a trick of the light or his imagination. Raising his face up just a bit to shield his eyes from the direct intensity of the rising sun, he gazes into the deep blue, cloudless sky that fills the frame, now in mid-March becoming more common above the still brown Michigan lawns. The blue endlessly resonant stretching from this Earth to the heavens.

He feels a tiny breeze on his face, like the breath of someone nearby, though the windows are shut.

"Thank you," he says, simply. Not to the imaginary breeze, or the blue sky or even to the sun, but to his own Father, out there somewhere beyond.

And then in a rush he thinks of that spirited old nun in the red and blue and yellow McDonald's and all she had said that he hadn't been ready to hear. The far-out stuff about Daddy and all. The *envelope* she had given him. Where had he put it? In the kitchen somewhere, he vaguely remembers. So, he gets up from the awkward position and ambles into the kitchen thinking, *Robbie's going to be up soon.*

He looks in the drawer of the little desk in the kitchen where the phone is, his hands thrashing through pens and paper clips, loose playing cards and Magic Markers, some AA batteries, thumbtacks that stick into his fingers without causing any real pain, and a little bottle of Elmer's glue. And, yes, the envelope, sealed shut. He rips it carefully open on one end and pulls out a clipping of some out-of-state newspaper from nearly two years ago, on the twentieth anniversary of the first moon landing, it says. On the top of the clipping, in a woman's cursive writing, *"How cool is this!"* The old hippie with her *far out!* and *how cool!* The headline reads:

ALDRIN RECOUNTS HUSHED-UP COMMUNION ON THE MOON

The article describes the scene of the Apollo 11 lunar module, resting on the moon's surface on July 20, 1969. Before Neil Armstrong and Buzz Aldrin climbed out of the little spacecraft and became the first humans to step onto the surface of the moon, Aldrin unpacked a small plastic container of wine and a piece of unleavened bread he had brought along on the journey, from a Presbyterian church near Houston, where he was an elder. Then he radioed back to Mission Control, requesting a moment of silence to "invite each person listening, wherever they may be, to pause for a moment and contemplate the events of the past few hours and to give thanks in his or her own way."

The article says that Aldrin had quietly read from the sixth chapter of the Gospel of John, while Armstrong, "reportedly a Deist, looked on respectfully but without comment." Aldrin then poured the wine into a little plastic chalice.

"In the one-sixth gravity of the moon the wine curled slowly and gracefully up the side of the cup," the astronaut recounted later. "It was interesting to think that the very first liquid ever poured on the moon, and the first food eaten there, were communion elements."

The story of the secret communion service was kept quiet until well after the mission, the news clipping says. Aldrin had planned to share the event with the world over the radio. But NASA hadn't wanted to tempt another lawsuit from atheist-extraordinaire Madalyn Murray O'Hair, fresh off her legal victory shutting down school prayer and Bible reading in U.S. public schools. Aldrin's microphone had been muted. Back at Webster Presbyterian Church, the article concludes, "Aldrin's communion service is still celebrated every July at a service known as Lunar Communion Sunday."

The part of the article referring to the astronaut reading from John 6 is circled and there's this in small but legible hand-writing: *"Not a symbol, but the <u>real</u> presence of the Lord. His own body and blood, soul and divinity. Receiving him is as personal as it gets, Tyler!"*

* * *

"Hey, I've been thinking. Let's go to Mass together tomorrow," Tyler suggests to Lyvia. They've been to Sunday service together several times since they started seeing each other, but it hasn't become the usual routine. "I'll pick you up at your place and then we'll spend the day over here."

She readily agrees, but asks him what made him think of this just now.

"Well, I have a new reason to better appreciate receiving Communion." He tells her about the hippie nun from the hospital and what they had talked about at McDonald's that one morning so many months ago. About the envelope she had given him, with the newspaper article about Buzz Aldrin and Communion on the moon. And what she had written: "… as personal as it gets."

"Nice, Ty. So good to hear you share all this. You'll have to show me that news clipping," Lyvia says, as she silently offers thanks for this encouraging little answer to her prayers.

54

Late April

    She cradles the ball in her two hands. Spring has arrived in Michigan triumphantly, lawns finally sprouting green, buds on trees beginning to burst, the sun hanging in the sky past the dinner hour. In the evening twilight, her eyes glimmer like emeralds inside the soft, brown relief of her cheeks and forehead.

    Nicki smiles occasionally as she recounts the latest goings-on around her. She has endured the winter and endless teasing at school. The other kids seem to be letting up on her a little even as her belly swells for all to see, her third trimester just begun. She lets the basketball drop against the driveway surface. Still speaking, she bounces it lightly, unconsciously, with gentle pulses from the spread fingers of her right hand, then her left. Never letting her palms contact the pebbled leather; her alert and capable fingertips make the ball obey. She dribbles it a little farther in front of her than she had three months before. Making room for her baby on board.

    The darkening blue sky above them provides a sacred dome, a private arena. They take turns shooting. Her first three shots are just short, grazing the rim and bouncing harmlessly away for Tyler to rebound and bounce sharply back to her. Weighted down by the extra mass in her belly, she must compensate, pushing a little harder from the balls of her Pumas to lift up onto her toes as she shoots. Then she finds her range and begins whipping the net with each shot. When one finally rims out, Tyler grabs it for himself, dribbling out a few feet beyond the free throw line. Nicki takes his place in front of the goal to rebound his shots. After a couple of misses, he too finds his range, knocking down several in a row from a variety of spots on the black asphalt.

They continue like this, wordlessly shooting and rebounding, while Lyvia and Robbie sit on the warm grass watching. Her left hand rests on the boy's shoulder, a tiny diamond twinkling in the scattered sunbeams.

On the asphalt driveway, knees bend, wrists flex. Fingertips on an extended right hand point the way home, the ball riding just the right arc. *Swish. Swish. Swish.* In the quiet of the moment, they understand each other perfectly. Content to get lost in the pleasure of each marvelous rainbow fulfilled. Neither attempts to follow and equal the other's made shots; no score is kept. The rematch long forgotten.

History doesn't repeat itself. But it often rhymes.

MARK TWAIN

EPILOGUE

One year later, on May 7, 1992, a massive rocket with two side-slung boosters launched Space Shuttle *Endeavor* on its maiden voyage into Earth orbit. Aboard that flight, astronaut Kevin Chilton carried three consecrated hosts in a gold-colored locket, inside his space suit. As *Endeavor* flew into the blackness above the dark side of the Earth, Chilton removed two hosts from the pyx and offered the Eucharist to the two other Catholics onboard the mission, and then received himself.

"It just made so much sense to me," he later reflected. "Going on this incredible adventure, you may not be coming back, you may die with the Eucharist in your pressure suit, with the Lord right with you. Or, if his will be so, how wonderful to receive the body of Christ while looking down on the marvelous creation of the Earth."

* * *

Tyler and Lyvia's story continues, many years later, in *Grace Rediscovered*, coming 2025.

#

Discussion Questions for Book Clubs

1. How do the many father-child relationships described in Scraps of Grace add complexity to the novel's fatherhood theme?
2. Does Tyler's short attention span make him unfit to be the story's protagonist? Why or why not?
3. The story is told in the present tense, and the narration features many detailed descriptions of circa-1990 living, including contemporaneous newspaper headlines, television programs and the like. What effect does the author achieve by writing in what he calls "the hyper now"?
4. Discuss the moon as a recurring symbol in *Scraps of Grace*.
5. Tyler can be as uncomfortable alone in the silence as he is in a noisy or crowded situation. How does this relate to his spiritual attention deficit disorder?
6. Consider the parallel motifs of war and the sanctity of life.
7. How is Linda McNeary similar to Nicki? How is she different?
8. What does Tyler learn from Cuhlman? What does he refuse to try to understand? Why?

About the author: Jon F. Harmon lives in Northville, Mich. and Bemus Point, N.Y. He is the father of five sons, a devoted husband, semi-retired corporate communications executive, and author of the acclaimed narrative business book *Feeding Frenzy: Inside the Ford-Firestone Crisis*. This is his first novel.

Milton Keynes UK
Ingram Content Group UK Ltd.
UKHW040743301124
451843UK00017B/325/J